UNSPOKEN
Endings

Book Three of the Unspoken Series

GABBIE S. DURAN

Cover art by ©Sarah Hansen at Okay Creations
http://www.okaycreations.com/
Editing done by Edee M. Fallon, Mad Sparks Editing
https://www.facebook.com/MadSparkEditing
Proofreaders: Missy Stegman and Janett Gomez
Formatting by Champagne Formats

ISBN-13: 978-0692288696
ISBN-10: 0692288694

Printed in the United States of America First Edition: September 2014 Library of Congress 1-1670050701

Author links:
Author page: http://gabbiesduran.com/
Facebook: www.facebook.com/authorgabbiesduran
Twitter: @gabbiesduran
Goodreads:
https://www.goodreads.com/author/show/7093957.Gabbie_S_Duran

Dedication

To my mother, Rosa. I love you.

Chapter One

Abigail

I CAN'T BREATHE. He's literally stealing the breath from me as his fingers tighten around my throat, his body pinning me down. His hand squeezes harder. My heart accelerates to a dangerous level, feeling as if it will burst from my chest, but I refuse to give up. I can't. It would mean he wins. With all the strength I have left, I keep trying to push his body off. My hands claw at his face and somehow I manage to gouge his eyes with my fingernails. With a wail, he rises off my body and loosens his grip around my neck.

With all my might, I swing my arm up and my fist makes contact with his face; it shocks him momentarily, allowing me to push him off enough to wiggle my way from under him. I'm still breathless, barely able to move, but my only thought is escape.

"Get back here, you bitch!" he shouts as he grabs onto my ankle, my body pulled to a stop. Turning around, I kick him with my other foot and manage to break free once more.

I don't have the strength yet to stand up, but I manage to frantically crawl from his grasp to keep him from pulling me down again. My fear and determination is what keeps me moving. Sucking in a deep breath of air, I force myself up to my feet and start to run.

I'm running for my life at this point. My feet are moving on instinct, doing what they know best as they attempt to put distance between us. I can hear him chasing me; his panting breathes mere steps behind me, but I keep running, never looking back.

"You think you can get away from me, Abigail?"

His words fuel my fear, causing my legs to pump harder and my body to move faster, the air swooshing by me, the world passing in a blur. I know he's no longer behind me, but I can still hear his panicked shouts.

"You belong to me! I'll find you and you'll regret ever leaving me!"

I rapidly sit up, escaping the nightmare of Bill. My lungs are gasping for air while my eyes adjust to the darkness of the room. My body is damp with sweat, while my chest still heavily rises and falls to catch up with my rapidly beating heart. Tears are threatening to break free as I sit wondering why I suddenly had the dream. The tears are still rising, but I refuse to cry because I know I'm stronger than my weakness. But, I cannot deny the fear still lingering in my blood. Even in my dreams, I can't escape him, and I hate it.

Sleep eludes me at this point, forcing me to hug my knees while I push the still lingering fear away. Instead, I keep asking myself: Have I made the right decision by coming here? A question I've been asking myself since the moment I stepped onto the plane and left Matt behind. With him, I always feel safe. Rarely fearing Bill would risk approaching me after that first time, but now I'm an open target.

With time, I come to the same conclusion as before. If I

ever plan to find myself, I have to follow my own dreams. I refuse to let the fear of failing, or being held captive in a controlling relationship, stop me from finding myself. I am Abigail Adams, and although I didn't know who I was six month ago, I know who I am now... I am a fighter, and I will reach that finish line, one way or another.

IT'S ONLY BEEN a couple of days since I'd left Portland, but New York is a wakeup call I didn't expect. The moment I stepped onto the plane and left the only past I'd known behind, was the moment I realized how much I'd grown to depend on Matt for stability. He'd been the one I'd gone running to in the beginning. He helped me discover love for the first time all over again. He was the rock I knew I would always be able to depend on.

The loneliness immediately began the moment after I checked into what would be my new home for the next couple of weeks. It was technically still a hotel, but you can equally compare it to a small apartment with all its equivalent similarities. I stood rooted to the spot at the entrance for the next couple of minutes, taking in its kitchen, dining room, and small living room, followed by two bedrooms, one on each side.

Julio had immediately gone into the first bedroom to my right, returning a minute later with a nod of approval. "It's clear." Two words I'm starting to believe I'm going to become accustomed to hearing during this trip now that he's in full body-guard mode.

With permission now granted, I enter soon after and toss myself on the bed, staring straight up into the ceiling. Missing Matt since this morning, I immediately call him hoping his soothing voice will help take the tension of the trip away. He immediately answers, but from the surrounding noise, I can already tell he isn't at home.

"Hey, beautiful," he says into the phone, tugging a smile on my lips.

"Hi," I reply, feeling a pang of disappointment that I'm not with him. "How did your trip go?" he asks as the noise slowly starts to tone down.

"Good. Where are you?"

"We decided to grab a drink at the Brewhouse. It isn't the same without you here, though," he tells me, making a smile creep up my lips.

"You're not serenading anyone else while I'm gone, are you?" I tease him with the smile still on my lips as I think back to the last time I was there.

"No one here worth singing to."

His words tug at my heart and an awkward silence grows between us. "Hey, Matt, your food is on the table," a voice similar to Trey's announces in the background. "Yeah, I'll be there in a minute," Matt replies to them, already causing me to grow disappointed knowing the inevitable will come. I will have to end the call with Matt.

"Can I call you later, beautiful?"

The dreaded question has caused my heart to sink. "Sure, but if I don't answer it's because I'm sleeping. I'm really exhausted from the trip," I tell him, truly feeling completely drained at this point.

"Of course. I'll just talk to you in the morning, then," he tells me. I'm about to tell him that I take my earlier words back and for him to just call me, but he's already adding, "Call me when you wake up. I'll talk to you then," gutting me in the stomach and adding to my already shattering heart.

"Promise," I force myself to reply, but barely manage above a whisper.

"I love you," he says into the phone. The sincerity of the words helps me reply with, "I love you, more," before we completely end the call.

THE ANNOUNCER REVS up the crowd by requesting more noise. The excited roar of screams and hollers travels through my body and ignites my blood. The feeling of being surrounded in a crowd of excited runners ready to cross the start line will always feel surreal. An excited tremble runs up and down my body, encouraging me to yell along with them.

My excitement is slightly broken when Julio begins speaking. "Why did you choose this morning, of all mornings, to run this race?"

"What's wrong with today?"

He raises his brow as if I'm the one not understanding the question. "The fact that I can see my own breath in the air suggests that it's too cold to be out running."

His words do remind me how cold it is, sending a shiver down my body. But I'm too excited to let it affect me. "Oh, come on. You'll warm up before you know it," I excitingly let out as the crowd starts screaming again.

"You'll have to remember to keep your pace slow. If you have to, walk," Julio orders. Appalled at his words, I look at him as if he's lost his mind. Does he really expect me to walk?

"Are you giving me this advice for *your* benefit or *mine*?" I ask in a teasing tone.

He snickers. "Both. If Mateo finds out I let you run this race and you injure yourself, he'll have my head," he replies, and from the way he's worriedly looking around, I honestly believe he's telling the truth.

I can't resist laughing at his comment. "Just look at this race as another one of our daily runs," I suggest, making him snicker once more. "It's just three miles. You can handle it." I hear no arguments this time, keeping me happy.

Ever since the night I went for a run with Matt, I haven't been able to resist running again. I'd done as my physical therapist had advised me to do when I'd planned on returning to running, but I quickly discovered running on a treadmill was not my thing. I grew frustrated of feeling like a hamster on a wheel. My legs were moving, but I felt stuck in the same place. If running without music felt frustrating, I soon discovered what could top that notion. Two tries later and I'd given up on the notion. I immediately called the hotel concierge to find a bike for Julio and have it delivered to my room, ASAP. Julio, on the other hand, was a little disappointed. He enjoyed having me run indoors. It gave him the opportunity to exercise and lift weights at the same time as I ran, and still manage to protect me by keeping an eye on me.

"Just keep my advice in mind," Julio reminds me, breaking my thoughts. "I still don't see why we're running this thing," Julio mumbles as his body shudders next to me.

Ignoring his bickering, I think hard for the answer to his question. Boredom. It's the reason why I'm running this race. I'd been searching for things to do in New York in hopes to help distract me and this small charity race had popped up. The race addict in me immediately signed Julio and I up.

I feel the crowd stepping forward, telling me we're about to begin. Looking to Julio one final time, I put one ear bud in and hold the other. "Follow my lead. I mainly stay to the outside, unless I get blocked. If that happens, I try to find an inside pocket," I explain.

He gives me a short nod in understanding right before the gun goes off and we start jogging forward. It isn't the sprint I would have loved to start off with, but I'm happy to be running the race at all, reminding me that I haven't felt this carefree in days.

New York wind in the midst of winter is brutal. It can feel as if needles are piercing your skin as it crashes against your body. With the distance we start putting behind us, my fingers slowly become numb. My nose is starting to drip with snot; graphic, yes, I know, but it's exactly what's occurring with every footstep I add to my mile. The sun is barely rising on the horizon. My body is protesting the need to be out at this moment, along with Julio who is now glaring off into the distance at no particular object.

My mind is lost to Tiësto's beat pounding in my ears; the lyrics of *All of Me* on repeat for my run. It's the only song I'm happy running to nowadays. The image of Matt is the boost of motivation to reach my daily goal as I run in the bitter cold of New York's weather.

Soon, my mind is quickly returning to the day I left Portland… And Matt.

"I really miss you, beautiful," Matt's sorrowed voice echoes in my mind.

They are the words that seem to be heard often now during my conversations with Matt. How can I blame him? They are the same words I feel repeating in my soul every minute of my day.

"How much longer until I get to see you?" The dreadful question he asked last night resurfaces in my thoughts.

"I don't know, Matt, but I miss you just as much," I answered back.

"I can't wait to hold you again in my arms." A painful reminder of where I miss being the most… His arms. I've tried to stay strong despite our distance; yet it's much harder than I expected. My mind can't help but think of him every chance I get.

"Abigail!" Julio shouts from my side, stopping me from crashing into someone in front of me. I'd been so lost in my thoughts I wasn't paying attention to where I was going. Weaving my way to their side, I keep running through the bitter cold air that continues to pierce my lungs. Taking a quick glance at Julio, my mind wanders once more, this time to our plane ride from Portland to New York.

"Here are the rules, Abigail. You may not like them, but you're paying me to protect you and I can't do my job if you don't follow my rules," Julio sternly orders. *"First and foremost, when I give an order, you follow it. No questions asked,"* he says, causing me to glower at him.

"You make me sound like a dog you're training," I irritably reply.

"It's for your safely, Abigail. Next. I lead. Always."

"What happens if I'm abducted from behind?" I joke, but wasn't expecting him to be so quick to answer.

"I'm always looking behind my shoulder for you. Plus, your instinct to reach out for me will take over," he explains, and his point does sound logical. *"Back to my original command. I lead, which mean I enter first. I only need two seconds to scan the room before we enter. The entire time I'll have my hand on my gun and ready to use it, if needed. So you'll need to get used to that."* The word gun makes me tense.

I'm already opening my mouth to voice my own concern on that matter, but he holds up his hand to silence me. "It doesn't always mean I'm going to pull it out, but I do need to be ready to, just in case." I have no choice but to accept his reasons.

Nodding in understanding, I ask, "How will we handle my shows? You think they will allow you to lead me down the runway?" I tease.

Without hesitating, he answers, "We'll continue as we have been. You'll remain at my side when moving. When we aren't, I'll keep to the shadows as I usually do." I expect him to go along with my joke, but from the stern expression still on his face, he's currently all business during this discussion.

"Which brings me to the next rule," he adds, verifying my thought just moments ago. "If I tell you to run, you will do so."

"I thought the point was to stay at your side at all times?" I taunt back at him.

He sighs with an impassive expression as he ignores my comment. "There may be a chance when I'm fighting off an intruder that I will order you to run. If I say run, you run," he sternly repeats. "You seek safety in a public place with a crowd. If you're being followed it makes it easier for you to blend in and harder for your attacker to find you." I'm still considering his words when he adds, "Your cell phone has a tracking device in it, along with the one the phone company has provided, just in case. I'll know how to find you if we get separated."

His words are appalling. "When the hell did you put a tracking device in my phone?" I ask, turning the device in my hand, expecting to find some sort of hint of the tracker.

"I didn't. Mateo did."

Snapping my head up, I pierce him with a glare. "He did it for your safety, Abigail," he replies, making me snicker knowing it sounds typical of Matt.

My thoughts go back to the day Matt came home with my new phone. Although it was to replace the phone he'd broken, I shouldn't be surprised he had a tracking device installed in it as well.

"There will be more rules depending on our location, but these are the most important," he instructs.

"How come you haven't given me these rules before?" I curiously ask.

"You usually had Mateo or another friend with you, which gave me the benefit of added security. One of them wouldn't have hesitated to put your safety first," he states, reminding me of Kelly and the mall incident. "On this tour, I'm alone. I need to be able to count on you to follow orders to keep you alive."

Deeply sighing, I agree.

Time quickly passes when you are lost to your thoughts. I'm brought back to reality when I hear the cheering of the crowd off to my sides as we near the finish line. With a wide smile on my lips, Julio and I both cross it and I feel better than ever.

"Your timing is getting better," Julio compliments as he tries to catch his breath. Nodding my head in agreement, I look down at my watch to confirm my pace. It's nowhere near as fast as I would like it to be, but it's improving with every run.

"We better hurry back so I can call Matt before he leaves," I say, walking my way through the crowd surrounding the finish line. It's much easier when you have a bulldozer of a bodyguard to guide your way. On the way, I grab onto a postcard an event person hands me.

Before I have a chance to view it, Julio asks over his shoulder, "Is he still nervous?"

"Yes," I answer with a light chuckle. "The rolls are now reversed between the two of us." My answer brings my thoughts back to my conversation last night with Matt.

"Matt, you're going to do just fine this week. Just go out there and be yourself." As much as I wish I could have been at his side to calm his nerves, he was alone because I had chosen not to be there because of my career.

"I sure hope so." The exasperated sigh following his statement tells me just how nervous he was, even after my encouragement. Soon we're back in my room and I'm dialing Matt's number, hoping he hasn't left yet.

"Hey, beautiful," his husky voice whispers into the line as he answers, my lips automatically pull into a smile.

"Hey, handsome," I answer, using the nickname I have adapted to calling him the last couple of days. "Have you left yet?"

"No. I should have, but I was waiting for you to call."

"You should have called me instead."

"I had a feeling you may have been on your run, but you know how I feel about that."

"Matt, please, I don't want to start arguing with you," I relay, debating whether I want to tell him I just ran a race instead of a simple run. "I promise I'm not pushing myself too hard. I just can't take running on a treadmill," I argue. "Would you like running on a treadmill?"

With a humorous chuckle in his words, he admits, "I've had to before, and I agree, it sucks. I worry you'll injure yourself again. But I guess I should be happy you didn't do that run you told me about." His words send a weight of guilt straight down to the pit of my stomach.

"Matt," I rasp out, fearful of telling him the truth.

"Why do I have a feeling you're going to tell me something I don't want to hear, beautiful?" he voices, the concern in his tone making me cave, no longer able to keep the truth from him.

"I did run that race with Julio," I blurt out.

I brace myself for the small lecture to come, but instead there is a dreadful silence followed by a disappointed sigh from his end, making me feel just as bad. "I hope you didn't run at your normal pace," he responds when he does speak.

Letting out the breath I was fearfully holding in, I answer, "I didn't. But I did miss you at my side," I remorsefully admit. "It didn't feel the same running it with Julio." I'm rewarded with a chuckle.

"He doesn't do it for you?" he playfully teases. Laughing at his words, I say, "No, he doesn't. I'd rather be huffing and puffing next to you."

I can hear his laugh this time, and as usual, I close my eyes to picture his expression. "Now I'm glad I wasn't on the phone listening to that," he replies, still slightly laughing into the phone.

"And why is that?"

His voice drops low as he answers. "Because you're usually huffing and puffing and instead of picturing you running, all I can imagine is you under me as you make those sounds. Which is where I would much rather you be."

His words make my heart speed up with anticipation of the image he's picturing. It's where I'd much rather be at this exact moment as well. "Abigail?" I hear him huskily ask on the other end.

"Soon, Matt. Are you still tired?" I ask, referring to how exhausted he sounded before we ended our phone call. Matt had called me immediately after checking into his hotel room near Lucas Oil Stadium. It had been late, but we had barely spoken throughout the day, so we were desperate to catch up.

"Not too much, but this hard-on I carry around the majority of the day from you not relieving it is not helping me sleep either."

Now I can't help but laugh. "You'll live."

"I just don't understand why you won't give me what I want."

Laughing at his request, I say, "I already told you. I'm not going to have video *or* phone sex with you when I know perfectly well that you jack off anyway."

Matt had admitted to masturbating while we have been apart, especially most recently since I left. He hoped it would lead to me finally giving in to his request to have video sex. Instead, it led to me almost peeing my pants in laughter and a very disappointed Matt.

"We'll see," he relays before adding, "I've got to go, beautiful. I'll call you when I'm done."

"Okay. Go show them who Matt Garcia is," I cheerfully reply, repeating the words he uses to give me courage. I can practically hear his smile radiating from his end of the line as he says, "I love you so much."

"I love you more," I say before ending the call. The silence that follows already pierces at my heart. I lay in bed with an image of Matt for the next couple of minutes, slowly continuing to torture myself. I pick up the postcard and finally get a chance to read it. The enticing words of a future race keep calling out to me. "*Run me.*"

My hopes of running a major race anytime soon seem near impossible, no matter how badly I wish to run it. Rotating my previously injured ankle in the air, I keep asking myself if I'm willing to push myself that hard ever again. Picking up the postcard sized race info up to once more concentrate on the date, I realize I will still be in New York.

Listening to my heart, I sit up and grab my phone, searching for the registration website. I start to do what I hadn't expected to do this morning and sign up for another race. When I tap on the confirm button on the screen, my heart flutters with excitement. I already know this isn't going to be easy to explain to Matt, but deep down inside I'm doing this for myself and it's what makes me happy. He always claims my happiness is what's important to him and if it's really true, then he will understand.

Chapter Two

Abigail

I'M BORED OUT of my mind while sitting and waiting for the set director to make his appearance. I'm surprised after my restless night that I'm able to keep my eyes open. It's getting easier to sleep through the nights without Matt at my side, but some nights, like last night, I get restless and don't sleep well.

I imagined I would make it up by taking a nap after my run this morning, but there was a damper in those plans when I returned and had a note waiting for me at the front desk. It was from the event coordinator in charge of the show.

Subject title: *First meeting.*

The time ordered barely left enough time for me to rush upstairs to shower and get ready before I was exiting the hotel again and hailing a cab with Julio. Apparently not many took the note seriously since there is only one other person besides myself who arrived on time. Glancing toward the girl sitting next to me, she's using her time to converse with someone on her iPad. Nosy and bored, I tilt my head back to get a better view of who she's speaking with and see a male on the screen staring back at her.

"How is your mother feeling today?" I hear her ask, the words coming out sounding as if she's heartbroken.

"She's feeling better. She says she sends her love," he says, looking a little saddened as he replies. The frown spreading across her lips is a well-known feeling.

My heart sinks from both their expressions. I fully understand how they both feel, which is why I turn away to give her some privacy, eyeing a man walking in my direction.

A couple of feet ahead of me now stands a skinny looking French man, who is deeply concentrating on the phone he's tapping away on. His fingers stop as he lifts his head up. "Okay everyone," he announces to the room. His eyes confusedly scan the room, causing his brow to furrow in frustration. "Where the hell is everyone?" he shouts to no one in particular.

Looking around the room, I'm still wondering the same thing. He looks over to an intern with an angered expression. "Find out where the hell the rest of the models are. If they don't get their asses here in the next ten minutes, let them know I'm replacing them!" The evident fury in his voice emphasizes his command.

The poor intern looks both terrified and confused as to how he's going to make it possible before he scurries off to proceed with the request.

"I would have expected you to be one of the missing ones," the skinny man proclaims.

"Who are you?" I snarl back, my sleep deprived moodiness getting the better of me. He draws his head back in shock, his eyes wide as saucers before they turn down to narrow at me.

"I take it you haven't gotten your memory back," he replies, more a statement than a question.

I sit, speechless and unwilling to answer his question, since he hasn't answered my own. For a moment, our eyes lock onto each other's, as if testing who will cave first. Fortunately for me, it's him that loses the battle.

"I'm Hans, the set director," he answers in a condescending tone. Before I have time to ask him to clarify his earlier comment, I see several models walking in, cheerfully laughing at something being shared between them.

"This better be the last time you're late," he bellows at them, but they roll their eyes as they each take a seat.

"Now that most of you are here, I suggest we go over the rules," he begins, back to what I'm starting to believe is his normal attitude.

For the next hour, we are given orders and lectured on what is expected of us. The entire time, I had to force myself not to fall asleep. After the first ten minutes of trying to keep myself from dozing off, I start scrolling the internet instead of torturing myself with having to listen to the lecture. It had not occurred to me until this morning what vital tool I was missing on this trip: an iPad mini so I can see Matt's face on a bigger screen. My phone just isn't cutting it nowadays. The only roadblock, which took up most of my time, was locating the exact hotel Matt was currently staying in. Thankfully, during one of our conversations he mentioned it was located near the training stadium, so it made narrowing down the specific hotel a little less stressful. With thirty minutes of research now paid off, I pushed confirm order on the screen. We would both have an iPad mini soon. You have to love technology.

"Adams, have you heard one word of what I've said this entire time?"

Snapping my head up at the director, I find myself looking back into a pair of eyes narrowed in anger. "Yes. Show up on time. Show up sober. Do my job, and do it well. No fucking up.

Period," I clip out. It was the last of his words, and to be honest, they were the only ones I had paid attention to.

I didn't think his eyes could narrow any lower, but I am proven wrong as they do, along with his lips that form into a very tight line. I'm expecting a lecture from that expression, but he surprises me when he starts to scan the crowd amongst us.

"As long as you follow those rules, we won't have any problems!" he barks out.

I've only just met the man and I already want to strangle him. Thankfully his words are a cue that the meeting is over, and I couldn't be happier that it is. Everyone starts standing to leave, but I stay rooted in my chair as the director's eyes have once again locked onto mine. They are slowly analyzing me and it's starting to creep me out. He begins walking in my direction and I soon feel Julio's presence standing directly behind me, giving me a sense of security, which is exactly what I need since I refuse to show this man any weakness. From the way he's snarling and commanding everyone, it's what he demands. His eyes briefly look above me, most likely at Julio, before they look back down at me.

"Miss Adams, being that I've had the pleasure to work with you in the past, I'm hoping we won't have a repeat of our last encounter."

His words silently shock me, causing my heart to suddenly pause for a moment before it rapidly speeds up. "You shouldn't judge people by their past," I say to him as I attempt to control the temper looming inside of me. "Because if that were the case, even though I don't know you, I'm pretty sure you'd be labeled an asshole," I add. I was only thinking the words that had uncontrollably come out.

I would have expected him to become furious from my words, but instead his eyebrows draw down in confusion.

"You don't remember, do you?"

"No," I curtly reply. I have never once regretted not knowing my past, until now.

Surprisingly, his voice softens as he replies, "So you haven't recovered your memory yet?" I don't know if it's sympathy he's now displaying, or if his sole purpose is to further irritate me.

Regardless, I still answer. "No," I repeat, before quickly adding, "But it doesn't mean I don't know how to do my job. So I suggest you put whatever past we have behind us during this little tour, or else you will be seeing the new me, and you won't like *her*."

He laughs, further irritating me. "I have a feeling that I'm going to like this new Abigail Adams," he replies with a hint of a smile before turning to walk away, leaving me to feel more confused than when we started.

"Was that supposed to be a compliment?" Julio confusedly asks behind me.

"I don't know, but I'm pretty sure it's the best I'm going to get out of him."

"Ms. Adams?" A petrified looking intern is now standing behind Julio's extended arm, as if he was blocking her from approaching me. His eyes scan her from head to toe as he keeps her from moving any closer. With her eyes locked onto Julio, she says, "Hi, I'm Tracie." She quickly introduces herself as she hands me a set of papers from her trembling hand.

"What's this?" I ask, taking the papers from her with an amused smile on my face as she continues to cautiously glance at Julio.

"It's your schedule. I would have given it to your manager, but I was told you don't have one," Tracie crackles out. Julio has taken his hand down now, but it's obvious she's still a little frightened of him as she continues to glance between the two of us. She next looks down at her clipboard, deeply concentrating. "It's noted here everything had to go to your manager's assistant Susan Waters, but I take it she is no longer with you since I don't see her here," she hesitantly adds.

"No," I bitterly clip out, causing her to flinch.

I hadn't meant to be so rude to her, but my earlier fury has returned full force with the reminder of who Susan really was. My temper must be showing since her frightful expression has returned, causing her to duck her head to sever our eye contact. I'm not mad at her directly, but her words upset me. I wasn't expecting them. The mention of Bill's assistant, Susan, has made my temper rise because it's brought back the memory of Bill. Looking down at the paper in my hands again, I take note that it's more than one page. It's five to be more specific. Scanning each page, it's filled with appointments, making my eyes go wide in shock.

"I'm sorry, but I'm still confused why I need this."

"I'm sorry, but I was just ordered to give it to you," she replies with a shrug of her shoulders.

"Thank you. I appreciate it," I answer, hoping I haven't labeled myself a bitch in her eyes because of my earlier reaction.

She gives me a brief smile before turning to walk away, leaving the verdict still open on that judgment. Letting out a huff of air, I start to scan the papers again, this time fully taking them in. The first thing that jumps out at me from the front page is an interview that is scheduled for three hours from now, followed by dinner with *"An exclusive party."*

It continues, page after page, with appearances or interviews pertaining to the show and it all seems overwhelming at this point. From the corner of my eye, I spot Hans walking by and I immediately stop him.

"Umm, I can't do the photo shoot scheduled on the Saturday before we leave for Paris. I already have previous plans," I tell him.

"Cancel them. This is more important. It's your job."

Shocked by his words, I answer, "My *job* is to model for the show. I wasn't told I had to do anything extra."

With an exasperated sigh, he replies, "We would have worked out all the details with a manager, had you had one. But since you don't, we're informing you now."

"So because of that you're just now telling me?" I irritably retort.

"Yes, it's part of your *job*," he states, using his fingers to quote the last word. "Photo shoots are part of the show, and with photo shoots come interviews," he clips out, as if he thinks it will make me cave. I keep my narrowed eyes at him while staying silent, refusing to budge.

"I'm not rescheduling my event," I sternly reply, shaking my head as I cross my arms over my chest, refusing to back down. "Either you reschedule or expect me to show up very late."

"Are you going to start making prima donna demands of us?"

"If that's what it takes to get out of them, I will," I curtly reply, still standing my ground.

He rolls his eyes at me before asking, "What is so important that you can't do what's best for your career?"

"I have a race that day."

He now looks confused, as if having no clue what I'm referring to. "Running. I'm running a race that day," I clarify in layman's terms so he can better understand. His eyes go wide as I finish speaking.

"You mean to tell me running is more important to you than

modeling?" he balks out.

"Yes, it is," I clip out.

"You can't honestly tell me you expect me to rearrange your schedule to accommodate your hobby?" he asks, sounding uncertain.

Stepping forward so I'm mere inches from him, he is forced to lean back a little as I practically growl at him. "Hobby or not, I'm a runner and running races comes with the territory. You either reschedule the photo shoot or expect me to not show up. It's up to you, but I know it won't be my ass on the line when Rebecca doesn't get her photo shoot," I state before turning to walk away, but not before adding, "Now *that* is my prima donna demand!"

Behind me, I hear the faint sound of a gasp, which only makes me smile.

Why do I have a feeling this schedule will be my hardest obstacle to overcome while in New York? Regardless of how hectic it will get, I refuse to let my *hobby,* as Hans had so clearly labeled it, be put on the back burner.

"Don't expect me to take on the role of your assistant as well, Abigail. That was Mateo's department for a reason," Julio teases, helping to push my tension aside.

"Yeah, well, Matt's not here," I huff out as I follow him out into the brisk winter weather. "I hope you're up for a run, because I need one."

"Another one?" Julio asks.

"Yes, another one. I've got a training schedule to cram in," I clarify.

Julio sighs knowing there is no arguing with me at this point. He's most likely upset from knowing he has no choice but to endure the bitter cold that New York has given us today, whether he wants to or not.

"YOU'RE LATE AGAIN," Hans snarls just above whisper into my ear while we both rush into the room. Everyone turns to face me as I enter, forcing me to greet them with an apologetic smile.

"Yes, I know."

I'd forgotten that I had to do this interview and gone for a run. It wasn't until I received a reminder from my phone that I remembered, which by then was a little too late. I'm only on my second day of this ridiculous schedule and I swear my head feels as if it's spinning from trying to keep track of everything. Thankfully, I entered all my appointments into my phone knowing I was bound to forget something at one point or another due to the overwhelming demand they have me under.

"I don't understand why I'm the only one with this out of control schedule," I irritably tell him as he leads me to a director's chair. He remains standing while we bicker at each other.

"Because you're the star model and it's expected of you," he states with his usual snotty attitude.

I don't have a chance to respond before I'm being pushed into a chair and I'm asked my first question. For the next hour, I'm asked many questions, but thankfully they never once bring up my amnesia. They seem more interested in what I was expected to bring to the show, which made me feel a little nervous. With the interview wrapped up, I'm already preparing to leave with Julio when Hans is standing at my side again, his usual pinched expression on his face as he starts speaking to me.

"I hope you're not fashionably late for tomorrow's party."

"What party?" I ask, already opening my calendar to see what I'm missing.

"The meet and greet!" he shockingly exclaims while holding his chest.

"I thought it was another meeting?" I screech, clearly surprised it's not. Of course he gives me a roll of his eyes.

"It's a cocktail party, so you're expected to dress up."

"Whoa. Nobody noted that on the schedule," I defensibly reply. "I don't even have a dress with me," I add, hoping it will help get me out of it, but of course, I'm wrong.

"You don't have a choice. It's mandatory for all models. It's part of the industry. You shouldn't complain. You get paid for the events," he throws at me as if it's going to help clear up the misunderstanding.

"Money is not the issue. It's the fact that you think it's okay to just spring this stuff on me," I irritably declare. "What makes you think I even want to do this thing?"

His lips go up on one side as he considerers my answer. "You really aren't the same girl I first met," he says, still not answering my question. "She would have demanded to be put on the list for these events."

"No, I'm not," I reply through clenched teeth. I hate how he keeps comparing me to my old self. It's really starting to get on my nerves. His eyes suddenly turn sympathetic.

"It's a small meet and greet for the event. Just show up, mingle a bit, and once you've rubbed elbows with a couple of people, you're free to leave," he explains.

Sighing, I reluctantly answer, "Fine," still through clenched teeth.

I turn to walk away when he stops me. "And, Abigail, remember that it's a semiformal event, so please dress appropriately," he clarifies, eyeing me from head to toe, taking in my jeans and hoodie. His eyes go wide when they stop at my Chucks. "Definitely not the old Abigail," he draws out. I ignore his condescending words and proceed to walk away, Julio picking up his pace to get ahead of me.

"You wouldn't fire me if I accidently popped him one, would you?" he asks over his shoulder. Taking a glance back at Hans who is now tapping away on his phone, I reply, "Not. At. All"

Within minutes, we're flagging down a taxi and when I'm inside I let my head fall back onto the seat and close my eyes. My phone starts ringing, alerting me that it's Kelly calling. "Hi, Kelly," I answer with a smile.

"Hey, chica. I thought I'd never hear from you again." Her words make me laugh from her typical Kelly humor.

"I'm sorry I haven't called sooner. My life has been a hectic mess," I grimly reply, remembering I now have to go shopping. "How are things going?" I curiously ask, trying to cheer myself up by changing the subject.

"Nothing new since you've left. You were the life of the party with your love life," she replies with a spark of sarcasm in her words. Now I'm fully laughing as I remember how entertaining she always claimed it could be. I use the next forty-five minute car ride back to the hotel to speak to her, allowing her humor to take my stress away.

Chapter Three

Bill

THE KNOCK ON the door surprises me since I'm not expecting it quite yet. I knew this new girl Amy was desperate, but enough to rush over here right away? I guess some people will do whatever it takes to get ahead in this world. Reaching the door, I'm excited from my vivid image of what's to come, but I am quickly disappointed when I see who is actually staring back at me. Although I'm a bit relieved he's here at all since it's taken him so damn long.

"It's about damn time," I irritably let out to prove how impatient I've grown waiting for him to show up.

"It's only been two days since you asked for the stuff," he throws back. "And they keep changing shit on me. I had to make sure it was up-to-date," he adds, sounding frustrated as he pushes his way past me into my hotel room. I have to admit, the kid's got balls to talk to me this way.

Seeing he's already holding something in his hand, I reach for it. "What do you have for me?" I'm denied as he quickly yanks the papers back and is now holding them up in the air.

"It's going to cost you two-hundred dollars more," he demands, keeping a firm grip on the papers, taunting me with them. His brow goes up, still holding his ground.

"We agreed on five-hundred dollars."

He casually shrugs before handing over the documents. "This is an old schedule anyway. If you want the current info you'll need to fork over the extra two-hundred," he says as he steps away. The little fucker is challenging me, and at this point, I know I have no choice.

"Fine," I bitterly answer, bringing him to a halt before I walk over to the counter to grab my wallet. Pulling out two extra hundreds, I hand it all to him and he reaches for his back pocket to reveal another paper.

Yanking it from his hold, I'm already asking, "What's the change?" before scanning it myself.

"The designer is trying to get the word out about her show, so she scheduled a meet and greet for the models and some high-class people. It's happening tomorrow night at the Regency."

Perfect. My lips curve up into a smile as I formulate my next plan. Quickly walking back to the counter, I scribble a name down on a notepad before handing it to him. "I need you to get this name on the list," I order, watching his brows go up again.

Taking the small paper from me, he tilts his head to the side, as if considering something. "It's going to cost you an extra hundred dollars."

"You sure know how to weasel money out of people."

"Interns don't make much and I'm not the one who's desperate to get to her," he relays with a shrug of his shoulders. Knowing I don't have much choice, I grab another hundred from my wallet.

"That name better be on the list," I command, still holding the bill in warning.

"It will," he clips out as he reaches for the money before turning to walk away, leaving me to watch him walk out the door. The moment I hear the click, I pull out my phone to make a call.

"Yeah, what's up?" Evan answers into the phone.

"I need a favor," I reply.

"When don't you?"

Ignoring his arrogant remark, I get straight to the point. "There's an event tomorrow night. Abigail will be there. I need you to gather some intel for me."

There's a pause from the other end before he asks, "And if she recognizes me?"

"Convince her she's lost her mind. It shouldn't be that hard. I just need you to find out specifically how much she knows."

Silence again. "Evan?"

"Fine," he lets out with a frustrated sigh that I can clearly hear. "But this better not get out of control, Bill."

"You have nothing to worry about," I inform him, not entirely lying.

"Where's the event?" he asks, sounding as if he's caved. Even if he hasn't, I know I can convince him.

"The Regency. There's going to be a lot of high society clients there, so it would be to your advantage as well."

I don't have to physically see Evan to know he's lighting up. It is apparent in his voice as he asks, "Really?"

"I just need you to make sure nothing has changed with her. I'll take care of the rest."

"Text me the information and I'll make sure to get back to you," he responds, not sounding convinced, but still willing to comply.

"Will do," I tell him, earning me an unsatisfied grunt before the line goes dead. Looking down at the paperwork in my hand, my lips curl up into a smile. It's then that I hear another knock on the door, but this time when I open it I find Amy.

"Good, you're early," I tell her, already pushing her back down the hall to the elevator. She looks excited as she asks, "Are we going out?"

"Sure. But first I have to stop by another hotel to leave an old friend a note," I say, already executing my next plan on the way over.

Chapter Four

Abigail

I CAN'T GET this text message to send. It keeps telling me network failure. I'm ready to chuck it onto the sidewalk, but then I wouldn't have a phone anymore and I'd be disappointed over that. Since I'm more focused on my phone than where I'm walking, Julio startles me when he shouts, "Abigail!" right before I slam into someone.

A loud "humph" comes from us both as a stack of paperwork scatters across the floor between us, followed by a slew of cuss words coming from the person I crashed into.

"I'm so sorry," I immediately say, feeling guilty about crashing into her.

"I tried warning you, but I guess I was too late," Julio says behind me as he kneels down to help the girl already kneeling on the floor. Feeling the need to also help, I squat down in an attempt to help them. With all three of us now gathering the papers, within seconds they are bundled and in a pile as we hand them over to her.

"I really am sorry," I say to the girl who is now stuffing the disoriented pile into a messenger bag.

"Yeah, whatever... It's not like I was paying attention either," she complains before she stands up.

"Victoria?" Julio asks, sounding unsure, her name rolling off his tongue in a Spanish accent. She stiffens for a moment before she looks up.

"Julio?" Her eyes go wide in surprise as she swiftly stands to give him a hug.

Now *I'm* confused. "You know each other?" I ask as I watch them embrace. When they pull apart, the girl happily nods her head. "Yeah, Julio used to work for my dad," she states, before her smile turns into a frown. "It hasn't been the same since he left," she immediately adds, the sadness spreading across her face.

"Has he gotten worse?" Julio skeptically asks.

She only nods her head, giving no verbal response.

Julio lets out a heavy sigh as he gives her a sympathetic look. "I hear he's in D.C. now. How's that going?"

By now I've managed to put two and two together. Victoria's dad must be the senator Julio used to work for. Now Victoria's dad is in D.C., exactly where Julio aims to be.

"More money, which means more women," she disappointedly answers, resentment clear in her tone.

"I'm sorry, Victoria," Julio says to her, a heavy frown still on his face.

"He'll never change. I learned that long ago, Julio, you know that," she says, but from the resentful tone in her voice, it's obviously still affecting her. "I just feel sorry for my mom. She's the one that has to deal with his cheating," she mentions, making my eyes grow wide.

"How's law school coming along?" Julio inquires, as if trying to change the subject. "It's going."

Julio looks around, as if searching for someone. "I see you haven't changed," Julio grimly comments, leaving me confused again.

"You know how much I hate having someone hovering over me every minute," she says, glancing in my direction.

"I'll talk to someone and have them contact you," he says, making her scowl.

"I've been doing fine on my own for a while now. I don't need security following me around like a puppy dog," she firmly bites back. "Besides, it's New York. It's easier to blend in," she declares, as if it will change his mind. She glances in my direction, her eyes analyzing me. "You're still doing security, I see."

Julio lets out a chuckle. "Yeah, but this one doesn't have me hiding anything for her," he states, leaving me wondering what he meant by the comment.

Victoria's lips go flat with a short nod. An awkward silence lingers in the air. Victoria looks down at her watch and her eyes go wide. "Oh shit, I've got to go. It was nice seeing you again, Julio," she says before quickly hugging him once more and walks away. Julio watches, eyes searching our surroundings like he usually does when he's with me.

"I take it her dad is that senator you told me about?" I have to ask.

"Yes."

When she has disappeared from our view, we resume our walk to our original destination; straight into Saks Fifth Avenue, the store I was dreading to go into, but according to the hotel concierge it was the best store to get my dress.

"So why the concern with her?" I ask, curiosity getting the best of me.

Julio looks as if he doesn't feel like discussing the subject, but still grants my request and answers. "Victoria has always been independent since the day I met her, sort of shy and quiet. She keeps to herself, but don't let that fool you. She's smart and doesn't let anyone push her around." When I look at him, he is considering his words with a tilt of his head. "You remind me a lot of her."

"I hope that's a good thing," I mumble, heading straight to the women's department, already dreading what is to come.

"It is. Most of the time," he voices before letting out a half-hearted laugh from the appalled look I shoot him.

"You're lucky I like you, Julio," I mumble under my breath, now earning me a full-blown laugh this time.

I'M TIRED, MOODY, and don't want to think of shopping for another couple of weeks. I thought I would be in and out, but when your name is Abigail Adams you're given your own personal shopper who thinks you need a whole new wardrobe. You're then walking out six hours later, even after I kept insisting I only needed *one* dress. At least Julio got the good end of the stick. He sat the entire time while the older ladies drooled all over him. His annoyed expression from how they were acting was my highlight of the day.

I've never been happier to hear the ping of the elevator announcing my floor, but my blissfulness soon disappears when we enter our hotel room. Julio comes to a complete halt, my dress bags dropping to the floor from his hands as he pulls out his gun and aims it at someone.

Within a millisecond, I hear the cocking of the gun as he shouts, "Freeze!"

Shocked, I'm frozen in place. My heart stops before rapidly

resuming, practically beating out of my chest. "I was only delivering your package," I hear a frightful voice squeal out from in front of Julio. Finding the will to move, I glance over Julio's shoulder to see a *very* frightened bellhop from the hotel holding both his hands up in surrender. Looking towards his side next, I notice a package sitting on the coffee table.

"Pick it up and bring it to me," Julio sternly demands, keeping the bellhop in a shivering state as he continues to point the gun at him. Without hesitation, he picks up the package and slowly starts walking over to us. "Were you expecting a package?"

Realizing what it might be, I say, "Oh, yes. Sorry." Shamefully apologizing to the bellhop, I grab it from his trembling hands. Julio lowers his gun and returns it to his holster.

"This note came as well," he says, still quivering as he hands me an envelope.

"You're dismissed," Julio curtly conveys to the employee.

I manage to whisper, "Sorry," as he rushes past me. I make a mental note to find out who the employee is and leave him a very hefty tip for what happened.

When the click of the door is heard, I say to Julio, "Well, at least you can't say you never got to use the thing," still trying to calm my racing heart.

"I'll do my usual check," he replies, choosing to ignore my comment as he makes his way into my room.

While he does that, I'm left picking up my clothes bags containing my dresses from off the floor. Julio exits my room, and with his normal nod of approval, he allows me to enter. Putting everything in its place, I toss myself onto the bed next, anxious to open the envelope.

"Emily, how much longer are you going to take?" Matt impatiently whines from my side, making me laugh.

"You're the one who insisted we spend time with each other," I remind him.

"When I mentioned spending time together, I meant it as a suggestion. Not for you to take it seriously," he mumbles in return, hoisting the bags he's holding from one hand to the other.

I shoot him with a glare. "Stop complaining. Oh, look, they're having their semi-annual sale," I enthusiastically say, already walking into the store and forcing him to follow. Behind me, I hear a disappointed groan come from Matt, but I ignore him. Browsing through the boxes for my size, from the corner of my eye I see Matt's eyes scanning the store. I've seen those eyes a lot most recently. They're what I call his "On the search for his next victim" eyes. The cheeky smile on his lips when a salesgirl approaches him confirms my prediction. Leaving him to his venture, I continue walking around the store. Minutes later, his eyes catch mine while still speaking with the same girl and he nods in my direction. My curious eyes are watching as he dips his head down to whisper into her ear, causing her to giggle. Shaking my head at his flirtatious actions, I go back to searching for what I need.

Thirty-minutes later we're both walking out of the store, happier than when we'd entered. I'd gotten a discount from the salesgirl thanks to Matt's flirtatious ways and he'd apparently gotten her number.

"Maybe shopping with you isn't so bad after all," he sarcastically lets out.

"Nice to know you're unashamed to use your sister as bait."

"You wound me," he says as he holds his hand to his chest. "What would ever make you think that?"

"Oh, please, Matthew. Ever since you've taken my advice and parted ways with Laura, you've become a typical man whore," I say, looking through the window of another store.

Through the reflection of the glass, I watch his eyes go wide as saucers.

"Emily!" Turning to face him, I'm now raising my brow to challenge him to prove me wrong. "I wonder if Sam is lucky enough to hear your dirty mouth," he says with a wag of his brows. Now I'm the ones with wide eyes, making Matt laugh.

"Dang, Emily. I do love you," he says through a fit of laughter, causing my heart to swell. "I really do miss spending time with you, though," he adds.

"I do, too," I whole-heartedly reply before sighing deeply.

"I really wish we didn't have to be so far apart from each other," Matt somberly says. "It sucks sometimes."

A sudden ache forms in my heart. I abruptly stop to hug him. My reaction dumbfounds him at first, but soon he is returning my embrace. "No matter where I'm at, or how far away I may be, I'll always be here for you," I promise.

"Dammit, Emily," he protests near my ear. "Don't make me cry like a pansy," he croaks out. I let out a burst of laughter from his choice of his words. His arms tighten around my body before he releases me to place a kiss on my cheek. "You know you'll always be my number one girl."

Smiling up at him, I say, "I'll make sure to remind you of that next time I want to go shopping."

Now groaning, he replies. "Anything but shopping."

Playfully swatting him on the chest, we both laugh before we start to walk way.

I sit on my bed as my lips curve up into a smile as I recall the memory. Now I know why Matt will make up any sort of excuse when I mention I need to go shopping. The thought makes me giggle. With the anticipation of reading Matt's loving words on the inside of the envelope, I glance over to the flowers he sent a couple of days ago. Impatiently ripping open the flap, my heart begins to race when I read the message.

Do you really think you can simply go back to being the person you were?

Deep down inside my mind recognizes the scrawl of lettering. My still rapidly beating heart is in denial, but my mind is screaming that it's him. I want to drop the letter, feeling as if it's burning my fingertips as I hold it, but I can't. Instead, I clutch it tighter, reading and rereading the words as if I'm trapped in a nightmare.

Julio's distinctive knock startles me back to reality, causing my breath to hitch. "Abigail, I'm going to head down to the gym for an hour. Is that okay with you?" he cautiously asks from the other side of the door.

Forcing myself to stand, I go to open the door, making sure to keep the note hidden. With a forced smile on my face, I greet him. "Sure. Would you like me to order dinner?"

"Not yet. Wait until I return," he answers, reminding me of his one rule while he's out of the room. *Never open the door for anyone, at all.*

"Okay," I reply, a fabricated smile still on my lips.

He gives me a quick nod as he says, "I'll be back soon."

Following him into the living room, I watch him leave. As soon as I hear the click of the door, I rush over to the fireplace, pushing the switch to automatically light it. When the flames are high enough, I throw the note into it. Standing in the silence of the room while the note catches the flames and evaporates into ashes, my fear and anxiety quickly take over.

When the flames no longer show any evidence of the note, I walk back into my room, needing to call Matt; I know his voice will push my worry aside. My eyes catch the package on the bed and I rush to open it with a slight smile on my face, anxious to see his smile instead. I spend the next couple of minutes setting up everything necessary on the iPad mini to FaceTime Matt. I'm soon pushing the call button on the screen, but instead of Matt's gorgeous smile staring back at me, I'm left with:

Matt is not available for FaceTime

My smile turns into a frown from disappointment. My earlier worry is now replaced with a tightening of my chest from missing Matt. Knowing I need to distract myself so I don't go crazy with worry, I grab my earphones off the dresser and plug them into the iPad to arrange my playlist. I'm not listening to the music for very long before Matt's picture is staring back at me, stating he's calling me back. Pushing the answer button on the screen, I'm soon seeing the smile I expected earlier, and it brightens my mood from the inside out.

"Hey, I've missed you."

"Thank you for the gift, beautiful," he beams back to me. "I'm sorry I missed your call. I went out to grab something to eat and saw on my phone that you were calling, so I rushed back here so I can talk to you."

His admission has my heart swelling. "I'm sorry I made you do that, but I won't lie, I'm happy you did," I happily admit.

"I wanted to call you sooner, but I checked the schedule you emailed me and saw you were in your interview."

"Trust me, I would have much preferred to talk to you," I grimace. Watching him laugh at my words tugs a wide smile across my lips. "So, what did you do today?" I pry as I usually do at the end of the day, wanting to know every detail.

"Oh, you know, the usual," he replies with a shrug of his shoulders. "Went to training camp. Got my ass physically kicked in training. Came back to take a shower, which is when I missed you the most," he teases with a wag of his brows, making me roll my eyes at the way he emphasized the words when mentioning the shower.

"Oh, really, and why was that?" I tease back, already knowing how he will answer.

"Because I would much rather have had you washing my body, instead of myself," he huskily answers as his eyes grow dark. He may be looking back at me through a screen, but my body instantly reacts to his words as if he were next to me.

"Is that so?" My breathing is slightly labored as the thoughts of showering with Matt roam my mind.

"Beautiful, if you keep looking at me like that, I won't be ashamed to take care of the little problem I currently have while I'm talking to you."

My breath hitches from the words, but I manage to ask, "And what problem would that be, Matthew?"

"The fucking hard-on I can't seem to get rid of when I talk to you," he answers in his low husky voice. The earphones emphasize every detail of the words and my body ignites with flames wanting him to do as he has teased.

"I want to see," I shamefully say. "Please," I plead, hoping my words will encourage him to comply with my request. His eyes close as he lets out a groan.

"Only if you'll do as I ask," he's managed to say, his voice dropping even lower.

My body is already pent up with desire from not being with Matt for the last week, so I'm weak and willing to give into any one of his requests at the moment.

"Yes," I impulsively say, hoping I have the courage to follow through. Because I already know what Matt will ask of me.

In the next second, Matt's face disappears from the scene and it's now shuffling before I'm graced with his erection staring back at me in its glorious salute against his stomach. Only a minute ago I was desperately containing my arousal, but I no longer can as a spark of desire shoots straight in between my legs. My eyes are still fully taking it in before it disappears from the screen and Matt's face is once more staring back at me. He has a smug smile on his face now.

"I know that look, beautiful. Did you like what you see?"

My pulse is racing and I'm forced to swallow so I can answer. "Of, course."

The smug smile has now widened. "Is that so? And what do you want me to do with it, Abigail?" His words cause my body to react with more sparks as if Matt were next to me whispering the words into my ear.

"I want you to touch it," I whisper back.

His eyebrows shoot up in surprise. "I'll touch it, but only if you touch yourself." My heart briefly stops as I nod my head to answer.

"Get naked, I want to know that you're naked while I touch you," he demands with the same tone as when he'd started encouraging me to do so. Obeying his command, I place the iPad down on the bed and quickly undress. Once done, I place the earphones back in since I love the way they delivered Matt's words directly into my ears.

"There, I'm naked. What about you?" Although I've asked the question, I'm already seeing the answer as Matt's bare chest is staring back at me.

Without hesitating, he begins. "Glide your hand up against your breasts and squeeze them."

Deep inside, I'm still hesitant to do as he requests, but my body is demanding I follow his instructions. Slowly, I run my hand up my body and grab onto my breast, giving it a tight squeeze. He must have seen that I complied because he shoots his next order.

"Now pinch your nipple. Pretend it's my mouth sucking on it. Close your eyes and envision me rubbing my tongue over it, sucking it hard."

His voice is low and full of desire, encouraging me to follow his every command. He's whispering the words to me and as he's ordered, I close my eyes and the image of Matt above me has replaced the darkness behind my closed lids.

"Do you like me doing that?" I hear him ask, causing me to lightly moan in response. "Now run your hand down your body and rub your finger against your clit."

My body is shaking with nerves as my hand glides down my stomach. With my eyes still closed, my fingers reach my clit and I gasp in shock from what I'm doing.

"That's it, beautiful," I hear Matt say into my ears. "Pretend it's my finger rubbing you down there. You're so wet and ready for me, aren't you?"

I can't answer with words since the sensation has overtaken my body. Instead, I let out a pleasured moan. "My hand is on my dick, pretending it's your sweet, warm mouth wrapped around it. Do you want me to lick you down there, beautiful?"

Shit. Pretending he was the one rubbing me was enough to make my body ignite, but from the words he's just given me, I'm about ready to go over the edge. He doesn't wait for my answer, but instead keeps talking.

"Fuck, beautiful, you taste so good."

"Oh, God, Matt," I whimper as I tell myself it's his mouth against my clit, instead of my finger.

"How close are you Abigail, because I'm about ready to fucking blow," he whispers to me. "Are you going to let me come in your sweet mouth like the last time?" His words take me back to the time I gave Matt a blowjob and how much I enjoyed bringing him to completion.

"Fuck, beautiful, I can't hold out much longer. Please, tell me you're with me and going to finish." His words encourage me to rub myself harder. My fingers are working full force to reach Matt's level. I can feel my body tensing like a bow and without answering his question, I scream at the top of my lungs from my release. My body explodes with fireworks and I can almost hear the pounding through my ears, but too late I realize the pounding is coming from the bedroom door as Julio suddenly burst through it. I'm now screaming, not from desire, but from mortification at seeing him staring back at me.

Grabbing for a pillow to cover my nakedness, my chest heaves as I try to catch my breath as I manage to scream, "Oh my God, Julio!"

I can hear Matt furiously screaming curses into my ears, forcing me to yank the earphones out. Julio is shielding his eyes with his hand, his body language telling me he's clearly embarrassed for walking in on me, but he stays rooted to the spot.

"I'm sorry, Abigail," he apologizes in his thick Hispanic accent he only uses when he's sympathetic. "I heard you screaming as I entered the hotel room and I was worried," he explains, "I'm sorry," he repeats, his head shamefully drops low, his eyes still covered as he exits the room, shutting the door behind him. I'm left shocked, still trying to catch my breath, as my eyes frantically scan the room. From the corner of my eye, I spot the iPad mini with Matt's furious expression screaming on the screen. Picking it up, he's no longer speaking, but angrily scowling back at me as I put in the earphones.

"Matt," I say, still dazed and confused.

"What the fuck is he doing just walking into your room?" he shouts back at me.

"Matt, he didn't just walk into my room," I reply, clutching the pillow tighter against my body.

"He just saw you naked, Abigail! I'm going to fucking kick his ass!"

Taking a deep breath now that my heart has managed to stop racing all over again, I explain, "I really doubt that is possible, but he didn't just come into my room. The door was locked, which is why he barged in."

"Why the fuck would he just barge in?" Matt's anger apparent in his expression and words.

"He says he heard me screaming and was worried," I quietly reply, now feeling ashamed over the entire situation. Matt rakes his hand down his face as I continue. "I told you this phone sex thing was a bad idea," I whisper back to him, now feeling mortified over the whole situation.

He doesn't reply, instead sighing as if reluctant to agree with my words. "I'm sorry, beautiful. No more phone sex," he answers, agreeing with me. My jaw drops in shock.

"Oh, no, Matt. You've proven just how much I need this. I'll just have to notify Julio of when we'll have our private little sessions so we don't have a repeat of tonight."

"Over my dead body!" he angrily lets out through clenched teeth. "He's already seen my girlfriend naked. I don't need him putting two and two together by you telling him you're having sex and he starts having fantasies of his own. *I am* going to have a talk with him when I see him again." I don't argue, but instead stay silent while Matt adds, "We'll just have to wait until we see each other again to have sex."

"And when is that going to be?" I ask.

"Soon," he says with a smile that quickly replaces his scowl, as if staking a promise. "After tonight it can't come soon enough," he adds, and I can't agree more. Exhausted from our little escapade, I stifle a yawn behind my hand. The smile on Matt's face widens. "Good to know I can still wear you out."

I let out a heartfelt laugh knowing exactly what he means. "Yes, you can."

Matt's face whips into another direction as I hear another voice. "I've got to go, beautiful. My roommate just showed up."

My eyes shoot wide open. "Matt, you're still naked," I sternly whisper back, hoping his roommate didn't hear me. Instead of looking ashamed from the realization, his eyebrows are wiggling back at me.

"I've got nothing to hide."

"You're such a whore," I playfully tease, clutching the pillow tighter to my chest as if his roommate would see me. "But I love you for who you are."

"I love you, too, beautiful."

Within seconds we're ending the call and I throw myself back onto the bed, still mortified over the entire situation. Letting out a huff of breath, I can only hope the time goes by quickly, because after tonight, I don't know if I can last much longer without Matt.

Chapter Five

Abigail

"SO WHAT IS this thing you're going to again?" Matt asks, a hint of jealousy in his voice, which makes me smile.

"It's a meet and greet," I answer with a chuckle, grabbing for the dress in the closet while juggling the iPad in my hands. An evident scowl crosses his face and I can't help but giggle.

"I still don't get why you're required to wear a cocktail dress to a *meet and greet*," he practically growls.

"It must be something the designer is demanding."

His lips go flat, but the sigh he returns tells me he's accepted it. "Alright," he voices, raking his hand down his face. "I guess I shouldn't complain much anyway. You're letting me go out."

"You make it sound like you need my permission or something," I say with a chuckle. From the way his teasing smile fills the screen, I have a feeling it was a test.

"Of course not," he quickly answers, trying to sound convincing, but somehow it seems far from it.

"Where are you going?" I ask, still curious since I don't know his plans.

"I'm going out with a group of guys to a local club," he calmly answers.

"Oh," I sorrowfully let out.

His brow is now high again. "You're not going to get mad are you?"

"No, but I remember the last time you were in a club and what *you* were doing," I playfully tease. Through the screen I watch his breath hitch and his eyes are now hooded as he looks back at me. He's about to say something, but is interrupted when we hear, "Let's go, Garcia!" as someone angrily shouts in the background. By the sounds of it, I know they're already impatient.

"I'm sorry, beautiful. I've got to go," he apologizes, but quickly adds, "I can't wait until I see you again. The things I'm going to do to you will put that night to shame." The promising words make me wet between my legs before the line goes dead. I let out a frustrated groan as I scurry off into the bathroom to get ready. I'm already late, but I don't care. I'm going to need the shower to help alleviate my sexual frustration.

"YOU'RE LATE. AGAIN. We didn't think you'd show up," a snarky intern, whose name is Charlie and is starting to get on my nerves, remarks.

"It's not your job to keep me on time," I snarl back, walking past him as Julio pushes him aside. I don't bother giving him a backwards glance as I walk my way into the room. The girl who was sitting next to me during the meeting spots me and gives me a friendly wave. I make my way straight over to her, feeling ashamed I never got her name that day.

"Hi," I greet with a friendly smile. I see her light up with a smile as well.

"I'm Sarah. It's so nice to meet you."

"I'm Abigail. It's nice to meet you as well."

She blushes as she replies, "I know. I was so excited when I found out I'd be working with you. You're the reason why I wanted to be a model," she shyly remarks.

"I like your dress," I quickly comment, hoping to break the awkwardness I feel between us from her comment.

"Thank you."

The next few minutes are spent getting to know each other, and within that time I come to admire Sarah. She seems confident of herself, but never shows an ounce of haughtiness from being a model. She's nothing like the other girls who walk around as if you should be privileged to be in their presence. It makes me wonder if that was how I once treated everyone around me.

She grabs a champagne flute from a passing waiter and hands it to me. "Here, you're going to need one of these to help loosen you up. Trust me, I'm still drinking mine," she says, holding hers up to emphasize her words.

I take the glass from her and take a sip from it, allowing the fizzy bubbles to trickle down my tongue. She eyes Julio who is only steps behind me as she looks him up and down.

"Does he follow you everywhere?" she asks in a whisper into my ear. With a chuckle, I give Julio a sideways glance before I answer.

"He has to. My boyfriend wouldn't have it otherwise."

Her eyes go wide in amazement. "Is *he* your boyfriend?"

"Oh, hell, no!" I exclaim, hearing Julio chuckle behind me.

Sarah now looks confused. "Where is your boyfriend, then?" She looks around the room as if she'd find him. I'm reluctant to answer, but from how humble she seems, I would feel guilty keeping it from her.

"He's in Indianapolis at some sort of football training camp," I casually answer, as if it's no big deal.

Her eyes go wide. "Is he a pro football player?" she curiously asks.

Her enthusiasm makes me giggle. "Not yet. But he will be soon," I confidently answer. She gives me a swooning sigh.

"You're lucky. Mine is a boring engineering major, but I still love him as if he were the sexiest man alive," she states as her earlier blush returns.

"Looks aren't always important," I tell her, and by the nod she gives me, she agrees. I'm about to ask where she's from when a gentleman is soon at my side. I can feel Julio close behind me.

"Abigail Adams. It's a pleasure to finally meet you," he states, tilting his head to the side, already holding his hand out for me to shake. "I'm Aaron, the marketing director for the Sprinter Running Company."

"Oh, the running company I did my first photo shoot for."

The man laughs while shaking his head. "I know for sure we weren't your first photo shoot, since it was *my* jaw dropping when they told me who they managed to book for the shoot. Regardless, I was honored you did the shoot in the first place," he states.

"I meant since I started doing photo shoots again," I feel the need to clarify.

"Oh, I remember that one," Sarah says, bringing my attention back to her. She ducks her head, as if ashamed of her comment. "Sorry. I sort of followed your career since I hope to one day be half as good as you are."

Her humble words make me blush. "She really was a natural when it came to that shoot."

Confidently smiling, I comment, "It's because I was doing something I love to do," I tell them both.

Sarah looks surprised by my statement. "So you really are a runner? Like for real?"

Her questions make me laugh. "Yes. My boyfriend actually got me into running. I love it."

"We appreciate that you do. It's rare when we get a model that is an actual runner. The new line we had you wear that day for the shoot has helped our sales skyrocket. But I'm pretty sure it's because you were wearing them," he claims. "So, thank you," he adds.

"It's my pleasure."

"Have you ever considered sports modeling for your permanent career? We may not be able to pay you as much as these big shots do," he says, waving his hand around at the crowd of people. "But from following your running events, I'm sure you'd be happy doing it. We'd love to have you be our official model, but it would mean being in a contract with our company."

I consider his words for a moment, but with a heavy sigh, I answer, "As much as I'd like to take you up on your offer, I think the runway is where I'm meant to be. But thank you anyway," I inform him.

He grows disappointed before reaching into his coat pocket to retrieve a business card, handing it over to me. "If you ever change your mind, please don't hesitate to give us a call," he says with a smile. "Good luck with your career and don't ever give up your one true love. Running."

"Never."

Sarah and I both watch him walk away, but her eyes stay locked onto him as she says, "Damn, if I wasn't already a girl spoken for, I wouldn't be ashamed of convincing him I can be his model," she states.

I love how Sarah can easily make me laugh. "There isn't anyone who can convince me of leaving my man," I say, still half-laughing.

"Is that so?" I hear a deep voice ask from my other side, startling me. When I turn around to see who it is, I'm greeted with another suited man, but this one makes the hairs on the back of my neck stand up. Julio had kindly backed away after Aaron had introduced himself, but my body language must have alerted him, because he's at my side once more. Normally Julio's hovering can annoy me, but from the way my stomach is turning, and not in a good way, I couldn't be happier he's invading my space.

The man gives me a smug smile before he reaches for my hand and lifts it to his mouth. The action makes my nervous stomach turn. "It's a pleasure to see you here tonight, Abigail," he coyly says. From the way he said my name, it's as if he knows me.

"I apologize, but I don't seem to recall who you are."

He brushes off my remark with a wave of his hand. "That's perfectly fine. I do understand the circumstances. Allow me to introduce myself. My name is Evan Donovan."

The name instantly sends a shiver down my spine. He looks over to Sarah and takes her hand to kiss it next. Instead of the forced smile I'd given him, her face still holds her bashful blush from his cavalier move. He's facing me again, and against all protest to run, I stay rooted to the spot with my fake smile as I desperately search my mind as to how I know him.

"And what is it you do exactly, Mr. Donovan?" I ask with a curious tilt of my head.

"I'm in advertising, Ms. Adams. It's how we knew each other so well in the past. It's a shame you don't remember."

His words stab at the open wound everyone in this industry

seems to remind me of. "Obliviously you must have not been important enough for me to remember," I smugly say with a smile. My comment doesn't faze him at all as he chuckles at my words. "If you'll please excuse us, Mr. Donovan, Sarah and I are required to mingle throughout the room. I'm sure you understand," I say, already tugging Sarah away, not bothering to wait for an answer. Sarah happily follows, but when we've put enough distance between us, I manage to glance over my shoulder to see his watchful eyes still on me.

"That was awkward," Sarah draws out from my side. "I take it you didn't like the guy?"

"No," I grimly answer. " I've been in more awkward situations than that," I mumble. Julio lets out a groan while I blush from head to toe from my own comment, remembering how many times he's apologized to me since last night.

"Oh, look! There's Hans," Sarah excitedly says. Finding him amongst the crowd, he is walking towards us, an artificial smile plastered on his face. My reaction is far from Sarah's. I'm ready to bolt as his eyes focus on me. I already know it's for a reason I may not like.

Reaching me, his high pitch voice squeaks out, "There she is. Just the girl we were looking for." Exactly what I was expecting.

From the tone of his words, I'm already dreading what will come next. "Ms. Ackerman here is from The National Society of Saint Smith Prep, a boarding school here in New York. She was just informing me she needs someone to present an award at their next social event and *of course* I thought of you, Abigail," he says, eyeing me with the same smile he walked over with.

It's taking every ounce of patience I have in my veins to not blow up in front of the sweet, old lady standing with us.

"That would be just wonderful!" she says as she claps her

hands together with excitement. My mouth is already opening to conjure an excuse, but Hans is already answering for me.

"She's honored to do it. Aren't you, Abigail?" I'm now piercing him with my signature glare.

Before I can deny her request, she's adding, "Wonderful. I'm going to go let my colleagues know," before quickly walking away.

My heart is pounding while my blood rises. "Why the hell do you keep doing this to me?" I angrily throw at Hans, ready to pound the smirk off his lips.

"We need good publicity for the show."

"You do, but I don't," I clip out.

His eyebrow slowly arches as he tilts his head and slowly lifts his finger. "This," he remarks, his finger swirling around at my body. "This is the old Abigail you didn't want to be, but are proving you still are," he retorts before turning to walk away, leaving me to stand there with my mouth gaping open.

"Do you want me to take care of him?" Julio amusedly asks from behind me, making Sarah laugh.

"I like him," she says, tilting her chin at Julio.

Lifting the glass of champagne up to my lips, I tilt the glass up and completely empty the contents into my mouth. The alcohol is warm and has lost its fizz, but at this point I don't care anymore. The least I can hope for is that it does its job so it can help calm my temper. If not, I may just walk over to Hans and strangle him. Looking down at my phone, I'm already counting down the minutes until I can leave and pray I don't kill someone before I do so.

Chapter Six

Matt

STILL SMILING FROM Abigail's open mouth gasp as I ended the call, I leave it lingering in my mind as I exit my hotel room and catch up to my roommate.

"Is that the girl who you have to keep checking in with?" Kevin, my roommate for the duration of camp, asks as we start to walk away. I've adapted to calling him, "*Crazy Kevin.*" From the moment we met, he's been nothing but crazy. There hasn't been anything he wouldn't attempt to try to succeed in getting noticed while the scouts have been watching us.

"Yeah, it was my girl," I answer as we step into the elevator. "But it's not like that," I push, somehow feeling the odd need to defend myself.

He grunts at my response. "You've spent more time on the phone than you do going out. It's a miracle I managed to get you out tonight." I keep silent, not daring to tell him the only reason why I agreed to go out was because I knew Abigail was going out as well. It was a mocking waiting to happen. "So, how long have you been with her?"

"A little over six months." He cocks his eyebrow, wearily looking at me. "Yeah, well, if you knew how lucky I am you'd want it too."

"So, it's that serious?"

"I'm going to marry her one day. She just hasn't agreed… Yet."

Shaking his head again, he asks, "You serious?" Again, I keep silent, knowing it isn't worth arguing over. "I don't know man. I don't see the point of wanting to settle down. You're still young and you'll have plenty of women throwing themselves at you soon. Why wouldn't you want to take advantage of that?" His last words come out more of a statement than a true question, but I ignore them. I know deep down inside Abigail is worth settling down for. "Trust me, dude. There isn't any girl in the world that'd make me change my mind. Even if she was hot."

"Trust me, I've had girls throwing themselves at me and it wasn't worth losing her over," I say as I pull out my phone to show him a selfie of Abigail and me on my locked screen. He tugs the phone up to get a closer look of the picture and I watch his eyes go wide.

"No. Fucking. Way!" he says, his face whipping from my face to the phone in disbelief. "Is that the model? What's her name?" he asks snapping his fingers.

"Abigail Adams," I answer with a nod as he continues looking at the phone as if he can't believe his eyes. "Is she the reason why you were naked the other night?"

"Yeah," I reply with a chuckle now that I can laugh about it.

Now looking suspicious, he asks, "How the fuck did you manage hooking up with her?"

The question should irritate me, but my smile returns as I think about the day she showed up at my door. "She found me, and it was the best day of my life," I reply.

He snorts before saying, "Good luck trying to put a ring on that girl's finger. It's all about the career with them," he utters, nodding in the direction of my phone.

This time my silence is due to the recognition of his words, and how it pertains to our current situation. Our love has endured many obstacles, and because of them our love is stronger. As much as I keep telling myself I have to let Abigail follow her dreams, is this only a glimpse of what our future will be like if I go pro? Us spending most of our relationship with distance between us? Somehow it feels like it will. Breathing deeply, I remind myself that the distance will only make our love grow stronger. It just really sucks that I have to keep reminding myself.

LOOKING DOWN AT my phone, I stare at the email confirming my plans for this weekend. Shooting off a text message to Julio next to make sure everything will be ready, I receive a confirmation from him telling me everything is set to go. Next, I'm placing another order of flowers to be sent to her, something I've been trying to do every couple of days to keep her smiling. They're not enough to show how much I miss her, but they will remind her I'm still thinking of her every moment of the day.

Turning my neck, I wince from the soreness in my muscles; a reminder of yesterday's brutal practice, but not as excruciating as the entire week as a whole. When the recruiter mentioned I'd be putting my skills to the test, he failed to mention I'd physically be torturing my body. But, I should have known from the details in the package he'd left me.

We'd been put through one test to another, our bodies barely getting a chance to rest. From dashes to test our speed and agility, to testing our strength by having us repeatedly bench press two hundred and twenty five pounds until we can't lift anymore, to going straight into jumping into the air to test how far up we can jump. That test was my favorite. Rolling on my side, I feel an aching pang shoot up my body. Add a slight hangover to the mix and I'm ready to be put out of my misery, which is what most likely will happen at the end of today.

This week I've been pushed beyond my limits, but I knew it was their way of testing us and in the end, it was all worth it. In all reality, I'm surprised I made it through until the end—not the case for more than half the candidates attending. Since today is the final day of the scouting trials, ending with interviews, I'm happier than when I'd arrived.

The blaring of *All of Me* announces Abigail's call. Instead of answering it as I usually do, I push ignore on the screen.

"Shut it up!" Kevin hollers from his end of the room right as my finger made contact. His resistance to wake up reminds me of Abigail, guilt stabbing at my heart for ignoring her call, but I have my reasons.

Kevin sits up as he yawns. "I thought you said she isn't an early riser," he groans, standing up to scratch his chest as he refers to our conversation last night. After several beers between us, the conversation ended up turning back to Abigail and I couldn't help but brag about how I liked waking her up on the days she was reluctant to rise early.

"She's getting ready to go on her run," I comment as I check the time, already grimacing from the thought. I'm not happy with her decision to be running again so soon, but regardless of the many times we've argued about it, she disregards my lecturing and somehow manages to always change the subject on me. That was one thing we were definitely going to discuss this weekend, whether she liked it or not. I blame the stubbornness in her for her defying everyone's advice to wait.

I force myself up and out of bed, heading straight for the shower. With the water running, I step in and allow the coolness to help further awaken me. With every deep breath I take, I can feel the alcohol threatening to come up from the hangover I've woken up with, but I force it back down reminding myself I need to pull my shit together before I leave for my interviews.

An hour later, I'm walking into the stadium, and as usual, I'm led in the direction of where I need to go. Today it's the conference room. For the next four hours, I'm interviewed by several different teams and asked question after question of what I expect out of my future as a professional athlete and what I plan to potentially give their particular team. After the second time of being asked the same routine questions, I learn to repeat the same answer with a smile on my face. It's what they expect and want, and I'm happy to deliver.

In between the interviews, I reluctantly cave to my eagerness to hear Abigail's voice and call her. Instead of her answering, it immediately goes to voicemail, as if she's ignoring my call. Pushing the resentment aside, I'm soon rewarded with a simple text message instead.

I'm in the middle of a meeting. I'll call you later. – Abigail

With a heavy sigh, I take in the answer as I'm once again reminded of my thoughts from last night. I'm not used to our lives being this way, either playing phone or text tag. I'm used to us having a routine schedule that always stayed the same.

Sure thing. I'll talk to later tonight. – Matt

I hesitantly reply, knowing I won't be calling her later tonight since I already have plans that will keep me from doing so. It's not the answer I wanted to give, but it's the only one I can respond with. The rest of the day goes as I had expected and my day is finally over. A few head coaches linger around to congratulate me on an excellent performance during the training process and from the smile on their faces, I'm hopeful. It's more than I had expected when I'd arrived, which leaves me knowing everything is going to go well. At least I hope it will, I think to myself as I leave the building with a smile on my face, thinking of what I'll soon be doing in a couple of hours.

Abigail

I ATTEMPT TO suppress another yawn, but fail miserably as I lift my hand to cover my mouth. The action makes me smile and think of the last time I yawned this many times. But just as quickly, my smile turns into a frown as a pang of guilt and sadness overpowers my emotions. My eyes catch a glimpse of Julio against the wall and he looks every bit full of energy, but then again he wasn't the one tossing and turning while plagued with every possible scenario of what Matt could be doing. I'd texted him a couple of times, and although he responded at first, I eventually didn't receive a response at all, which only threw my thoughts into a turmoil of possibilities. I finally gave up on the notion of sleep and waited until I saw the first glimpse of sunlight cascading into my room to get up and get ready for my run.

What should have been a simple three-mile run was not simple at all due to my lack of sleep, but I pushed myself beyond my limits and completed the run; exhausted, but proud of myself. It's now that I'm paying the price from my lack of sleep. I'm forced to attend an *emergency* meeting, ordered by the designer to go over the details of the show for tomorrow night.

My phone starts to vibrate and on the screen I see Matt's

face smiling back at me. With a quiet groan to myself, I push ignore, and I hate having to do so. I quickly send off a text telling him why I couldn't answer the phone and within seconds he responds. Even though I can tell through his words he understands, I hate not being able to speak with him. I don't get much time to dwell on the subject before Rebecca Russell, the designer, walks in as I'm stifling another yawn behind my hand. Her eyes catch mine as she turns them down into a narrowed slit; clearly irritated with me for some reason. I simply ignore her since it seems to be how she reacts to something she dislikes. Apparently, my one requirement as her top model to be fully rested at all times is the cause of her dislike for me at the moment.

"I need everyone's attention!" she demands with an added clap of her hands. Her eyes are still directed at me, as if her command is for me more than anyone else. "Tomorrow's rehearsal is our last before our show here in New York, but we are going to do things different than planned."

Although her words catch my attention, I can't help but start to yawn again. Great, the designer Nazi in her is going to start bitching my ass out any minute. I've managed to keep from having her wrath directed at me until now.

"Will someone please get Abigail a Red Bull?" she commands while rolling her eyes at my yawn. "And make sure it's sugar free," she adds, as her eyes roam my body.

"What the hell is that supposed to mean?" My sleep deprivation has caused me to snap.

With her nose pinched high, she states, "I don't like my models consuming any unnecessary calories. I need you as fit as I can force you to be."

My blood is now boiling. I know for damn sure I'm in the fittest shape I can be in. My bones may not be protruding from my body like more than half these girls, but I'm lean and in my opinion am lacking an ounce of unnecessary fat. Shit, I've already gone more than a week without eating Matt's pancakes; the lack of that meal is torture enough on my diet.

"I run enough to make my own decisions on my diet choices," I irritably say through clenched teeth as my eyes stay locked onto hers. The room is now silent and you can practically cut the tension with a knife. No one has ever dared speak back to Rebecca from fear of the outcome. She is a force to be reckoned with, but I cannot care less at this moment. I can be just as feisty when I want to be.

Her eyebrow arches high before responding. "You're correct, Ms. Adams. I appreciate it, unlike the rest of you who chose an unhealthier lifestyle," she declares, now scanning the room, eyeing the remaining models.

I notice how she used my last name. She's only ever called us by our first names, if she even remembers them at all. Most of the time she refers to the girls as, "*Hey you,*" with a snap of her fingers.

At that moment, a *sugar free Red Bull* is shoved into my hands, causing me to roll my eyes. Opening the can, I take a giant gulp from it, savoring the sweet taste.

"Back to what I was saying. My show for fashion week will be my biggest yet. It's the most important show of the season," she beams with a smile on her lips. "So I've asked the stage manager to change the layout of the runway to accommodate the attendees. That means today I need you models to practice… Practice… Practice," she demands with another set of claps from her hands. "The last thing I need is for you to use the excuse that you fell on your face because you're not used to it. Lord knows it's probably because you're high," she tries mumbling the last words under her breath. I should be rolling my eyes at them, but in all reality they will most likely be true. Not all of them, but a majority of them either show up drunk or high, which is why I'm labeled the prude because I don't partake in their pre-show activities to help with the nerves.

She soon dismisses us, shouting demands at the intern following closely behind her as everyone begins to slowly start to depart in their own directions. I stay seated in my chair, continuing to sip on my Red Bull.

I can now feel Julio standing directly behind me and I don't have to turn around to know he's probably eyeing Bob, the stage manager who is now standing in front of me. "You know the show is only as big as it is because of you."

Confused by his remark, I ask, "What do you mean, *me?*"

He snorts at my response. "Abigail, when we scheduled this show, we were lucky if we got two hundred people interested to attend. Now I have to accommodate over five hundred people for the show. It's not a coincidence as to who's bringing them here."

"Isn't it the designer?" I sarcastically let out before bringing the can up to take another sip.

He rolls his eyes. "Isn't it obvious? It's because of you. Believe what you want to believe Abigail, but I was surprised when I found out they'd contracted you for the show. Face it, everyone is curious to see if you've still got it," he replies before turning to walk away.

His words stay with me for the next couple of minutes as I watch everyone scatter around me. It explains all the lingering stares I've gotten over the past week, especially during the meet and greet. Curious as to what changes will be made with the stage, I stand and make my way over to the wall blocking it, taking a quick peek around it, noticing how what was once a small runway in a straight line is now a rectangle.

Placing my earphones in my ears, they're now playing the

only song that can bring me the serene calmness I crave when I start to fidget from being nervous. It's starting to become a recurrence before anything I do when it comes to my modeling. From the corner of my eye, I notice Charlie, one of the interns suspiciously eyeing me as he usually does.

"What are you listening to?" Bob asks from my side, startling me. Yanking the ear buds from my ear, I place it into his. A smile spreads across his face. "So is this what you're into?"

"What do you mean?"

"Electric?"

I still have no clue what he's talking about. "Who's the artist?" he asks.

"Tiësto," I say, still trying to figure out what the hell he's getting at, but I never get the explanation I was looking for as he turns to walk away with a smug smile on his face, leaving me still confused. The guy has clearly lost his marbles.

Glancing over to Sarah who is now standing at my side, I ask, "What was that all about?" She shrugs her shoulder at me while looking at the stage. "Hell if I know. He's in his own little world sometimes." Her eyes focus on the entrance of the stage.

"Are you nervous?" Sarah asks, and from the hesitation in her words, she clearly is.

"Is this your first show?" I can't help ask as I watch her nervously bite her lip. Her nervousness is ironically calming me knowing I'm not alone.

"I've done small shows for local bridal events, but never anything like this."

"Then this should be easy for you."

"Are you kidding me?" she croaks out, wide-eyed.

Giggling at her reaction, she snickers knowing I was teasing her. "So, I Googled you." Her confession makes me nervous. "Are all the rumors true?" she cautiously asks. Normally her question would irritate me, but knowing that it's Sarah it doesn't.

"Depends on what you read," I mumble, bracing myself for her answer.

"I read that you have amnesia," she shyly states, as if ashamed that she was stalking me. "But there were also pictures of you at some of the races you did recently. I particularly like the one with you and that guy in Portland. It looks sweet," she says with a smile. "Is that your boyfriend you were talking about?"

Thinking of which picture in particular she's speaking of, it immediately brightens up my mood. It's the same picture as my background on my phone. It gave me a purpose to never give up after I was injured and doubted I'd ever run again.

"Yes," I happily admit with a smile.

Sarah's eyebrows squish down. "But the tabloids always state him as your assistant."

I'm now the one blushing as I clarify. "That's what we told everyone at first, but he's my boyfriend."

"Do you miss him?" her words sound raspy, and I understand the reason behind them as I nod my head and turn away to look back out to the stage to hide the tears now clouding my vision. I hadn't expected to become so emotional over discussing Matt, but I now have a painful pang in my hollowed heart.

I text Matt, but just like the last five messages, I get no response. Instead, I try calling him, but his phone goes straight to voicemail, my heart plummeting from the rejection. Today is the first day Matt has ever done this and the dismissal is slowly destroying me.

"Adams! Five minute warning call!" I hear someone shout from behind me, startling me from my thoughts.

"What's the point of this again?" I ask Sarah as we both rush to the front of the line to take our places. I can hear the familiar screeching of Hans's voice, lecturing everyone to treat this as if it were the show. I don't know whether to roll my eyes or take him seriously. That man is clearly going to give himself a heart attack with how much he screams.

Sarah is back to nervously fidgeting behind me as she answers, "According to the schedule, it's a mock run for the show tomorrow night."

"It's their way of catching our flaws and mistakes now, so we don't embarrass them tomorrow," she murmurs. Taking a peek around the wall I will soon be walking around, I can see the director now in his chair, queuing the music producer to start the music.

"Good luck," she says as the line manager holds up his hand to start counting down the five second warning.

"And, go!" the production manager shouts, bringing me back to reality. My adrenaline is pumping. The music is blasting. Right on cue, I step onto the platform of the runway, adrenaline pumping through my veins. I'm halfway on the runway when I hear the director start yelling.

"Wipe that smile off your face! It's a runway show, not a photo shoot." His eyes pierce straight behind me as he lectures Sarah, who always has a smile on her lips. When I turn my first corner, my eyes glance at her and her normal radiant smile is replaced with a frown; one I know she isn't faking.

I make it backstage without a lecture, and although I should feel relieved, I know I still have five more walks to go. One hour later, I'm doing my last walk and with minimal complaints, we're all done and being called to gather for one final meeting.

"Alright, everybody! I do hope tomorrow night isn't as disastrous as it was just now. And to guarantee it isn't, we're doing it again!" the director shouts before everyone groans in unison. He obviously ignores us as he walks away shouting, "Line up in ten!" over his shoulder.

Grabbing the bridge of my nose, Julio walks up to me and says, "I have to go do something really quick. Where is your phone?" When I hold it up to show him it's in my hand he gives me a quick nod. "I shouldn't be more than five minutes."

"Bathroom break?" I tease.

His lips slightly quirk up, his eyes smugly staring back at me. "Something like that." I don't bother continuing to tease him as he rushes away. He must really need to go.

"I'm so over this shit," one of the other models complains as we stand around waiting for them to order us to line up again. I ignore her whining as I check my phone to see if I've missed anything from Matt. Her next words catch my attention. "Damn he's hot. I know what I'll be doing tonight, and it's him," she purrs.

Curiosity gets the best of me as I turn to see what's caught her attention. My heart stops, but just as quickly beats back to life. "Matt?" I ask with a fluttering in my stomach.

His dark eyes never leave mine as he pushes his way over to me and when his lips go up into his smile that I love so much, I know it's him. Rushing to help close the distance between us, I practically throw myself at him. He lifts me up so I can wrap my legs around his waist, holding on for dear life as my lips slam down onto his, needing to reassure myself he's real.

"I take it you're excited to see me?" he utters, laughing against my lips.

"Please tell me I'm not dreaming," I say against his lips as I kiss him again, still not believing it's really him. My heart is uncontrollably pulsating as I keep kissing him.

"If you're dreaming, then so am I," he says, squeezing me tighter against his body.

I pull away to stare down into his eyes, his beaming smile

matching my own. "Happy birthday, beautiful," he murmurs. My once racing heart has suddenly stopped in disbelief, my mind searching to remember what day is today.

"But my birthday isn't until tomorrow," I croak out, surprised I even remembered.

Matt throws his head back and lets out a full-blown laugh. "Don't worry, beautiful, we can always start celebrating early," he declares, reaching up to briefly kiss me.

"Yup, this is definitely the boyfriend," Sarah voices with a giggle at our side, distracting me from Matt. It also reminds me we still have an audience surrounding us. Slowly unwrapping my legs from Matt's waist, I lower myself back down to the ground, but he keeps his arms tightly wrapped around my body to keep me close.

Looking over to Sarah I introduce them. "Matt, this is Sarah."

"Nice to meet you," he answers with a nod, unwilling to relinquish his hold on me, but I don't complain. It allows me to lean into his body and savor him a little longer. Suddenly a thought occurs to me. "Is this why you haven't answered your phone all day?" I suspiciously have to ask.

"Yeah. I was scared I'd end up caving and telling you I was on my way. You have no idea how hard it's been keeping this from you."

"I still can't believe you're here."

"There was no way I was going to miss your birthday," he replies before leaning into my ear. "As I said before, you can be the icing on the cake," he whispers, his warm breath caressing my neck and sending a shiver down to my toes as I remember the last time he used those words. I quietly let out a moan that only he can hear. From the way his body stiffens against mine, I know he's received my message.

"You better stop making those noises or else I'm going to drag you out of here and not look back," he warns, placing a kiss below my ear. I'm about to drag *him* out of the room, not caring what anybody thinks, but my plan is brought to a halt when I'm reminded of why I can't leave.

"One minute warning call! Take your positions!" an intern orders.

I groan into Matt's neck, earning me a chuckle in return. "How much longer do you have left?"

"I don't know," I miserably mumble.

Giving me a kiss on the corner of my mouth before he pulls away, he says, "Go do your job and I'll wait here with Julio until you're done," then squeezes my ass before shoving me lightly, urging me to walk away.

I'm already mourning the loss of his embrace as I walk away from him. Taking one final look over my shoulder, I see Matt smiling back at me, making me want to rush back into his arms and stay there for the next couple of days.

I take my first step onto the runway, a smile on my face, uncaring of what the director thinks. I have a reason to smile this time, and he's currently waiting for me only steps away.

Chapter Seven

Matt

"I CAN'T WAIT to be inside of you," I breathlessly tell Abigail as we both savagely kiss each other. Abigail's warm tongue glides against my own as she whimpers into my mouth, urging my hands to tighten their grip on her waist as she grinds her hips against my body. "How much longer until we get back to your hotel room?" I desperately ask, unable to control my patience, wanting to rip her clothes off in the back seat of the car.

Grinding harder up in between her leg, she breathlessly responds, "I don't know." The answer frustrates me knowing it's New York and it can take forever. If I have to, I'll take her here and now. Fuck decency. I'm pretty sure once they hear Abigail screaming they will get the point and keep driving. The thought is broken though when I feel the car coming to a stop, telling me we have arrived at our destination. A groan escapes Abigail's lips, which only makes me laugh.

"Miss me that much?" I ask before kissing her. A quick knock on the window tells me Julio is waiting on us. "Let's go finish what we started, beautiful," I tell her, earning me a cute little pout of her lips. Opening the door, Julio helps her climb out of the car, allowing me to follow her. Her hand is tightly clasped in mine as she leads me to the elevator. I'm surprised she's still controlling herself as the doors enclose the three of us in.

When the elevator doors open, she holds me back to allow Julio to exit first, something she has explained is now routine. Entering the hotel room and heading to the room on the right, you can hear the opening and shutting of doors before he exits soon after with a simple nod. My body is yanked by Abigail's hand into the same room and within seconds I'm slamming the door shut with my foot. Crashing my lips down onto hers, her hands are already demanding I take my clothes off, my own doing the same with hers. The only time our lips break apart is to lift our shirts over our heads before we're back at it again.

Practically ripping her jeans off, I have her naked and lift her against the door, entering her in one hard thrust, making us both groan with pleasure. The warmth of her warm walls completely surrounds my cock as I start grinding in and out of her. Her gasps are my reward as I start pumping hard and fast, just the way she likes it. Her legs tightly wrapped around my waist help her meet each and every thrust I give her as my hands massage her ass.

Within minutes, I feel her tighten around my dick. Her nails dig into the skin of my shoulders as she throws her head back and moans my name. I hadn't wanted to finish so quickly, but the week since I've made love to her has felt like years and within seconds I'm soon emptying myself inside of her. Bringing myself to a stop, I use every ounce of strength I have left to hold Abigail up and walk us over to the bed to collapse on it.

Her body is lethargically laying on mine as I feel both our hearts hastily beat against one another's chest and run my hands up and down her back, needing to feel every inch of her body.

I'm practically panting as I say, "I can't wait to do that again."

Her little giggle from my words sends a warm shiver down the throat her lips are now trailing kisses upon. "Hmm, hmm," I feel her say. "I love you," she whispers, the words already making me twitch inside of her as I begin to grow hard, her rocking urging me into our next round. Thankfully, we have all night to make up for the time we have been apart.

ABIGAIL'S HAND SLOWLY glides up and down my forearm where my tattoo rests. She's half draped across my body, where I positioned her.

"How come you didn't tell me you were coming?" she asks, no hint of resentment in her question.

Placing a kiss on her head, I answer. "I wanted to surprise you for your birthday," I tell her as I grind her core against my leg.

"It was the best surprise and birthday present ever."

I let out a small laugh as I clutch her thigh. The warmth against my leg has been teasing me for the last couple of minutes, but after that last round, I know we both need some time to recover. She lifts her head to rest her chin on my chest as she looks me in the eyes, the moonlight coming in through the window illuminates her beautiful smile.

Looking curiously at me, I can see a question forming in her mind. "How did you manage to get into the showroom? They weren't letting anyone in because of the media," she says, reminding me that Julio had to pull strings to get me on a special list. Brushing my fingers through her hair, I say, "Julio knew I was coming, so he arranged to meet me. We had to use the assistant ruse to get me through the door," I answer with a chuckle as

I watch her nose scrunch up, hating the term we used in the past.

"They've been getting on me to get one," she glowers.

"Yeah, that's what he told me."

Her eyes slowly blink, as if struggling to stay open. Her chest is slowly rising and falling, telling me she's exhausted, but from the rumble of her stomach I know she's hungry. I'm starving myself, now that I think about it.

"Want to eat?" I ask her, but she doesn't immediately answer. Lightly shaking her, she gives me an angered grumble as she mumbles, "I'm not hungry."

"Abigail, you're not trying to starve yourself now that you're here, are you?"

Her head snaps up, looking agitated. "When have I ever needed to do that?"

"Good," I say, squeezing her thigh and pulling us both up. "Because I'm hungry and you're eating with me." She lets out an exasperated sigh before her eyes light up, looking hopeful.

"Are you making pancakes?"

"Why would I make you pancakes now?" I ask, arching my eyebrows in confusion as I look towards the darkening New York sky outside our window.

"Because I'm pretty sure I've earned them." I throw my head back and laugh at her proclamation. She irritably digs her finger into my ribs, making me wince. "Well, I did," she urges.

Digging my finger into her side, she squirms away from me as she yelps. "As I recall, it's usually running that earns you my pancakes," I state. With a wiggle of my brows, I add, "But if cardiovascular activities were the case, then yes, you did earn your pancakes, beautiful. But I don't have the stuff to make them," I remind her.

She crawls up onto me, straddling my hips before she reaches past me to the side table. Her breasts are in perfect alignment with my mouth and I take advantage by taking her nipple into my mouth, urgently sucking on it. She digs her nails into my shoulder as she lets out a moan and arches her back, thrusting herself into me. The warmth between her legs rubbing against my cock triggers it to awaken, but I mentally order it to calm itself when I hear her stomach rumble again. Releasing her nipple with a pop, I glance up to see her opening her eyes, looking disoriented.

"Food first, then sex," I explain, watching her pout down to me. Kissing her breast as I chuckle from her reaction, she lightly shoves me before placing a pen and notepad into my hands.

"Write down all the ingredients and I'll have Julio give it to the concierge so they will know what you need. I'm getting my pancakes, Mr. Garcia," she orders, rubbing herself against my cock before she quickly climbs off me. Now I'm the one left pouting as I watch her naked body walk away from me as she goes to turn on the light.

Blinking my eyes to adjust to the light, I'm now looking at the notepad and start scribbling down what I need. "Even if they were to get all the items, it'd be really late by the time they deliver them. I'm hungry now," I protest as I keep writing.

Rolling her eyes, she says, "I know that. The hotel has a twenty-four hour kitchen that delivers room service and according to Julio, they make a killer steak."

My eyes light up at the mention of steak, boosting me to write faster.

"DAMN, THIS STEAK is good," I say before stuffing another piece into my mouth. The moment it hits my tongue my eyes close with delight from the mouth-watering flavors exploding in my mouth.

Swallowing the piece he's chewing on before he speaks, "Told you," Julio states. Abigail rolls her eyes with a mouthful of salad she ordered for herself.

"Why are you eating a salad?" I ask, confused because she doesn't usually only eat a salad.

"Because you're not around to help me burn the extra calories."

Eyeing her, I'm confused because she looks exactly the same as I'd seen her a week ago. Putting my utensils down so I can pull her into my lap, I say, "I know that isn't the real reason, so tell me the truth."

Dropping her head as if ashamed, she mumbles, "For some odd reason those other girls intimidate me. They're always eyeing me as if they're looking for my flaws, and I hate it," she grimly declares.

Lifting her chin to look at her, I ask, "Has it ever occurred to you that maybe they do it because they're jealous of you?" She doubtfully looks at me, causing me to continue. "You're beautiful, Abigail, and I'm pretty sure they know that."

She lights up with a smile and links her arms around my neck so she can tug me forward to kiss her. Pushing my tongue into her mouth so I can deepen the kiss, we're soon forced to break apart when Abigail's phone starts ringing from the room. Sighing after she pulls away, she stands saying, "That's Hans. I better answer or else he won't stop calling," already walking towards the room.

My eyes follow her until she disappears through the door. I turn back and I'm now facing Julio, which reminds me I still need to talk to him. Narrowing my eyes down at him, I start speaking. "About the other night," I start off. "It better not happen again… Ever."

His body tenses from my statement. "I've repeatedly apologized to Abigail and I owe you an apology as well. I'm sorry, but it only happened because I thought she was in danger. Otherwise it wouldn't have happened at all," he explains. "The moment I barged in, it only took a split second to realize she wasn't in danger, which is why I closed my eyes."

"How much did you really see?"

"Not everything, if that's what you're wondering." My eyes go wide making him laugh. "And I'm glad." I'm still skeptically looking at him, wondering just how much I truly still trust he's telling me the truth.

He lets out a heavy sigh. "Mateo, I know what you're thinking and you have nothing to worry about. It's awkward enough knowing what happened and I will have to live with the guilt of violating her trust on that matter. You should know by now that I see Abigail more like a daughter that I will continue guarding with my life more than anything else. So you can let that thought go," he reprimands, pointing his steak knife at the room. "I like this job way too much to do anything that would jeopardize it."

"Is that so?" I ask, almost challenging him to see what his next answer will be.

"You kidding me? I get paid to sit on my ass most of the time and my greatest source of entertainment is your love life. I wouldn't get that in the field I'm usually in," he says with a chuckle. His declaration allows me to let out the breath I was holding the entire time.

"That's good to know," I tell him and he replies with a short nod before going back to eating his steak, leaving me to do the same. Minutes later, Abigail is exiting the room looking irritated.

"What's wrong?"

"They want us on set an hour earlier than scheduled," she

complains. "I hate that they always pull this shit with us. They think they can just order us around."

I desperately want to ask if all this was worth it, but the last thing I want is to piss Abigail off and cause her to resent me the entire weekend. Instead, I pull her to sit back down on my lap and kiss her below the ear to help her relax.

"Is there anything I can do to put a smile back on your face?" I ask, trying to distract her while images of what I'm already imagining of doing to make it happen spin around in my mind.

Tilting her head, she mutters out, "You can go for a run with me in the morning."

Julio slants his head as if remembering something. "Abigail, isn't tomorrow—" Julio is cut off as Abigail snaps her head up and glares at him. Julio's eyes widen before he clears his throat to say, "I'm going to go finish eating in my room." Lifting his plate, he walks straight into his room. "Better you than me," he mumbles before the door shuts.

"What was that about?" I ask, confused out of my mind as I look back at Abigail.

"Julio just hates running with me."

"But what did he mean by tomorrow?"

"Do you really want to keep talking about Julio now that he's gone, or do you want dessert?" she asks, swinging her leg over my legs so she's straddling my waist. "Because I'd much rather have my dessert now than later," she whispers into my ear, roughly grinding herself into my body.

I've completely forgotten what it was we were speaking about as Abigail's lips close around my earlobe, still rubbing her body back and forth against my hard cock that is demanding I take her back to the room. Who am I to ignore its request? Standing up with her, I start walking us back to the room and I hear her giggle into my ear as we enclose ourselves in the room to enjoy our dessert.

Chapter Eight

Abigail

WHISPERING INTO MATT'S ear, I say, "Get up sleepy head."
He turns his body and tugs me back into his side as he murmurs
back, "Happy birthday, beautiful."

"Thank you," I reply, but before I can repeat my request, his
hands are roaming my body and his head snaps back.

"Why do you have clothes on?"

"Because I plan on going for a run this morning," I tell
him. Normally my statement would prompt him to join me, but
instead he surprises me.

"Take them off and let me give you your birthday present,"
he says, already trying to tug my shorts down. I try protesting
by wiggling myself away from him, but that doesn't help. He
tightens his arms around me, trying to keep me trapped against
him. "Your wiggling is making me hard," he says, proving it by
pushing his hips into my body. Sure enough, I can feel his erection pushing up in between my legs.

Knowing I have to leave soon, I try another tactic. "Fine,
you stay in. I'll just run this race by myself," I declare, shocking

him and allowing me to escape, but not far as he holds onto my wrist and tugs me to look at him. His eyes are demanding an answer.

"What race?"

"I signed us up for a race today," I proudly say, hoping to damper the wrath now radiating in his eyes. My smile quickly fades when he says, "You aren't supposed to be running races yet, Abigail."

The enthusiasm I'd awoken with has now vanished with the tone he's used. Resentfully, I yank my hand from his hold so I can step away from him. My body is trembling from how furious I'm feeling while I search for my shoes.

"I'm running this race with or without you, Matt," I pronounce through clenched teeth. "I'm not stupid and wasn't planning on sprinting the race like I would have in the past. I just want to run. Why can't you understand that?" I tell him as I throw on a light jacket, my back facing him the entire time.

Matt slips his arm around my waist, pulling me back against his chest. My eyes close as he leans in and his mouth finds my neck; his warm breath hits my skin and sends a shiver down my back. I try to resist surrendering to the weakness of easily pushing my resentment of his words aside.

"I just don't understand why you're being so stubborn and pushing yourself so hard," he somberly whispers into my ear. He continues before I can reply. "And I never said you were stupid, beautiful. I just don't want you pushing yourself too hard just yet."

Turning me so I'm now facing him, my arms automatically loop around his neck. "I promise to run it at a slow pace," I say, pouting up at him as my last resort to convince him, because regardless of how this ends, I will be running this race. He looks down at me with apprehension, the tilt of his head letting me know he's still contemplating my words.

"Alright, but only if you promise not to push yourself."

"Promise."

"Good," he smiles while kissing the corner of my mouth. "I'll go speak with Julio to make sure you keep that promise."

Sheepishly looking at him, his brow arches up in question. "Julio's not running with me anymore," I explain, biting my lip to keep from laughing at how his brows draw down. "I'm not running it alone. You're running with me," I smugly answer, giving him a quick kiss on his lips.

"This is why Julio was acting strange last night, isn't it?"

"Come on," I playfully whine out. "It's not like you can't run a simple race."

"Are you crazy? It's fucking freezing out there!" he says, hitching his thumb in the direction of the window.

"It's not that cold out there, you big baby. You live in Portland. How different can it be?" I tease, knowing personally from previous runs that Portland is nowhere near as cold as New York, but I'm not going to admit that to Matt.

"It's balls freezing cold out there compared to Portland," he answers with a hitch in his words.

"Then bundle up."

Half an hour later, we're walking through the lobby and out of the hotel and hit with a gust of cold wind.

"No way. We're not running in this cold," Matt proclaims, trying to tug me back inside.

"Are you scared of a little cold?"

I feel his body stiffen at my teasing. "This isn't just cold, Abigail. This is dick numbing cold, and I'd rather keep it warm by keeping it inside of you." He is still trying to pull me back inside, but I tug in the opposite direction while laughing at him.

"You're starting to whine like Trey," I say, winning in the

tug-of-war game, Matt now following me.

Stopping, I reach up and say into his ear, "I'll tell you what. If your dick freezes, I'll make sure to use my mouth to defrost it." My promise causes him to stiffen and his brow shoots up. His reaction permits me to tow him away into the direction I need him to go.

Matt shouts out to Julio in front of us, "How about we trade places?"

"No way. I'm lucky you're here to run this one with her," he replies over his shoulder. "It's not so bad once you start running. It helps warm you up," he adds.

Groaning at his loss, his eyes look back at me. "Fine, but you owe me big time for this, *Abigail*," he says through clenched teeth. I have to bite my lip to keep from laughing at his childish whine. "How do we get there?"

Briskly leading the way, I already know where we need to go. After signing up, I researched all the information needed for the race. "It's not that far from here. Just a little over a mile walk. That should help warm you up."

He grunts as he keeps up with me. As we near the corner to what should lead to the starting line, I can already see other runners walking in the same direction. Not having any clue where to pick up my packet, I stop someone to find out.

"Do you happen to know where same day packet pick up is?"

The gentleman whom I've stopped considers my question and points me in the direction I need to go. Quickly thanking him, I head in the direction he's pointed me towards and see the registration table within view; along with a huge banner indicating which race it is.

"You never said this was a marathon," Matt surprisingly lets out.

"This isn't a marathon. It's a *half-marathon*," I clarify, not chancing a look at him because I can already feel his eyes narrowing down at me, clearly unhappy with my response.

"It's still more than you should be running," he clenches out.

Crossing my arms over my chest, I draw in a deep breath to help calm my frustration to his response. "I'm up to running six miles now. *At a slow pace*," I emphasize before he can lecture me about the distance. "And as I told you earlier, I'm not running this race for a personal record. I'm running it for fun."

"Running a 5K would be logical if you're running a race for fun," he throws back at me. "What the hell are you trying to do, Abigail? Break you ankle for sure?" His question makes me feel like a child being scolded.

"My timing was pathetic during that race, but I was happy with it because I earned it," I reply. "I'm running this race today, Matt, and I don't need you lecturing me about my pace. It's embarrassing enough I have to live with it," I say as I glare at him before turning to face forward again.

Julio, who is standing at my side, is speaking under his breath. I can't quite make out the words, but I'm pretty sure he's mumbling about Matt and me.

Since I'm currently in a bad mood, I don't hesitate to remark, "You know, Julio, you sound like a grouchy old man sometimes." Thankfully, his chuckle tells me he isn't upset with my comment.

"You make me feel like one sometimes with the way I have to put up with the both of you," he teases.

Wondering what his true age is, I chance asking. "Just how old *are you*, Julio?" He's skeptically staring back at me, as if contemplating whether to answer the question or not.

"I'm old enough to be your father."

I'm shocked. "Really?" I ask, earning me a snicker. "I mean you don't look that old." This time I hear a grumble. "At least you're in good shape for your age," I add, trying to soften up the mood I have sent him into. "Maybe I should stop now before I hang myself any further."

"Yes, that would be a good idea. Remember, I'm the one with the gun," he teases as we step forward.

"You're lucky I like you, or else I'd fire you for that comment," I playfully tease back. His eyebrows arch even higher, if possible.

"I wouldn't let you fire him," Matt proclaims from my side.

"Along with thinking you have the right to order me around, you're back to thinking you have control over my decisions as well?" I furiously retort.

Slumping his shoulders forward, he attempts to speak "Abigail—" is the only word I allow him to get out before my hand shoots up to silence him.

"You better hope I run off my anger this morning or else you'll be sharing a room with Julio."

Matt's silence is acknowledgment of his defeat.

"I swear, Abigail, this has to be the most entertaining job I've ever had," Julio says, as if trying to break the awkwardness now floating in the air. One step forward and we're now next in the pickup line. Ten minutes later, Matt and I have our bibs. Still ignoring him, I head to the starting line.

"Here, let me do it," Matt offers as I fumble with my bib, grabbing for the pins. He uses the opportunity to tug me forward, closing the space between. His lips close over mine as my mouth unconsciously relinquishes to his kiss, completely forgetting I'm mad at him. Seconds later, breathless and incoherent, I'm staring at him as he smiles back at me.

"What was that for?" I eagerly ask, wondering what the

motive is behind it.

"Just because I love you," he comments, making me smile, completely throwing all bitterness aside. He returns to the task at hand as my body blissfully flutters while watching him, remembering all the times he's done it before.

"There. All done," he whispers, kissing my nose and stirring the feeling in my belly.

"Come on, Emily. I run enough during practice. Why are you making me run with you now?" Matt utters, sounding as if he's containing himself from whining.

"Because I read somewhere it's relaxing, and according to my physician I either find a way to bring my blood pressure down or he's putting me on medication. You know how much I hate taking pills," I explain.

"So take up yoga or something," he suggests.

I roll my eyes at his comment. "Shouldn't you be encouraging me instead of complaining?"

"I wouldn't be complaining if you hadn't gotten me up so fucking early," he mumbles under his breath. He doesn't think I've heard him, but I prove otherwise. "Watch your mouth, Matthew. You may no longer be a little boy, but I can still punish you," I scold.

"Oh, yeah?" Matt says before scooping down to pick me up and toss me over his shoulder. He quickly starts spinning us both around as fast as he can, all while I'm screaming and pounding at his back. "Matt! Put. Me. Down!"

He spins us a couple more times before he stops and we're both swaying, leaving me in fear of landing on the ground if he drops me. A couple of seconds later, I feel him grip my legs and lower us both to the ground to allow me to climb off. With a huff, I compose myself before I look up into his face to see him joyfully smiling back at me. I hate the fact that with a smile, like the one he is currently giving me, I can never stay mad at him.

"Alright, Em, I'll run with you this time, but don't expect it to become a habit. I'd have to be crazy to take up running. I do enough of the shit during practice," he declares.

"Language," I clip out, making him chuckle. I can only shake my head at his response. Even if it's only this one time, it's still one more thing I get him to do to spend time with me.

The memory fades and I return to the same smile I was given moments ago in both the memory and reality, but it quickly turns down into a frown as if realizing where my mind had wondered off to. The hands resting on my hips gently tighten while he sincerely looks at me.

"Which one was it this time?" he rasps out, as if hesitant to ask.

Before answering, I grab onto his face to tug him down to kiss me. My sole purpose is to remove that frown from my lips. "The very first time you ran with her," I say against his lips with a heavy heart.

Leaning his forehead against mine, he replies, "Who knew I'd come to depend on it for my sanity?"

"Or be forced to do it as you were back then?" I remind him of our bickering from this morning. I'm rewarded with a heart-filled laugh.

"Obliviously I can't push you because of your ankle," he voices, already trying to change the subject. He puts his lips to my ear and whispers, "But you owe me for making me run this thing."

"What exactly is it that I'll owe you?" I playfully tease. The crowd starts to cheer as they gradually start counting down for the race to begin. My already fluttering stomach is adding to the excitement coursing through my veins as we look around at the roaring crowd.

"I expect that earlier promise," he murmurs into my ear before he pulls away.

"What promise?" I ask, searching my mind, wondering what I've missed or can't quite remember at the moment. His finger comes up to my mouth, slightly tracing my lips.

"The one where your mouth is going to warm me up later," he says over the roaring cheers.

I gawk at him. "It wasn't a promise!" I shout back. Ignoring my protest, he begins putting his ear buds into his ears. "Matt! I never promised anything!" I continue to argue. His brows go up in question, as if indicating he hasn't heard me. From the smug lift of his lips, he knows why I'm shouting at him.

"You shouldn't have suggested it," he replies before jogging off with the crowd already taking off.

For a moment, I'm rendered speechless and watch him jog a couple of step ahead of me. "Ugh!" I huff out as I start to jog after him, wondering what I've just gotten myself into.

"I LOVE YOUR laugh," Matt mumbles against my skin, making me giggle again. Lifting his head to look at me, his deep brown eyes are contently staring back at me. My stomach takes the chance to rumble, announcing its demand to be fed.

"Someone's hungry."

"I am. But I'm too exhausted to move."

"Someone pushed herself a little too hard this morning."

I laugh as I remember this morning. "It was worth it to see you struggle," I tease as my mind returns to this morning and the constant grumbling I heard coming from Matt's side. Holding my medal up in the air to admire it once more, I smile. "They sure are addictive," I tell Matt as I glide my thumb across the lettering on the emblem of the race's logo.

"Yes, they are," he replies, his teeth nipping at my stomach, breaking me from my thoughts. Yelping, I shove his head away.

"Stop it!" I tell him, earning me a bout of laughs. My stomach growls immediately after coercing Matt to climb off my body.

"Come on, beautiful. You've earned your pancakes so it's time to feed you."

Although I'm exhausted, the thought of eating Matt's pancakes is motivation enough for me to get up and out of bed. Heading for my dresser to retrieve a pair of underwear, I pull open the drawer and rummage through it, but only find socks and sports bras.

"Crap," I huff out, remembering I'd used the last pair yesterday. Biting my lip, I search the room for an alternative and see Matt's duffle bag. Rushing straight for it, I dig for a pair of his boxer briefs.

Feeling victorious when I find a pair, I quickly start pulling them up, already hearing, "What are you doing?"

"I don't have any clean underwear and I used my last clean pair of running shorts so this will have to do until dry cleaning delivers my clothes later today," I explain, giving him a peck on the lips as a thank you, even if I didn't ask to use them.

"What are you supposed to wear for your show?"

"I'm not allowed to wear anything at all. They claim it interferes with the wardrobe."

Matt's eyes widen in shock. "They expect my girlfriend to prance around commando in front of hundreds of people?"

I giggle at the thought he has portrayed with his choice of words. "Matt, it's only under my dresses," I say, still laughing at his reaction as I leave the room. He follows me as he states his claim. "You don't care?"

Stopping, I turn to face him. "Matt, you can't tell because I'm completely covered up," I tell him while wrapping my arms around him. "I know you probably don't like it, Matt, but you need to stop overreacting so much," I dispute.

Embracing me back, his teeth start nibbling at my collarbone. "The only problem I have is knowing that you'll be bare underneath your dresses and I have to sit back and watch you prance in front of me. Can you imagine the hard-on I'm going to have?" he mutters against my skin.

"Stop that!" I convey to his nibbling at my neck. I would drag him back to the room if it wasn't for my protesting stomach demanding to be fed.

His hands start roaming across my butt before gripping it. "How about you just wear these underneath?" he asks, stepping back so he can better take them in. "I never thought my boxer briefs would look so sexy on someone."

Tilting my head, I arch my eyebrow up. "Am I the only one that's ever worn your boxer briefs?" He opens his mouth to answer, but quickly clamps it shut as if choosing to not answer instead. "Never mind, don't answer that," I clip out, knowing I'd rather he not as I pull away and resume walking over to the kitchen area.

"If it makes you feel any better, you're the only one I'll let keep them."

"Do you want a pair of mine in exchange?" I tease, needing to break the tension that would have come otherwise.

It works when Matt throws his head back to laugh, making me follow soon after. Minutes later, we're wiping tears from our eyes when Julio walks in the door.

He eyes us in confusion, only making us laugh again. "What's for breakfast?" he asks staring at us with a perplexed expression, as if he's trying to figure out why we're still laughing. My stomach grumbles with his question, causing both Matt and me to burst out laughing again. I swear I may just pee my pants if I can't get myself to stop.

"I'm making Abigail pancakes," Matt tells him around a chuckle.

Julio perks up with a smile. "I think I'm going to like him visiting," he replies while heading to his room. "I'll be right back out. Extra for me," he shouts over his shoulder before the door closes.

Matt shakes his head. "You both make me feel like I'm your personal cook sometimes," he playfully mumbles. Locking my arms around his neck, I ask, "Would you prefer I cook for us?"

"No," he clips out faster than I'd expected. My mouth drops open as I swat him on the chest.

"Thanks for the vote of confidence," I say, feeling dejected as I walk away to open the fridge and grab the ingredients he needs.

"Yeah, you're definitely keeping those boxers. I like your ass in them," I hear Matt draw out behind my back, making me smile.

CLOSING MY EYES and taking a deep breath, I prepare myself for my cue. The first beats of *Red Lights* immediately opens my eyes and my lips go up into a wide grin. I quickly push it aside as I take my first step. The flashing lights and the shuttering sounds from the photographers snapping pictures are silent as my body absorbs the bass and I lose myself to my zone.

The eyes of the audience are following my every move, as

if waiting for me to make a mistake. It's almost intimidating, but it's not enough to damper the rush I feel inside. Suddenly my eyes find Matt's, the smile on his face is brighter than any of the flashing lights aimed at me. The pride radiating off him completely illuminates me from the inside out. I'm unable to control the smile I was fighting to contain as I briefly stare back at him before rounding the last corner that leads me backstage.

As rehearsed, I rush to the curtains standing as a makeshift wardrobe. Hands quickly tug at me from every direction as they strip and dress me in my next outfit. In record time, I'm rushing back into line to walk back out and do it all over again. My earlier exhaustion from my run has completely vanished, replaced now by adrenaline.

Waiting in line to be queued for my second walk, a tinge of soreness travels through my bones; a result of my near sleepless night and overachieving run this morning. My thoughts are broken with the shout of my name ordering me to go.

Close to an hour later, I'm walking the final walk next to the designer as the crowd proudly gives her a standing ovation. My body is beaming with elation after the walk. Stepping off the runaway, Charlie immediately thrusts a set of roses into my arms.

"These are for you."

Perplexed, but still excited from receiving them, I pluck out the card tucked inside of the roses expecting to read a message from Matt. Instead, it's the familiar scrawl from earlier this week. *"Happy birthday, but how many more will you have?"*

The blood drains from my face as I drop the roses and hastily walk away from them, not caring if they get trampled on. The corners of the card are digging into my hand as I crush it within my palm, my heart pounding in my chest. Stepping into my wardrobe station, I quickly strip from my dress, carefully handing it off to a wardrobe assistant and put my own clothing on. The curtain suddenly swings open and my heart stops.

"Damn, you're dressed already," Matt huskily says to me with a smile. My heart starts up again in relief that it's him, but my earlier shock is still lingering upon my face. "What's wrong?" he worriedly asks, taking in my pale expression.

I force a smile. "You scared me. That's all," I truthfully respond. With a chuckle, he lifts me up into his arms and slams his lips down onto mine, stealing the only breath I managed to hold onto from moments ago. Holding onto his shoulders as I return his kiss, I can still feel the card in my hand.

"I'm so proud of you," he says as he pulls away. His prideful words make me smile, helping push some of the worry lingering inside of me away. Giving him another kiss, I need him to push the remainder of it to the back of my mind. It's soon accomplished as I feel him groaning into my mouth, making me laugh.

"Have I ever told you how sexy you look while working?" I hear him say, his lips leaving my mouth as they trail across my jaw. My body is already reacting as a tingle shoots between my legs. Digging my fingers into his forearms to hold myself up, my now weak legs threaten to buckle on me as he continues to trail kisses across my skin. My only response is a soft moan as he continues to breathe down my neck; his nose gently nudging itself against me.

His lips are now at the hollow of my ear as he whispers, "Can we leave now so I can hear you scream my name instead?" Actions speak louder than words as I pull him out of the curtained area and past everyone to the exit. An amused chuckle is heard behind me as I tuck the card into my pants, praying Matt didn't see me doing it.

"Abigail!" Hans shouts my name, bringing Matt and I to a

halt. "Where are you going? You have an after party to attend."

"I'm not going," I say, throwing a glare at him. He opens his mouth to most likely give me his usual cocky response, but I cut him off by declaring, "I don't care if it's part of my *job*." Walking away, I don't give him the opportunity to argue.

"Damn that was hot," Matt says as we walk away.

Within minutes, we near the car and Julio is already waiting with the door open for us to enter. I'm climbing in when I hear Matt ask him, "Is everything ready?"

"Almost," he replies to Matt.

"Have the driver take the long way back then," Matt tells Julio before he climbs in after me.

"What was that about?" I ask, wondering what Matt has up his sleeve. With a smug expression, he shrugs his shoulders.

"I have no idea what you're talking about."

My mind is swiftly distracted when Matt pulls my body to straddle his hips and I immediately feel his erection brushing up into me. I can't resist digging my hands into his hair as I deeply kiss him, making us both moan as our tongues meet. His hands fasten on my hips as he grinds me harder against him. Impatiently, my hands reach down to unbutton his pants and my hand digs inside to wrap around the silky warm skin to start stroking him.

"I can't wait to get back to the hotel tonight," I mumble against his lips as I continue to tantalize Matt. Unbuttoning my pants, he reaches into them and starts rubbing my clit.

"Maybe I like the idea of you not wearing any underwear after all," he says before pushing his finger inside of me, but just as rapidly he's yanking his hand out and starts shoving his pants down.

"Matt, we can't do this in here," I frantically let out, looking behind me to the closed patrician knowing Julio and the driver are on the other side.

"I'm not waiting until we get back. Take these fucking pants off now," he demands, pushing me off him and throwing me onto the seat next to him so he can push down his own pants. My pants are barely around my knees as Matt growls, "That's good enough," and I'm yanked back on top of him, this time facing forward.

"Matt, I don't think this is going to—" I try to say, but I'm unable to finish what I'm thinking as he brings me down onto him, filling me completely. The groan we both let out was most likely heard in the front seat.

"Shhh!" Matt warns. Biting down on my lip to try to contain my moans doesn't help much as he wildly lifts and lowers me onto his cock. We suddenly stop when the driver slams on the brakes, causing Matt to slam deeper into me. This time I uncontrollably let out a loud moan of pleasure.

"I warned you," he says before his hand covers my mouth to stifle my groans.

The dominating feeling of his hand tightly clasped on my mouth while he uses the other to lift and pull me down on his hips sends me spiraling higher and higher until the walls of my core are clamping around him and I'm screaming into his hand. Matt continues his unmerciful thrusts, building me up to another climax, this one feeling stronger than the first as I explode around him and continue screaming into his hand. From the grunting vibrating into my back, I know Matt has also found his release. Seconds later, I feel his warmth releasing into me.

Exhausted and my mind spiraling out of control, I slump back onto Matt's chest trying to recover my breath. He removes his hand from my mouth, allowing me to take a deep breath. The same hand glides down my body to wrap around my waist.

"I love when you give me what I want."

I'm still too incoherent to understand his meaning as I

mumble. "Hmm?"

My whole body shakes as Matt lets out a laugh; my thoughts are still jumbled. "You screaming my name."

Now understanding what he meant, I laugh along with him. He's right. I do like giving him what he wants, especially if it means I get rewarded as well.

Chapter Nine

Matt

I'M FULL OF nerves, hoping everything is perfect and Abigail likes it. I've been planning this dinner for over a month, but it was supposed to take place at home. Instead, I've had to improvise and make do with what I have here. Regardless, the end result is to have a smile on her face at the end of a memorable night.

The ding of the elevator breaks my thought and I hold Abigail back in the hallway while Julio goes and checks the room. I've already spoken to him and he knows the plan. He's to complete his sweep of the room, leaving afterwards to allow us some privacy. I've already rented him another smaller room in the building so he's still nearby if needed. I wanted the entire suite completely to ourselves, not having to worry if Julio feels awkward if I want to spontaneously do something in the dining room.

Abigail's eyes follow Julio as he disappears into the room while I keep her leaning against the hallway wall with me. "Why aren't we following Julio?" she asks, shyly smiling back at me.

"Does it have something to with my birthday?" she suspiciously asks with a smirk, most likely already aware I have a surprise waiting for her.

"You'll just have to wait to find out." Her lips go into a pout. I'm about to kiss it away when I see Julio exiting.

"All clear," he relays with a quick nod.

Pulling away from the wall, I lead us both to the door. "Thanks man," I tell him with a smile as he leaves us. Gradually, I push open the hotel door Julio left ajar and allow Abigail to enter first. She immediately lets out a gasp as she enters. Quickly closing the door to shut out the light of the hallway, we're engulfed by the illumination from the glow of the candles. Rose petals have been spread randomly across the floor and several bouquets fill the room, the bedroom mirroring a similar appearance.

She looks over to me with a look of astonishment in her eyes, but an elated smile on her lips. "Oh, Matt," she whispers, taking me into her arms and kissing me. "Thank you," she says before giving me another kiss.

"You're welcome, beautiful. I knew you'd probably want to eat in instead of going out," I say, nodding my head in the direction of the dinner waiting on the table. I've learned when it comes to Abigail that she would much rather stay home than go out most of the time. I've offered plenty of times in the past to take her out to dinner on a date, but her answer was always, "Can we just stay home instead? I'd rather just be alone with you."

She slowly takes in the room again, growing more excited as she takes in every inch. I give her another couple of seconds to take it all in before I lead her over to the dinner table. I stand there with her in my arms, cherishing how lucky I am to have her in my life.

"You hungry?" I quietly ask her. Eagerly, she nods while craning her head around to curiously look over what's on the table. "Come. Let me feed you."

Taking a seat, I pull her into my lap. I want her as close to me as possible. Lifting the lid off the plate, her eyes light up at what's underneath.

"Pancakes!" she excitedly says, making me laugh.

"Yes, that's why I made extra this morning. I knew you would have earned them tonight."

"But I usually only earn them either running,"—she lowers her head—"or in bed," she hoarsely says into my ear. Gripping her thighs, I attempt to help control the carnal images coursing through my head.

"Would you prefer to go earn them first?" I ask her as my hand glides up in between her legs. She squirms in my lap, making me grow hard.

She bites her lips, contemplating her answer. Her eyes avert to the pancakes with a yearning, letting me know she's hungry. "How about we burn them off instead," I suggest instead, making her smile. Ripping a piece of pancake, I offer it to her. Her lips wrap around my fingers. "Sorry if they don't taste fresh."

Quickly chewing and swallowing the piece in her mouth, she's soon answering, "It's okay. Even if they were days old, they're *your* pancakes." Her statement pleases me. Tearing off another piece of pancake and feeding it to her, she gladly takes it as before. She does the same with me and soon the stack I'd saved for us is completely gone.

"That's it?" she disappointingly asks, lifting up another cover and pouting when she doesn't find pancakes. Instead, she finds what I planned for dessert.

Looking skeptical, she asks, "What's this?"

"Cronuts."

She gives me a puzzled look. "I couldn't get you your favorite donut from Portland, so I did some research and this is just as gooey as that one," I explain, already reaching for one and lifting it up to her mouth. She sinks her teeth into the crusty creation and her eyes immediately close with a blissful moan. "That good?"

She pulls away, eyes still closed, and slowly chews as she nods her head. Her lips turn up into a smile as she opens her eyes to look at me then grabs for my hand to push the pastry to my mouth. Taking a bite, I now understand why she had that reaction. The mouthwatering flavors of the fruity filling within the crusty donut layers surrounding it practically explode in your mouth.

"Good, huh?" Abigail asks. I give a muffled 'Yes' through a mouthful of dessert. She pulls the Cronut back to her and takes the next bite.

Our mouthwatering dessert is all thanks to the concierge. I had no clue what a Cronut was until I asked him for a recommendation of the best dessert in the city. When I'd requested if he can have some delivered for tonight, he happily responded, "Of course, sir. And I'll make sure there's plenty. You can never eat just one." Now I know what he meant. Had he only had one delivered, I would have had to suffer not having more than the one bite.

Abigail stuffs the last bite into my mouth before she reaches for the next Cronut. When we've both had our fill, she lets out a contented sigh, looking delightfully happy. She loops her arms around my neck and I contently look into her eyes. "I've got to be the luckiest person in the world that you found me."

Even with the candlelight, I can see the blush creeping up her cheeks.

"I love you, Matt," she shyly replies.

"I love you, more," I say as I lean in to kiss her. "I've got your present in the room," I say against her lips. She yanks her head back, completely surprised.

"I thought you showing up here was my present?"

"You honestly thought I wouldn't get you something for your birthday?"

She sincerely looks at me. "But I wasn't expecting anything," she voices.

Pulling her to stand with me, I lead her to the bedroom. Another gasp is heard from her lips as she takes in the room, but I don't give her enough time to fully take it in before I lead her to the bed so she can sit. Going to the desk drawer where I hid Abigail's present when she wasn't looking, I pull it out and walk back to her. Wrapping my arms around her from behind, I hand her the present and wait while she opens it.

Like an excited child, she starts ripping at the wrapping paper then lifts the lid to the box. "Oh, Matt," she utters, taking in the album I've given her. She opens it and her hand immediately goes to her mouth to cover another gasp. She's staring down at the picture of me holding her in my arms at the finish line for the Portland Marathon. Cautiously, she turns the page and it's a picture of our *very* first race. Silently, she continues to flip through the pages one by one, taking a couple of seconds to take each one in. Most of the photographs are of our races, but many are candid pictures taken by our closest friends.

"Do you like it, beautiful?" I hesitantly ask, hoping I haven't failed in satisfying her. Snapping her head up to look at me, she has a heartfelt smile on her lips.

"Oh, Matt. It's perfect."

"I got the idea from you," I explain, feeling pleased. "From the album you gave me of Emily and me. I wanted you to have something of the both of us." A tear slowly trickles down her cheek. Using my thumb to brush it away, I kiss her, hoping to take her sadness away.

Turning so she can climb onto my lap, she gently places the album on the side table. "It's perfect," she says while wrapping her arms around my neck and pulling me in for a kiss.

Somehow, it doesn't feel the same. "I'd planned this whole big dinner with all your favorite things we've shared together, but when you said you'd be here in New York, I had to modify everything. I was going to wake you up with pancakes in bed. Order your favorite pizza and have your donuts for dessert, but I had to improvise with what we had here."

"Everything was perfect because you're here to celebrate it with me. That's all I could ever wish for on my birthday," she expresses, her lips meeting mine while my hands slowly roam inside her shirt and against her skin.

Breaking our kiss and gasping for air, our hands become frantic and start tearing at our clothes, demanding they come off. Within seconds, we're both naked, only the glow of the candlelight illuminating our skin. She pulls me back to lie above her on the bed, her hungry eyes filled with a craving I'm all too familiar with.

Usually I would thrust myself into her, impatient to be one with her, but this time I want it to feel as if it were the first time I make to love her. Her legs impatiently pull at my body, demanding I plunge myself faster, but I ignore her request, keeping my slow and steady pace. Her nails are digging into my back as she moans my name. My eyes never leave her face, wanting to take in every second of me making love to her.

She's meant to be treasured and every second patiently taken. Needing to taste her, my mouth finds her lips. I push my tongue into her mouth and match the rhythm of my thrust. Her sweet taste is like nothing I've ever experienced before. She is my one and only. No one will ever compare to her.

"Oh God, Matt," she moans, starting to grow frantic and desperate for me to send her to her release. Always wanting to satisfy Abigail's every need, I quicken my thrusting. Her nails dig into my skin, an indication that she is nearing her climax. Reaching down to widen her legs so I can push myself deeper inside her body, my thrusts are now desperate to send us both over the edge. I can feel my balls tightening and my cock demanding I release inside of her, but I refuse to allow myself to finish without Abigail.

"Fuck. I love you, beautiful," I groan into her ear. She responds with a grunt of my name. I feel the walls of her core squeezing me below and I can't resist pushing harder, deeper inside of her.

She throws her head back as she screams, "Matt!" My name coming before a moan that has no resistance, making me follow her over the edge. Feeling every ounce of myself emptying inside her, I continue until I know I have nothing left.

Spent and exhausted, my body hovers above her. Taking her contented appearance in, I know there is no more beautiful sight than when she's panting from screaming my name. Pushing her hair from her sweaty forehead, we're both breathless, but I manage to whisper down to her, "I love you." Watching her eyes widely beam, my lips slam down to hers to kiss her.

Her hands grip my waist, as if resisting letting me go, but I know my weight is too much for her. Landing on the bed besides her, I pull her snug to my side and give her another kiss on her temple before her slow breathing tells me she's now falling asleep. Reaching over to grab for the album, I start flipping through the pages, reminiscing over every memory that corresponds to the matching picture.

I don't know how much time has passed, but the glow of

the candlelight is now low and my eyes are growing heavy. Placing the album back where Abigail placed it, I wrap my arms back around her, adding yet another memory to my mind. With the remaining candlelight dancing across the walls, I pray that Abigail and I will have the rest of our lives to celebrate our birthdays together… Never apart.

Chapter Ten

Abigail

MATT'S RUMBLED GROAN vibrates against my cheek as my phone continues to ring. Hans is the only one designated with the basic ringtone. There are no words I can find to relay the bitterness I feel inside when he calls. At this very moment, I may just murder the man if he's calling simply to give me a lecture for missing last night's after party. Choosing to ignore it and let him lecture away in a voicemail, I tighten my arm wrapped around Matt's waist as I snuggle closer to Matt, using the warmth of his body to help send me back into my slumber. However, I'm vastly disappointed when my phone starts ringing again with the same annoying ring.

"You better answer that," Matt suggests, shaking me awake. "It may be someone important." With an angered grumble matching the one he had moments ago, I sit up and reach for my phone.

"This better be worth waking me up for," I angrily say into the phone, not caring how the words sound. It's Hans after all.

"It should be since it's your career we're talking about."

His comment does not faze me one bit as I lie back down at Matt's side and try to get comfortable.

"What now?" I gripe into the phone.

"There's been a change of plans with the show." The simple declaration already has me groaning as I think of the possibilities of what other demands they will throw at me. "The designer's father passed away last night so she's postponing everything for now. The show has been cancelled until further notice," he says, completely surprising me instead.

"What does that mean?" I ask sitting up.

"It means we'll give you a call when everything is back on."

Unable to contain my excitement, my lips widen into a smile. I shouldn't feel so excited under the circumstances, but I can't resist since it means I no longer have to leave for Paris, or leave Matt behind. "No problem."

Hans ends the call and I'm still radiating inside as I snuggle back into Matt's arms. Throwing the phone to the other side of the bed, I lay against Matt's chest, too excited to go back to sleep.

"Matt, what time does your flight leave?"

He doesn't immediately answer me and now I'm the one trying to shake him awake. "Beautiful, if you want it, you have to climb on top this time. I'm too exhausted," he mumbles, attempting to pull my body up above his. Doing as he asks, I straddle his waist, but drape myself across his chest so my mouth is next to his ear.

"Actually, I'd rather go home than fall back to sleep," I whisper into his ear.

His body stiffens and his arms give me a shake. "What do you mean by home?"

"I want to go home," I repeat. "Back to Portland," I clarify.

Rising so we're both in a sitting position, he asks, "Who just called?"

Trying to contain my excitement so I'm not joyfully screaming out the words, I say, "It was the director. He said the show has been cancelled until further notice."

Matt's exhilaration towards my answer matches my own. "Are you serious?" Kissing me fully on the lips, he quickly pulls away. "What are we waiting for then?" he excitedly lets out, already pushing us both from the bed.

"Let's go home," I say with a smile, already rushing around the room with him to pack all my stuff.

Matt

TILTING MY HEAD so I can get a better look at Abigail's face as she sleeps on my shoulder, I smile. The content feeling pouring through my body, knowing she's returning with me to Portland, has been enough to keep me smiling since the moment she told me she was coming home with me. She lets out a whimper followed by a shudder. Suddenly she's sitting up gasping for air, terrifying me. Her wide eyes are searching her surroundings as her chest rapidly rises and falls.

"Beautiful?" I worriedly ask, not wanting to frighten her further. Her shoulders slump forward and she leans back into my welcoming arms. Running my hand up and down her back to comfort her, I say, "Tell me what it was about."

She trembles, her arms gripping me as if afraid to let me go. "It was just a nightmare. I'm fine now," she utters, but I know she's not being completely truthful.

"Was it about Bill?" I hesitantly ask. She slowly nods her head and the blood drains from my face. I can do nothing more than continue to stroke my arm up and down her back, trying to contain my anger. It's not her I'm angry at, but the fact that even in her dreams she can't escape him.

"I'll be much happier when we're home," she says, surprising me with the meaning of her statement.

"Why is that?"

"Because I'll be home with you."

"I can't wait," I say against her temple, smiling before giving her a brief kiss. She gives me a contented sigh, I'll take it for now. The rest of the flight is spent in silence.

Hours later, David is pulling up to my house after picking us up from the airport. The scene in front of me does not surprise me. Somehow, I should have expected it.

"Doesn't he know you're coming home tonight?" Abigail asks, looking at the blocked driveway at all the parked cars lining the street. David lets out a snort.

"You think that would stop Trey?"

"True," she mumbles.

Grabbing her hand, I open the door and pause. "You going to stick around?" I ask David before climbing out.

He shakes his head as he says, "I'm picking up Kelly in an hour and taking her to dinner."

"Thanks for the ride, David. Will you tell Kelly I'll call her tomorrow so we can get together sometime this week?" Abigail asks him.

"Of course. Good luck with Trey," he teases, looking towards the lawn where a set of drunken girls are stumbling, laughing the entire time. A group of guys soon follow them and help them up before leading them away.

"I'm so going to kick his ass," Abigail threatens.

"Let's go kick his ass together," I say, laughing at her annoyed expression as I tug her out of the truck. Grabbing the luggage from the back of the truck, I follow Abigail up to the driveway with her protectively at my side.

"Where's Lola?"

"She's locked up in the garage with Eleanor," I tell her, watching as she lets out a sigh of relief. "Come on. You two can reminisce in the morning. I'm beat."

"Me, too." A couple of steps later, I hear her say, "This reminds me of the night I moved in." Her declaration causes me to pause at the entrance and stare at our closed door as the image of her that night returns. When I look at her, she's staring back at me with a smile on her lips, the opposite of the frightened expression I'd opened the door to that night. Dropping our luggage, I grab her face and remember that night clear in my mind as I kiss her deeply.

She giggles against my lips. "I love you," she says, still giggling as I continue feathering her with a couple more kisses.

She pulls away with a smile. "Come on. I'm tired and I want to sleep in my own bed tonight," she urges, already reaching for the knob. The moment the door opens, the music intensifies and we're greeted by a mass of drunken partiers scattered throughout the living room. Abigail doesn't bother looking at them, heading straight for the hallway leading to our bedroom with me just steps behind her. She surprises me though when she stops in front of Trey's bedroom, pounding on the door with all her might. Trey's holler to 'Go away' can be faintly heard, but she ignores it and continues to bang on the door, kicking it shortly after. This time we don't hear any shouting, but instead stomps leading to the door.

"What the fuck!" As naked as the day he was born Trey is now yelling in our faces. His eyes light up at the sight of Abigail before he picks her up in a bear hug. "Supermodel, you're home!" he shouts as he bounces her up and down in the air like a rag doll. He lowers her back down to the ground and I shove at his shoulder when her feet hit the floor.

"Go put some fucking clothes on!" I yell, putting myself between Abigail and Trey to shield his naked body from her eyes.

"She was the one banging on my door. She should've known I was naked from the screaming coming from the room!"

"I was banging on your door to tell you the house better be clean in the morning when I wake up, or else I'm going to make sure it's you screaming my name when *I kick your ass*!" she shouts over my shoulder before I feel her pulling at my arm, leading me to our own room.

"Welcome home, supermodel," Trey bellows behind my back.

Abigail reaches for the doorknob to our room, but I stop her, producing my set of keys from my pocket.

"It has a lock?" she asks.

"I had it put in before I left. I had a feeling Trey was going to throw a party, so I made sure to lock up the room before I left," I explain, remembering the last time he had a party and I came home to find our bed occupied, but I'm not going to tell Abigail that little fact. Shutting the door after entering, my eyes watch Abigail throw herself onto our bed, letting out a blissful groan. Leaving the luggage on the floor, I walk over to join her.

"I'm so glad to be home," she mumbles into my chest as I pull her flush to my body, kissing her on her head.

"Me, too," I reply, closing my eyes with a peaceful smile.

Chapter Eleven

Bill

THE RINGING OF my phone disrupts me from my concentration. The number is blocked, alerting me it may be someone important.

"Bill here."

"Bill, it's Charlie," he says into the phone, sounding winded, as if running. "I was calling to tell you she left."

"What the fuck do you mean she left? When?" I ask, knowing she was still in New York just last night.

My plan failed last night. I wasn't expecting for her little boy toy to be there. She hadn't showed up with him, and from how Charlie had reported she'd been moping around, she wasn't expecting him either; so him showing was unexpected.

"The show has been postponed so she must have left."

Already knowing the answer to my next question, I still ask. "Where did she go?" There's a pause, as if he's thinking.

"I'm trying to find out, but she didn't even tell the director."

"Don't fucking worry about it. I have an idea."

Her returning to Oregon is going to put a hindrance in both

my schedule and budget. I already had to rearrange everything to coincide with New York, now she was going to have me flying back to the west coast. This bitch is pushing my limits, but I still need her, and I plan on getting her back. And when I do, she is going to pay.

"When is the show postponed until?" I question, wondering if it's worth flying back for.

"I don't know. They're not disclosing any information to anyone. Not even the models. Everyone is on standby under further notice."

"What kind of bullshit is that?" He sounds as if he's about to start explaining, but I cut him off. "Never mind. Just get me her new schedule," I demand into the phone.

"I already told you. Nobody has a schedule," he relays, sounding frustrated. He doesn't understand the meaning of frustrated.

"Then call me when you fucking have one!" I roar before hanging up on him. Taking my frustration out on the phone, I toss it across the desk, watching it skitter across the paperwork in front of me. Her leaving me stirred the rumors labeling me controlling and demanding. I had determination, which is why I'm controlling and demanding. It's the only way to succeed.

Thankfully, they didn't know the true reason why Abigail left. She's done a well enough job of using the *"contract met"* excuse to anyone who asked. She wasn't as stupid as I expected her to be. I'd predicted for her to sell our story to every tabloid that would pay. She's done it in the past. Abigail wouldn't have hesitated to make sure she made that front page and stay in the spotlight, the opposite of the girl she seems to be now. It makes me wonder if she has any drive left in her to succeed in this industry.

Narrowing my eyes into the air ahead of me, I have no

choice but to resort to patience. If I keep to my plan, Abigail Adams will cease to exist when this is all over, which is what should have happened over a year ago.

Abigail

TREY'S KNOCK ON the door startles me awake. Seconds later, I feel Matt disengage himself from under my arm wrapped over his chest and is shortly opening the door.

"I'm headed over to Andrew's to help him move. Tell supermodel I'm sorry about the mess, but I've got to go," Trey declares just loud enough so I can hear.

"Yeah, I'll let her know," Matt tells him before he shuts the door.

With a protest, I mumble under my breath, "Bastard."

Matt's booming laughter fills the room, helping to awaken me. Sitting up and rubbing my eyes, I watch Matt already searching through our closet. I didn't expect to come home and have to immediately clean, but knowing there's a mess out there is driving me nuts.

"I've only been gone for a week and he's already turning it back into a bachelor pad," I complain to Matt. Dressed in basketball shorts and a black muscle shirt, he walks back over to the bed and sits next to me. He looks out the window with a frown upon his lips and I follow his gaze. The weather is gloomy and it's pouring rain outside. It isn't the most ideal weather to go for a run, so that's out of the question.

"I guess I'm cleaning today," I mutter, remembering the chaos we walked into last night. Lord only knows how bad it got after we passed out. "You want to help me clean?" I ask with a sweet smile.

Looking apologetic, he says, "I have a new video game I've been wanting to test out."

"Fine, you go play your video games," I say, already climbing off the bed, feeling dejected.

"I am a guy. Most guys like to play video games, beautiful," he says, yanking me back to sit on his lap, kissing me below the ear.

"Don't try to sweeten me up. I already know you don't like cleaning so I'm not going to make you do it," I say with a chuckle, kissing him on the lips. "You're lucky I don't make you take me shopping," I say with a smirk, watching his eyes go wide as I tease him, remembering Emily's shopping memory.

"Anything but shopping," he pleads.

Laughing, I stand up from his lap. "We'll see," I say, grazing my finger down his tattoo. The sight of his wing always makes me tingle inside. "How about I play video games with you," I probe, testing to see what his answer will be.

"Oh yeah," he says with an arched brow, his eyes roaming down my body with a tilted head. "You *would* pull off being a sexy Black Op, but since you don't like guns, I don't think you'd be brave enough to take out the opponent."

I roll my eyes at his remark. "Point taken. I clean, you play your video game," I reply before leaving the room with Matt right behind me.

Entering the living room, the blood drains down to my toes as I take in the entire house. I can't help but cringe at the sight. "How in the hell did you manage to keep the house clean when I moved out?" I gripe to Matt who is already picking up bottles from the coffee table.

Matt stops in front of me, blocking my way to the kitchen. His arms wrap around my waist while he looks me in the eyes. "I didn't want it to be dirty in case you ever decided to come back. I made sure to have a maid service come once a week to keep it clean," he admits. His admission makes my heart swell from knowing he did it for me. "I know how much the mess bothers you. Leave it and I'll see if I can get someone out to clean it up today."

"It's okay. I'll clean it up."

An hour later, the trash is all thrown out, the kitchen is clean and I'm moving back into the living room to wipe everything down. With the music blasting in my ears to keep me motivated, I take a quick glance at Matt staring at the television with the control in his hands. He hasn't once looked in my direction as I've moved around the house, but it doesn't surprise me. The handful of times I've seen Matt playing video games with Trey he gets so engrossed with it, it's as if I don't exist; boys and their toys. His eyebrows furrow as he starts to grow frustrated, telling me my chance to wipe down underneath the flat screen is coming soon. Throwing his hand up in the air, I know he's died. I'm still watching him as he widens his eyes, encouraging me to move.

"Beautiful, you're in the way," I faintly hear through my music, making me glance over my shoulder to see him craning his neck as his fingers pound away at the control. *S&M* has begun to play in my ears and my resolve to test Matt's ability to ignore me any more rises. Keeping my back to him, I move, but only to the side where I'm still in his line of vision. I'm cleaning, but start provocatively dancing to the lyrics of the song. When I quickly peek over my shoulder, Matt's hooded eyes are locked onto my body. Further testing him, I start sashaying in Matt's direction, never taking my eyes off his. My body is already igniting with desire and my mind has now come up with a completely new purpose other than cleaning.

I'm standing in between his legs as I keep swaying to the music. The game has completely been forgotten at this point as Matt keeps his eyes locked on my body. Rihanna is bellowing out the final lyrics, letting me know that it's about to end as he glides his hands up my thigh to cup my ass. Removing my ear buds and tossing my phone alongside Matt's control, I slowly start to remove my shirt. His eyes grow dark and hungry before I turn to give him my back again, slowly reaching behind me to unclasp my bra. Looking over my shoulder to tantalize him, I can hear a faint growl escape his lips, making me chuckle. Hooking my fingers into the waistband of my shorts, I deliberately take my time to bend over and pull them down; just as slowly standing back up to turn and face him. Gradually gliding his hands up my thighs, the heat of his palms leaves a trail of a shivers over every inch of skin he touches.

My body is tugged to straddle his hips and the friction from his shorts rubbing against my naked core sends a tremor up and down my spine. Holding onto his shoulders, I grind harder into him as I throw my head back to moan. His hands on my hips lift me up and my eyes snap open in shock wondering why. Leaving me still hovering over his body, he pushes his shorts just low enough so his engorged cock comes out. Pulling me back down, I guide him inside me, groaning from the pleasured sensation of him filling me. Wanting him as bare as myself, I tug his shirt off and over his head.

His hands are back on my ass, coaxing me to rise and fall against him. His mouth finds my breast and suckles first on one nipple before he moves onto the other. Our movements become frantic and my whimpers grow louder as he keeps thrusting his hips higher, trying to push deeper inside me. The feeling of my body tensing is telling me I'm nearing my climax, and the digging of Matt's fingers into my skin lets me know he is just as close. I know my climax is Matt's weakness. I scream, allowing my body to release its hold. He closely follows me over the edge with a grunt of my name and a few final thrusts before slowly coming to a stop. Slumping down onto Matt's chest, I continue to tremble from my release, feeling the thumping of our hearts pounding against each other. Matt's labored breathing matches my own as I feel the beating of my heart in my ears.

"And this is the reason why I can't play video games when you're around," he breathlessly comments.

"Huh?"

"You're a distraction." Realizing the meaning behind his words, I giggle. "But I should keep the house dirty from now on if this is the end result," he huskily says into my ear. His warmth breath gliding down my sweaty body sends a shudder down my spine.

"I say next time I sit on the couch while I watch *you* clean," I breathlessly respond. Matt lets out a full-blown laugh, making me chuckle along with him.

"As long as I get my reward for doing it," he replies, squeezing my ass to notify me of the reward he has in mind.

Chapter Twelve

Abigail

I SEE MATT storming from the room, looking furious. "What's this?" he asks as he holds something up in his hand.

The blood drains from my face as he stops in front of me and I take a better view of the object in his hand. I'm rendered speechless, unable to come up with a plausible answer just yet. His eyes widen, demanding an answer.

"Where did you get it?" I force myself to rasp out.

"I was emptying out your pockets so I can do laundry and found it in your pants. Who sent it to you?"

"I don't know," I lie, trying to figure out a way to diffuse his anger. His head snaps back in shock as if he knows I'm not being truthful with him.

His eyes narrow down at me. "When did you get it?"

Swallowing, I answer. "The night of the show," I say just above a whisper.

"And you didn't tell me!" he roars, causing me to flinch.

"I got distracted," I throw back at him, which isn't entirely untrue. Matt does have a way of always distracting me.

Holding the card higher in the air, he yells, "This isn't something you keep from me, Abigail!"

Damn... He's used my name. He's truly pissed.

"Was this the first time?"

Shit. Closing my eyes knowing I can't lie to him again, I shake my head in response.

"When did you start getting them?"

"I got the first one earlier this week," I truthfully admit.

"What did it say?"

Forcing myself to remember exactly what it said, I answer him. "Something about me not being able to be the same person as before," I reply. "I thought maybe it was one of the other models, so I didn't think anything of it."

He looks at me skeptically. "Anymore after that?" he asks through what I'm sure are clenched teeth.

"Another during my first rehearsal," I quietly admit, remembering the note. *"I'm always watching you,"* I rasp out, bracing myself for his reaction.

"Does Julio know about them?" he angrily asks.

"No," I whisper. Had Matt been one of those animated cartoons, I'm sure he'd have smoke coming out of his ears, his face a mask of stone. Stepping away to pace the room, he tightly clutches the paper in his hand, his knuckles turning white from the action.

Snapping his head, he turns to glare at me. "You're not leaving the house until I find out who sent the notes."

"What?" I shockingly let out. "You can't order me to stay locked up!"

His face is back to looking like a stone. "Take it how you want, Abigail, but I refuse to let you risk getting killed over you being careless."

My mouth drops open to gape at him. "Careless? Is that

what you think of me?" I furiously throw at him as he begins pacing the room again.

"I don't mean it like that," he says as he rushes to close the distance he'd put between us. "Abigail, I love you too much to lose you to him." His hands hold onto my waist as if fearful I'd run.

"But we have no proof that it's really him. It could just be one of the other models I was working with," I suggest, but somehow deep in my heart I know I'm lying to myself as well.

"Regardless, there's someone making threats and I don't like it," he growls.

"You can't keep me caged up like an animal, Matt."

A heavy sigh escapes his lips. "You're right. I can't," he confesses. "But I'm afraid you're back to the old rules. I meant what I said, beautiful. I refuse to let *anyone* hurt you," he declares, slowly pulling me to his body.

Automatically wrapping my arms around his waist and leaning into his body, I silently stand there in his arms. Minutes later he sternly instructs, "Just don't keep any more notes from me."

It's hard to agree to, but I do so with a nod. He's embracing me tighter into his chest and places a kiss on my temple as if it will make all my troubles go away. I know it won't, but a girl can hope.

Matt

I'M PLAYING WITH Abigail's bracelet as she lies draped across my chest, still arguing into the phone. The ringtone indicated it's the director she is talking to. With her head resting sideways, I run my hand through the strands of her hair to try to calm her. It helps until I hear, "And I'm telling you *again*. Since I had nothing on my schedule for this week I decided to leave the city. How was I supposed to know you'd spring a photo shoot on me last minute?"

Tilting my head to get a better view of her face, the sight is utterly comical. She looks ready to strangle someone as she stares off into the distance, grimacing while she listens. I'm biting down on my lip to refrain from smiling. She looks so cute when she's agitated.

"Have you even heard from her?" She releases an exasperated sigh as she demands to know more information. "Email me the information. But you have to stop pulling this shit!" She's rolling her eyes at his response, making me lightly laugh this time because of her sassy attitude. I already know Abigail can be a force to deal with when she's pissed, which is why I don't dare bring it out of her unless I have to.

Right when I think she's done arguing with them, she adds, "You may be paying me to do the show, but I still have the original offer and nowhere does it state I was obligated to do extra shit on the side on demand," hanging up the phone, effectively ending the call after her last statement.

She still looks furious as she lets out a frustrated growl. Wanting to take her frustration away, I dig my fingers into her side, tickling her. "Matt! Stop it!" she angrily yells as she tries to squirm her way out of my hold.

Wrapping my arms and legs around her, I trap her. We're both now laughing as she continues to attempt escape. Suddenly, I remember the last time I was tickling her like this on the couch and when she lifts her head to look at me, I kiss her. Looping my hand behind her neck to hold her in place, I tilt my head to deepen our kiss. This is what I should have done the very first time I tickled her on the couch. It's what I anxiously wanted to do, but my fear of losing her if I broke her heart as I had purposely done with every girl who'd come my way stopped me from doing so. Every day, I fought so hard to keep her at a distance, to keep her safe, but it caused us to make mistakes.

I pull away, left breathless from the beautiful smile she's giving me. "I love you," I say, my heart swelling as I say the words to her.

"I love you, too," she says in return before kissing me again.

The heat of the moment reminds me of something else I'd wanted to do back then, and can easily do now... Make love to Abigail.

My hands are already inside her shirt gliding against her warm skin, lifting it over her head as the doorbell goes off.

Glancing at the door, she turns to me and asks, "You expecting someone?"

"No. You?"

She tenses above me as her eyes stay locked onto the door. Sliding her onto the couch, I stand up and head towards the door. "Go to the room and lock the door," I order her. Without questioning me, she gets up and practically rushes down the hallway. Glancing over my shoulder, I make sure the door to our room is completely shut. I've been meaning to put in a peephole and right now more than ever, I regret not doing it sooner.

Reaching the door, I grab the bat I'd placed there the other day, having it ready but hidden behind the door as I slightly open it. Through the crack of the door, I see a FedEx delivery guy holding an envelope in his hands.

"Matthew Garcia?" he curiously asks, waiting for my reaction.

"Yeah, that's me."

He hands me the envelope, practically forcing me to take it before thrusting his little machine at me. "Sign here, please," he orders next. Placing the bat under my armpit, I sign my name. Wishing him a good day, I shut and lock the door, already seeing Abigail peeking from the hallway.

Disbelievingly arching my eyebrow at her, I'm disappointed she's standing there. "I didn't hear any arguing so I figured it was safe," she says with a nonchalant shrug of her shoulders. "What did you get?" Abigail asks, already at my side.

"I have no clue," I answer as I tear open the envelope. Inside is another envelope. After opening that one, I start reading the letter it contains. My eyes quickly scan the words and my heart halts to a stop before it hastily starts up again.

"Is this good?" she asks.

Still speechless from the letter, my hands begin to slightly tremble. All I can do is nod as I force myself to take measured breaths, because if I don't, I may just past out from the lightheadedness I'm feeling.

Finding my voice, I scan the letter again. "They only invite the first round players to the draft. It pretty much means you're guaranteed to be picked up by a team." The words come out barely above a whisper as I'm still in shock.

"Oh. My. God!" Abigail shouts as her arms wrap around my neck, hopping up and down in excitement. If I weren't already breathless, she would have extracted every ounce of breath from how tightly she's hugging me. I'm still in shock from what I've just read, but Abigail's feathered kisses spreading across my face bring me back to reality.

"Holy. Shit!" I roar out.

Abigail is still bouncing up and down at my side. "I guess we're both going back to New York!" she says in an excited squeal.

Just as excited, I reply, "I guess we are," still unbelieving of how lucky I am right now. Trey walks through the door and

Abigail is already shouting the exciting news.

"Matt got invited to the NFL draft!"

His eyes go wide in shock. "No. Fucking. Way!" he whoops, rushing to grab the letter from my hands. Surrendering the letter, he looks just as shocked as I felt when reading it. "Dude, it's during the week of spring break," he declares. "I want to go," he states in a light plea, looking between Abigail and me.

"Of course!" Abigail shouts back to him, already digging her phone out of her pocket and calling someone. "Kelly! You'll never believe what Matt just got," she says walking back into the living room, excitedly giving her the details. "I know right!" I soon hear her say, making me chuckle.

Trey engulfs me in a hug, shaking me from my astonished state. "Congratulations, man."

Guilt hits me as we pull apart. I stare at Trey before looking down at the letter again. "Thanks, man," I guiltily reply, feeling a pang of regret it isn't him as well. Trey looks up at me with a frown on his lips, which at first worries me.

"What's wrong?" he confusedly asks.

"I don't know, man," I answer, shrugging my shoulders as I rub at the back of my neck and look down at the floor. "I just feel bad because all this is happening to me and not you too," I truthfully admit.

"Yeah, I'll admit I'm a bit jealous," he confesses. When my head snaps up, he has a playful smirk on his lips. "But you're like a brother to me, man, and I couldn't be happier it's you. I know if it was me you would feel the same way."

Nodding at him, I smile. "Of course I would be," I truthfully answer.

Abigail rushes back to our sides, looking more excited than earlier. "I invited Kelly and David as well."

"Damn, supermodel. You're just making a party out of

this," Trey jokes.

"This is a very important thing for Matt, and they insisted on coming."

For a moment, I felt a heavy ache inside from not being able to call Emily to give her the great news. It's the first thing I would have done in the past, but looking at Abigail's excited gleam lightens me up just the same. It's as if Emily is also here next to me. Her eyes meet mine and she's still radiating excitement before throwing herself into my arms. I may not physically have my sister at my side any longer, but what she's given me in her place is satisfying enough and there is nothing better in the world.

Abigail

LOOKING AROUND THE room making sure I've packed everything I can think of, I turn my attention back to my suitcase, already doubting it will close easily. Standing back while I crossly stare at it, I refuse to be defeated by a piece of luggage. As I'm contemplating what I should try next, I hear Matt chuckling behind me.

"Here, you sit on it while I zip it up," he suggests.

"Why didn't I think of that?" I huff out as I throw my hands up in frustration.

He laughs as he lifts me to sit on the suitcase. "Next time don't overpack," he proclaims, already zipping it closed under me.

"I need options this week," I tell him, remembering everything I've packed. I'd ordered the largest suitcase I could find for this trip, wanting to take as many options as the luggage will allow me to pack.

He pulls back from me, looking skeptical. "Since the day I've met you, you've never cared what anyone else thinks about what you're wearing."

Hanging my head in shame, I know he's right. "That was before. During the week I was in New York, everyone around me crudely looked at me because of the way I was dressed," I confess around the lump now forming in my throat as tears threaten to emerge. "I just want to look nice for your event," I admit.

The memories of the looks I received pass through my mind as Matt lifts my chin, forcing me to meet his stare. "You don't have to impress anyone. If they don't like you for who you are, then they don't need to be in your life. You're beautiful inside and out. Don't let anyone make you feel like you aren't," he says to me, followed by a kiss. When he pulls back, the sincerity in his eyes and the smile on his face makes me light up, pushing any doubt I had aside—including the tears. It reminds me that I don't have to please anyone but him, and if he loves me for who I am, then so should I.

I lift my legs up to wrap around his waist, pulling him towards me to close the gap between us. My hand reaches inside his shorts to wrap around the warm skin of his shaft. "Beautiful," he manages between our kiss. "We're going to be late," he mumbles against my lips, making me giggle from the strain in his voice.

"We rarely get to have quickies," I murmur back. "I think we need to have one right now," I suggest.

Using my legs and feet, I push his shorts and boxer briefs down, leaving him exposed and ready for me. I know I've won when I feel his hands yanking at the button of my jeans. Unhooking my legs from his waist so I can help, I lift my hips so they can come off. In my mind, I think Matt is going to lower me back down next to the luggage, but I'm proven wrong when my ass is dropped onto it and he's pushing himself between my legs, guiding himself into me. The roughness of the material is digging into my ass as he frantically rocks back and forth. I already know this will not end well on my rear end, but the pleasure I'm feeling may just be worth it.

MATT LAUGHS AS I wince from trying to get comfortable. "Shut up," I say with a glare, only making him laugh harder. Normally his laugh would make me smile, but right now it's irritating me since he's the reason why I'm wincing. The person behind me causes me to give another cringe as my seat is shoved forward.

Normally I fly first or business class, but since the entire gang was coming, it was more economical to fly coach, leaving me very limited space between Julio and Matt.

"I need to go to the bathroom," Julio informs us before standing and leaving us alone.

Matt leans down, his lips merely inches from my ear as his warm breath caresses my skin. "How's your ass?" he huskily whispers. Although the question is sending shivers down my spine, I still playfully shove at him. "You're the one who wanted a quickie. I delivered," he proudly proclaims.

I glare at him as I fight to contain the smile that wants to creep up my lips. "I didn't ask for my butt to be rubbed raw," I retort. "I wouldn't be surprised if you took a layer of skin off of my ass," I say with a grimace, remembering the pain mixed with pleasure as Matt kept pounding into me. Half of my screams were from the chafing on my butt gliding back and forth over the rough material.

"I'll gladly kiss it better once we're alone in our own hotel room," he promises while placing a kiss on my neck. His words make me smile as I envision him keeping that promise. Entwining his fingers into mine, he asks, "Are you excited about this week?"

I nod my head in reply then ask, "Are *you* nervous?"

He lets out a deep breath through his lips. "Nervous as fuck. There's only one team I really want to play for, but at this point I'll take anything," he answers.

No matter how much I've insisted he tell me which team he wants to play for, Matt never divulged the information claiming he didn't want to jinx himself. I squeeze his hand to comfort him. "All that matters is that you're going to get picked," I reassure him.

He answers with a nod as I lean in to kiss him, causing me to wince again. Matt chuckles against my lips and I give him another playful swat. "I'm sorry. I can't help it," he laughs out.

"You just wait until I put *your* ass on a carpet and ride you. I'll be the one laughing when you have rug burn on your ass," I throw back at him, turning to face the seat in front of me.

"I look forward to it," he answers. Rolling my eyes, I realize my life is never boring with Matt in it, and I don't want to imagine ever being without him again.

Chapter Thirteen

Abigail

I STARE AT myself in the mirror as I rotate my body from side to side, unsatisfied with my current choice. Removing the dress as fast as I can, I toss it onto the floor and grab for the next one, hastily putting it on. Rushing back to the mirror, I proceed with the process of analyzing the dress as I'd done with the previous one.

"Damn, you look sexy," Matt's deep voice says to me from the bathroom. He's only wearing a towel around his waist, his hair still slightly damp from his shower.

Looking back into the mirror again to take another look, I ask, "Are you sure?" Doubting he's telling the truth.

In the reflection of the mirror, I see him move behind me, his hands now resting on my hips. His hooded eyes lock onto my reflection, sending a jolt of shivers down my naked spine.

"I think it's perfect," he huskily responds, taking his hand from my waist. I feel his finger touching my lower back right were the material meets my tailbone. His finger gradually starts to float up my back inch by tantalizing inch, making my body ignite with flames. A gasp escapes my lips as my heart rapidly speeds up.

Lowering his mouth to my ear, he whispers, "I don't know if I like the idea of you not wearing a bra. I can see how hard your nipples are from here, which means everyone else will, too."

My eyes shoot to my breast and staring back at me are my hardened nipples beneath the silk material of my dress. The spark of desire coursing through my body has rendered me speechless and unable to defend myself. Matt's hands spread across my ribs and into my dress, gliding to the front of my body. Cupping my breasts in each one of his hands, he roughly squeezes them. I throw my head back to land on his shoulder and let out a pleasured groan. Since my hair is already up and styled, Matt's lips slowly start tormenting me with kisses across the back of my neck. My hands reach behind to grip his waist and I pull him up flush to my body. His hardened erection is pressing against my butt, jumping every couple of seconds.

"I think you're wearing too much," I say, yanking the towel from his body and reaching for his shaft, rubbing my hand up and down his silky skin. A moan leaves Matt's lips as he bites my shoulder and fiercely grasps my breast. I feel him tugging me in the direction of the bed before he turns me and shoves me forward, my hands landing to catch myself.

The silk material of my dress glides up my thighs before the brisk cold air hits my legs. "Hmm… No underwear again," he says as I feel the tip of him finding my center. I hadn't gotten that far in getting dressed. As expected, he pushes forward and in one hard thrust, I'm completely filled at the same time there's a knock at the door.

"Are you almost ready? The car is going to be here any minute!" Trey shouts as he bangs on the door. Without giving a response, Matt starts plunging in and out of me, ignoring Trey's statement. I'm biting down on my lip, desperately trying to contain my moans as he pounds into me, but it's no use. He's so deep inside of me that I start whimpering louder than I intended.

My fists grip the sheets for dear life as he rocks me faster than he ever has before, our wild groans echoing through the room. With every second, I feel my body demanding to shatter and I throw my head back as I explode with fireworks from the inside out. Matt's grunts tell me he's found his release as well, coming at the same time as me.

Matt's warm lips kiss my back, making me shudder. "This dress is perfect," I hear his deep voice express, pulling himself away from me as he lowers the dress back down my legs. Hauling my body up from the bed to stand, I lean against his chest for support as I struggle to stay upright. "I want to remember what we just did every time I look at you today," he adds, my body shivering from the thought.

"Okay," I reply, wanting to satisfy him.

There's another pounding at door and I already know it's Trey from how it was delivered. "Why do you guys always do that shit when we have to go somewhere?"

We both laugh at the lecture, but it was worth it. "We better hurry," Matt says into my ear. His deep voice vibrates off my skin. I'm about to lose it as the sensation travels down to my core, regardless of having just finished. I'm left disappointed when Matt pulls himself away and lifts the towel off the ground. "No time for another shower," he says, already cleaning himself. "But I can't say I'm going to complain knowing I smell like you."

He laughs as I scrunch my nose thinking about his statement. "Sorry, beautiful, but you don't have time for a shower either." Looking over to the clock, I groan knowing he's right.

Matt pulls me to him with a smirk on his lips. "And make sure to not wear any underwear," he instructs before walking away. With a low grumble, I go back into the bathroom. The least I can do is hastily freshen up in the minutes I have left.

Checking my make-up and hair, satisfied I don't have to do much, I'm ready to go. Exiting the bathroom, I'm left frozen in my steps the moment I take in Matt. The outfit he has chosen is simple, but still leaves him looking breathtaking. The dark semi-faded jeans and dress up shirt were only the beginning as he now adds a black blazer for a touch of professionalism. When his gaze finds mine; his dark eyes and sensual smile are the finishing touch.

Originally, I suggested he wear a suit, since it was what most athletes wear to this event, but Matt grimaced at the suggestion. I knew even if he had chosen my idea, he wouldn't have felt comfortable the entire day.

Feeling lightheaded, my heart races with desire as I resume walking over to him. "Now you, Matthew Garcia, look very handsome," I purr to him, my hand already on his chest.

He shyly blushes at me. "Handsome enough to let me have my way with you?"

I throw my head back and laugh. "I was ready to throw myself at you the day I met you in shorts and a cut off shirt," I inform him.

"Had I known that, I would have done what I wanted to do that day," he says, nibbling down my neck. I knew that same day he would be my downfall; but this downfall I will happily accept.

"I can't wait to rip these clothes off of you," I say, using one of his lines.

Tilting my head, he tortures us both by continuing to kiss his way along my shoulder. "Is that so?" he mocks as his warm breath caresses my skin. Breathless and even more lightheaded than before I stepped into his arms I nod. With a final quick, opened mouth kiss that sends shudders down my spine, he pulls back to greet me with his dark, hungry eyes.

"Let's go. The sooner we get there, the sooner we can get back so you can keep that promise," he murmurs with a wag of his brows.

Trey's banging on the door startles me from my trance of carnal thoughts, reminding me we must leave. "You're very lucky we have a car full of people or else I would hold you to that promise the moment we stepped into the car." His suggestion makes me bite my lip as I quietly whimper from the thought.

"We really should go. The last thing I want is to arrive late and make a bad impression," Matt says, already tugging me to the door.

MATT IS ANXIOUSLY bouncing his knee up and down, clearly nervous. Who wouldn't be? We're patiently waiting in a private green room the executives put us in. Madison Square Garden is buzzing with excitement from the anticipation of today's event. In a few moments, they will go live with the announcements of the draft. Until then, we are ordered to patiently wait. Entwining my fingers with his, I bring his hand up to kiss the back of his palm. I'm rewarded with a genuine smile and a quick kiss.

"When are they going to call your name?" Trey impatiently asks for the fourth time.

"You asking over and over again isn't going to help," David lectures. Trey pierces him with a glare, but it doesn't affect David at all as he sits there, expressionless. I know he's just as nervous as Matt. All of us are.

Suddenly there's a light knock at the door and Julio goes into high alert before slightly opening it. "I'm here to film the live footage when they call his name," a man says from the other side. A brief moment later, Julio allows the cameraman to enter and the atmosphere of the room suddenly changes. It's obvious from his presence that things are about to begin. Our nervousness has now been replaced with excitement.

"You stay at the entrance of the door. Nowhere near Matt and Abigail," Julio orders. The guy looks as if he's about to argue, but with the challenging glare Julio is giving him, he has clearly thought otherwise.

"That's fine. I can get a good shot from here," the cameraman mutters as he lifts the camera. "Would you mind standing up so I can get a better angle of you?" he asks Matt.

With my hand locked with his, Matt stands, bringing me up with him. Nervously, we stand side my side and I can do nothing more than rub my hand up and down his forearm to comfort him. David heads over to the flat screen on the wall that is broadcasting the live footage. He turns the volume up and the commentators are still talking away about the various candidates. They announce they are now going to begin and my stomach rolls as the screen changes to show a man walking to a podium.

The seconds it takes for him to fumble with his papers and welcome everyone feels endless. Matt seems calm and collected as we wait, but the moment the announcer names the first team and their choice, his body tenses.

Minutes later, with several teams and their choices behind us, the announcer calls out the next team. "The San Diego Chargers select…" It's as if time has frozen and everything ceases to exist as Matt goes rigid. It's at that moment I know which team Matt is eagerly waiting for. This is the team he's been wishing to play for. My eyes stay locked onto Matt as he anxiously stares at the screen. "Matt Garcia, for their selective quarterback." With the words being delivered, Matt releases a gush of breath as he tugs me into his arms.

"Congratulations," I whisper. Tenderly, he places a kiss below my ear, as if telling me thank you. I'm reluctant to let him go, wanting to savor the moment. When we do pull away, I can barely see through my tears of joy. With a last quick kiss, Matt turns to receive congratulatory cheers from everyone else in the room. He's given enthusiastic pats on his shoulder and ecstatic smiles from their faces. I couldn't have asked for anything more for Matt. The cameraman has somehow managed to push past Julio and is now circling around all of us, taking in every possible view of our moment.

From the corner of my eye, I see a familiar face and I tug at Matt's arm to get his attention. His eyes meet Eddie, the man who had invited Matt to the NFL scouting combine, and in his hands is a Chargers jersey, already embroidered with Matt's last name. He heads straight to Matt and hands him the jersey. I'm just as breathless as Matt looks as he takes it from him.

"This is for you," Eddie tells him, looking proud as Matt takes it from him.

"Thank you so much," Matt says with wide eyes.

Clapping him on the shoulder with a smile, Eddie says, "You earned it."

Matt's eyes have yet to leave the jersey in his hands as he continues to stare at it in awe, but still manages to say, "But you gave me the chance," finally lifting his head to meet Eddie's eyes.

Eddie gives him an acknowledging nod before saying, "Welcome to the NFL, boy," his hand still tightly clasped on his shoulder.

They exchange one last handshake and a half hug before Eddie exits the room, leaving us all alone to admire the jersey. A couple of minutes later, a crew steps in to interview Matt. The entire time Matt is composed and answers every single question with a beaming smile on his face. Twenty minutes later, the camera crew exits the room and the NFL executives for the Chargers are handing a set of papers to Matt for him to sign, informing him he has seventy-two hours to look over the details of the contract and make a final decision before we are finally free to leave.

We head back to the hotel room to celebrate Matt's draft with plenty of alcohol and mocking stories of how he'll forget us all when he becomes famous. It doesn't take long before we're seeking our beds. David and Kelly claimed they were tired, but from the way they were tearing at each other's mouths, I doubt they were going to sleep. Matt keeps gripping my thighs as I sat across his lap on the couch, letting me know he has the same idea.

With a heartfelt good night, we all head to bed. Since the trip was last minute, we were only able to find a suite with two rooms, leaving Trey and Julio to seek refuge on the couch. Upon arriving, we all agreed that David and Kelly would take one room, while Matt and I took the other.

The faint click of the door causes my stomach to flutter with anticipation of what I know will come. The faint glow of the city lights entering through the translucent curtains covering the window illuminates Matt's handsome form as he predatorily walks over to me.

"Wasn't there something you promised to do when we got back?" he asks, his deep voice breaking the silence in the room. He wraps me in his arms as his lips find the hollow of my neck. "I've been waiting all day to get you alone again."

A jolt of electricity rapidly travels through me, causing

my legs to go weak and my stomach to flip flop. Impatiently, my hands start yanking at Matt's shirt, quickly fumbling with the buttons until it's open and I'm running my hands across his chest. Our tongues glide back and forth against each other's as I explore every inch of Matt's mouth. The mixture of the beer he'd been drinking earlier and his own unique taste is like ambrosia I will never tire of tasting. The cooled air caresses me as my dress falls to the floor, leaving me completely naked and shuddering with eagerness.

My fumbling hands finally manage to push Matt's pants from his body and my hand reaches toward his center wrapping itself around his shaft, gripping him tightly. Matt lets out a gasp into my mouth as I start moving my hand up and down, deliberately teasing him while leading him towards the bed. Turning us so his back is facing the bed, I give him a light shove. He lands on the bed and I quickly climb above him. I guide him into my body and ride him, sending us both to our favorite land of ecstasy.

Chapter Fourteen

Matt

CAREFUL NOT TO wake Abigail, I detangle myself from her sleeping body. I've been unable to sleep, my mind a turmoil of thoughts since this morning. Even with her in my arms, I can't push them away. Picking up my jersey that is sitting at the edge of the bed where I'd placed it upon coming back to the hotel, my eyes stare down at it contemplating what I should do. For years, I've wanted nothing more than to play for them, but these last couple of weeks have made me rethink my wish.

Running my fingers across the embroidered lettering of my last name makes my heart sink. Since childhood, I've loved playing sports. I'd trained hard. Played hard. Made sure I always gave one hundred percent no matter what I did, but it wasn't for me. I did it all to make Emily proud. She would cheer me on from beginning to end, always the loudest person in the crowd and never once missing any of my games; even in college. When my parents passed away, Emily chose to get me involved with sports to help distract us both from our loss. At first, I resisted her, not having the spirit or will to play, but she was persistent and won in the end. I soon discovered that I enjoyed doing something for her. It was the reason why I stuck with it. Eventually, I grew to love playing any type of sport.

With a heavy sigh, I wish my sister was still alive to see me play again, but the reality that she isn't makes me wonder if it's even worth doing anymore. While clutching the jersey tight in my hands, I feel the bed move behind me. Looking over my shoulder, I see Abigail crawling her way towards me, stopping to kneel at my side. Wrapping my arm around her waist, I tug her to straddle me, needing the feel of her body to comfort me. Digging my face into the crook of her neck, I inhale her sweet scent, letting it soothe me.

"Whatcha thinking about?" she asks, her sweet voice now sounding somber.

"Nothing," I shamefully lie to her, not wanting to admit that for a brief second, I considered giving it all up. Her hand reaches in between us to take the jersey. Pulling back so she can get a better look at it, her lips turn up into a smile. As I'd done only moments ago, her fingers brush across my name.

"What does it feel like to wear it?" Her question takes me back to this afternoon when I'd put it on for promotional pictures.

Wearing the jersey had felt like one of the proudest moments of my life. Without thinking, I pull the jersey up and over her head. She stands, giving me a full view of her body as the jersey falls just above her thighs. It engulfs Abigail's tiny form, but nevertheless, she looks beautiful as always.

"Now that has got to be the sexiest thing I've ever seen," I breathlessly say. Knowing Abigail is completely naked underneath the jersey makes me close my eyes to catch my breath. When I open them again, she's shyly biting down on her lip and tugging at the hem. My earlier thoughts of giving up have completely vanished. Reaching for her waist and tugging her between my legs, I look up at her.

"I will never be able to look at my jersey the same again."

She giggles, using her hands on my shoulders to keep steady as my fingers find the center of her heat. "Is that so?" she breathlessly asks, her eyes now closed and her head thrown back as I continue to tease her.

"I feel sorry for the guys in the locker room with me because I'm pretty sure right before I put my jersey on, I'll be sporting a hard-on." She lets out a bout of laughter, but it's followed by a gasp as I pinch her clit. Taking my hand from her body, I pull her back down onto my hips and rub her core against my semi-erect dick as she sits down on me.

"How about I give you something else to remember before you put the jersey on?" she asks in a seductive tone.

I'm already pushing inside of her as I say, "How about you do."

Abigail

OUR BREATHING IS settling into a soothing rhythm; I'm both exhausted and satisfied as I contently lie across Matt's chest, the material of his jersey the only barrier between us. Lifting my head to look at him, I calmly ask, "Are you happy?"

"Yes," he answers, bringing his hand up to brush the hair from my face.

Still feeling doubtful, I ask, "Excited?"

"Of course," he says with an arch of his brow.

"Nervous?" I continue to probe. Instead of immediately answering, he chuckles. "Why all the questions?"

Resting my head on his shoulder, I consider what to say next. "I don't know. I just want to make sure you're happy," I convey. "I know Emily would be proud of you right now." The words cause my heart to sink with sadness.

Matt pushes me onto my back and is now staring down at me with tender eyes. "I *am* happy. I don't think I've ever been happier in my life, beautiful, but it's because I have you in it. Without you, my life isn't worth living."

My heart swells and I can't help but smile up at him. "I can't imagine my world without you either, Matt," I whisper back to him. "I love you." I pull him down to kiss him, proving just how much I love being with him.

HIDING MY YAWN with the back of my hand as the make-up designer applies her final touches, I hear Matt laugh. "Tired, beautiful?"

With a smile, I answer, "Yes, but it's worth it." When the brush leaves my lid, I open my eyes to find Matt returning the same satisfied smile with a gleam in his eyes. Even after yawning, I can't resist doing so again.

"Do you want me to go get you some coffee?"

"A sugar free Red Bull would be even better," I inform him with begging eyes. This time he laughs as he stands and walks over to me.

"Your wish is my command," he says, placing a kiss on my lips before heading out the door. I watch him leave, already longing for this shoot to be done and over with so we can go home.

"All done," the make-up designer informs with a satisfied

smile. "You're not needed on set for another few minutes so just relax until someone comes to get you. I'm pretty sure you'll want to take advantage of the time when your man comes back," she says with a wiggle of her eyebrows. "Just don't mess up your makeup or I may just strangle you both," she sternly lectures before leaving the room.

I laugh at her, knowing she's probably right. I will most likely take advantage of my time when Matt gets back. With a contented smile, I look into the mirror to take in my outfit. Earlier, I'd put on the dress ordered and was ready to head out onto the set, but Charlie had informed me that the shoot was slightly postponed due to the photographer not being able to find his camera. The make-up artist had then decided to take a little more time adding a few more touches to my make-up.

Looking down at my dress to make sure I don't have any lint on it, I hear the click of the door shutting behind me. With an excited smile, I turn to face Matt, but my heart immediately stops before racing back to life when I take in Bill instead. My eyes search for an escape, but as I look around the room, I know I'm trapped. When I look back at him, a gun is now pointing at me. My frantic mind prays Julio will soon return from wherever it was he left to. Bill furiously stalks his way to me, his body language full of rage. There is no hiding the evident anger radiating from his eyes.

"It's nice to see you again, Abigail." The sound of his voice sends me back to that very first day I heard it in my coma. A set of shivers courses through my body knowing his sole intention is to harm me.

"You shouldn't be here, Bill. I'd hate to see what would happen if Julio caught you near me," I bravely state through clenched teeth while I attempt to control them from rattling in fear.

"Your little bodyguard won't be coming back soon. I've made sure of that." The words worry me the instant I absorb them and my body demands I move as I try to sidestep past Bill, but he lunges forward and fiercely grips my arm. His fingers forcefully dig into my skin as I continue my attempt to escape, to no avail. My scalp radiates with pain as he digs his hand into my hair and yanks. With his mouth brushing up against my cheek, I feel his dirty, warm breath as he says, "The only way you're leaving is with me."

"Fuck you!" I angrily growl.

He laughs at my exclamation. The eerie feeling of his breath running down my neck sends an unwelcome shiver down my spine. Grabbing onto his wrist, I try my best to free myself from his grip, but he tightens his hold, sending another jolt of pain down my scalp. This time I let out a wail in hopes someone will hear me.

He strikes my face with the hilt of his gun and I almost black out. "Shut the fuck up, bitch!" he shouts, tugging again on my head and urging me to walk. I try to dig my heels into the ground, but it doesn't do any good and I soon feel something being shoved into my ribs, urging me forward with another jolt of pain. I already know it's the gun digging into my ribs and fear is what motivates me to move.

"We're leaving this room now. If you try to call out for help, Abigail, I won't hesitate to pull the trigger," he proclaims while shoving it deeper into my side, making me whimper from the pain.

My worst nightmare has come true. The fear of Bill finding me again is now a reality. Every precaution I took to keep safe seems worthless at this point as he drags me to the door. When he opens it, Charlie, the slimly little intern, is guarding it.

"Is it clear?" Bill asks him. He answers with a nod and Bill wraps his arm around my waist, but keeps the gun pointed at my ribs with the other. The feeling of his body next to mine disgusts me. His smell making my stomach churn and revulsion now replaces my fear. We don't make it too far outside my dressing room before I hear my name shouted.

"Abigail!" I recognize the voice as Clara, the only intern I'm friends with.

Bill brings us to a halt, but leaves our bodies slightly turned so he's able to keep the gun pointed at me. "You're expected on the floor in five," she notifies me, but as she takes in the sight she grows confused. "Who are you?" she asks Bill.

"I'm just an old friend of Abigail's. We're just going to take a walk to catch up."

She doesn't look convinced, but Charlie immediately jumps in by suggesting, "Why don't we leave them and go make sure everything is ready on set," as he practically pulls Clara away. She allows Charlie to lead her away, but not before taking one last glance over her shoulder. My heart sinks knowing my only hope has just walked away.

"Keep moving," Bill orders.

"Why are you doing this?" I desperately ask as I'm left no choice but to start walking again. "Please, Bill. If it's money you want, I'll give it all to you. Just let me go," I plead while trying to hold back my tears.

"Oh, that's exactly what you're going to do, Abigail," he says, vengeance evident in his tone.

With every step, my eyes scan for the perfect escape, but I'm left defeated when we near the exit. He removes the gun, places it into the waistband of his pants and pushes the door open. In that split second, I make my move. Lifting my foot, I stab him in the shin with the heel of my shoe. He releases a howl and loosens his grasp. I don't hesitate to turn and slam my knee into his groin. As if expecting it, he blocks my hit and the only contact I make is his thigh. He reaches for me and wraps his hand into my dress, but it is a mistake. I slam my fist into his face; the contact shoots a bolt of pain up my arm, but it frees me again and this time I run. Or at least attempt to; the five-inch heels I have on severely slow me down. It allows Bill the opportunity to catch up to me and grab a hold of my hair again, but I don't give up and continue to fight his grip.

It's then I hear footsteps running towards me and my body is pulled free from Bill's grasp as someone punches his face. Looking to see who's come to my rescue, I see Julio struggling as Matt pulls me away.

"He hit you," he says as his fingers gently touch my cheek. The contact makes me wince in pain as I remember that Bill struck me there.

"I'm fine," I say before we hear a grunt.

Julio is holding Bill with his arm around his neck and he's struggling for air. A feeling of relief courses through me until I see Bill reach down into his pants where his gun is nestled into his waistband. Time freezes when I see him point the gun in our direction.

My eyes stay locked onto his finger as he slowly pulls the trigger, my life flashing before my eyes: The day I had my first memory of Matt, leading to the day I went knocking on his door the first time. Next, the day Matt told me he loved me and chose me in our bathroom. The day he proposed and I had foolishly turned him down, regretting that choice at this moment. The day I drove away from him, having to wait to see him again. But most importantly, the day he said the words that will stay in my heart forever... even after I die.

"I don't know what's going on in that beautiful head of yours, but whatever it is, it brought you to me, which makes you

mine now, and I always protect what's mine, Abigail."

The sound of the gun firing rings in my ears as I feel myself falling to the ground. Someone screams my name in the background as my back slams onto the floor. My head is pounding with pain as it makes contact and my breath is completely taken from my lungs. I struggle to open my eyes, but when I do I feel Matt on top of me.

"Oh, my, God!" Kelly shouts above me, already rolling Matt off me.

Her panicked cries to call 911 are worrying me. Crawling completely out from under his body, I kneel at his side and scream. Matt's lifeless body is covered in blood. My own blood drains from my face as I panic. I'm barely given a second to register what has happened before I hear a grunt at my side, forcing me to look in the direction of where Bill and Julio are still struggling. Bill is giving Julio a fight as he uses all his force to push Julio off his body, allowing Bill the chance to lift the gun again and point it back at me.

Julio slams down on his hand, causing the gun to come skidding across the floor, landing mere feet from me. The fury inside of me wills me to crawl over to it, picking up the cold metal in my hands. Lifting my head, I see Bill looking straight at me as Julio yanks him up and back into a chokehold. I don't hesitate to lift the gun and point it straight at Bill. Now I'm the one full of vengeance as I wrap my other hand around the hilt. It's now his eyes that go wide before I pull the trigger. I close my eyes, the booming sound of the pistol going off in my hands is the only sound I hear behind my darkened lids. I'm praying I've shot Bill and not Julio, but I'm too frightened to open my eyes to find out.

I don't know how much time has passed. Seconds. Minutes. Maybe hours. Julio's thick accent calling my name pulls me from the darkness.

Snapping my eyes open, I find him standing in front of me. He wraps his hand around mine, silently requesting for me to release the gun. I relinquish it, my thoughts now returning to Matt as I scramble back to his side again.

"Call 911!" I shout again, repeating Kelly's demand as I place his head in my lap. "Matt, please wake up," I beg, the tears streaming down my face as I shake him. Kelly is applying pressure to his chest with her jacket looking just as frantic as I feel. "Please, Matt. I can't lose you. Please, wake up," I continue to beg, kissing him on the lips as if I can magically make him wake up.

He looks lifeless, but I continue to kiss and beg him to obey my commands. My tears have completely obstructed my vision as they continue to fall on his pale looking face. I hear more footsteps and soon there are paramedics at Matt's side.

"Ma'am, I'm going to have to ask you to move so we can work on him," they order, already shoving me away.

Reluctantly, I release his head and move away, but only enough so they can work on him. They cut open Matt's shirt and attach wires to his chest while Kelly sits at my side, holding me in her arms as we kneel on the cold concrete floor. My eyes never leave Matt's body as I watch the paramedics' every move. A slight beeping comes from a machine they've placed on the ground next to his body; a faint indication of a heart beat on the screen.

"We've got to move him fast," one paramedic says to the other as they proceed to lift him onto a gurney. Just as quickly, I stand and follow them out as they take Matt to the ambulance. It's when I'm about to step into the ambulance behind Matt, refusing to let them take him without me, that I hear the dreadful… *beep…beep… beeeeeeeeeeeeeeeeeeep.*

"He's coding!" the paramedic shouts, already grabbing for some paddles. The other paramedic looks at me. "I'm sorry, ma'am, but we can't take you," he says, shoving me away to close the doors.

"I'm not leaving him!" I shout back as I try to open the door. "Ma'am, we can't take you while he's coding. Please. We need to get him to the hospital before he dies on us," he explains before turning to run to the front of the ambulance and into the driver's seat.

My body is numb as I scream like a lunatic as the ambulance drives away. Julio's arms are tightly wrapped around me as my mind goes blank.

Have you ever heard of the saying, 'When you're going to die, life flashes before your eyes?' Well, that is exactly how I feel at this moment. The rain is pouring down with a velocity of a vengeance, as if Mother Nature is angry at the world. We can barely see the hood of the car as Sam proceeds to stubbornly continue to drive.

"Sam, why don't we pull over?" I beg as I look out the window, unable to see in front of us.

"Emily, we're almost home. Look at the streets. The last thing I want is to be stuck in the car while the rain floods around us."

I ignore his protests and continue to plead. "Sam, I'd rather lose the car than our lives," I argue.

He turns to look at me, but his eyes soon go wide. Turning to see the cause of his fear, I see the glare of another car's lights beaming through my window and my world darkens. When I open my eyes, I feel the rain hitting my body, feeling as if needles are piercing my skin.

"Ma'am! Ma'am, what is your name?" I hear someone asking.

I can barely think at this point, but the only name I manage to whisper is, "Matt." The thought of leaving him behind keeps running through my mind as my will to keep holding on is slowly slipping from my gasp. I can't keep my eyes open any longer. My last thought as I hear, "We're losing her!" is of Matt and my promise to never leave him behind.

I raised him to keep every single one of his promises—to always honor his word—but as I lay here feeling myself slowly slip away, I have only failed to prove my own example. I can only pray he will not hold this promise against me.

Chapter Fifteen

Abigail

THE POLICE OFFICER is skeptically eyeing me as I wait for an answer. "I've already told you everything I know," I irritably tell her.

"I understand, ma'am, but we just want to make sure we get our facts straight," she replies, making my blood boil within my skin.

The moment they drove away, I was unwillingly pulled away to be questioned by the officer. They didn't even spare a moment to let me catch my breath before they hit me with question after question. I wanted nothing more than to rush off to the hospital to be with Matt, but they wouldn't allow it. I killed a man and they wanted answers.

"I just want to be with my boyfriend and make sure he's okay," I plead as I've been doing for the past hour. Kelly has already tried calling the hospital for an update, but they refuse to give her an answer, which only frightened me.

"We understand, ma'am, but a homicide has occurred and we can't allow you to leave until we get all the details."

"I've already told you it was self-defense," I repeat for what feels like the hundredth time. "He was trying to kill me. I had every right to defend myself," I snarl.

At this point, the officer is sympathetically looking at me, but it doesn't change the fact that I feel like a prisoner under interrogation. Several times, I've had to explain how I knew Bill and why he possibly wanted to kill me. At least it earned me her sympathy. It still wasn't enough to allow me to leave, though. Julio, on the other hand, was being grilled just as intensely because he was holding Bill when he was shot.

"We understand, ma'am, but we need to make sure to get a full detailed report in your defense."

A tremble travels through my body as I remember everything that happened. Kelly's arm tightens around my shoulders as she tries to comfort me, but still manages to give the officer the stink eye before asking, "What's going to happen now?"

My head is hanging as I stare down at the concrete floor, unable to keep it lifted anymore from exhaustion. "We still have to interview the other gunshot victim for his statement, since he was also a witness. Hopefully, he's made it," she expresses. Her words make my head snap up to glare at her.

"*He will make it*," I growl out.

Kelly's hand squeezes my shoulder as she remarks, "Of course he will," her sobering words making me want to cry again.

From the corner of my eye, I see Julio making his way over to us and I feel a little relieved.

"Unless you have any reason to detain her, we'd like to go to the hospital now," he sternly relays to the officer.

Her lips go flat as she eyes Julio. The expressionless mask he's currently wearing tells me he's not willing to allow her to challenge him. "You have our information, officer. Feel free to contact us if you have any further questions," he states before he urges me to walk away. Lowering his head, he whispers into my ear, "She can't arrest you and she knows it, which is probably pissing her off."

Eagerly walking to put distance between us and the officers, I don't dare take a look back. We've nearly left the room when Hans enters. He rushed over after everything happened. His lips are pinched in agitation, telling me I now have another roadblock ahead of me.

"Obliviously, the photo shoot has been rescheduled for another time. Can you please make sure to keep your psychotic life at home next time? We *are* on a schedule."

I step towards him, my face mere inches from his. "Don't fuck with me right now, Hans. I've already killed one man tonight and you're really testing me to do it again," I say to him, watching him turn pale. I can feel fear radiating off him and it's enough satisfaction for me at the moment. Shoving him to the side, I walk past him, not caring what my outburst will do to my career. My only focus at this time is getting to Matt.

Soon, we're in a taxi and rushing to the hospital. The time it takes to get there feels never-ending with the added New York traffic. Before long, I'm rushing up to the emergency desk with my heart racing faster with every step. Reaching the desk, I blurt out, "Matthew Garcia! He was brought in with a gunshot wound. Where is he?" I demand.

The nurse behind the desk gives me a skeptical look. "Who are you?"

"I'm his girlfriend."

"I'm sorry, but we can only release information to relatives."

"He's my brother," Kelly quickly announces, forcing the nurse to look over to her. Believing Kelly's statement, she immediately starts tapping away at her keyboard before looking back to us.

"He was in critical condition when they brought him in. He's currently in surgery. Fourth floor," she says, pointing to the elevator. I barely have time to thank her before I'm rushing off in the direction of the silver doors. Julio beats me to it and is already pressing at the button as my heart practically jumps out of my chest. If he's in surgery, then it's good news. I grow impatient as I stare at the metal doors in front of me, willing them to open, but they grudgingly don't listen.

"I can't take this," I deliver before searching for the doorway indicating the stairs. Julio must have read my mind as he pulls at my arm.

"Over here," he proclaims, already leading me in the direction we need to go. With every step up I take, I keep praying he's okay. I have to keep reminding myself that if he's in surgery, then he's still alive. Reaching the fourth floor, I look left to right, realizing I never asked exactly where I had to go. I see a lady in nurse's scrubs approaching us and I don't hesitate to stop her.

"Excuse me, ma'am. Can you tell me where surgery is?"

"It's down at the end of this hall, but the waiting room is through there," she indicates, pointing a couple of doors down.

"I need to know how my boyfriend is doing," I plead to her. I stand there clutching at her arm, my eyes begging for her help. Her lips go flat as if considering her thoughts before she looks at the doors leading to the surgical ward then back at me.

"If you can give me his name, I may be able to get some information for you."

Letting out the breath I was holding while waiting for her response, I tell her Matt's name and watch her disappear behind the doors. I do as she asked and wait in the waiting room. Thankfully, the room is empty upon entering, allowing me to immediately start pacing the room as every imaginable scenario travels through my mind.

"Abigail," Julio says, his deep accent breaking my worst thoughts. "Maybe you should take a seat."

I look at him and notice he looks just as worried as I feel. Tears are falling down my face now and I'm pretty sure I look like a hectic wreck at this point, but I don't care. Julio holds out a box of tissues with a slight nod of his head, ordering me again to sit. This time I obey while grabbing for the tissues and start dabbing at my eyes. What feels like an eternity later, the nurse returns with a regretful look upon her face; it doesn't look hopeful. Quickly standing, I meet her halfway, waiting for her to speak.

"They're still trying to stabilize him. The thoracic surgeon is delayed and they're waiting on him to try to dislodge the bullet. If they continue without him, they risk the chance of the bullet traveling or cutting a major artery."

The words make no sense to me. "What does that mean?"

Her lips go flat before answering "I can't really promise anything at this time. But it doesn't look good since it's only half an inch from his heart," she answers. My knees give out and I collapse to the floor, my sobs echoing in the room. I feel Kelly's arm around my shoulder as she comforts me, but it's not her I want to take the pain away. It's Matt.

"I'm sorry," I hear the nurse apologize above me. "I've informed one of the surgical nurses who's in the operating room that you're here. She's promised to keep you updated." Her words don't make me feel better.

"We appreciate your help. Thank you," Julio informs her as I continue to kneel on the floor, whimpering in misery.

Kelly forces me to stand as she leads me to a chair as I continue to cry. The minutes tick by feeling like hours and soon I've completely lost track of time. With all the crying I've done, my eyes now feel heavy and it's difficult to keep them open. Eventually, I doze off as my mind succumbs to the exhaustion of the day. Before long, I'm being shaken awake. When I slowly blink my eyes open, I see another person in surgical scrubs standing in front of me.

"Are you Mr. Garcia's family?"

"Yes," I answer, bringing myself fully awake.

"I'm Dr. Turner. We've just completed the surgery. Although it was touch and go a couple of times, we managed to get the bullet dislodged from his chest. It barely missed his heart, he's a very lucky man. He still isn't out of the woods, but for now he's been moved to ICU until further notice. I can take you to see him now if you'd like," he conveys. I let out the breath I feel I've been holding from the moment he began speaking.

"Yes, please," I say, already standing. The doctor eyes me as if wondering whether he should allow me to follow him or not.

"Are you family?" he skeptically asks once more.

Before I have the chance to respond, Kelly is once again stating, "I'm his sister, and this is his fiancée." He looks over to Julio with an arched brow.

"I'm her bodyguard by order of Mr. Garcia."

He pauses as if considering our responses. "Okay, follow me please," he states, leading the way to the ICU.

We are taken to another floor of the hospital, "Intensive Care Unit," displayed over the door as we near the hall. The eerie atmosphere of the hospital rooms stays with me every step of the way as the doctor continues to lead us.

Reaching what must be his room, the doctor stops us from entering. "Only one person at a time is allowed to visit with the patients," he sternly notifies us, eyeing all three of us standing at the door. "Go," Kelly states, nudging me forward to enter the room. Without looking back, I take the steps needed to lead me to Matt.

The sight when I enter takes my breath away. Matt is lying on a hospital bed looking as if he's peacefully sleeping, but seeing his body and the slow rise and fall of his chest makes the tears return. My steps are hurried as I rush to him, my lips going straight to his. I let them linger for as long as I can before I can feel his face soaked with my tears, forcing me to pull back to wipe them away. I want to demand he wake, but deep down inside I know it would be useless. I can do nothing more than wait.

"He most likely won't awaken anytime soon due to the anesthetic. We will need to monitor him for the next couple of days for any signs of complications, but for now, everything has gone well," he explains.

Looking behind me to ask the doctor a question, I find I'm now alone in the room. Desperately needing to be closer to Matt, I climb into bed next to him, careful to not touch the upper part of his injured chest as I wrap my arm around his body and lay my head on his shoulder. Closing my eyes, the tears continue to silently trickle down my cheeks as I pray for Matt to wake up soon.

I HEAR A screeching sound in my sleep, and before I can open my eyes, I'm being shouted at. "Move!" My body is yanked from its slumber and shoved aside. Julio's familiar arms are catching me and practically dragging me away as I'm too sleepy to comprehend what's happening.

"He's coding! Charge the paddles!"

"What's happening," I shout. "I need to know what's happening," I demand, but am ignored as someone pushes me out of the room and closes the door, leaving me once again screaming into the air.

Chapter Sixteen

Matt

THE LIGHT IS brightly shining, demanding I open my eyes. When I do, I cautiously take in my surroundings. What seems to be an endless meadow of beautiful lush flowers are below my feet, spreading for what looks like miles around me in every direction. Slowly turning to find a familiar face, I instantly spot Emily a few footsteps away, greeting me with a heartfelt smile.

Closing the distance between us, she engulfs me in her arms. Returning her embrace, I stand with her in my arms, shell shocked and confused. Pulling back to place a kiss on my cheek, her eyes are next tenderly looking back at me.

"It feels good to hold you again, mijo. Most of all, to see you," she calmly conveys with a smile still on her lips.

Trying to find my voice, I nervously swallow as I say, "I'm happy to see you, too, Em. But why am I seeing you?" I somberly ask.

Her chest rises and falls in a deep sigh. "Walk with me," she states in more of a command than a request. Without hesitating, I follow her as we both silently begin to walk.

"How have you been?" I ask, feeling the need to break the silence between us.

"Good," she replies, but with a lack of sincerity in the response.

"Is there something wrong?" I ask, earning me another heavy sigh.

"As much as I've desired to see and hold you again, I just never imagined it would be so soon," she admits. Her anguished words painfully strike at my heart as I ponder the meaning behind her statement. As if knowing my thoughts, she adds, "Patience, mijo. You'll understand soon enough."

Taking in her words, I glance around at my surroundings. "Where are we, Emily?"

"There isn't really a name for this place," she answers. Still walking next to Emily, my eyes wander off into the distance and see what looks to be a replica of Abigail sitting on a stone staring off into the horizon. Running, I try to reach her but fail, the distance never closes between us. Growing tired, I surrender and stop as I stare at her. She continues gazing off into the distance, looking absent and unhappy. I shout, scream, and do everything I can to catch her attention, but she doesn't once turn in my direction.

"She can't hear you, Matthew." Emily's words force me to look back at her. The shock of the situation leaves me puzzled, and wanting answers.

"Why can't she hear me?" I breathlessly ask as I look back to Abigail.

"Because she's not really here," Emily answers. It's not the answer I was expecting and I look back at her, wanting a further explanation. "Come," she states, now taking my hand and leading me away. Hesitantly, I allow her to pull me away, but not without looking over my shoulder one more time, still seeing

Abigail perched on the rock.

Seconds later, we're standing at a small pond in the middle of the meadow, the water lightly rippling ahead of me. Taking a moment to remember what I was doing before I woke up, my heart suddenly sinks to the pit of my stomach as I realize why Emily is standing next to me.

"Please tell me I'm dreaming," I plead.

The hand still entwined with mine gently squeezes, as if comforting my sorrow as I remember every detail of what happened before I opened my eyes.

I was already on my way back to Abigail with her Red Bull when Julio spotted me. "Why aren't you in the dressing room with Abigail?" His reprimand coming out as a lecture more than a question. I'm about to answer the reason why when an intern rushes up to us, concern in her eyes.

"I think Abigail is in trouble," she blurts out, already turning to walk away, as if leading us to where we need to go.

"What do you mean in trouble?" I demand. She quickens her steps, but still manages to answer. "There was this guy with her claiming to be her friend, but something was off. Before I could ask, Charlie was pulling me away. I just barely managed to sneak away to find you," she explains.

"Is there any other way into the building?" Julio asks before I had the chance.

"There's an emergency exit in the back, but if you have keys to deactivate it, it won't go off."

We're already nearing Abigail's dressing room and when I see Abigail, my body goes numb for a spilt second. She's struggling to escape Bill.

Julio and I rush towards them. Julio reaches them first and pulls Abigail from his grasp, already attacking Bill. Catching her, I make sure to put some distance between them and us be-

fore I start to assess Abigail.

Satisfied that she isn't physically injured anywhere on her body, I look up into her eyes and see the tell tail sign of a bruise forming on her cheekbone.

"He hit you," I growl as my finger reaches up to gently touch the spot. She winces from the pain I'm sure she's already feeling.

"I'm fine," she bravely says before we hear a grunt, forcing me to look to see how Julio is doing.

The moment I see Bill lift the gun and point it right at Abigail, my heart stops. Without hesitating, I move in front of her as I hear the gun go off. At the moment, I didn't know if I made it in time, but my sole purpose was to protect her. As I had promised I always would.

"Are you okay?" Emily's voice brings me back to the present and my eyes close to engulf the darkness clutching at my heart. My lips are trembling as I struggle to contain the tears building in my throat. I'd known what my intention was when I'd thrown myself in front of Abigail, but I had never expected the outcome. How am I supposed to continue to protect her if I can no longer be at her side?

Emily is now embracing me, knowing I need the comfort. Wrapping my arms around her in return, I finally let the tears fall. I don't know how long I stand here with her. It could have been seconds, minutes, maybe hours. When my tears have finally subsided, I'm still tightly wrapped in her arms—refusing to let *her* go.

When I have the strength to pull away, I look down at her to ask, "What's going to happen now?"

"Sit with me, please," she requests, already pulling me down to sit at her side. My heart is still shattering inside my chest. The loss of knowing I may never see Abigail again is slowly tearing me apart.

"When I get lonely I come here to cheer myself up."

Looking around, it finally occurs to me that we're alone in the meadow. "Where's Sam?"

She grows saddened and now it's her eyes looking glassy. "He chose to continue on. I stayed here where I can watch over you until I was ready to meet up with him. I couldn't bring myself to leave just yet," she explains.

"I'm proud of you for putting yourself before Abigail when the gun went off. It showed how selfless you have always been when it comes to those you love."

"Selfless or not, it still cost me," I bitterly say.

Tilting her head, she looks over to me. "Would you do it all over again if you had to?" Emily questions.

"Of course!"

Giving me a satisfied nod, she looks back to the water. "It does get lonely here sometimes," she somberly says with a sigh.

"Well, I guess it won't be lonely anymore."

She releases another sigh before she begins to speak again. "It's a shame I'll never get to hold what is a part of us," Emily murmurs, leaving me confused.

"What do you mean a part of us?"

A tender smile creeps up onto her lips. "Your child, of course. Technically, it holds your blood, making it a part of me as well since I'm your sister," she proudly states as I struggle to comprehend her words.

Linking her arm under mine to wrap around my waist, I throw my arm over her shoulder to hold her at my side. She leans her head against my shoulder as she speaks. "You know I love you, right?"

Now I'm more confused than ever and I pull away to look down at her. Her eyes are still glassy, but it's evident she's holding back tears.

"And you know you can always count on me, no matter if I'm not always with you, right?" Still confused by her statement, she doesn't allow me a moment to ask what is really concerning her before she continues. "Matt. We all make our own choices and I don't want you regretting yours."

"What is that supposed to mean, Em?" I finally manage to ask.

She leans up to kiss my cheek and hugs me tight. Her expressions and words are concerning me, leaving me with unanswered questions.

"I want you to remember I love you, mijo, and it was my choice to let you go," she murmurs before squeezing harder, as if she is afraid of releasing me. My lips find the top of her head and I manage to kiss her before my world goes dark.

I awake gasping for air. Abigail shouts and my eyes immediately search for her. Above me are doctors and nurses staring down at me as if they are waiting for my reaction.

"Don't let him die. He can't die!" Abigail's frantic shouting can be heard in the distance. Her words... Where I was just moments ago comes back to me.

"He's back," someone says above me as my eyes continue to take in my surroundings.

The white plain ceiling and bleak walls tell me I'm no longer in the meadow. Faintly, I hear Abigail's continuous sobs over the noise around me. I want to cry out to her; Tell her I haven't left her, but my eyes grow heavy and it's difficult to keep them open any longer. As they slowly begin to drift close, I hear, "His pulse is slow, but steady. I think he'll be fine now." Those being the last words before I'm dragged off into the darkness once more.

Chapter Seventeen

Abigail

STARING DOWN AT Matt, my mind is exhausted since I've barely slept in the last twenty-four hours, fearing a repeat of yesterday. I've nearly lost him twice. I fear the saying, 'third time's a charm', which is the reason why I refuse to leave or allow myself to sleep. If the fear wasn't enough, I can also add guilt to my emotions. With Matt still in critical condition, our friends have barely left. Trey and David immediately rushed to the hospital after Kelly called them. Everyone is camped out in the waiting room, waiting for Matt to wake up. I told them to go back to the hotel, but they insisted on staying.

With my body demanding its rest, I cautiously climb back into bed with Matt, knowing I'm risking a lecture from one of the unfamiliar nurses. However, it's a risk worth taking to be able to hold Matt. After the dreadful scare of the code blue yesterday, I was ordered to stay off the bed, but of course, I couldn't stay too far from him. Being next to Matt was the only comfort I could find to keep me from going insane while I waited.

Carefully adjusting my body to get comfortable without

moving him, I wrap my arm over his stomach and lay my head next to his on the pillow. Surrendering to my exhaustion from the day, I begin to drift off into sleep when I hear Matt groan. Panicking, I frantically sit up thinking I've hurt him. His eyes are still closed, leaving me to think I may be hearing things. I'm startled breathless as I watch him lift his arm up to his chest to rub at it.

"Matt?" I rasp out, unbelieving he's awake.

He responds by letting out another groan, this time sounding as if he's responding to me. "Matt," I repeat, and this time I know he's responding as I watch his lips slowly tug up into a smile.

"Hi, beautiful," he slowly croaks out, barely above a whisper.

My heart lights up and every ounce of exhaustion is replaced with adrenaline as my heart races with glee. Too excited, I kiss his lips, forgetting about his injured shoulder as I lean against him. Hearing him groan in pain, I pull back.

"Oh, God, I'm so sorry," I say. I'm about to pull myself off the bed when his hands clasp my wrist to stop me.

"Don't leave me," he says, the words sounding like a desperate plea. My heart somberly stops for a moment.

"I'm not going anywhere," I reply, kissing him once more.

Knowing I need to notify a nurse, I push the call button, letting them know he is awake and feather him with another kiss.

"Matt, I have to climb off the bed or else I'm going to get in trouble again," I reply with a giggle against his lips as he holds me in place. Giving me a muffled groan of disappointment, I chuckle before pulling away. Trying again, I attempt to climb off before the nurse enters, but it's too late as the sound of the curtain being pushed aside is heard, informing me I'm in for a lecture if it's the rule-keeping nurse.

"No naughty business allowed yet, Mr. Garcia," Lucy, the nurse currently on duty, playfully remarks. Lucy also happens to be the nurse I encountered on my first day on the fourth floor. Thankfully, she's a little more lenient when it comes to the rules. "It's nice to finally meet you," she greets Matt while checking his I.V. bag. Satisfied, she looks down at him. "On a level of one through ten—ten being the worst—where is your pain level?"

"Like shit," he replies.

My eyes go wide at his unexpected answer, but Lucy simply laughs at his response.

"Okay, I'll make sure to get you something for the pain," she replies. After taking his vitals, she's about to leave the room but turns to him and says, "I'll let your friends know you're awake. As long as you all promise to be quiet, I'll let them visit for a bit."

"I promise," I reply with a thrilled smile. A few minutes later, everyone is filing in with apprehensive expressions on their faces. Taking them in, Trey looks exhausted, the lack of sleep is clearly showing on his face. David has Kelly tucked at his side and she looks as if she's just awoken as she rubs at her eyes. Julio looks like he can use some rest as well. They all stand at the foot of the bed looking down at Matt with worried eyes.

As usual, it's Trey that breaks the ice. "Glad you made it back to us," he announces, his tone quiet and lacking his normal sense of humor.

"Did you miss me?" Matt teases.

"Fuck yeah, I did. It'd be a shame to lose you. Nobody knows how to give head like you do," Trey playfully replies.

"Fuck you," Matt throws back.

"You can't. The doctor told Abigail no sex for four weeks," he jokingly answers.

The playful bantering helps break the dreary setting we're

surrounded in as we all laugh. Matt is holding onto his shoulder as he grunts. "Fuck, this hurts," he groans, throwing his head back onto the bed looking miserable.

I begin to worry and I'm about to go search for the nurse when she walks back into the room with a new I.V. bag. "Brought your magic juice," she says, wiggling the bag up in the air for him to view. "You'll be loopy in no time."

"I like her," Matt responds.

A pang of jealousy hits me as I watch him smile up at her, but I just as quickly push it away, blaming my attitude on my lack of sleep. When she's done switching the bags, she informs him that he may grow sleepy again.

"Have you been here the entire time?" Matt asks as he looks me over. Looking down at myself, I'm wearing a simple tee with yoga pants that Trey brought me so I could change out of the bloody dress I'd arrived in.

"She hasn't left the room," Kelly tells him.

"When was the last time you slept?" Matt asks, making me wonder if I truly look as bad as I feel.

"She hasn't," Julio replies, making me pierce him with a glare.

"I'm fine," I say aloud to no one in particular.

"You look like shit, supermodel," Trey snorts.

"Yeah, thanks," I clip out.

Reaching for my hand, Matt gives it a reassuring squeeze. "Why don't you go back to the hotel and get some rest. I can already feel the drugs starting to kick in and I'm pretty sure I'm going to go back to sleep."

"I don't want to leave you," I somberly say. I'm about to argue again that I'm fine, but Matt's pleading eyes are staring back at me when he asks, "Please? For me?" I'm unable to deny his request since I'm too exhausted to argue.

Wanting to take a shower to wash the stench of blood I know is still lingering on my body, I surrender to his request. "I'll be right back after a quick nap and shower," I inform him before I kiss him and climb off the bed.

"I'll be waiting here," he jokes.

Taking one last glance over my shoulder as Kelly urges me away, most likely knowing I will not go willingly, Matt's contented smile looks back at me. My steps are heavy as I walk with her to the elevator feeling the need to return to Matt's side, but my body is agreeing with him and demanding its rest.

I don't recall the car ride back to the hotel, nor do I remember climbing into bed. I was beyond exhausted by the time we'd walked into the hotel room, and the moment my head hit the pillow, I was instantly dragged into a deep slumber. My last thought before I surrendered to sleep was how grateful I was to have Matt in my life, and happier that Bill was now a part of our past.

Matt

I WATCH ABIGAIL walk out of my room, when I know she's far enough not to hear, I turn to Julio to ask for details. "What happened?"

Julio apprehensively looks at me and it takes him a few moments to answer. "He's dead. After you were shot, I was still struggling with him, but I managed to knock the gun from his hands before he could fire again."

Knowing he didn't answer the question I really wanted an answer to, he continues. "The gun was close enough for Abigail to pick up and she fired back," he grimly tells me, his words sounding pained.

He doesn't need to further explain for me to figure out the rest of the details. The blood feels as if it's drained completely from my face and my heart is now resting in my stomach. I'm left speechless as I imagine the scenario.

When I find my voice again, I ask, "How is she handling it?"

Julio's lips go flat for a moment as he shrugs his shoulders. "I don't think she's had time to completely process it. Her main concern was getting to you after they took you away."

Confused, I ask, "She didn't come with me to the hospital?"

Shaking his head with saddened eyes, he says, "She was about to climb in the back of the rig when you first coded. They didn't allow her to tag along. It gave the cops an opportunity to drag her away and start questioning the both of us for details.

"I thought she was going to have a reaction while being questioned, but she kept calm the entire time. To be honest, it's worrying me. I'm afraid when she finally does have time to process everything, she may not take it so well. I know from personal experience, killing someone will eat at your conscience, even if it was in self-defense," he explains.

Understanding his meaning, I can only imagine how Abigail would react. She may hold the persona that she's strong, but I know deep down inside she can be fragile sometimes.

"She's a strong girl," I tell him, more to reassure myself than anything else.

He nods in agreement and I soon start to feel the drugs taking effect as my eyes slowly start to drift shut.

"I'll let you rest and make sure to bring her back in a couple of hours," I hear Julio state before I open my eyes once more to look at him.

"Thanks," I tell him as I watch him leave the room.

Although my eyes close, I don't immediately fall asleep as I wonder what would have happened to Abigail had I not returned. I'm grateful to Emily once more for giving me another chance, because in all reality, it's because of her I found Abigail again.

Chapter Eighteen

Abigail

I'M LOOKING AT Matt as he fiddles with my phone, thinking back to the trials of these last couple of days. Almost losing Matt has given me a whole new perspective. At this point, I don't think I could ever live my life without Matt, and I don't think I ever want to find out. Looking back down at Matt's phone in my hands, I finish the task of choosing my ringtone. When I look up, I find him deeply staring at me.

"Have I told you how beautiful you look when you smile?" he huskily says to me. I hadn't known I was smiling and his question causes my body to light up. His lips slowly tug up to the side as he continues to keep his eyes locked onto mine, handing me back my phone and I return his.

Today Matt is finally being released from the hospital. Although we don't actually get to go home to Portland because I have to stay behind to fulfill my obligation of the photo shoot that never occurred, we no longer have to endure being stuck in this room. Another commitment I still have to satisfy is the event that Hans had voluntarily obligated me to. I had wanted to back out of the commitment, but Matt insisted I go, not wanting to draw any bad publicity towards myself. So now, we are spending the remainder of spring break in New York.

Already dialing Matt's number, we're soon listening to the lyrics of *Cupid's Chokehold.* I have to bite my lip to keep from laughing out loud when I take in Matt's shocked expression. "Now, that is just cruel. You know I can't laugh right now and it's taking all my will power not to," he states, still listening to the final chorus. Not wanting to risk making Matt laugh, I bite down harder on my lip to keep from letting my own out.

"I thought you'd be upset about the words."

With an arched brow, he looks at me. "Being that I won't be able to make love to you for a couple of weeks, it's suitable."

I sigh as I remember the doctor's orders. "The doctor said four weeks to be exact, mister," I lecture him.

"I've had to wait that long to make love to you before and I swear it was hell. I'm not going through that again," he complains.

"You kept count?" I ask, surprised by his statement.

"Of course I kept count. I had to jack off during that time. It wasn't the same."

Unable to resist any longer, I hunch over and let out the laughter I was containing. I swear he's going to make me pee my pants at any moment. My eyes are full of tears that I have to wipe away and my stomach is cramping up from laughing so hard. When I can see clearly again, I notice Matt clutching at his shoulder as he winces, but the smile that spreads across his face is priceless. Standing up from the chair, I sit next to him on the bed to give him a kiss.

"I'm sorry, buddy, but the last thing I need is for me to kill you from having a heart attack during sex," I say on his lips.

He angrily complains while trying to sit up. "It's not fair."

"You need to stop trying to sit up," I lecture at Matt as I gently shove him back, earning me a scowl.

"I need to go pee again," he informs me.

"Oh. Sorry."

He chuckles, causing him to grasp my shoulder while wincing. Waiting for him to bring his hand down, I take it into my own as I usually do when I'm going to help him up, but this time he pulls me down to land on top of him. His other hand wraps around my neck to hold me in place as he deeply kisses me. Pulling away, but leaving our lips mere inches apart, I feel him say, "Now tell me if you're going to be able to wait, four fucking weeks for me to satisfy that craving." I now have an agonizing ache in between my legs and he knows it from the chuckle that soon follows his words.

Playfully shoving him back down, he lets out a groan, most likely from the impact of hitting the bed. Normally his groans would worry me, but from the laughter in his eyes, I know he isn't really in any major pain. At this point, I see it as equal punishment.

"If you're trying to get me to feel sorry for you, it's not working," I shamefully lie to him, knowing damn well that it is. "Guilty, maybe, but not sorry."

"Why would you feel guilty?" My silence is his only answer. I don't want to reminisce as to why I feel guilty. I don't need to as I stare down at Matt's chest.

"Come here," he beckons, tapping at the spot next to him on the bed. Unable to resist, I'm about to sit on the bed when he pulls me further onto it so I can climb on top of him.

"Matt, this is not right. We can get in trouble. And I already told you I'm not having sex with you," I whisper, as if someone would hear my words, looking over my shoulder at the door as I try to wiggle my way out of his grasp.

He digs into my waist to keep me firmly planted on his body. "It's not my shoulder that hurts anymore," he states, lifting his hips for me to feel the erection now rubbing between my thighs.

Narrowing my eyes at him, I ask, "Is this why you wanted me to climb on you? So I can dry hump you to finish?"

He throws his head back in full-blown laughter, ignoring the pain he must feel in his chest. "Fuck!" he groans out next.

"That was your fault," I reprimand. When he's recovered, I feel him tenderly tuck my hair behind my ear as he looks up at me with a slight smile tugging at the corner of his lips.

"I love just staring at you. I could stare at you all day," he says, causing me to blush. He manages to make me light up from the inside out with his tender words, which I love.

"Now tell me why you feel guilty."

I carefully choose my words before I speak. "You wouldn't be in this hospital bed if it weren't for me. You almost died, Matt," I confess, holding back the tears now lodged in my throat.

Matt pulls my body to drape across his and his hand starts to rub up and down my back to comfort me. "It was my choice to put myself in front of that bullet and I would do it all over again in a heartbeat for you. You may have almost lost me, but I swear I would keep fighting to come back."

Deeply sighing into his chest, I'm soon saying, "I love you."

"I love you just as much."

We lay in Matt's hospital bed for a couple more minutes until I feel him pushing me to sit up. "I really have to pee and your pressing on my bladder."

"Oh," I reply, realizing I'm still straddling him.

"If I didn't have to go, I'd keep you right here. That dry humping idea doesn't sound so bad now that I think about it," he relays with a wink of his eye. Lightly swatting his stomach, I quickly hear another grunt.

"Serves you right, you pervert. I swear you always have sex on your mind," I answer as I'm starting to climb off.

"How can I not when my girlfriend is hot!"

This time I actually help him up from the bed while shaking my head at his response. I'm flattered, but I'm also realizing we may not make it to the one month mark after all with that attitude. Matt doesn't need much help walking. The only struggle he has is with the I.V. machine.

"I can't wait until they take this stupid thing out," he frustratingly mumbles.

Understanding his frustration, I simply agree. The sight of him is a reminder of when I'd awoken attached to an I.V. Those were not happy memories and I hope to never be in the same predicament again. When he's settled back into bed, the nurse walks in—my favorite nurse, Lucy, to be precise. She's the only one who hasn't lectured me when I've climbed up into bed to sleep next to Matt at night.

"Hello, Matt. You ready to leave us today?" she cheerfully asks.

"More than ready." She laughs at his response while starting to remove the I.V. from his arm.

"Now remember to keep up with your pain meds or else you're going to feel like doo-doo again," she says with a twinkle in her eyes.

Looking over to me, she repeats, "Make sure he takes his meds, or else he'll be crying like a big baby. That injury of his is no joke."

"I will," I say with a smile, knowing full well what she means by the comment. With the I.V. removed, she begins the process of having Matt sign all his paperwork and with a smile says her final goodbyes a couple of minutes later. Trey walks in the door with Julio, both of them excited Matt is ready to go home.

Since it was still spring break , Trey is able to stay in New York another couple of days with us. Kelly and David had left the day after Matt had fully woken up. They both originally planned on visiting with her family after Matt's draft, but the Bill incident postponed their plans. Plus, it was also an important week for David. He was planning to propose to Kelly, but wanted to ask for her father's permission first. He looked like a nervous wreck just telling me. I can't imagine how he was going to react while popping the question. His only fear was that she'd say *no,* but I think I was to blame for that idea. My eyes find Matt and with a forced smile, I remember the day he proposed, feeling guilt-ridden all over again.

"Hey there, fucker," Trey greets Matt as he stands at the edge of the bed. "You ready to blow this popsicle joint?" he asks with his usual Trey humor.

"Fuck, yeah," Matt replies, making us all laugh.

"Abigail, can I speak with you for a minute?" Julio asks, looking concerned.

"What's wrong?" Matt immediately demands before I can reply. Julio looks torn whether to answer, but Trey gives him a curt nod.

"There were several paparazzi hanging around outside the exit when we arrived. I think it has to do with how much the media has been blowing up the news of the shooting."

"What are they saying?" I have to ask since Matt and I haven't exactly been watching the news. We've sort of been avoiding watching anything to do with the shooting since we were starting to get upset at how out of proportion they were making it.

"They haven't stopped talking about how your manager tried killing Matt out of jealousy," Trey says. "They're claiming he was so in love with you that he shot Matt and then offed himself because he couldn't live without you."

My knees go weak and I practically collapse. Julio, being only a couple of steps away, catches me and sets me down on the bed next to Matt who is already pulling me into his arms. The shock of Trey's words leaves me breathless, my heart feeling as if it's plummeted to my stomach.

"But that's not true," I squeal out when I can speak again.

Trey snorts. "Of course it isn't, but somehow the cops are not telling them it isn't true. At least for now it sounds better than the world knowing you killed the dude. Imagine if the paps got a hold of that info. They'd have a field day with it."

Trey's sarcastic words don't lessen the mood, instead I now feel as if I'm going to throw up and the room is uncontrollably spinning. Matt's doing his best to comfort me by rubbing my back.

"I've already spoken to hospital security. They're aware you're leaving soon and the car is already outside waiting," Julio notifies us.

"Sounds good," Matt tells him as if the whole situation doesn't faze him.

It takes me some time to get my thoughts and breathing under control. The entire time Trey's words kept repeating in my mind and I don't know what sounds better: The love stricken story the press has been releasing, or the fact that I've killed a man and it's being covered up like a secret for now. I know eventually the truth is going to be leaked out as Trey had so kindly put it, and I know they're going to have a field day with it when it happens.

Eventually, Matt is dressing and we're soon leaving the

room with Matt being wheeled to the exit, the entire time grumbling he can walk perfectly fine. The nurse ignores him and keeps pushing, insisting it is hospital policy. Before we reach the exit, I see a hoard of paparazzi standing outside the hospital doors patiently waiting with their cameras in their hands.

"Shit," I let out as I take in the sight. When Julio had mentioned there were several outside, I merely thought maybe a handful, but there must be at least a dozen, if not more.

"I'm getting up here," Matt tells the nurse and she stops wheeling him, allowing him to stand with my help. He wraps his uninjured arm around my waist and protectively holds me against his body. "Let's go," he says over to Julio and Trey, leading us towards the door. As soon as the first cameraman spots me, he holds up his camera to start snapping pictures, the rest of them soon follow suit.

As if they had the exit already planned, Julio and Trey take up guard in front of me, and Matt walks snuggly beside me. The minute the sliding doors open, you can hear the sound of the non-stop clicking of cameras. Recently I had come to love that sound, but today I am loathing it. It's a reminder that I'm now the old Abigail Adams; the one who chose to always be in the spotlight.

"Abigail! Is it true you were still in love with your manager?"

"Are you still grief stricken?"

"Do you still plan on modeling?"

"What's going to happen now?"

They all start hammering me with nonstop questions before I can take one step out of the door. I'm tempted to yell back at them to leave me alone, but I know it would only fuel their fire. My only goal at this point is to get Matt into the car as quickly as possible. I can already feel the tension in his body with every footstep as his grip tightens around my waist. I know at this point it isn't to protect me, but from the anger and animosity of the situation. He's probably struggling just as badly as I am to not shout back at them.

When we're finally in the confines of the car, I let out the breath I was holding as I exited the hospital. Why even after his death does Bill not fail to remind me of the past I had with him? The scene before me as we drive away is a replica of the day I'd left the hospital in Seattle, and all because of him. Taking a deep breath, I force myself to calm down. I have to remind myself it's my past and he's no longer a part of it. Thank God.

Matt

TUCKING ABIGAIL PROTECTIVELY at my side, I ignore the paparazzi shouting at us. Their questions are enough to make me want to rip them to shreds for asking them, but shouting back at them isn't going to win us anything. Right now, my only concern is getting her into the car. Within seconds, Julio is shutting the door behind us and I'm finally able to lay my head back on the headrest to let out my breath. Even through the blackened tint of the windows, I can still see and hear them shouting at us. Another minute later the driver is cautiously driving away. I would have preferred silence for the car ride back to the hotel room, but since we have Trey, it isn't possible.

"Well, that was fun," he sarcastically mocks, breaking the silence in the car. "So, what's for dinner?" he quickly changes the subject. Neither Abigail nor I immediately answer, causing Trey to continue with his bantering. "I guess it's my choice," he announces. "You all like sushi?"

Ignoring his words, I tenderly kiss Abigail on her temple, hoping to reassure her everything will be okay, but deep down inside I have no clue what will happen from this day forward. I can only pray Abigail will have the strength to deal with it, especially knowing she's still choosing to ignore the subject for now. But that is soon going to change because the first chance I get I'm going to talk to her about it. I already know she isn't going to be happy with having to face the demons of her past.

Chapter Nineteen

Abigail

MY EYES ARE glaring back at Hans as he stares down into the screen of his phone. I've only been back at my hotel room for a little over an hour and he's already hounding me about rescheduling the photo shoot. To be honest, he's been hounding me for the last couple of days, but I'd purposely been ignoring his phone calls and text messages while Matt was in the hospital. My daily answer to him was: I'll let you know when Matt is released, until then, leave me alone.

He wasn't happy with the answer, but it was the same every day.

"I've already told you, Abigail, I don't think I can manage rescheduling the shoot on such short notice. You either stay in New York or you fly back when I have a confirmed date."

"No," I clip out for the fourth time since he's told me the same demand. "It's either you schedule it for tomorrow or the day after while I'm still in town, or you don't get the shots. Once I return to Portland, I'm not coming back. My boyfriend is still recovering and I'm staying at his side until the show in Paris,"

I clarify.

Grabbing at the bridge of his nose, he replies, "It's bad enough I have to deal with Rebecca still grieving like a diva and refusing to proceed with the show, I now have to deal with *your* diva demands."

"Take them how you want, but those are your only options from me. You're lucky Matt is still alive, or else you would have two *grieving divas,* as you have so kindly labeled us," I throw back at him.

I rub at my temple in hopes it will help ward off the headache he's managed to give me as the minutes tick by. "I've already told you. It's not like I planned on my boyfriend getting shot," I proclaim through clench teeth. "We wouldn't be in this situation in the first place if you didn't hire shady people."

"How was I supposed to know that Charlie was an accomplice in plotting a murder?"

The word *murder* makes me cringe. It's a reminder of how close I came to dying—how close Matt came to dying. My thoughts are broken when Hans continues the conversation.

"I thought with the gorilla you had with you all the time, you were fully protected." The sound of an angry growl comes from behind me and I don't have to turn to know it came from Julio, making me smile.

"I'd watch what you say, my gorilla owns a gun."

Hans rolls his eyes before grabbing at the bridge of his nose again. I hope his damn headache is worse than mine. At that moment, Trey walks out of the bedroom and heads straight to the couch to sit. He curiously looks back and forth between Hans and me.

"What going on?"

"Hans is bitching about the photo shoot again," I answer Trey, earning me an amused nod as he throws his arms on the back of the couch.

"I'm not bitching. I just don't understand why you're being so difficult," Hans screeches back.

Trying to calm myself from his response, I take a quick deep breath before I answer. "I wouldn't be so difficult if you'd stop throwing last minute shit at me. Since the day I arrived you've done nothing but demand things out of me. I'm tired of it. I need to time to breathe!"

Hans opens his mouth to argue back, but he's cut off by Trey. "You don't have to do it, Abigail."

"Yes I do. It's part of the show," I sadly reply.

"Yes, she does," Hans throws out at the same time I respond.

"No, she doesn't," Trey clips back to Hans. "The contract you sent her never stipulated any additional appearances or promotional work she was required to do. Therefore, Abigail is not obligated to accommodate your additional demands. Her job was solely to perform for the runway show, and that's it. By law, you have to present her with the offer and it's her right to choose whether she wants to do it or not. You're the one who keeps throwing all this other shit at her and she's been doing it like a dumbass," Trey announces.

My mouth drops open in shock from Trey's proclamation. I don't know if it's from him pointing out that I'm a dumbass or the fact he used such highly intelligent language. Either way, Hans immediately goes stiff as if being caught in a lie.

Trey's eyebrows are raised and he's staring straight at Hans, as if waiting for him to argue. The silence is now thick in the room as we all wait for someone to speak. Not surprisingly, it's Trey who does so first. "From now on you have to give Abigail forty-eight hours' notice, and don't be surprised if she says she doesn't want to do it."

"It's not like we don't pay her. She gets paid fairly well in my opinion to do everything." Hans pinched nose goes up high after saying the words.

"I really doubt supermodel does it for the money," Trey states, now looking over at me.

I nod in agreement before I say, "I don't."

"See? She doesn't have to do shit for you besides strut her ass on that platform on the scheduled days you gave her."

I should be angry at the way he described what I do, but instead I'm beaming for the first time in days. Hans still looks furious as he speaks. "She already said she would do the photo shoot. It's Abigail who is being difficult and backing out now."

"I never said I wouldn't do it. I just said I was tired of you thinking I was at your beck and call."

"And she isn't," Trey adds. Looking over to me, he asks. "When do you want to do the photo shoot?"

"Tomorrow."

"There you have it. She's willing to do it tomorrow," he claims with a tilt of his head as he answers.

Hans grows more irritated when he realizes he's losing the battle. "I already told her, it's too short notice!"

Trey shrugs his shoulder at him. "Take it or leave it, dude. Shit happens. People were shot and you're lucky Abigail isn't suing your ass for the lack of security on set that allowed someone besides Julio to get near her with a gun. If I were you, dude, I'd take Abigail's offer of tomorrow and make it happen, or else we're leaving and you're going to be screwed."

"Fine!" Hans exclaims as he stomps from the room. "I'll call you later with the details."

"Email!" Trey yells back at him. Hans stops in his tracks and turns to face him.

"Fine, I'll email them," he growls as he turns and leaves the hotel room.

I'm still mildly in shock from what's just happened when I turn to face Trey, who has a smug smile on his face. "You're welcome," he says.

"How in the hell did you know all that?"

He simply shrugs his shoulders as if it's no big deal. "I'm good at deciphering contracts," he smugly replies. I'm still looking at him dumbfounded. "Matt left a copy of your contract on the counter after you sent it to him. I was being nosy and read it. I majored in business management so that shit is easy for me to understand."

Julio's booming laughter vibrates throughout the room as I say, "Trey Johnson, for the first time ever, you have ceased to amaze me."

His smug smile grows wider as he shrugs again. "You'd make a really great manager," I tell him before standing up and heading straight to my room. When I enter it, it's still dark from when Matt began to fall asleep. Standing against the doorway for a moment to allow my eyes to adjust, I can hear Julio and Trey's deep voices holding a conversation. Not wanting to be away from Matt any longer, I head towards the bed. Climbing into bed next to him, his arms automatically reach out and tuck me against his good side. Digging my nose into the hollow of his neck, I take in his familiar scent and quickly begin to grow sleepy.

"I love you," I whisper into his neck right before I drift off into sleep.

Matt

MY EYES FOLLOW Abigail as I sit in bed and she frantically rushes from one end of the room to the other, clearly looking for something. I know it's her bracelet. She removed it from her wrist earlier to clean it and placed it to dry on the counter. I picked it up while she was in the shower to admire it while I waited for her. Cruelly, I haven't told her I have it because I like watching her prance around the room in nothing but her strapless bra, thong, and stockings. Her hair has loose curls at the end cascading down her back, making her look sexier than ever.

She lets out an exasperated huff, and from the way she's now biting her lip as she heads to the bedside table, I know she's on the verge of tears, causing me to cave.

"Looking for this?" I ask, dangling the bracelet on the tip of my fingers.

I had expected for her to joyfully light up, or at least be relieved to see it, but instead her eyes bore into me as if she's ready to kill.

"You had it this whole time and you didn't tell me?" she yells out, already reaching for it. I yank it back as far as my body will allow, causing Abigail to stumble onto my body as it escapes her grasp. "Matt! Give it to me!" she exclaims, telling me there is something more than just the fact that she couldn't find her bracelet that is bothering her. Still clutching the bracelet, I pull her body to mine.

"Come here," I command, urging her to straddle my waist. With a final huff, she does as asked, but still looks distressed.

"Now, tell me what's wrong?" From the way she's still biting her lips, I know she's considering her words.

"I just wish you could come with me," she states. "I want

182

you to rest, I truly do, but I feel bad for leaving you alone to-night. You sure you don't mind staying?" she asks with grave looking eyes.

"I'm sure," I tell her. "Anyways, I wouldn't be much fun with me swaying on my feet every now and then."

She reaches up to run her hand through my hair, causing me to shiver from her touch. "The pills still keeping you high?" she asks with a light chuckle. Her pointing out exactly how I feel most of the time is a bit disappointing.

"Yeah," I grimly answer, hating having to admit it. I know I have to take the stupid pills to keep me comfortable, but I dislike knowing they keep me high half the time. It's how I've felt since I woke that first day. They keep me in a fog, and I'm getting tired of it. "I'm going to stop taking them tomorrow morning."

She sits up straight, now looking concerned. "No, you need them for the pain," she utters, running her hand across my bandaged chest.

"It's not as bad as before. I'll just take some over-the-counter Motrin. It's the same thing."

"It's not the same," she argues.

Chuckling at her reaction, I say, "You're right, it's not the same. The difference between the two is one isn't going to make me feel like an addict."

She sighs as her shoulders slump in defeat knowing how much the fact disgusts me. "You're right. The last thing I want is a boyfriend who's addicted to pain pills," she somberly admits. We both stay silent from the acknowledgment. Wanting to push the dark cloud away, I slowly start gliding my hand up her thigh to help distract us.

"I'll just stay in with you," she reiterates, as if it's going to convince me to change my mind. "Plus, I don't really want to go to this thing alone."

"Trey will be there to keep you company," I answer, but just as quickly she's looking at me with a wrinkled nose. "I know it's not the same, but I trust him to not let anything happen to you," I explain. Her brow arches and her lip skeptically goes up the same time.

"Why do I have the feeling I'm going to be babysitting him more than he would me?" she disputes.

"Is that all that's bothering you?" I ask, already gliding my hand up inside her thigh. The warmth of her skin against my palm is awakening my dirty mind and my cock begins to stir between my legs. Her flattened lips and saddened demeanor is a distraction from my carnal thoughts.

"You know what? I'm calling them and telling them I can't go," she huffs out before attempting to climb off.

I grip her thighs to keep her in place. "As much as I wish you could stay with me tonight, you need to go so you can show them you have nothing to hide," I inform her. Her shoulders slump forward in defeat once more.

"You're right," she admits.

"Just go do what they need you to do and leave an hour later."

"Are you sure you're going to be okay here alone?"

"I'll miss you, but you can make it up to me when you return." I emphasize what will be waiting for her by lifting my hips and rubbing my semi-erect cock against the center of her legs.

Rolling her eyes, she says, "No, doctor's orders. Now, may I please have my bracelet back?" she asks, holding out her hand.

"I want you to earn it," I answer, giving another lift of my hips to grind up against her while I feather kisses against her lips.

She playfully giggles in return as she replies, "I already did this morning," as she takes the bracelet from my hand. Remembering exactly what we did, I let out an unsatisfied grumble.

"As I recall, it was you finishing and me who was left hanging."

She throws her head back and lets out a full-blown laugh as I watch with a smile. When her eyes look back down at me, she clarifies, "The doctor ordered no sex for you, mister. And if I recall, you were not left hanging. It was still standing when I climbed off your face," she reminds me, holding up her index finger to demonstrate exactly the position my cock was left in.

"Not helping," I growl, grinding my now fully erect dick back up into her one more time.

"No dry humping, either," she orders, already climbing off my body.

"I don't want to wait," I playfully whine out loud.

"Pity for you," she replies with a mocking pout.

Wincing, I climb out of bed as quickly as I can to pinch her on the ass, making her yelp. "I'll remember that in the near future when you're begging me to make you come." With her mouth now gaping open, she's about to protest, but is distracted by a knock at the door.

"The car is down stairs waiting," Julio says through the door.

"I'm almost done!" Abigail shouts back, already walking into the bathroom. I follow her and stand behind her to flank my arm around her waist. Still going about her business, I watch Abigail through the reflection of the mirror as she fumbles to put on her bracelet. The sight of her in front of me sends me back to one of my most favorite memories with her.

"Do you remember the first time we were alone in a bathroom together?" I ask into her ear before my lips kiss her neck.

"The restaurant?" she confusedly answers.

Lightly chuckling, I wonder who really has sex on their mind. "It was the night I told you I love you for the first time," I remind her and I immediately feel her lean into my body. Still trailing kisses along her silky skin, I can see slightly above my line of vision into the mirror's reflection as she smiles back at me.

"Yes. It was," she recalls.

Slowly, I start gliding my free hand against her bare stomach, further torturing us both. Her head is now thrown back, resting on my shoulder and I can't resist gently nipping at her earlobe with my teeth. She quickly turns her body as she gently pushes me away with wide eyes.

"Why are you tormenting me?" she asks with a playful smile and quickly escapes my embrace.

I laugh as I realize I had unintentionally pushed us both to the verge of caving. "I swear I didn't do it on purpose this time," I declare, remembering all the times I *did* purposely tease her in the past week hoping she'd give in to my request.

"Sure," she drags out, now reaching for her dress in the closet and pulling it on. Leaning my body against the doorframe of the bathroom to take in the show, she adds, "I promise, when the time comes, I'll make it worth the wait."

She's now fumbling with her zipper and wanting to help, I make my way over to her already taking over the task. With the zipper in place, she turns to face me, rewarding me with a kiss. "If you're a good boy for the next two weeks, I'll make sure I finish what I started this morning," she whispers in my ear.

Shit. If my dick wasn't already hard and threatening to burst, the vision from her promising words are enough to make me hard in seconds. Playfully shoving me to the bed, she says, "Now let me finish getting ready. The sooner I leave, the sooner I can get back to you."

Doing as she commands, my legs are now walking me back to the bed to lie down, leaving me to count the days left until I can be inside Abigail again. I don't care what the doctor has ordered, I know damn well I won't have the strength to hold out that long, and I'm pretty sure Abigail doesn't, either.

Abigail

WATCHING TREY GIVE another tug at the collar of his tux causes me to bite the inside of my cheek to keep from laughing. I've lost track of how any times he's tugged at it. He looks miserable in his suit, but handsome nevertheless.

Letting out a miserable sigh, his eyes roam the room. "How much longer we got to be here, supermodel?" he miserably asks.

"I've already told you, after I present the award I have to stay at least another hour so it doesn't look like I'm intentionally ditching the party."

"And when is that?" I'm about to tell him to shut it when my attention is requested from my side.

"Ms. Adams, we're ready for you," a young lady politely informs me, making me smile.

"Quit asking," I clip out before I stand to follow the attendant now patiently waiting for me to follow her. Julio is following closely behind as we leave Trey sitting amongst the partygoers waiting to hear the upcoming announcement.

Ten minutes later, I'm nervously making an announcement honoring some governor for his contributions throughout the year. Strangely, it isn't a man coming up to the stage to receive the plaque, but a girl who looks vaguely familiar. I can't place exactly where I've met her, but she has a smile on her lips as she gladly receives the plaque from my hands.

"On behalf of my father, I'm honored to accept this award. I've spent many wonderful years at Saint Smith Prep, and although my father isn't here to accept this award, I know he is just as honored to be recognized for his contributions. Thank you," she finishes saying with what looks like a forced smile on her lips.

Following her off the makeshift stage, I'm met by a proud looking Julio who greets the girl with a hug.

"Hey, big guy. It's nice to see you again," she says with a giggle.

"Victoria, are you drunk?" Julio asks, looking shocked.

She grimaces back at him. "I've only had two drinks, Julio. Don't start lecturing me. You know damn well I dislike these people," she quietly snaps back. My eyes go wide watching the awkward encounter before she reaches out for a champagne flute from a passing waiter.

His eyes roam around the room as if searching for someone. "Where is Andrew?" he asks.

She rolls her eyes at his question. "He was scheduled to come, but he called to tell me he couldn't make it, which I'm pretty sure is a lie," she says before lifting the glass to take a sip. After swallowing, her eyes stare off into the distance as she comments, "I'm pretty sure he's kindly following my father's footsteps."

Julio's brows shoot straight up, but his eyes just as quickly grow sympathetic. "I'm sorry, Victoria," he tells her. Waving off his words, she takes another sip of her drink as Trey shows up at my side.

"You ready?" he asks, looking eager to leave.

"Would you stop trying to rush me," I say through clenched teeth.

"I just don't understand why we have to stick around now that you've done your thing," he disputes.

"Trey, quit being a baby. It isn't much longer. Aren't you always saying how you're never one to turn down a good party?" I lecture back to him.

"This isn't a party, supermodel. This is a room full of stuck up ass kissers."

Victoria lets out a snicker. "And clearly you're not one of them," she says to Trey before taking another sip of champagne. He looks at her, his eyes analyzing her from head to toe.

"Obliviously you're right at home," he throws back at her.

My mouth is threatening to drop, but I quickly compose myself. "Trey, stop it," I warn, now glaring at him to shut up, but he clearly ignores my threat.

"What? She started it!" he exclaims, pointing straight at Victoria like a child. Victoria takes the high road by keeping silent and ignoring his words. I, on the other hand, shake my head since it doesn't surprise me he would blame someone else.

"Look, if you don't mind, I'm going to take off," he says.

"Fine with me," I throw back at him. "Just make sure you don't get into any trouble," I add before walking away, already irritated with him.

He snickers as I walk away, leaving him behind with Victoria while I pray he leaves without saying anything that would shock her into a coma. Finding a private spot outside, I make a phone call to check on Matt. Feeling reassured he's doing fine, I'm soon returning to the party. Looking around the room, I don't see Trey, which tells me he didn't take long to disappear.

Continuing to look through the crowd of people, I hope to spot Victoria so I can apologize for Trey's behavior, but she too has disappeared, leaving me to find another way to distract myself while I count down the minutes before I can leave.

"Victoria didn't seem very happy tonight and she looked a little sad when you mentioned that Andrew guy." Julio cautiously scans the room before answering.

"Andrew is her boyfriend, but I think it's more of an arranged relationship pushed on her by her father," he quietly voices for only me to hear.

His comment brings back Victoria's earlier words. "What did she mean by Andrew following in her father's footsteps?"

Julio lets out a sympathetic sigh this time. "Her father is constantly having affairs. It was one of the things I was in charge of covering up, but Victoria always knew," he explains with a guilt-ridden sadness.

"That sucks. Where is she anyway?" I ask scanning the room again.

"She's never been one to stick around longer than she has to at these things, so it wouldn't surprise me if she's already left."

Taking one last look around the room, I feel the need to escape as well. "Do you mind if we leave?" I ask, not caring anymore what anyone thinks. Trey was right, I feel completely out of place in the current crowd and I want nothing more than to get back to Matt.

"Of course," he says, already guiding me towards the exit. On the way out, I find the event coordinator and thank her for the opportunity. With a pleasant smile, she wishes me a goodnight.

Before long, we're back at the hotel and entering our suite. As I'm about to leave Julio behind, bidding him goodnight, we hear a roaring moan come from Julio's room. Both shocked and confused, I watch Julio head straight for the door, following closely behind him because I'm nosy. He tries to turn the knob, but it doesn't turn, causing Julio to bang on the door.

"Trey!" Julio shouts at it, but it's soon covered up with the urgent cries from the other side. Knowing he's been defeated,

Julio gives up. "He could have at least left me my pajamas," he says while still staring at the door.

From the living room, we both hear Trey's name being shouted to move faster.

"That's it, I don't need to hear anymore," I voice, already walking away.

"Do you think Matt would mind if I used some of his sweat pants?" Julio asks as I walk away.

"Not at all. Let me get them for you," I say, already entering our room.

Matt is completely passed out as I search in his luggage for a pair of workout pants for Julio to wear. Seconds later, I'm returning to the living room to hand them over to Julio with an extra blanket.

"Thanks."

Hearing another round of demands from Trey's guest, I sympathetically look over to Julio. "Good luck sleeping to-night," I tell him, hearing another scream come from the room before disappearing back into my own. The last thing I need is sound effects to encourage my images of what Trey is currently doing.

Quickly closing the door behind me, I strip off my clothes and wash my face. I climb into bed on Matt's right side. Snuggling as close to his body as I can without stirring him, I lay there in the dark thinking back to tonight and Trey's appalling comment. How he labeled everyone in the room leaves me wondering where exactly I fit now. I know deep in my heart I'm not the same person I was a year ago—a *stuck up, money hungry girl.* Would continuing to stay in the same career I was in then make me revert to my old ways? Fearfully, I hope not.

Soon, my wayward mind is painting images in my head of being a wife with kids, happily living at home. The thought leaves me feeling happy, but deep down inside I know I'm not ready for that step just yet. In the last couple of months I've regained the passion for what I love doing most. The last thing I want is to give up after I've fought so hard to find it again. Pushing my dream of a family and kids aside, I remind myself that I'm still searching for who I truly am, and until I fulfill my current dreams, a happy family may just have to wait.

Chapter Twenty

Abigail

STARING DOWN AT my phone as I read the daily news, I take another sip of orange juice as I hear the door to Julio's room open. My eyes automatically shoot up expecting to see Trey walking out scratching his chest, or balls as in most cases. Instead, I see a blushful looking girl whose eyes are locked onto the floor and her hair cascading down to conceal her face. Her shoulders are hunched forward and her steps are quick to reach the exit to the suite.

"Victoria?" Julio's croaks out from the other end of the room, leaving me to choke on my orange juice I'd been swallowing. The sound of his voice causes her to practically run the last couple of steps before she's swinging the door open and leaving us behind.

With my mouth hanging open, I look back at the door, still in shock from the situation. I would have never expected for it to be Victoria leaving the room this morning considering how they were both practically tearing each other's eyes out last night.

My eyes snap over to Julio sitting on the couch. My gaping

mouth is far from the flattened lips and narrowed eyes now lock-ing onto his opened room door. If looks could kill, he's doing a good job of strangling Trey to death without him being physi-cally visible.

"She's a big girl, Julio. It was her choice," I remark, know-ing the look of wrath is going to be aimed at me next. His nos-trils are still flaring as his eyes snap over to me.

"I know that, but it doesn't mean I have to like the idea of her now being one of Trey's victims." I'm about to risk defend-ing my earlier statement when Trey comes charging out of the room in only a towel wrapped around his waist.

"Where did she go?"

I'm speechless as my finger points toward the door, des-peration on his face to find the girl that has just left his room. Without hesitation, he rushes out the door as Victoria had done just moments ago. A few minutes later, Trey is banging on the hotel door as Matt is leaving our room.

"Why are you out in the hallway half-naked?" he confused-ly asks him.

Trey lets out an angered snort, completely ignoring Matt as he stomps back to the room, slamming the door behind him. Julio stands up and follows him into the room, fury still radiating from him. There's another slam of the door after Julio enters. Matt takes a seat next to me, looking more confused than ever as turns to me for answers.

"A girl just did the walk of shame out of Trey's room then he went chasing after her," I explain, watching Matt's eyebrows rise in shock.

Biting my lip to suppress the giggle threatening to escape my lips, he considers my explanation. "Are you sure he went chasing after her?" he asks, sounding doubtful of my explana-tion. From the room you can now hear the shouts of a heated argument. It's impossible to make out the words through the closed door, but it's clear they're both angry.

Minutes later, Julio is exiting the room with an agitated look on his face. "I'll be down at the gym for a little while. Call me if you need me," he snips out, walking right past us, completely avoiding eye contact.

Julio doesn't slam the door as he exits the hotel room, but from the force he used to pull it open, it's clear he's frustrated.

"What the hell is going on?" Matt drags out.

"The girl who left the room was Victoria," I tell him. Of course Matt doesn't know who Victoria is so I continue to explain. "She's the daughter of the last guy Julio was protecting. When he wasn't protecting Victoria's dad, he was in charge of Victoria. I think he saw her more as a daughter like he does me," I say with a shrug of my shoulders.

"And Trey fucked her last night?" Matt questions. I simply nod to answer before he asks, "How did Trey even meet her?"

"She was at the event I was at last night. They were ready to claw each other's eyes out when Julio and I left them so I could call you. She would have been the last person I'd expect Trey to bring back last night," I comment, still confused over the situation.

"If I remember correctly, we were at each other's throats most of the time before we made love for the first time," he reminds me with a wag of his brows.

His words make me laugh as I remember all the times I wanted to both strangle Matt and practically rape him at the same time. Matt chuckles before he reaches over to kiss me. "Make up sex is the best in my opinion. Especially because it's with you."

"Yes, it is," I say around a chuckle and on his lips. When I pull away, I let out a sigh as my eyes glance at the door. "I don't know what happened last night, but from the way Trey looked when he came rushing out of the door, she must have made an impression on him."

Matt is about to voice his opinion, but his words are cut off when I hear the ping notifying me of an email. Picking up the phone to look at the message, my lips drop into a frown. "Looks like the photo shoot is scheduled for this afternoon," I grimly say.

Matt's reaction is different from mine as he perks up. "That's good. It means we'll still make our flight tomorrow."

"Is it crazy that I'm not looking forward to this shoot?" I murmur.

I feel Matt's hand tug at my wrist, pulling me to sit on his lap. Wrapping my arms around his neck and leaning my head down onto his shoulder, his nose starts nuzzling at the hollow of my throat. The warmth of his breath and the grazing of his nose against my skin makes me giggle, but also sends a flutter of shivers through my body.

"I'm not surprised, but I'll be there this time. You have nothing to fear," he says into my ear.

"I'm just not as excited anymore."

"Maybe you should look into doing something else," he says. "When you did the photo shoots for that running company you looked happy, beautiful. The entire time you had a smile on your face. When it comes to anything for Rebecca I rarely see you smile. It's as if you don't like it," he expresses.

"It's not that I don't like it. It's what they are starting to demand out of me."

Squeezing me tighter, he replies, "I like it better when you smile. But like you said, it's part of your job so I guess it's what you have to do."

Sitting in Matt's lap, I take in his words, unable to respond.

He's right, though. My job entitles me to give whoever is paying me what they want, but do I really enjoy certain jobs over others? Still sitting on his lap, I think back to last night and remind myself: You're choosing this for your future.

THE SHUTTER OF the camera and flashing of the lights do nothing to help send me to my familiar zone. The photographer's lecture lessens the chance of me getting there. "I want fierce. Angry. Sexy. Do you really want these photos to look like shit?" he shouts.

Letting out the frustrated sigh I've been holding in doesn't please him at all, but I don't care. He's done nothing but bitch and complain about every expression I've given him, regardless of how I try to ignore his scolding comments of advice. "Imagine your dude over here just cheated on you!" he voices, making scowl that he would stoop so low as to use that example.

"Perfect!" he says, the camera rapidly shuttering away. "Now give me lust."

Trying my best to deliver his command, I think of Matt, but it's not satisfying enough for him. "That's it? I want your *'you've just been fucked'* look. "

Staring at the photographer as if he's lost his mind doesn't earn me points with him. "Is that seriously how you look when you're being fucked?" he sarcastically asks. My mouth drops open as I stare gaping at him from the question. The photographer's eyes are now looking in Matt's direction. "You must not be doing your job right if that's all she can give me!"

"Turn!" is the photographer's next demand. His camera shutters away for the next minute before he's next shouting,

"Take ten for a wardrobe change!" leaving me happier than I've felt for the last hour as I walk my way back to my dressing room.

"Tell them we need a minute," Matt says into my ear as soon as I'm done changing.

"Um, can you guys give me a couple of minutes?" I politely ask the interns in the room.

They look confused at first, but with a shrug of a shoulder the first one leaves the room with the other soon following. Matt walks with them to the door. "Make sure they don't come back in until I open the door," Matt orders Julio before I hear the click of the shutting door.

Turning to face me, he has a mischievous smile on his lips as he leisurely stalks his way back over to me. "What are you doing?" I somehow succeed in asking with the butterflies now taking over my body. His silence and hooded gaze staring back at me are making my body scream with yearning of what will come.

"Face the mirror," he commands in a low tone, sending a ripple down my spine. Facing the mirror over the counter, my eyes go straight up to meet Matt's. He stops to stand directly behind and the familiar spiced aroma that is uniquely Matt's is radiating off his body, driving my senses wild as I breathe him in. Wrapping his arm around my waist to pull me closer to his hard chest, my back feels every inch of his chiseled body. Closing my eyes to allow my senses to take over, his warm breath caresses my ear. "I'm claiming what you owe me."

Snapping my eyes open in confusion, I look back into his eyes. "The race," he reminds me. "I'm going to make sure you look like you've just been thoroughly fucked when you go back out there," he utters into my ear.

"Matt, we can't have sex," I say, trying to sound stern as I remind him of his doctor's orders. But my words are full of bluster as I push myself into his stiffened erection rubbing my butt. A small moan of satisfaction vibrates down my throat from the contact.

"Who said anything about me fucking you? I'm just going to make sure you come," he huskily promises.

My eyes close, engulfing me in darkness, my sense of touch taking over as Matt's warm hands glide against my body. They stop at my breasts, now grasping and teasing them while his mouth trails kisses along my neck. My shudders intensify with every inch of skin he touches.

"I love the way your body responds to my touch," he says, his deep tone vibrating into my ear. "And the little sounds you make drive me wild," he adds, pushing himself into my body.

Knowing what we're doing is wrong, completely forbidden due to doctor's orders, I struggle to pull away from Matt who tightens his grip, forbidding me to move. "You're not going any-where until I'm done with you," Matt growls into my ear.

"Matt," I whimper as he nips at my neck. "Please, stop. This isn't fair," I plead.

"What's not fair?" he asks. "I'm simply giving that asshole what he wants. I'm going to make you look like you were just fucked. You're going to show him how beautiful you look when I'm done with you."

Immediately after he delivers the words, my body is pushed forward and onto the counter, forcing my hands to catch me. His hands are impatiently tugging my dress up my waist and within seconds I feel the cool breeze against my bare legs.

"Matt, stop," I demand. My protest is replaced with a des-perate whimper when his fingers brush my center and start ex-ploring, leaving me breathless and unable to speak.

"Damn, beautiful. You're so wet and warm," his deep voice rumbles behind me while his fingers travel deeper inside my walls. Soon they're pumping back and forth with determined force. It's Matt's familiar way of pushing me towards my completion. "Open your eyes," he demands. "Look at how beautiful you look right now."

When I open my eyes to look at myself in the mirror, it spirals me higher to my peak. "I want you to see what you look like when I make you come."

My eyes obey his command and stay locked on my reflection. The sight of Matt standing behind me intensifies the pleasure roaming through my body. I can already feel myself stiffening and an exhilaration slowly starting to build. Matt's fingers quicken their thrusting as they pump inside of me with abandon. Feeling my body ready to explode, my head drops down as I continue to moan. Matt's hand digs into my hair and jerks my head back up. "I told you to keep your eyes open, and you're going to listen to me."

The possessiveness in his words should scare me, but instead I instantly shatter and I'm coming around his fingers as he quickens his movements. I ride out my orgasm as Matt refuses to stop until I have nothing left in me. The hand tightly wrapped in my hair loosens its grip and I slump down onto the counter. His fingers slowly pull from my core while my body is still shuddering from my mind-blowing orgasm he just gave me.

Pulling my body flush to his chest, his lips are now kissing me below my ear. "I hope you remember what you looked like," he conveys with a smile on my lips. I'm still too weak to speak, let alone move any part of my body.

"Come on. Back to work, beautiful," Matt says with a chuckle, now pushing my dress back down to cover my lower body. Finding the strength to move, my butt brushes up against the still evident erection bulging in Matt's pants.

"I hope you don't plan on walking out there with this," I

huskily whisper into his ear while gripping it in my hands. He lets out a frustrated groan.

"I thought the time apart from you left me with the worst case of blue balls, but I've been proven wrong today."

"I'm not the only one counting down the days until you can thoroughly fuck me," I relay into his ear. He groans again and I feel the bulge in my hand jump. A demanding knock sounds at the door, breaking our conversation.

"Time's up in there," someone shouts from the other end. Matt angrily pulls away, already stalking his way back to the door. Pulling it open, the photographer is now staring into the room.

"You were due on the set ten minutes ago," he angrily lets out.

"We were discussing something," Matt nonchalantly tells him.

Not bothering to look at Matt, but at me instead, he says, "Having sex isn't the job she's getting paid to do."

Before I have a chance to snarl back at his remark, Matt is in his face with fury radiating off his body. "You talk to her like that one more time and I'll make sure to deck you so hard you won't be able to speak anymore."

He's about to say something, but Julio cuts him off next. "And I'll make sure to help him."

Silently, his eyes flash between Matt and me before he turns to stomp away like a child who was just scolded. Matt walks back to me to take a hold of my hand with a satisfied smile. Remembering the condition Matt was in before he'd opened the door makes my eyes look down to find it no longer there.

"Being pissed at that asshole made it disappear," Matt informs me and somehow I'm still managing to blush from knowing he's caught me looking for his erection. "Don't worry, beautiful, when you deliver what he's asking of you, I'm pretty sure I'll be hard again in seconds."

I'm now walking out of the dressing room with a thoroughly fucked face, exactly what the photographer was demanding of me earlier. Maybe this job is only satisfying when I have Matt on the set with me—something I should take into consideration when I schedule them.

Chapter Twenty-One

Abigail

I FEEL EXHAUSTED... Tired. My eyes begin to slowly drift closed again when Matt says, "Almost home," as he squeezes my hand. My exhaustion is now replaced with excitement from the notion of almost being home. Tired as I am, I knew we were heading home this morning, which is the only reason why I'd woken up so early.

Matt's discomfort from not sleeping well is now affecting me. He'd awakened every so often to adjust himself while letting out painful groans, which alarmed me to awaken every time it happened. I kept insisting he take one of his prescribed painkillers instead of the over-the-counter ones, but he still refused. He was sticking to his declaration of no longer being doped up on the addicting pain medication.

I understood his dilemma of not wanting to get addicted to them, but seeing him in pain was upsetting with the grimacing expression he always seemed to carry around now. Looking out the window as I use the scenic route leading to our home to distract me, my lips form up into contented smile.

Our home...

I never thought I'd be catching myself saying the words, let alone think I'd ever have a place to call home. But since the day I moved in with Matt, it's all he's ever made me believe. Sometimes I wonder how my life would turn out if I had not found Matt. I know for sure it wouldn't have the blissful happiness I feel everyday I'm with him as I do now. When the town car pulls onto our street, my eyes find Matt's.

"Welcome home," I croak out from the emotion already built inside of me.

The car has barely come to a stop and Trey is already climbing out while Julio opens Matt's door to help us out. Taking in Julio's form, he looks just as exhausted as I feel and he must from the ordeals we've been through this week.

"Why don't you take the next week off? Take a vacation with your mom," I suggest. He lights up a little at the proposition, but quickly grows skeptical before asking, "You sure? What's going to happen if I leave town and you need me?"

"I really don't feel like doing anything but lounging at home. So you're safe to ignore me," I say with a smile.

"What about your runs?"

Crap, I hadn't really thought of that. "I'll live. We've been through enough this week. We both deserve a vacation," I state, knowing how true those words are.

With a short nod, Julio agrees. "Thank you."

"You're welcome. Go have fun and tell your mom I said hi." He waits until the driver is done taking our bags in before giving me another nod goodbye and climbs back into the car for his ride home.

"That was nice of you," Matt says to me while leading me inside.

"I haven't given him any time off since Christmas, and after the week we've had, he deserves it," I genuinely say.

The moment we walk in the door, Trey is already trying to exit it. "I'm off to get some ass," he states, brushing by us. "I'll make sure to get enough for the both of us Matt," he shouts back to us, already at his Jeep. I swear, sometimes that boy drives me to want to murder someone, but nevertheless, he's grown on me.

Matt is already pulling me to the room after we shut the door. "Want to go have sex?" The enthusiasm he put into the question makes me laugh as I shake my head. "I'm serious," he continues.

I roll my eyes. "I'm pretty sure Trey will keep his word and have sex for the both of us. Come on, I'm tired and I need your chest to sleep," I mention, already pulling him to the bed. With most of our clothes off, we climb into bed and Matt's hands are starting to work their magic to fuel my desire.

"Matthew Garcia, if you don't stop trying to provoke me you're going to end up sleeping in the spare room again. Sleep!" I order, earning me a frustrated groan.

"I swear, woman, my balls may be shriveled up and useless by the time I can fuck you again." I simply chuckle from his comment, too tired to dispute him. Even if his statement were possible, I'd make sure to remedy the problem when the time came. Until then, all I want to do is spend quality time with the person I love and almost lost.

AS USUAL WHEN I'm bored, I scroll the internet. Sometimes it's perfect to help the time go by, but other times it can be a curse. This afternoon it's the latter.

'Former manager shot dead my supermodel, Abigail Adams,' the headlines read, draining me of the blood in my body.

My heart stops beating. My throat feels as if it's constricting and forbidding me to breathe. The world around me is beginning to spin out of control and the banana I'd eaten just minutes ago is already coming up. Reaching for the trash bin Matt keeps at the side of the bed, the contents of my stomach come completely up, leaving me dry heaving with nothing left.

I'm still dizzy as I wipe my mouth with the back of my hand and slump myself back onto my bed. Trembling, I bring the iPad mini back up to look at the screen, hoping my eyes were deceiving me. When I open it up again, I am proven wrong as I stare down at the headlines across the screen.

With my heart now beating out of control and pounding against my chest, my mind is racing with turmoil as I ask myself how in the hell did they find out. I was told by the police department they would keep the records private, yet here I am reading the details of what I've done splattered across the headlines.

As much as I don't want to read the article, I know deep down inside I must. Clicking on the link while holding my breath, I take in the outlined details they've written. They've left out the most important part of it all: How I'd defended myself. To them, I've killed a man and I'm considered a murderer.

Refusing to keep reading the article, I move onto another, but it's not much different from the first one. Every article I proceed to scan through pretty much detail the same events, as if they've been sold a similar story and refused to get the actual details. It shouldn't surprise me. To them this is a prime story as it's currently written and anything different wouldn't get them the front page story where it's currently sitting.

The tears flowing from my eyes are now obstructing my vision and I'm convulsing from the crying that began minutes ago. I'm desperately trying to gasp for air, but it feels useless.

Instead, I spend the next hour miserably crying before my phone rings. The lyrics to *Umbrella* are singing to me, telling me it's Kelly calling.

Picking up my phone to answer the call, I glide my finger across the screen to answer. Instead of speaking, I whimper into the phone. "Hang in there, Abigail. I'm on my way," she sympathetically expresses.

"Okay," I muster through my tears before hanging up the phone, not realizing I didn't even tell her goodbye. I'm too distracted to even think straight. I don't know how much time goes by, but as Kelly promised, she is soon walking through my bedroom and straight to me to wrap her arm around my shoulders.

"I tried calling Matt, but he didn't answer. He texted me back. Do you want me to tell him to come home right away?" she asks, but I frantically shake my head knowing how important it is that Matt stays in class. "Trey is already on his way home, though," she finishes saying.

Immediately after she says the words, I hear the front door slamming, making me flinch as Trey's distinctive stomps make their way to my room. He stops at the doorway, his piercing blue eyes looking back at me. He looks furious, his fisted hands hanging to his side looking ready to punch something.

"How did they find out?" Kelly's question floats in the room. At first I think she's asking me, but when I look up to answer she's already staring daggers at Trey.

"I don't know, but I'm going to find out," he angrily growls. "Abigail, I need your phone," he orders, already holding out his hand for it.

"Why?" I rasp out around my tears. "I'm going to start making phone calls to your people at the design show. That asshole is already scared of me, so it will be easy to get it out of him," he proclaims as I hand him the phone.

Grabbing it from my hands, he turns to stomp away, already cursing the world. Within minutes, Trey returns with a glass of water and some pills.

"Take them, they'll help you sleep."

"What are they?" Kelly confusedly asks.

"They're Matt's pills."

Shaking my head in refusal, I try pushing them away. Trey is persistent and shoves them into my hand. "Take them. They'll knock you out. You need it, supermodel."

I look from Kelly to Trey and both their eyes are encouraging me to take them. Doing as told, I throw the pills into my mouth and swallow them down with the water. I know I shouldn't be taking them, but at this point I just want to shut out the world and I know sleeping will help me do that.

Satisfied that I've taken the pills, Trey leaves me alone with Kelly. Twenty minutes later, I feel the effects of the medication. In that time my convulsing has slowly begun to calm down, left with only the shuddering aftereffects of my crying. My mind is slowly starting to feel like I'm in a fog and my eyes are growing heavy. With Kelly's continuous soothing, I'm soon succumbing to the darkness demanding to take me and I willingly submit.

Matt

CONFUSED, I LOOK down at the text message Kelly sent me immediately after I'd ignored her call. She knows I'm in class, so why would she call me? Reading the message, I'm beginning to wonder if it has something to do with Abigail.

Make sure to come straight home after class. – Kelly

Is Abigail okay? - Matt

She doesn't immediately respond, which is only pissing me off. Why would she text me only minutes ago and not respond when I've texted her back right away? Needing an answer, I text Trey next wondering if he'll know anything.

Kelly just texted me, is there something wrong? - Matt

I send it off and wait. Minutes later, I'm still waiting. When I look down at the time I take notice that I have fifteen minutes left until I'm done with class, but those last fifteen minutes endlessly drag by. Right now, I'm wondering if I should have taken the doctor's advice of medical leave from school. When he'd suggested it, I'd kindly refused, knowing I was almost done anyway. There was no way I was letting something stop me from graduating.

Impatiently, I wait for the minutes to tick by. The first chance I get, I exit the class and walk as fast as I can to my car and race home. The moment I walk in the door I see a frustrated looking Trey screaming into the phone demanding information. Kelly is sitting on the couch looking both somber and worried, but Abigail is missing, sending my heart to beat out of control.

"Where is she?" I ask, already walking to our room.

Kelly stops me halfway down the hall. "She's asleep," she quietly whispers, as if afraid someone would hear. Pulling me back into the living room, Trey is still pacing the small space in front of the fireplace.

"Trey gave her some of your pain meds and it knocked her out."

Jerking my head back in shock, I ask, "Why would he do that?"

"We wanted her to calm down. It worked, and thankfully she quickly fell asleep."

Still confused, I ask, "What's going on?"

Kelly's shoulders drop in worry as she takes a deep breath

and sits back down. "The media found out about Bill. I tried to get here before Abigail found out, but by the time I called her she was a mess," she explains.

The room starts spinning and my earlier shock has doubled.

"Yeah, it was that bad," Kelly says.

Looking back towards our door, I ask, "How long has she been asleep?"

"Not long. Those pills of yours must be really strong. They kicked in almost immediately."

Nodding my head, I remember how fast they make me groggy, which is why I slept most of the time. I still don't have the full details of what is happening, but I still need to know she's okay.

"I'm just going to check on her," I inform Kelly, not caring what she thinks of me disturbing Abigail. When I enter the room it's completely engulfed in darkness as I take in Abigail's sleeping form. Shutting the door behind me, I walk my way over to the bed and carefully climb in on my good side. The moment my arm wraps around Abigail her body turns into mine.

I place a kiss on her temple. "Everything is going to be alright, beautiful," I whisper to her. Kissing her on the corner of her lips this time, I can taste the remainder of her salty tears.

When I brush my lips over her swollen eyes, she lets out a light whimper, breaking my heart. Trying my best to soothe her without having to move my injured side, I feather kisses along her skin, knowing how much she likes that.

Satisfied that she's fine for now, I'm soon cautiously pulling myself from Abigail's tight embrace, giving her one last kiss on her temple before exiting the room. Heading back to the living, I find that David has arrived, but what surprises me the most is seeing Julio amongst them.

I give him a nod of greeting. "I thought you were taking the week off," I say on my way to the fridge to grab a much needed beer.

"As soon as I saw Abigail's name on the news, I came right over. Vacation or not, her safety is my concern. It's my job," he answers as I'm already walking back into living room drinking my beer. Another minute later, Trey hangs up the phone and he looks livid as he rakes his hand down his face.

"What happened?" I ask.

He lets out an exasperated sigh. "I think I may have just screwed myself over and became Abigail's manager," he grimly answers. I practically choke on my beer.

"How the hell did that happen?" Kelly screeches out.

"They wouldn't put me through to the slime ball director unless I was someone important and I convinced them I was legit. They're getting bombarded with a shit load of phone calls from the media about Abigail. It took me repeating over and over again that I was her new manager to get me through to him," he explains. We're all still gaping at him as he continues. "I finally got through to the weasel and he's denying he leaked anything. From the way he sounded, I'm pretty sure he's telling the truth. He sounds just as shocked as we are. He's practically losing his mind with trying to get his own press release out to clean up the bad press linking their show to the shooting." I take another swig of beer trying to take everything in.

"So how did you become her manager again?" David skeptically asks the one question we still haven't gotten enough clarification on.

"Everywhere I called I dropped the title with my name and number and eventually I was getting phone calls from all of them. If that's what it takes to keep the hounds off her, then yes, I'm now her fucking manager!" he proclaims before looking straight at me. "I want fifty percent of her earnings," he orders.

"Fuck you," I throw back at him.

"Forty?"

Rolling my eyes at the joke he's made, I go along with it. "You're lucky if I let you get two percent."

"Shit, I'll take it," he announces with a fist pump to the air. Everyone laughs at his response, lightening the mood for a moment before his excited expression turns into a frown. "Don't get mad at me, but I told them she would release a statement from our end. I think it will help if she tells her side of the story," Trey expresses.

I'm now glaring at him. "No," I clip out.

Defensibly holding out his hands, he claims, "Now think about it. If she stays quiet, she's pretty much admitting that she murdered him. But if she gives her side of the story, which is the truth, it'd show she isn't hiding anything."

"I hate to admit it, but I agree with him, Matt. Abigail does have the right to tell her side of the story," Kelly states, defending Trey.

I don't like the idea, but at this point I'm defeated. Giving Trey a curt nod, he lightens up at my approval. "Don't worry, man. As her new manager, I'm going to make sure she doesn't get fucked over," he claims. The title he's happily taken upon himself makes me groan as I watch him tapping at his phone and starts calling someone. I can only imagine the circus this is going to turn into to, but better he deal with it instead of Abigail dealing with it herself. With a heavy sigh, I sit and think about the trials that I know will soon come. Tilting my head to the side to look at Julio, I say, "You're going to have your work cut out for you."

"Nothing will change," he replies.

For the next couple of minutes, I sit drinking my beer until Trey is announcing, "Okay, everything is set. I've contacted a

PR guy. Don't worry, I checked him out and he's legit," he proclaims, as if knowing how skeptical I'm feeling about the declaration. "He wants her statement by tomorrow so these hounds will get off her ass. I'm making him sign a NDA, non-disclosure agreement for those of you who don't understand," he mocks over to Kelly and David, but they're already rolling their eyes. "And in the contract I'm putting in there that if he doesn't issue the exact statement that Abigail presents, I'm suing his ass. He's agreed," he proudly states, looking as if he's just won a medal.

I have to admit, his actions are surprising me. I've known Trey was taking up business management as his major, as I have, but I thought it was because it was forced upon him by his family to keep running their business back home. I guess he is going to put that degree we're earning to use sooner than he'd expected.

"See, I knew me not falling asleep during all those stuck up classes would come in handy. Abigail's life is going to be turned upside down, but I'll be there to make sure she doesn't puke."

Kelly lets out a snort while David laughs. I, on the other hand, sit there silently cursing from how he's explained how Abigail's life will soon be. Right when I think she is finally at a point in her life where she doesn't have to fear for her safety, here she is the center of attention all over again. It makes me wonder if Abigail will ever be able to live a normal life. Or if she even wants one.

Chapter Twenty-Two

Abigail

I'M STARING OUT the kitchen window overlooking the front of the house. The sight of the construction workers assembling the gate darkens the cloud already looming in the skies outside. Matt comes up behind me, leaving not an inch between our bodies as he locks me in his embrace. His lips immediately find the hollow of my neck as they usually do when he first comes up to me. The feel of his lips brushing my skin would normally send shivers through my body, but today it's otherwise; today, not even Matt's touch helps to soothe my hopeless mood.

Lifting his head after giving me a kiss, his eyes are now looking in the direction mine are currently locked on. "They're almost done," Matt says next to my ear.

A sigh leaves my lips while continuing to watch the men at work. Ever since I'd released the statement with my side of the story, the media has practically exploded with wanting to see a glimpse of me. My words were not enough to keep them happy. Somehow, the media had discovered where we lived and that same day they started hounding the house. Julio was currently taking up residence in the spare bedroom because Matt refused to allow me to stay home alone while he and Trey went to school. I hadn't planned on leaving the house when I'd returned from New York because I'd wanted to relax, but it's difficult to relax when you have people circling the house and trying to peek in through the windows. Even calling the police wasn't doing much for my protection. They could only order them to stay on the street when they arrived, but the minute they left they'd ignored the police's orders.

Most were disappointed we weren't giving them an exclusive interview. They kept throwing higher offers at Trey for an interview, as if they thought I was holding out for the highest bidder, but it was far from that. Money was not the issue. It was keeping my life private that I truly wanted.

Leaving the house had become challenging, even with Julio. The first time I tried to leave the house for a run to clear my mind, I never made it to the trail. Thankfully Julio was driving, because with how crazy the paparazzi was driving around me to get the perfect shot, I would have definitely crashed into one of them. Not purposely, but from being so distraught. So we were forced to return to the house where they were brave enough to follow me up the driveway and have been doing so ever since. It took Julio calling the police to get them off the property, but they couldn't do anything about them being at the end of the street. The moment Matt got word of what happened, he called a security fence company to have one installed ASAP.

Now as I stare out the window as they lift the iron wrought fence, the sight is another definition of how trapped my life will be. Even with him dead, Bill is still keeping me from being happy.

"Do you want to watch a movie with me?" Matt asks, kissing his way down my neck. I somberly nod my head, not because

I want to watch a movie, but because I know it will allow me to be in Matt's comforting arms for the next few hours. Matt pulls me away from the window as if knowing he has to force me or else I won't willingly move. Leading me to the couch, he sits me down and begins searching for the remote. Julio is already perched on the smaller part of the sofa on his laptop.

"Are they almost done?" he asks over to Matt, inquiring about the gate.

Triumphantly holding up the remote, he shows me that he's found it.

"Almost. It shouldn't be too much longer," he says as he makes his way to sit next to me. His hands pat his chest and the action makes me chuckle at how he knows how I'd prefer to be with him on the couch.

"Good. Thankfully I knew the guy, or else I don't think they would have been able to do it right away."

"How do you know the guy?" I curiously ask Julio, already draped across Matt's chest.

"He worked for the same security company you found me at, but it's his family that owns the fence company. It's through him that they get a lot of business because of the type of clients we work with," Julio explains.

"Makes sense," I reply.

"Yeah, we can never be too safe. I'm surprised you didn't put up a fence a long time ago," he states over to Matt.

"When Abigail first arrived, she was pretty much hiding out. Not many people knew the details of her personal life until recently," Matt answers.

"I bet you didn't think your life would get this exciting when I first hired you?" I tease, thinking back to the first couple of weeks when I'd hired him and he looked bored most of the time.

Nonchalantly shrugging his shoulder, he says, "It's been interesting, but it's the best job so far. I get to do what I love. Even with you," he teases in return. "Just don't expect me to be your nanny when the time comes. I draw the line with that type of babysitting," he sternly adds.

Matt's chest is vibrating from his booming laughter, but my body has completely tensed from his remark. It reminds me of the most important appointment I was supposed to keep, and had completely forgotten about. Mentally counting the day since I got my last Depo shot, I realize I should have gotten another over a month ago.

Frantically climbing from Matt's body, I'm now rushing to the room, panicking with every step. Matt's footsteps are quickly heard following me.

"What's wrong, beautiful?"

Reaching the room, I signal him to shut the door and I'm already biting on my thumbnail, nervously choosing how to tell Matt. I'm so lost in my thoughts he's able to sneak up behind me and trap me in his arms, forcing me to look at him. His wide eyes are demanding I answer him.

I take a deep breath before I answer. "I forgot to get my birth control shot updated," I quietly croak out. His eyes grow wide and his body is now rigid against mine.

"When were you supposed to get it?"

"Over a month ago. I think?"

A silence overtakes the room for what feels likes minutes as Matt's eyes become lost in thought. "Have you gotten your period?" It takes me a moment to think of an answer as I think back over the last month.

"I've spotted, but it wasn't a full period." Matt's lips go flat and at first I'm frightened he's angry with me.

"I'm so sorry."

217

His head tilts to the side and his once flat lips are now turned down into a frown. "Would you be upset?" he asks.

I don't know how to answer the question, but somehow I feel as if it's entirely my responsibility. "This is all my fault. I should have kept track of when I had to get it renewed," I guiltily claim.

Taking me in his arms, he whispers into my hair, "We'll figure this out."

"Matt, I need to take a test. Just to make sure."

I feel him sigh in my arms. "I could run out and buy a test for you, but I'm afraid the paps will follow me. Pictures of me buying a pregnancy test all over the front of their magazines is the last thing I want right now."

I agree. Dreadfully closing my eyes trying to figure out what the hell we're going to do, I think of the one person they haven't hounded leaving the house.

I pull myself from Matt's arms so I can leave the room. "Where are you going?" Ignoring him, I nervously march my way over to his door and start knocking. Matt quickly figures out my plan. "Are you sure that's a good idea?" he shockingly asks while we wait for Trey to answer.

He answers it with an arched eyebrow. "What?" he irritably growls.

I don't know what's going on with him, but some days he can act like a grumpy bear.

"Abigail, I'll just ask Julio," Matt voices from behind me as he tries to pull me away.

I turn to Matt to argue my case. "No. They'll follow him, too," I clip out and then just as quickly turn back to face Trey who now has his arms crossed over his chest. "I need you to go to the store for me," I tell him.

He shakes his head and I grow disappointed. "I'm not buying you tampons or pads. No way!" he states, already stepping back and trying to shut his door. Using all my force, I push it back open and his eyes are widely staring back at me.

"I'm not on my period," I quickly reply and he now looks relieved. "I actually need a pregnancy test," I blurt out, watching him go pale. He looks over my shoulder to Matt.

"Are you fucking kidding me?" His booming words make me wince.

"Trey, please. We would go, but we can't," I desperately plead, throwing in a pout of my lips for good measure.

He looks ready to cave to my request when Matt also pleads. "I'm sorry, man, but we can't leave the house without being followed," Matt explains. Trey narrows his eyes at both of us and I'm already believing he won't do it.

"Never mind. I'll call David or Kelly to do it," I declare, stepping away from the door, hating the situation I'm in.

"No, I'll go. But you just upped my two percent to five for this shit," he lets out before turning back into his room to grab his wallet and keys off his dresser. I know I shouldn't be gleefully smiling, but I can't help it as I watch him walk down the hallway and out the front door.

Julio is heading to the bathroom in the hallway, but not before asking, "Where's Trey going?"

"He had to run to the store for something," Matt answers without any further details. Julio accepts it and shuts the bathroom door, leaving Matt and I to walk back to our room to impatiently wait. I'm already an impatient person and the time it's going to take for Trey to return might just drive me nuts.

Trey

I'M DRIVING AWAY from the house mentally cursing to myself for the situation I've volunteered myself for. Actually, I know I would have been forced to do it whether I wanted to or not, but Abigail's pleading will make me do anything for her. She may not know it, but that girl has us *all* wrapped around her little finger without her even trying.

Looking in the rear view mirror to make sure none of the paps are following me, I head in the direction of the pharmacy, seeing that it's clear. I can't believe the fucking chaos our lives have turned into since the day she's moved in. If it's not one thing, it's another with that girl. Sometimes I think her life is the perfect soap opera. Pulling into the parking lot of the pharmacy, I take one last look around me to make sure I wasn't followed. When I know the coast is clear, I make my way inside.

This has to be one of the craziest fucking requests I have ever gotten from a girl. I wasn't joking when I told her I wouldn't buy her tampons, but I never expected them to throw buying a fucking pregnancy test at me. At this point, the fucking tampons would have been a better request.

Walking past aisle after aisle with no luck finding what I need, I'm forced to stop an employee to ask where I need to go.

"Um, excuse me. Where would the pregnancy tests be?"

With a cheerful smile on her face, she answers, "Aisle fifteen, by the feminine products."

With a thankful nod, I continue on. What the fuck did she mean by feminine products? I ask myself, but soon find out as I turn the corner onto aisle fifteen and find myself walking straight past tampons and maxi-pads. Letting out an exasperated sigh, I think to myself… Fuck my life.

As she indicated, the pregnancy tests are at the end of the aisle, but when I take in their selection I'm left speechless. There has to be over twenty different kinds. Feeling lost and indecisive over which one to buy, I call Abigail.

She immediately answers. "Are you on your way back yet?" she asks, sounding desperate.

"No, I'm not on my way back yet," I sarcastically answer. "I barely got here."

"Then hurry up," she impatiently orders into the phone.

I can hear Matt mumbling something in the background and it sounds like he is telling her to be patient and using his corny nickname for her. The first couple of times he started calling her the nickname I wanted to gag and roll my eyes, but just as quickly I caught myself using my own for her.

"I seem to have a problem, supermodel," I say into the phone. I'm about to explain when she begins rambling into the phone. "Were you followed? Oh, God. What if someone sees you? Just leave, Trey. Never mind," she frantically continues to ramble on. I'm about to tell her to calm down when Matt speaks into the phone.

"What's wrong," his calm collective voice a total opposite of Abigail's.

"Dude, there has to be over twenty different kinds of test here," I explain.

"Fuck."

"Exactly. I don't know which one to buy."

"And I'm supposed to know?" Matt throws back at me, sounding just as confused as I feel staring at them. Raking my hand down my face, I think of an idea.

"How about I just take a picture of each one and let you guys decide?"

"That would take too long. Beautiful, calm down, I've got

this," he clips out. Abigail must be driving him nuts.

"Just pick one, Trey. I don't care. I'm pretty sure they all work the same," Matt orders. I feel as if Matt is going to say something, but I cut him off when something catches my eyes.

"Dude, this one has a little screen that talks to you," I say into the phone. "Oh, this one is like the ones on the commercial. *Results six days before your missed period*," I mimic how the girls says it on the commercial. "When is Abigail supposed to get her period anyway?" I ask, wondering if it will work. If it's too soon maybe it won't. Then it occurs to me that's probably why I'm here.

"Just pick one," Matt growls into the phone, now sounding frustrated.

"Dude, you need to calm the fuck down with that attitude. You're not the one standing here," I clarify.

Matt sighs into the phone. "You're right, I'm sorry," he tells me and I savor the moment. It's not often he admits I'm right. "Look, can you just hurry up? Abigail is starting to freak out and I don't want to drug her up again. *If* she is pregnant, it may not be good for the baby," he explains.

"Alright. I'll just pick one. But don't go blaming me if the shit doesn't work," I say before hanging up the phone.

Letting out a frustrated growl, I stand there staring at the boxes with my hands on my hips, contemplating which one to buy. "Fuck it," I say out loud, grabbing one of each.

With the cluster of boxes in my arms, I make my way over to the register, ready to leave this building. Thankfully, when I reach the counter there is no one in front of me, allowing me to dump the bundle in my arms onto the counter. The same lady who directed me to the tests is staring at me with wide eyes.

"Better safe than sorry," she claims before sarcastically adding, "But then again, had you been safe the first time you wouldn't need these."

I narrow my eyes at her for her comment. "Just ring me up," I tell her through clenched teeth. Her smile turns into a frown as she snickers and does as ordered. Minutes later, she's facing me with the total. "That will be two hundred forty-two dollars and thirty-two cents."

Practically choking from the total, my mouth is slightly gapping open. "Are you fucking kidding me?"

She's glaring at me, most likely from my language. "I'm pretty sure one of these will do the job just fine," she suggests.

"She's not sure," I explain. "Here, put it on this," I say, handing her my credit card I have for emergencies only, thinking this better be considered a damn emergency if they have me pulling this shit.

I was joking earlier when I declared I wanted a cut of Abigail's earnings. What she paid me was not an issue. Running errands for her and having to pay for them out of pocket would be. My family is not as loaded as the both of them and I barely manage to get by on what little side jobs I pull here and there. If I was going to have to keep up with their spending habits, I was demanding a company credit card.

And a car.

Yes, maybe I can convince them to buy me a car, too.

Lord knows I need both, because there is no way I can afford to pay for her lifestyle on my non-existent salary.

Chapter Twenty-Three

Abigail

THE MINUTES TICKING by until Trey returns feel endless. Plus, I was going to have to wait for the results once I took the test. Today may be the day I go insane. I'm reminded of when I'd gone to the clinic to get put on birth control and they made me take a test and wait. I'd known then I wasn't pregnant because I was already on my period, but to not know for sure this time and having to wait… Yeah, I'm going to lose it.

I'm still fidgeting as I lay on the bed next to Matt while we wait, but not too much later we hear the front door open and close.

"Honey, I'm home," Trey playfully shouts from the living room as I jump up from the bed and rush out into the hallway. He's holding up two grocery bags full of items.

"You owe me two hundred and fifty dollars," he announces, handing me the bags.

"Sure," I say, already grabbing them from him. "Thank you," I manage to mumble before completely disappearing into my room with Matt on my heels. He shuts the bedroom door and follows me to the bathroom as I'm dumping the contents of the two bags out onto the bathroom counter. My eyes go wide in astonishment from how many different tests Trey has bought.

"Did you tell him to buy out the whole store?"

Matt picks up a box to read it while I do the same to another.

"It looks like he bought one of each," Matt says now looking at another.

"Screw it, I'll just use this one," I say while staring down at the box stating it to be 99.9% accurate. Tearing open the box, I grab for a skinny package and tear it open. This isn't like the test I'd taken at the clinic. There they had me pee in a cup and sent me back to my room after putting it through a little window.

Lifting the instructions that were inside the box, I carefully start reading what to do. "It says here I have to pee on the stick," I say, looking down at the stick I've retrieved from inside the package.

"Well, get to it," Matt teases from my side.

Piercing him with a glare as I look at him, he simply chuckles back at me. "It doesn't sound that hard to do," he says to me, watching as I stare at him. "Unless you need help."

I scrunch my nose up at him. "No, I don't need your help," I screech back. "What I need is for you to get out so I can pee on this stick," I order, holding up the stick in my hand.

"I thought I'd be with you to take the test," he says back.

"I'm not peeing in front of you," I say, already trying to shove him out of the bathroom.

"Come on, I've peed in front of you," I hear him say as I shut the door.

Ignoring him, I make sure to lock the door so he doesn't come barging in while I'm doing my business. It's bad enough he knows when I pee, but I refuse to go pee in front of him anytime soon. Taking a deep breath while I pull down my pants and get to business, a minute later I'm placing the test down on a massive amount of toilet paper on the floor.

Cleaning myself up and washing my hands, I wait…

And wait….

And nearly go insane as I continue to wait and stare down at the stick as if I take my eyes off of it, it's going to magically disappear.

A knock at the door startles me and soon Matt's deep voice is booming through the wood. "Beautiful, can I come in now?" he asks, already jiggling at the doorknob.

Unlocking the door, I let him in and the first thing he does is look down to the counter. "Where is it?"

Pointing at my feet, he looks down and his eyebrows furrow.

"Really?"

"What? I didn't know where else to put it."

He lets out a booming laugh, which only irritates me. We both kneel on the ground and watch as the color changes across the center. Soon the little words, *Not Pregnant,* appear on it.

I let out the breath I swear I've been holding for the past hour, but just as quickly I'm rendered speechless when Matt says, "Maybe it's wrong."

Pointing at the stick still sitting on the floor, I reply, "It says the results right there on the stick."

"Yeah, but maybe it could be wrong," he argues. "Take another."

Rolling my eyes, I grab for another from the same box, but Matt stops me. "No, not those. Try these. The box says six days before your period," he points out.

Yanking for the stick Matt is now handing me, I'm ordering him back out of the bathroom. The second round is much harder than the first since I've probably peed out everything my bladder had the first time, but the nervousness in me manages to get enough on the stick to wet it. That's satisfying enough for me.

This time I place the stick on the counter, but as before this one is also sitting on many layers of toilet paper. Letting Matt back in again, we stand and wait. We get the same results as before and although my heart is jumping with excitement, Matt doesn't look too satisfied.

Somehow, I think he was expecting a different result. "Are you mad?" I bravely ask, not knowing what to expect from him at this point. He's still staring down at the test in front of us, expressionless.

"No," he says just above a whisper.

I know Matt too well to know he isn't being completely honest. Turning him to face me, I see a set of disappointed eyes looking back at me, and it's then I realize why he had me take another test.

He wanted it to be positive.

"Matt, I'm sorry," I guiltily say, as if it's my fault.

Grabbing for my waist, he tugs me to him, holding me tightly in his arms.

"You have nothing to be sorry about. I'm not going to lie, for a little while I was hoping you'd be pregnant, but only if it was meant to be. It's obvious it isn't."

Laying my head against his chest, I wonder how I feel about this entire situation.

"I can't wait for that day to come, though," Matt says, the sincerity in his confession making my heart swell. We're both silent as we pull away and stare into each other's eyes.

"I really doubt me being fat and pregnant would be so appealing to you," I joke to him.

Pulling back as he shockingly looks down at my body, I'm thinking I've proven my words until he says otherwise. "There isn't anything more I'd love to see than your stomach swollen with a life we've both created. I have wanted it since I found out Lisa had lied to me. That entire time I kept wishing it was you instead," he confesses, pulling me back to him.

"Can we just let nature take its course for now? I don't want to rush into things," I declare. He nods his head and kisses me on my temple before his lips start trailing down to mine. Of course, Matt's kisses always have a way of distracting me from my worry. Add the fact that his hands are now cupping my butt and pulling me tight against the bulge in his pants and I'm ready to do something more than just kiss him. Thankfully, Trey's booming knock startles me to pull away.

"Not today, lover boy. You still have some time before we can play," I remind him, giving him a quick kiss on the corner of his lips.

Giving me a groan in return, he says, "I swear with the blue balls I'm carrying around, if you ever want kids from me, I won't be able to give them to you."

I laugh at his little speech while I walk away to answer the door. Opening it up, I find an anxiously waiting Trey looking back at me for an answer. "So, am I going to be a godfather or not?" I answer with a disappointed shake of my head. "Well, damn," he replies before looking over my shoulder to Matt. "The gate guys are done. They want to talk to you," he notifies him and then walks down the hallway.

"I'm going to go talk to them, but in the meantime, just think of how much I love you," he declares before briefly kissing me, leaving me to wonder exactly what he's supposed to mean by those words. Leaning against the doorframe while all three of the men walk outside, I let out a heavy sigh as Matt's words repeat in my head. I don't need to think about how much Matt loves me. I already know. My dilemma is how I'm going to prove to him that it was me making a mistake about our future. That's what I'm left thinking of instead.

Matt

I'M STARING DOWN at the email I've just received as I lie in bed with Abigail. It's the one I've been looking forward to for the past four years. Although it's a tentative email, I know it's as true as it states.

"What are you smiling about?" Abigail purrs at me while lying at my side. She tightens the leg that is wrapped on top of me, telling me all my teasing is working to bring her walls of resistance down.

"It's my graduation schedule."

She excitedly sits up. "Really?"

With a wide smile, I nod my head. Pulling her on top of me to straddle my waist, it's the closest to being one with her that I'm going to get for the next couple of weeks of misery I have left. When she's comfortable, she grabs the phone from my hands and begins to read the same email I've read only moments ago.

"I'm so excited!" she shouts out. "We have to plan a party!" Her eyes light up and somehow the wheels of her imagination can be seen from where I'm sitting.

Shocked, I look up at her. "You want a party?"

She chuckles. "It's not for me silly. It's for you, Trey, and David," she replies. "Graduating from college is a big accomplishment. We should celebrate!"

I can't help but laugh at her excitement. "Sure," I say, not wanting to disappoint her by denying her request. It's the last thing I want to do. Her excitement keeps the smile on my face for only a couple of seconds more as I remember the last time I celebrated anything. It was when Emily threw a party for my high school graduation.

The house has more balloons than I've ever seen in my life, the gold and blue of the school colors overtaking the entire house for my graduation party tonight. Entering the kitchen, I spot Emily putting a tray into the fridge and the sight of her makes me smile. After closing the fridge, she turn and is already wiping at her brow. She looks exhausted and tired. A pang of guilt hits me in the gut knowing all she's been doing in preparation of this party. She spots me entering the kitchen and her eyes light up.

"Matt, are you excited for tonight?" The enthusiasm in her question would fool me if I didn't know how stressed she's been the last week.

"Of course," I truthfully tell her, but it doesn't show how guilty I now feel. "Emily, you promised me you wouldn't overdo it," I remind her.

Snickering, she begins opening the packages of disposable plates. "You made me promise not to invite a ton of people. The guest list was all you," she proclaims.

All I wanted was my friends to come over and celebrate, and maybe for Emily to leave so she wouldn't have a heart attack when my friends showed up with the alcohol. As if she's read my mind, she states, "And there better not be any alcohol at this party, Matthew." The scornful tone she used when she spoke my full name is nothing to mess around with.

Groaning, I say, "Emily, I have no control over what my friends bring."

She pauses to glare at me. "I mean it! No alcohol. You can have all the alcohol and parties you want when you've reached the legal age, but as long as you still live in my house, you will follow my rules." I can't resist laughing at how aggravated she looks. "Don't you dare laugh at me, Mr. Garcia."

Now laughing harder from her using my formal name, I walk over to her and embrace her in my arms. Kissing her on her temple to lighten her mood, I feel her body ease into mine and she sighs.

"I love you, Emily."

She squeezes her arms around my waist. "When did you grow up?"

"According to you, I'm still a kid," I tease.

She lets out another heavy sigh. "Mom and Dad would be so proud of you."

I hardly remember my mom and dad anymore, but Emily makes sure to remind me of them every now and then. "They would be proud of you, too, Em."

I spend the next minute holding Emily before she pulls away to look up at me. "Promise you won't forget me when you leave for college?"

"There is no possible way I can ever forget you, Emily. I'm pretty sure you're going to be calling me every day," I mock. Swatting me on the chest then pushing me away, she returns to what she was doing.

"I'll remember that when you're calling me and begging me for something," she teases in return.

"I don't beg, Emily."

Pausing once more, her brow is now arched. "Oh, there will be a day when you'll be begging a girl for a certain some-thing," she coyly proclaims before opening the box of utensils.

My eyes go wide from her declaration and when she notic-es, we both let out a bout of laughter. We laugh so hard that there are tears coming from our eyes when we stop. Wiping at my eyes and still attempting to catch my breath, I say, "I'm pretty sure

I'll have the girls begging."

She delivers another snicker before replying. "That, I'm sure of." Finishing up her task, she takes in the room with a contented smile. "If you think this is overdoing it, wait and see what I plan on doing for you when you graduate college."

"What if I don't graduate?" I ask, still teasing her because I already know what her reaction will be, and as expected, she delivers.

"Oh, you're going to graduate, Matt. If not you're a dead man," she scolds.

"I refuse to be denied the opportunity to throw a party I will be planning for the next four years."

"Dear, Lord," I say, pushing myself from the counter I was leaning on and already walking back to my room to get ready.

"Just you wait, Matt. It's going to be the party of the century!" she exclaims. I can only laugh knowing she's teasing. At least I hope she is.

"Matt, you okay?" Abigail's somber words draw me back to the present. All I can give her is a forced smile as I look back at her.

"Of course, beautiful," I respond, pulling her down to kiss her. She gently lowers herself down onto my chest, careful as always to not put too much pressure on my injury.

Normally the position she's in and the way she kisses me would make me grow rock hard in seconds, but right now I don't have it in me to be cheerful. Not when the one person I'm wishing were here to help me celebrate is no longer with me. Abigail must have sensed my sadness. When she pulls away from our kiss, her hand comes down to run across my cheek to say, "She'll be watching over you from above, Matt. I just know it," she proclaims, knowing that's exactly whom I'm thinking of.

My eyes turn glassy and I have to blink away the tears fighting to leave my eyes. Abigail leans down one more time to kiss me while rubbing herself against my groin. The movement and knowing I'm sitting in between her legs works this time to tempt me. Clasping my hands on her hips to rub her harder against my body, she lets out a tantalizing moan.

Now my dick is hard.

"How many more weeks until we can make love?" she desperately asks against my lips. I've lost track of time at the moment.

"I think our time is up," I tell her, turning to roll her under me.

Trailing kisses across her chin, she lifts her head, giving me better access. Her little whimper is torture as my balls tighten up. I wasn't kidding when I told her last week I had the worst case of blue balls, and with every day and night I'm next to her, it only gets worse. Every time I get her naked and willing, her senses come back to life and she forces me to stop.

As I feel Abigail's hands in between us reaching for the waistband of my shorts, my mind does a little victory dance thinking this is it, she's finally going to cave and we're going to make love again. Her hand reaches inside my shorts and wraps around my dick and it's now me whimpering as she glides her warm palm up and down my shaft. My hands are reaching for the button of her jeans when her phone starts ringing.

"Ignore it," she says into my mouth and I've never been happier to hear her say it. I'm already pushing her pants down as the ringing stops, but within seconds it begins ringing again. Leaning my head against her forehead, I let out a sigh knowing she should answer it.

"Answer it," I tell her, throwing my body to lie next to her thinking: There goes my chance of getting laid.

My dick is still rock hard as I watch her speak into the phone while perched on the side of the bed. At first, she looks confused as she has a back and forth conversation, but soon her eyes are lighting up and agreeing to something with the person on the other end. Lying patiently while she continues her conversation, it isn't long before she's ending the call with an excited smile.

"Who was that?"

Excited, she looks over to me. "That was Aaron. He's the marketing director for Sprinter Running Company. I met him at a party I had to go to for the designer, but he was the one in charge of my first photo shoot you contracted for me."

For some reason, her enthusiasm is bothering me, but with a smile, I keep listening. "He said his company is a sponsor for a series of races that are held throughout the United States. They're having a race in Seattle in June and they want me to represent them by running it and do a photo shoot for the race." Her excitement is beaming off her as she finishes explaining. I, on the other hand, am not as excited as she is.

"Marathon?" I calmly ask even though deep down inside I'm apprehensive over the entire situation.

She sees the apprehension radiating off me. "I'll be fine, Matt. He knows about my injury and said I wouldn't have to run with the elite. They just want me to do a promotional shoot for the race and wear their products while running. They said they'd even pay me for it!" she exclaims, still trying to convince me.

I'm still skeptical, but seeing how excited she is pushes some of it aside.

"June?" I ask, thinking about how soon that seems to be.

She ignores my question and begins searching for information on her iPad mini. "Oh my God, Matt. They even have one here in Portland. They're all over the place," she claims, turning the screen so I can look at it. I can't focus on what she's showing me. My worry is overtaking my thoughts.

"Do you think you'll be ready for it? You'd be actually representing a company. I know it wouldn't be as fast as an elite, but I really doubt you're going to want to run it at a slow pace."

Her smile quickly turns into a frown as she nervously swallows while considering my question. "I'll make sure I'm ready," she says with determination, but disappointingly looking at me.

"Come here." I beckon her to climb back on top of me, but her head is hung as she speaks.

"You don't want me to run it, do you?" she somberly asks, and from the breaking in her voice, I know she's on the verge of tears. From the ways she's repeatedly swallowing, I know she's strongly forcing them back.

Her question nearly breaks my heart as I force myself to step back and look at the situation. She only wants to do the one thing she's come to love, something I pushed her to start doing. Lifting her chin up so I can see her face, her eyes are glassy and my heart completely shatters knowing I'm keeping her from doing what makes her happy.

"You really miss it, don't you?" She nods her head slowly to answer. "I understand. I may not be able to train with you, but I'll make sure you're ready," I say to her, watching her eyes light up.

"Really?" she giddily asks, as if needing clarification.

"Only if you promise not to push yourself too hard. You can always do that later," I tell her.

She never does promise me as she throws herself at me and wraps her arms around my neck, screaming with excitement into my ear. The excited screech makes me wince, but laugh at the same time. Pulling back, her beaming smile has now returned. Her eyes wander and then go wide.

"Your appointment. We have to go or else we're going to be late. I'm excited to hear what the doctor has to say," she says, already climbing off the bed and me.

I'd forgotten my routine checkup was today. Since the bullet came so close to my heart, they have me going in every week to have an EKG. It was more an order from the NFL to make sure I wasn't going to have a heart attack on them while training. So far, everything was coming back normal, but I was still ordered to check in every week. I already know I won't be one hundred percent ready to play the opening season, but rookies rarely do. So it gives me time to completely heal and be ready for next season.

This is the first appointment Abigail is going to be able to come with me. The previous ones I'd forced her to stay home because of the media camping outside our house. Ever since everything has calmed there was rarely anyone lingering outside the gates. Abigail was finally able to go on a run at the beginning of the week. Of course, I made her take a few extra friends along to help Julio out, and other than one camera man taking a candid shot when she was leaving the trail, everything had gone okay.

Standing up from the bed, I'm right behind her as she bends over, most likely looking for her shoes, but I'm unable to resist rubbing myself up against her ass. Abigail snaps straight up and faces me, glaring right at me.

"Matt, stop teasing me!"

"Me teasing you? I'm the one left with a hard-on most of the time," I throw back at her, trying to sound upset, but I'm biting the inside of my cheek to keep from laughing.

"I'm going to make you start sleeping on the couch if you don't behave," she huffs out before turning to walk away.

"The day I sleep on the couch is the day hell freezes over!" I shout to her retreating back walking down the hallway.

Shaking my head, hating how she always gets the last word, I'm left staring down at my straining dick pushing straight up under my basketball shorts. I let out the same exasperated huff Abigail just gave me. "I'm sorry, man. I'm trying," I say down to my dick. As if sympathizing with me, it jerks up before I go to dress for my appointment.

If I had enough time, I'd jump into a freezing cold shower right now. Damn. I already know this is going to be a long day if I don't learn how to control my thoughts.

THE DOCTOR IS looking at me with a satisfied smile. "Well, Mr. Garcia, everything looks good and no signs of distress on your heart. Another couple of weeks and you'll be done." He takes notes on his iPad then looks back up to me. "Any questions?"

"When can I start having sex again?"

He lets out a small chuckle. "As I told you last week, Mr. Garcia, you're required to refrain from any sexual activity at least until you receive your clearance. According to your EKG, your heart is in excellent condition, but unfortunately, it's for your own good to wait."

Of course he'd answer with a medical opinion since he's old enough to be my grandpa and probably isn't even having sex anymore. How does he know what it's like to walk around with the biggest case of blue balls?

"See, Matt, stop asking," Abigail lectures from my side. I turn the tables on her as I pierce her with a glare she would have given me for that comment. She sticks her tongue out at me, making me laugh.

Stepping over to me, the doctor is now patting my back. "I don't blame you, boy. With a girl as beautiful as this one, I'd be asking the same question. See you next week," he says before walking out of the door.

Hopping off of the table to take off the hospital gown they gave me, I start to throw my shirt over my head, wincing as I stick my left arm through the sleeve.

"I'm sorry, Matt. I swear when the time comes, I'll make it up to you," she says before placing a quick kiss on my lips. "If it makes you feel any better, I have to suffer through it with you."

Snapping my head back in shock, I say, "If I recall, my mouth has been down in between your legs more often than yours has been in mine."

She clucks her tongue at me. "Touché."

"Touché, my ass. We'll see how badly you're begging when you're horny," I tell her.

"If it makes you feel any better, I think Trey has been holding out along with us." Her comment surprises me.

"What makes you think that?" I curiously ask.

She gives me a simple shrug of her shoulders, but from the laughter in her eyes, I know she's holding out on information as well. I grab her and turn her body so she's trapped against the exam room table and my body. "Oh, no you don't. Tell me what you know," I say, nipping at her neck.

She immediately giggles as my fingers start to wiggle into her ribs.

"Matt! Stop it," she screeches and giggles.

"Tell me what you know," I playfully demand with another wiggle of my fingers. Her nails are now digging into my forearms as she tries to push me away, but I suck up the pain as I continue to torture her.

"Okay, okay," she screams out while still laughing. I briefly stop, but when she doesn't speak, I give a slight wiggle to warn her I could easily start again. "I saw a girl stomping from the bathroom at the Brewhouse the other night. At first I thought he'd been kinky with her, like we'd done, but she looked pissed. Like unsatisfied pissed. When I asked Trey about it later, he snapped at me and told me to mind my own business. When he walked away, he was mumbling something about her not doing it for him. I think he only mumbled it because he was already drunk. I don't think he actually had sex with her, though," she explains. My eyebrows are arched as high as they can go, and for some reason I want to believe her words, but since it's Trey, I'm skeptical. "And he's been looking miserable since we've left New York. In my opinion, I think that girl that left the hotel room messed with his head. He hasn't been the same since," she adds.

Thinking back on it, she has a point. Trey's been acting as if he's got a thorn stuck up his ass. He has his good days, and his bad, but the bad are practically intolerable. Abigail lets out a sigh. "I think he just needs to find the right girl and settle down already."

"Maybe you're right, but we can't force Trey. You know how he is. He claims he'll be a player for life."

She's now smirking at me. "If I recall, you used to say the same thing to me at one point." Remembering how many times I used that phrase with Abigail to push her away makes me now laugh.

"You're right, but I think I was just telling you that to lie to myself. You had my heart the moment you walked into my house. Thankfully, I came to my senses."

"Well, hopefully Trey will come to his senses soon, too. If not, I'm going to knock some sense into him," she retorts. The determination in her words make me laugh again. That's one thing I've always loved about Abigail, she will not give up on something she believes in. Thankfully, she never gave up on me, no matter how many times I fucked up with her, or else I'd be the one acting like I had a thorn up my ass.

Chapter Twenty-Four

Abigail

I'M LOUNGING ON my bed watching my guilty pleasure—a Spanish soap opera—when there's a knock on my door. "Come in," I shout, too lazy to get up and open the door.

Trey enters, his eyes catching a glimpse of the flat screen on the wall. With a quirked brow, he looks at me and asks, "Seriously?"

"Don't judge me. I don't tell you shit when I hear the screams and moans of your porno flicks coming from your room." I expect him to look horrified, or at least embarrassed that I know, but instead he lets out a snort.

"I've got nothing to hide."

"Neither do I," I retort. "Whatcha want anyway?" I ask, getting straight to the point.

"I got a call from the director about the show," he states. I perk up, somewhat excited from the news. It's been weeks since we've heard anything. I quickly discovered what Julio had to go through with being on standby for my calls.

"It isn't good news."

Dreading what he'll say next, I still ask, "What did they say?"

"They set a date for Paris, but you're not going to like it," he explains.

"Why?" From the frown on his face, I know he's being as honest as he can with me.

"It's the day of our graduation," he proclaims.

"Are you sure?" I ask, as if needing clarification.

Silently, he gives me a short nod. My lips are starting to tremble from holding back my tears as I tell myself *I'm not going to cry.*

I refuse to cry.

Trey can still be wrong.

As if reading the doubt in my eyes, he declares, "I'm sure, supermodel. I even asked them to send over the itinerary for that week. It's the same day. I've confirmed it." It isn't the answer I wanted to hear. I continue to sit in silence, stunned as I stare into the air ahead of me.

"What do you want me to do?" he asks, forcing me to look at him.

"I can't, Trey. I don't want to miss Matt graduating," I rasp out around the lump in my throat. "It's too important to him."

"I don't think you have a choice, Abigail. You signed a contract," he reminds me.

He's right; I'm obligated to do the show. I signed my name on the line promising to do so. The sound of footsteps draws my attention to the hallway. Thinking it's Matt, I'm somewhat relieved when I see Julio instead. He's sympathetically looking at me, as if understanding my dilemma.

"I'm sorry, Abigail," Julio apologetically says to me.

"He was in the living room when they called," Trey says, as if needing to explain how Julio knows. I don't care if *he* knows, the only person I don't want finding out about the news is Matt. I know I promised to no longer keep secrets from him, but this is one I can't face him knowing. Not yet. It will break both our hearts.

"Please don't tell Matt. If he finds out he won't want to walk at graduation and I can't risk him giving that up. Not for me," I say to both of them. They look torn from my request. "Please, promise me," I plead.

They look at each other, and for a moment I think they are going to defy me.

"Of course," Julio answers first, followed by a nod from Trey.

Their promises help calm my frantic mind. Scrambling up from the bed, I head over to the bathroom to wash my face, hoping it will help calm me a little. I don't know how long I must have been leaning on the counter contemplating how I should tell Matt, but as if knowing I was thinking of him, he's now walking into the room.

"Beautiful?" he ask, sounding as if he is searching for me. Forcing a smile on my lips, I walk out of the bathroom to greet him.

"Hey there. How was school?" I'm already asking while wrapping myself into his arms.

"News has gotten around that I got drafted. Suddenly I'm the cool kid in town," he answers with a mocking tone.

"You've always been the cool kid. And the jock who had every girl chasing you," I tease him.

"True." Giving him a light swat on his uninjured side of his chest, we both chuckle. "I may have had all the girls chasing me, but there's only one girl I like chasing in return," he declares with a wag of his eyebrows. The words make my heart swell.

"I am worth chasing," I say in return, playfully going along.

He throws his head back to laugh. When his eyes meet mine, he mocks, "Who's the cocky one now, Ms. Supermodel?" This time I'm fully laughing with him at the thought.

With a contented sigh, he's managed to push all my sadness to the back of my mind. I lay my head on his shoulder while we happily hold each other. The entire time I'm debating whether I should tell Matt right now, but I'm not given the chance when he says, "Want to go grab a bite to eat?"

"Sure. But I get to pick this time," I demand, knowing if I were to let him pick we'd end up at the Brewhouse because some game was on.

"Fine, but it better have good dessert." His eyes roam my body, making my stomach flop from the hunger in his eyes. "It doesn't matter. My dessert is right here," he states, pinching me between my legs and making me yelp.

"Matthew Garcia, you're intolerable," I lecture, pulling away and leaving him to follow me.

"So does that mean I'm going to get lucky tonight?"

Ignoring him, we reach the living room and Matt is already asking Julio and Trey if they want to join us for dinner. Taking up the offer, I pray they keep their promise because deep down inside, I'm not ready to break both our hearts when I share the news with him.

I'M STARING DOWN at the contract I've signed, reading it for what seems like the hundredth time. No matter how many times I've read it, the words never change. It's only been a couple of days since Trey informed me of Paris, and with every day that passes, it becomes harder to find the courage to tell Matt.

"You're going to go nuts if you keep reading that thing," Trey's voice startles me from my thoughts. Giving up for the moment, my body slumps back into the recliner I'm sitting in, my lips letting out an exasperated sigh. Oddly enough, when I'm frustrated I find myself curling up into this stupid thing, and lately I've practically lived in it while Matt is at school. It's the only time I'm allowed to wallow in the misery of my situation.

A couple of times he's caught me staring off into space as I keep thinking of ways to tell him, but when he asks me what's bothering me, I find myself fabricating an excuse to distract him. Lately he thinks it's the pressure I'm feeling from the race I've committed myself to running. Which, ironically, even the training runs for it haven't managed to take my stress away for more than an hour or so.

"Did you contact them?" I ask Trey, thinking back to yesterday when I'd asked him to contact them to see if there was any way out of it.

My mind is easily lost as it returns to the first day this all started. He'd immediately called them that night and informed them of my dilemma, believing they'd be sympathetic of my situation and release me from my obligation, but it was a failed attempt. They'd only laughed at him from the other end of the phone.

He'd tried again, practically begging on my behalf, asking them to move the date to the following week, even a couple of days later, but they'd disagreed. Trey had bravely flat-out told them I wasn't doing the show then, and they'd come back with a legal order from their lawyer stating I was obligated to do the show or else they would sue me. The blood had completely left my body the moment I was served with the paperwork and I'd read the order. I'd asked Trey if we should hire a lawyer to fight it, but he'd sympathetically replied, "We can try, but as they pointed out, your signature is on this contract saying you'd do the show. It can turn nasty with the media and I don't know if you want that to happen."

The last thing I need is for the media to get ahold of this story and blow it out of proportion, as they did with Bill's death. Trey was still currently trying to clean up that mess, even with my statement. Poor guy was learning the ropes of being a manager quick. Fortunately, he never complained to my face, but some days I saw the frustration in his eyes as he stormed around the house yelling into his phone with my *new* publicist. He'd managed to find someone who was just starting out and at first I was skeptical, but he assured me the guy was good and everyone has to start somewhere. I told him if my ass got publicly screwed over, I'd degrade his income back down to two percent, where he'd started.

I only had two days left until I was scheduled to leave and the only thing keeping my sanity together was helping Matt plan his graduation. I was also planning a small party at our house for everyone and their families who were flying in. I'd originally suggested the Brewhouse, but Matt insisted we have it at our place so everyone could relax. I couldn't complain. The guys all volunteered to barbeque and the parents had said they'd take care of the sides. It just sucked I wouldn't be here to celebrate with everyone. But planning the party was the least I can do before I left. It would leave Matt something from me.

"Yeah, I just got off the phone with them to tell them you're ready to go, even though we both know that isn't true." Trey's voice breaks me from my thoughts once more. "You can't keep it from Matt much longer. It's bad enough he's going to be pissed that you kept it from him for this long," he declares and there is no arguing the simple fact.

As if knowing we're speaking about him, Matt walks

through the door with a jubilant smile spread across his face. "I'm officially a college graduate!" he shouts with his hands held high into the air.

"Whoopty. Fucking. Doo! So am I!" Trey's comment makes me laugh knowing that he's worked just as hard as Matt to earn the right to say it.

"What the fuck is up with you?" Matt bitterly bites back to him.

Trey's lips turn down into a frown as he looks over to me. "Good luck," he proclaims before walking away. Pausing when he reaches Matt, he claps him on the shoulder. "We'll go celebrate tonight, *if* you're still up for it," he says to him as his eyes briefly look over to me.

Matt seems confused as he looks back and forth between Trey and myself, but he shakes it off and is now looking back at me. I'm already standing up to greet him with a hug and kiss. "Congratulations," I whisper into his ear. Engulfing me in his arms to hug me tightly, I'm trying my best to hold back the tears building inside of me. This conversation is not going to be easy, but it's finally time I stop hiding.

Kissing me below my ear as he does when he hugs me, the shiver and tingles emerge throughout my body, helping to push some of my dread aside.

"Can we have sex to celebrate?" Matt eagerly asks into my ear.

Jokingly, I reply, "Alright," not thinking he'd instantly scoop me up after the words came out. "Matt, put me down! You're not supposed to be overdoing yourself!" I shout as he rushes to our bedroom. My voice echoes in the hallway as he ignores my protesting along the way and soon we're in our room with the door being slammed behind us. The entire time Matt has managed to keep me laughing with his excitement of thinking I'm really going to go against his doctor's orders.

My body is soon descending onto our bed with Matt just as quickly following above me, doing his best to strip me of my clothes. His eagerness is hilarious, keeping me laughing the entire time I playfully fight his hands to stop.

"I love it when you laugh," he says, already digging his fingers into my side to keep me giggling and squirming. I attempt to buck his body off me to stop his torturous tickle attacks, but it's impossible with my body being locked under his. Instead, I do the next best thing I know to stop him. I kiss him. The moment I slide my tongue into his mouth and the warmth of our mouths mix together, he completely stops, telling me I've won.

The ceiling above me disappears when he turns me to straddle his waist, our mouths still tightly fused together. Remembering what my intentions were just moments ago, I pull my mouth from his, panting as I look down into his eyes. The lingering smile that was once on my lips evaporates as I think of the words needed to begin.

"Matt, I won't be here for your graduation," I blurt out, watching his smile quickly disappear.

"What do you mean you won't be here?"

Holding onto the newfound courage, I repeat, "I'm not going to be here for your graduation. I have to go to Paris."

He's staring up at me with a perplexed expression. "You leave the day of the graduation?"

"I leave the day before your graduation," I clarify.

His eyes are searching the room as if thinking of an alternative. "Well, good thing I have my passport up to date." Just as I'd predicated, he's already thinking of coming with me, which is why I've already prepared my reply.

"You can't come with me," I inform him.

His brows furrow. "Why the hell not?" he practically shouts

back.

"You have to stay here and graduate, that's why."

His body has completely gone tense underneath mine. "Being with you is more important than me graduating."

Now he's just pissing me off. "How can you think not graduating is more important than being at a runway show? You have worked too damn hard for you to not walk that graduation line. And if you think for one second it's not important, think of how your sister would feel if she heard what you were saying right now," I throw at him, knowing the question will make him rethink his decision.

Dumbfounded, his head snaps back as he angrily narrows his eyes at me. I'd expected him to argue my statement, but his silence is puzzling as he lies beneath me.

"I promise I tried to get out of it, Matt. I truly did, but they've involved their lawyers and there's nothing I can do at this point," I somberly state, hoping he'll say something. I'll take anything at this point.

Closing his eyes as he lets out a sigh, he throws his arm over his face. "Why can't anything in our relationship be easy?" he asks. Understanding his meaning, I sigh with him. When it comes to our relationship, we've had to face one obstacle or another to hold onto our love. When will it ever be easy?

"Remember when you asked me if our love was worth fighting for?" I ask, remembering that day very well. It wasn't one of our happiest days, but it was the day Matt reminded me of how much we do love each other. "I think it is."

Taking his arm from his face, he looks up at me. "Yes, it is," he agrees. "But it still doesn't change the fact that I'd rather go with you."

"You're going to walk that graduation line for me, your sister, and every darn person who has ever been there to encourage you to graduate, mister," I order, gently pushing my finger into his chest. Matt is now chuckling at my words, making me feel a little better. "Promise me," I add, hoping this will keep him from changing his mind.

He's silent for a moment—too long for my liking—but eventually his chest rises and falls before he mumbles, "Alright, but I'm only doing this for you," making my lips go up into a triumphant smile.

Sitting up, our faces are mere inches apart. "It's not going to be the same without you, beautiful," he admits.

"I know, but you have to remember that the people you love don't have to be physically at your side for you to know their heart is with you," I state, rubbing my palm against his tattoo. He looks down at the same spot my eyes are currently focused on and we both sit in silence for the next minute before he pulls us to lie back down on the bed. My cheek rests above his chest as I listen to his heartbeat thump into my ear, thinking of how close I came to almost losing him. With every day that passes, I cherish every moment I can with Matt, because I can't imagine a day without him.

Chapter Twenty-Five

Matt

MY EYES FOLLOW Abigail as she slowly moves around the room, checking and double checking her surroundings as if frightened she'll forget something. A silence has taken over the room since this morning when we'd awoken. Her answers have been short and to the point, occasionally a tinge of bitterness was added to her responses. She'd profusely apologized for her attitude, but I'd brushed it off knowing it was the resentfulness she was carrying that was speaking.

These past few days have been both bitter and sweet. Abigail had wanted to make sure she was completely involved with every detail of the preparations for my graduation tomorrow, and I'd willingly allowed her to have full control of it all; anything to keep a smile between us.

She pauses to take another turn around the room for the fourth time since I've started counting, her left hand tightly clasped around the bracelet on her right wrist. The sight tugs at my lips, a smile forms knowing how much she loves that thing. She rarely takes it off except for when she runs or is ordered by her job to do so.

She's still fiddling with her bracelet when I command, "Come here," beckoning her with my fingers. She lets out a sigh before she starts walking over to me. Reaching out for her wrist, I tug her down on top of me and as she always knows to do, straddles my waist.

This time, though, I pull her into my arms so she's flush against my chest. "I'm going to miss you," I say into her hair, my nose inhaling the sweet scent of her shampoo. The arms wrapped around my waist tighten as she says, "I'm going to miss you, too." Her somber words full of sadness.

My hand is already gliding up and down her back in a desperate need to comfort her, but in reality I feel the need to touch her to comfort myself.

"I really wish I didn't have to go," she rasps out. By the sound of her voice, I know she's holding back tears.

"It's fine. It's only a graduation where I'll be sitting around for four hours trying not to fall asleep."

She pinches my side, making me wince. "It *is* a big deal."

"Says who?" I tease. She groans into my chest knowing she can't answer. "If you want, we can FaceTime the entire time I'm sitting there," I suggest.

Her silence worries me, but I'm given an answer as to why she's quiet when I hear a slight sniffle come from her. Pulling her chin up to look at me, I see her tear stricken eyes blinking. "Don't cry, beautiful," I plead, but my request only makes it worse as she lets out a whimper with her next breath.

Wanting to stop her crying, I kiss her. My sole purpose is to kiss her as if it's the last time I will see her so the memory will stay with her until she comes back. Rolling her body so she's now under me, I grab her thigh to wrap her leg around me, thrusting my body between her legs. My tongue slowly dances

251

against her own, exploring every inch of her mouth. The barrier of clothing between us is frustrating and I want nothing more than to tear her clothes off, but Abigail is already beating me to the task as she starts tugging my shirt up and over my head. Her warm hands rub against my ribcage, sending a spark of shivers through my body. My hands have already found their way into her shirt and are kneading her breasts, while Abigail's hands are unbuttoning my pants and reaching inside to wrap her hand around me. I let out a groan into her mouth, praying she's not going to make me stop this time.

"Please, Matt. I need you," she pleads, pulling me tighter into her body with her leg. She already has my pants halfway down my ass when I realize she is still fully dressed. There is definitely something wrong with this situation. Breaking our kiss as I yank my body back, I tug her to sit up, my hands pulling her shirt up and off. She helps me with her bra and next I'm impatiently tugging down her pants. She's about to reach for my own pants when I stop her to take a moment to stare down at her in front of me. Her body is nothing but perfection as it lays naked and ready for me.

Craving the taste of her skin, I lower my head and start kissing at her collarbone, slowly working my way down between the valley of her breasts. I can smell the faint floral scented lotion she applies after showering; the scent is pure torture to my senses as I run my nose close to her skin. Slowly, my tongue glides and tastes every inch on its way down her body as I leave a trail of kisses behind. Her little mews of pleasure are encouragement enough to keep tantalizing the both of us.

My rock hard dick is demanding I strip myself of my remaining clothes, but my desire to please Abigail first always overtakes my own needs. Abigail suppresses a giggle when I reach her stomach and swirl my tongue around her belly button.

Her hands are attempting to shove me away to keep from tickling her, but the action pushes me further down her body to the spot my mouth has been searching for.

Using my hands to fully spread her legs open, I take one quick peek up her body and her lust filled eyes are staring back at mine. Making sure my eyes are locked onto hers, I lick the center of her heat and I'm rewarded as I watch her throw her head back to moan.

My cock jumps from the sound and taste, but it's not enough. I want more. Clamping my lips down on her clit, my tongue swirls between the center of her folds. I can feel her nails digging into my hair, gripping and pulling, as if she fears I'll move. Her body is wiggling under my mouth, causing me to reach under her and take her ass into my hands to keep her still. I can't resist squeezing her ass as I bite down on her clit. She lets out a yelp and tries to pull away, but I keep her firmly locked in place as I suck the spot to relieve some of the ache. I know she's nearly ready to come from the sounds she's making and the way she keeps pushing herself harder into my mouth. Already knowing her body well and what it takes to make her reach her peak, I have her screaming within seconds as she starts coming into my mouth. I nearly come myself when I hear her pleasured screams. Her body is now lightly twitching as I lap up the remaining juices left between her legs, making sure I take in as much of her taste as I can.

When I sit up to look at her again, her body is limp and her chest is rapidly rising and falling, but her eyes are still closed as she takes in her breaths. Stepping off the bed, I push down my pants and boxer briefs to shuck them aside before I slowly climb back over her. She welcomes me into her open arms while her legs tug me forward. My cock is resting against her center where my mouth was just moments ago, and her heat is torture as my cock lies in its warmth.

Abigail lifts her hips, urging me to enter her and I no longer have the willpower to resist. Entering in one hard thrust, my dick is surrounded by the warmth of her walls; the one place it's been waiting to be in for the last three weeks. As much as I want to rapidly pound in and out of her, I force myself to slow down, needing to savor every second of making love to her. The last thing I want to do is come so fast inside of Abigail that she believes I was a greedy bastard just wanting to fuck her. No, I don't want Abigail thinking sex is all I ever want from her. It's not. What I crave is her touch… her presence next to me… her soul. That's what I look forward to when I wake up each morning next to her and at the end of the night as I fall asleep in her arms.

Her whimpers turn desperate. Her nails dig harder into my back as she holds onto my body. With her legs tightly wrapped around my thighs, she's urging me closer to her, her hips moving in an equal rhythm to my plunging.

"More, Matt. Oh God, Yes!" she screams as I push deeper inside of her. My lips slam down onto hers to kiss her as I obey her command and increase my speed to push us both over the edge. It's been so long I can't hold out any longer and I can feel by balls tightening up, ready to release inside of her.

"Please tell me you're close, beautiful. I'm about to finish," I warn her. Her moans become louder and the walls of her core are tightening around my shaft, as if answering my question. With a couple more thrusts, she's screaming my name and squeezing every ounce of come out of me as I explode inside of her. For a split second my world darkens and spins out of control as every muscle in my body stiffens with my release.

When I've released the last of myself inside Abigail, I slowly bring my body to a standstill, both our chests rising and falling as we attempt to catch our breath. My heart is racing out of control as it pounds against my chest and I look down into Abigail's beautiful face. I see her slowly opening her eyes with a smile, leaving me more breathless than I already am.

Pushing the hair from her face to better see her, I say, "I love you, beautiful." She reaches up and places her palm on my face in return.

"I love you, more." A smile radiates from her lips as she reaches up and kisses me.

When I pull my lips from her to end the kiss, the smile I was returning to her turns into a frown when I hear a knock at the door. I don't need to ask who it is because regardless of who's knocking, it's a reminder that Abigail has to leave.

Reluctantly pulling away from Abigail, I wrap myself in our bed sheet as she rushes to the bathroom. When I open the door, I see Julio standing at it.

"I'll let the car know to give you guys a couple more minutes to say goodbye," he says before turning to walk away.

After shutting the door, I walk over to the bathroom and join Abigail in the shower. The entire time it's spent in silence as we quickly wash each other. When we're both dressed again, I help her carry her luggage out to the living room, handing it over to Julio to take out to the car.

I'm about to walk Abigail out when she stops me and says, "Do you mind staying inside? I have to keep telling myself it's a quick photo shoot in order to be able to walk away from you," she explains.

Understanding how hard this is on her because it's just as hard on me, I give her a nod in agreement. Although I've agreed to stay behind, I'm still full of anguish as I watch Julio follow her out to the car. When the front door shuts behind them, I stand in the middle of my foyer, alone, with only my agony to keep me company.

Abigail

IT FEELS LIKE déjà vu all over again, but this time Matt isn't standing at the end of the driveway to watch me leave. I didn't allow him this time. It was hard enough the first time when I'd left for New York. This time would have torn me completely to pieces.

The drive to the airport is a blur as the scenery outside the car speeds past me. Instead of allowing myself to wallow in the agony of my heartache, I keep repeating the memory of what Matt and I shared before I'd left. It's the only thing keeping me from breaking down. *Four days, three nights, ninety-six hours. That's all I have left until I'm back in Matt's arms. I can make it. It will be over before I know it,* I keep telling myself. The hardest part of that equation is the day after tomorrow, one of the most important days of that calculation.

An hour later, I'm sitting next to Julio in the airport terminal counting the minutes that go by until it's time to board my plane. I'm staring at my phone debating whether I should call Matt. In my heart, I'm craving the sound of his voice, but I'm afraid the moment I hear him on the line my heart will return to the dreadful ache of his loss from my side.

No longer resisting my temptation, I start pounding away at my screen and soon I hear Matt answering, "Hi, beautiful." The words alone make me light up.

"God, I miss you already," I quietly say to him.

"I missed you the moment you walked out the door."

"How much longer until I get to see you again?" I ask in a teasing tone, but my heart is far from wanting to laugh.

We spend the next couple of minutes discussing the difference in the time zones, trying to coordinate our next phone call.

It isn't long before they are announcing my boarding call and my heart sinks knowing I have to end the phone call. Since I'm flying the first part of the trip as a first class passenger, they are announcing for me to board first.

With one final *I love you* for the day, I dreadfully push the red button on the screen, already missing his voice. With a heavy sigh, I look over to Julio as he walks by my side to the entrance of the terminal. As he usually does in these situations, his pain stricken eyes are looking back at me. With heavy steps, I lead the way up to the plane and we take our seats.

The flight attendant is ordering everyone to buckle up in preparation for takeoff. She briskly walks right by me when my phone starts ringing to the lyrics of *I'm Sexy and I know It,* and my eyes roll as far back as they can go. Retrieving it from my purse, I see Trey's face staring back at me I ask myself why I ever allowed him to handle my phone. Remembering, I let out a sigh. He'd changed his ringtone the day shit hit the fan with the media and I let him use it to contact everyone. The flight attendant has already returned to my aisle, piercing me with a glare as I lift the phone to answer.

"Ma'am, all devices need to be turned off. We're taking off shortly." I nod to acknowledge that I've heard her as I say, "Hello," into it. My gut is telling me to take this call. She isn't too happy with my raised finger asking for a second.

"Have you gotten on the plane?" Trey asks, sounding breathless, as if he's been running.

"Yes, I'm on it now. Why?" For some odd reason I hold my breath as I wait for him to answer.

"Get off it, now!" he shouts into the phone.

Puzzled, yet still silent since he didn't give me an answer, I frantically ask, "What's going on?" My heart is now beating out of control as I fear something has happened to Matt. "Trey answer me!" I demand. Time freezes and it feels like an eternity while I wait for his response.

"You don't have to go, supermodel. I found a way for you to get out of doing the show," he breathlessly replies, sounding as if he's running.

"Are you sure?" I doubtfully ask.

"Yes. I'm here at the airport to pick you up. I came as soon as I found out." The sound of the airport announcements can be overhead through the phone.

I'm still sitting in my seat with my breath still stolen from my lungs as I stare at the seat in front of me in a daze, trying to register his words.

"Abigail?" Julio's thick accent at my side brings me back from my trance. Looking around, I see them already shutting the door to the plane, making me jump up from my seat.

"Stop!" I shout over to the flight attendant at the door. The flight attendant at my side and the one I'm shouting at are looking at me as if I've lost my mind, as is Julio.

"Ma'am, you need to take your seat. We're about to take off," she insists.

At this point, I'm tugging at Julio to stand up. "We're getting off!" I shout. He looks perplexed by my order, but slowly stands. Shoving at him, he finally starts to move towards the exit.

"Ma'am, once you exit the plane, you won't be able to come back on."

"I won't need to get back on," I say, urging Julio to move faster.

"Abigail, what's going on?" he worriedly asks, already reaching for our carry-on bags overhead.

I don't immediately answer as I urge him to hand me my bag so we can get off the plane. The few passengers we pass on the way out are looking at me as if I'm crazy. Stepping into the terminal gate, my heart is uncontrollably racing and my mind is in a whirlwind of emotions; the most powerful being excitement.

"Abigail, are you sure this is a good idea?" Julio continues to interrogate from my side as we briskly walk out to the departure area.

"I don't know, but there's no going back now," I reply, watching from the window as the plane starts pulling back on the runway. For some odd reason, knowing I'm not on the plane feels as if the weight of the world has been lifted from my shoulders.

Remembering Trey said he was at the airport, I quickly turn to head towards the main entrance, practically jogging to get there. When I see Trey anxiously waiting amongst a crowd of people, I've never been happier to see him in my life.

When he sees me rushing towards him, he has the widest smile I've ever seen on Trey. His head is already nodding with enthusiasm when he says, "I can't wait to get you home. Matt is going to shit a brick when he sees you." His words make me laugh. It's so typical of Trey to always find a way to do so.

"How did you get me out of the contract?" I enthusiastically ask.

With a shake of his head, he replies, "I'll tell you on the way home. Let's go, traffic is a bitch right now."

My steps cannot be quick enough to get me back to Trey's Jeep. The minute we're enclosed inside, I'm already grilling him for details. With a light chuckle, he starts to explain.

"They fucked up by stating *weeks* on a contract that was dated when signed," he states. I'm still confused by what this means and he sees it on my face. "In the contract it states you were to spend *one week* in New York and the *next two weeks* finalizing the show in Paris," he emphasizes. "You see? They fucked up by not specifying the length of the contract. I didn't realize that at first because it never occurred to me. I know, rookie manager mistake," he states holding his hand up. "I've learned my lesson. Had I caught that from the beginning we wouldn't have had to go through the headaches we went through. Anyway, that's how I was able to get you out."

"Are you sure?" I hesitantly ask, although I'm beaming from head to toe from his explanation.

He nods his head. "I'm sure. Like I said, I spoke to one of the law professors at the school who happens to have a brother who specializes in entertainment law. By the way, he's your new lawyer in all this shit," he clarifies. "We called him on the spot and he's already issuing the paperwork needed to counteract the shit their lawyer sent you. He's assured me you're no longer obligated to satisfy the contract and he's also going to hit them with charges for them making you do all that last minute shit that wasn't in the contract. If they want a fight, we're ready for them this time."

"I told you we should have hired a lawyer from the beginning?" I utter at our stupidity.

"Like I said, a rookie mistake that I won't be making again," he repeats in his defense.

"We had a lot of shit going on these past couple of days with them threatening you, Abigail. Between you and Matt bickering the entire week and me trying to figure out how to get you out of this, I'm surprised my head hasn't exploded. This shit is making me rethink my five percent only salary," he smugly says, making me laugh at his response. "I'm pretty sure big boy here gets paid more than I do," he adds, hitching his finger towards the back seat.

"I'm on salary, it's not the same," Julio throws back at him with a hint of amusement.

"Well, that sucks," Trey, replies.

I roll my eyes at their playful bickering. When Trey turns onto our street and into our driveway, my heart feels as if it's ready to explode from the thought of seeing Matt again so soon. Trey hasn't even turned the Jeep off before I'm swinging the door open and climbing out of the Jeep. I practically run to the front door and rush inside. Matt is sitting on the couch playing video games when I enter. When he turns to see me, he stands and his face goes pale as if he's seen a ghost. I catapult myself into his arms and he catches me, but loses his balance and stumbles back down to sit on the couch. We're both laughing into each other's mouth as we kiss.

I'm still giggling against his mouth when he says, "Damn, that was the fastest week ever," making me laugh harder.

"Yes, it was," I playfully play along, kissing him again. He pulls away after the kiss, stunned as he looks at me.

"As happy as I am to see you, why are you back so soon?" he asks, and I give a playful pout from the question. "Not that I'm complaining," he quickly adds.

"Trey found a way to get me out of the contract," I burst out with excitement. For a moment, Matt looks shocked, but just as quickly turns to Trey.

"How did you manage that?"

For the next half hour, Trey is forced to explain everything all over again, but this time I happily listen as I sit on Matt's lap, tucked against his chest. His arms have been tightly wrapped around me as if he's afraid of letting me go. Last night's lack of sleep has already caught up to me and with the rumble of Matt's deep voice vibrating against my ear, I'm soon falling asleep. This time, though, I'm falling asleep with a smile on my face, something I haven't been able to do since the day I found out about the show.

Matt

"ARE YOU SURE there is absolutely *no* way Abigail is going to get in trouble for not being on that plane right now?" I quietly repeat, hoping Trey has heard me. I'm trying not to raise my voice since I know Abigail has fallen asleep. Her warm breath against my neck has slowed and her body is lax in my arms. I'm happy she's finally sleeping. She's been restless at night for the past week and it was affecting me as well since it would constantly wake me.

"Dude, I told you, I've got it taken care of. Abigail has a lawyer now and if those fuckers want a fight, we're giving them one."

His statement doesn't leave me convinced, but now that I have Abigail in my arms, I'm reluctant to let her go. So my only choice is to believe him.

"This better not blow up in her face," I say, knowing how upset Abigail will be if the media got ahold of this story. Since the day I met her, she's always avoided being in the spotlight unless it was required for a job. If this got messy with lawyers, she'd be talked about for months, and it's not the type of publicity she needs. "I don't know, man," I say, still doubtful as I stare off into the backyard.

"Look, Matt," Trey sternly says to catch my attention. Snapping my head to look at him, he's already continuing. "I know what I'm doing. Trust me. I may be new to this shit, but I'm not stupid. It's her career on the line and without it, I don't get paid. I wouldn't be doing this if I knew it would blow up in our faces," he conveys.

"Plus, I know how much she wants to be there tomorrow. How *we all* want her to be there tomorrow. It's the reason why I never gave up," he admits.

"Thank you," I tell him, understanding why this past week he's been acting like an asshole half the time. He was just as frustrated from dealing with the situation as Abigail.

"No problem," he answers with a light smile. "Just don't expect me to buy you a graduation present now, fucker."

My response is laced with humor. "You didn't have to buy me anything. A blowjob would have been just fine," I reply.

He perks up. "Is that what you're giving me?"

We both bust up laughing, making Abigail stir in my arms. We freeze, our laughter immediately dying in fear we've awoken her. Rubbing my hand up and down her back to soothe her back to sleep, my eyes look towards Trey as he stands.

"Thanks, man," I repeat, watching him curtly nod and head in the direction of his room. Sitting on the couch, I think to myself how much I've missed my playful bantering with Trey. He never fails to make me laugh during the worst situations.

Kissing Abigail on the temple while I continue to hold her, my eyes wander off to stare out into the air ahead of me. With a smile on my face, and happier than I've felt in days, I think of how much I'm actually looking forward to graduating now. Something I haven't felt in the past year.

Chapter Twenty-Six

Abigail

MATT STEPS UP behind me and starts nuzzling my ear. Soon he's trailing warm kisses across my neck, making me giggle from how his light stubble is tickling my skin.

"Matt, stop it!" I say. He stops, but soon my neck is being bitten on, making me laugh. "I'm going to cut myself if you keep tickling me," I lecture him.

He lifts his face from my neck and releases a heavy sigh.

"Why are you doing all this? David and Trey's mom's already said they'd help chop everything when they get here," he reminds me.

Ignoring his protest, I keep chopping. "I know, but I just feel bad for making them do anything at all. I'm almost done anyway," I state, placing the last vegetable on the cutting board. Matt's chin is now resting on my shoulder as I finish and transfer the chopped pieces to a container. Closing it up, I hand it to Matt.

"Here, make yourself useful and put it in the fridge," I order.

He snickers, but takes it from my hands while I begin cleaning the counter. The last thing I want is the house to look like a mess when everyone arrives.

"What the hell, beautiful? Is this why you came to bed late?" he asks, referring to the full fridge. I had indeed stayed up late preparing everything for today. My body is exhausted and ready to collapse from being sleep deprived, but I'd gone back on my word of allowing the parents to help and done it all myself. The original plan was because I'd thought I wasn't going to be here for the celebration, but now I felt responsible to do everything since it was at our house.

When I finish wiping down the counter, I turn to see a scowl on Matt's face as he returns from the garage.

"I had to put the container in the spare fridge."

"Thank you. I'm almost done. Why don't you go start getting ready," I suggest, already turning and looking for the next task I need to complete.

"You are done," he states from behind me as I feel my body being lifted off the ground and thrown over his shoulder.

"Matt! Put me down, you're going to hurt your shoulder!"

"You're on my good shoulder," he conveys before he smacks my ass. The smack of his hand is sharp and fast, leaving a lingering sting on the cheek.

"Ouch! That hurt!" I bellow before going back to my earlier protesting. Julio's laughter can be heard as we disappear down the darkened hallway to our room. The entire time the only view I have is of Matt's ass. I stop complaining as I take in the view.

After entering our room, he spins around so he can shut the door then turns again before he tosses me onto the bed. "You have to stop throwing me on the bed like a caveman," I giggle as I lift myself up on my elbows to look at him. He has an amused smile on his lips as he starts taking off his shirt.

"What are you waiting for?" Matt asks, stopping with his

hands on the waist of his shorts.

"I'm waiting for you to take off your shorts," I reply.

"Tit for tat. I've taken off my shirt, now take off yours."

Doing as he asks, I take off my shirt and toss it to him while I lay back on my elbows, wiggling my eyebrows for him to continue. He slowly starts pushing his shorts down and my eyes never leave the center of his body where his erection is now upright and pointing back at me. Matt slowly starts climbing onto the bed, his dark eyes now commanding I stay locked onto them. He hasn't even touched my body yet and it's already igniting from head to toe. A spark of shivers explodes inside me when his hand briefly touches my skin to pull my yoga pants down. Lifting my hips so he can drag them down, I have to bite down on my lips to hide my whimpers. The entire time his smile never left his lips and his eyes look hungry... the meal being me.

Swallowing, I say, "Matt, we're going to be late."

"And..." he huskily replies before he lowers his head to bite down on my earlobe.

Oh... Dear... God... I've completely lost all control with that one single word as I pull Matt down and demand he kiss me. His mouth slams down onto mine and I let out the whimper I've been containing. His hand is now reaching in between my legs and suddenly I feel Matt's fingers probing at my entrance, deliberately teasing me as he glides his fingers up and down my inner lips. I'm about to scream for him to quit teasing me when he slides his fingers inside of me and I let out a moan into his mouth.

"Someone's warm and ready," he says just above a whisper. The rumble of his deep voice mixed with the shivers shooting down my body to where he's currently inside me makes my blood rise to find my peak. I can feel his erection pushing up against my thigh and from the force of its throbbing, I know it's demanding it replace his fingers. Lifting my leg to wrap around his back, I urge him closer, his hand trapped in between our bodies.

"Someone's also desperate," he murmurs against my lips. I pull him down again to answer, but I'm quickly denied my request when he demands, "I want to hear you beg," he says. My form of begging is adding pressure to my already tightened leg wrapped around his hip. "Say it," he huskily demands.

Throwing my head back in frustration, I say, "God, Matt. Please!"

Within a split second, his fingers are gone and he's plunging into my body, the hilt of his cock hitting me perfectly on my clit. I'm expecting him to begin rapidly pounding into me, but he surprises me by slowly rocking back and forth as if needing to take his time. One hand is at my head, extending his body up so he can keep looking into my eyes, and the other tightly grips my ass as he lifts me to meet each and every thrust. His mouth starts trailing kisses along my shoulder and my sleep filled daze I had been walking around with all morning is quickly replaced with a course of fireworks exploding through my body. It's then that Matt's thrusting increases and I'm thrown over the edge once more as he's grunting my name.

His rocking slows, eventually coming to a stop. Throwing his body to land beside me, we lay side-by-side, breathless as our hearts race out of control. Grabbing my body so he's now spooning me from behind me, his lips are once again laying kisses along my shoulder.

"Beautiful, there's something we need to talk about," he voices.

My once racing heart has stopped in fear as my body goes rigid in his arms. I don't know what to expect with those words.

"Have you decided on our future yet?" The dreaded question causes my heart to sink to the pit of my stomach. I haven't even had time to fully process my answer before he adds, "Because we haven't been using protection and I don't think you've gone back for your shot," before placing a gentle kiss on my shoulder. This time his lips linger longer than expected. My heart has starting beating again, but just as rapidly as before as I take in the realization of his words and I'm shocked into silence. I told myself I'd go back and get the shot again, but I knew I had time since Matt wasn't supposed to be having sex yet. Then I'd gotten distracted with having to deal with the designer and I'd completely forgotten. Matt has a way of making me lose all coherent thoughts of responsibility; leaving me on the verge of begging him to take me.

"I'm sorry," I guiltily reply, feeling like the most irresponsible person in the world. I feel him tense up against my back and a dreadful feeling of him being angry crosses my mind, but just as quickly I feel his body relax and I'm soon being turned to face him.

"What do you have to be sorry about?" he confusedly asks. The pang of guilt is still lingering with his question, causing me to look away. He turns my head to face him. "I wouldn't be sorry," he whispers down to me.

I'm left confused by his words, until he clarifies. "Would you be mad at me if I told you that I knew each time I should have used a condom, but I didn't want to?" he asks. My breath catches for a moment at his admission before I raise my hand up to brush against his cheek.

"No, Matt, I'm not mad at you," I truthfully reply. As if relieved by my answer, he drops his head down onto my chest. I place my hand along his arm where his tattoo is at as I contemplate my next words, but I'm unable to say them as Trey begins banging on the door to remind us it's almost time to leave.

Reaching for my phone on our nightstand to check the time, my eyes go wide. "Shit. Matt, we're going to be late," I say, already scrambling from the bed.

Instead of reacting as I expected him to, he instead lays back down on the bed with his arms crossed behind his head. Looking over at him, he is relaxed and without a care in the world. "Matt, get up! We have to take a shower," I scold, rushing over to my dresser to grab some underwear.

"I'm thinking of skipping the shower. I want to graduate with your smell all over me." I stop dead in my tracks on the way to the shower and turn to face him with a disgusted look.

"No. It's not happening," I tell him.

"Why not?" I hear him ask as I begin walking again.

Turning on the water and checking to make sure it's the right temperature, I take a peek out of the door to find Matt still where I'd left him, but now looking smugly back at me. Knowing Matt, he most likely isn't getting up from the bed to try to prove his point. So I do the one and only thing that will get him up. I bribe him.

"If you come take a shower, I'll give you a blowjob in here!" I yell before stepping under the water.

YOU OWE ME some really *good sex for this – Matt*

I already gave you sex this morning. – Abigail. Immediately shooting off another text. *Twice* – Abigail. I add for clarification.

Blowjobs don't count because you're not screaming my name. - Matt

I start laughing uncontrollably from the words on the screen. Kelly looks at me as if I've lost my mind and Mrs. Johnson snaps her head in my direction and narrows her eyes at me to behave, forcing me to suppress another giggle. My phone vibrates again and when I look down, I see a picture of Matt pretending to be sleeping, his tongue hanging out. I clamp my lips as tight as I can and hold my breath to contain the bout of laughter tightening in my chest.

I am so going to strangle you when we get home. Mrs. Johnson is ready to punish me for laughing this much! – Abigail.

I push send as Mrs. Johnson glances at me once more, her narrowed eyes still watching me. She's already had to tell me twice to behave. When I tried to explain it was Matt who was making me laugh, she told me to put my phone away. I really couldn't because there was no room left in the clutch I'd brought, the space in it was being taken up by the graduation picture of Matt and Emily; the first picture I'd ever seen of them together. At the last minute, I'd run back inside the house and grabbed it. Inside my heart, I felt some part of Emily needed to be here, even if it was only a picture.

My phone vibrates again, breaking my thoughts.

You tell Mrs. Johnson the only one allowed to punish you is me. I'll let you strangle my dick anytime. You don't even have to ask. ;) –Matt

My eyes go wide from his response. My phone vibrates as I'm trying to reply, but instead of it being Matt messaging me, it's someone else. Clearing out of Matt's message screen, I see it's Julio who has texted me. I look to my side where he's sitting and with a forward tilt of his chin, he commands for me to read the message.

If you keep it up I may have to use bodily force to protect you from Mrs. Johnson. I really don't want hurting such a sweet woman on my conscious. – Julio

Looking back at him, I snicker. His eyebrow raises and

he points his chin in Mrs. Johnson's direction, and when I look she's eyeing me. I give her an innocent smile and she seems satisfied as she looks back towards the podium.

Matt wasn't kidding when he said this would be boring. If it wasn't for his text messages I probably *would* have fallen asleep. My eyes are staring down from the seats high up in the stadium to find Matt. As if he's sensing I'm staring at him, he looks and flashes me with his smile. My body melts from head to toe, and my insides turn upside down. Our eyes stay locked onto each other's for another minute and our connection is broken when they announce they will soon be calling the names. Although Matt's name is towards the middle, he's graduating with honors, which puts him at the front of the calling order for the commencement.

Ten minutes later, Matt is standing at the head of the stage waiting for his turn, the entire time my heart is swelling with every heartbeat. He looks up at me as he waits to step up and flashes me with a smile that he's soon clenching with wide eyes as if he's nervous. The sight makes me giggle from how he's not taking this seriously, but he takes a deep breath as if preparing himself as the person in front of him is now leaving the stage.

I'm holding my breath the moment his name is called and my body is overjoyed with happiness as he takes the steps up onto the stage. Clutching my purse, I imagine Emily at my side watching him walk across that stage. The built up tears are obstructing my vision as I think of how close I came to missing this moment. Emily may not be here to witness him graduating, but I know deep down in my heart and soul she's here spiritually. She wouldn't miss this for the world. My heart feels as if it's going to burst from my chest from how proud I feel watching him take his diploma and look down at it with pride. A second later, he's looking back up at me and holds it high in the air. Our little group hollers to him and he walks off the stage with an excited smile on his face.

I stand there watching him make his way back to his seat, telling myself this is only the beginning of his journey in life. Although Emily won't be here at his side throughout it, I know without a doubt there is a reason why she sent me to Matt. I was going to make sure to not disappoint her. I love them both too much to do so.

Two boring hours later and several text messages of convincing Matt to stay put and ride out the rest of the ceremony, we're finally exiting the stadium. Trey's acceptance had to have been the most entertaining of them all. He acted more like an elementary student accepting his diploma than a college student. His, "Fuck Yeah!" holler, while saluting two rock star fingers high in the air, could probably have been heard outside. My little group of friends might have been laughing, Trey's father included, but Mrs. Johnson's eyes looked as if they were going to pop out of their sockets as her body turned three shades of crimson from embarrassment.

Once outside, I spot Matt already walking over to me and I rush to meet him halfway, practically catapulting myself into his arms. My eyes are swelling up with tears again as I hold him tight, refusing to let him go just yet.

"I'm so proud of you, Matt," I say into his ear. His arms tighten around my waist, acknowledging my words. "I love you," I add.

"I love you, too, beautiful."

When we pull apart, Julio is patiently standing at Matt's side and he holds out his hand for Matt to shake. Willingly he obliges, but adds a half man hug with it. Julio slaps him on the back, also congratulating him. After several rounds of hugs and kisses to everyone else, we are now leaving the school grounds and are on our way back home to celebrate.

Slowly, our home begins to fill with friends and guest, the sound of conversations and laughter overtaking the entire house. Seeing how hard I had worked to prepare everything for everyone's arrival, Mrs. Johnson insisted I enjoy my time with Matt while she and the other moms take care of everything else. After the glares she gave me in the stadium, I knew there was no arguing with that woman, so I obeyed and kept myself tucked at Matt's side.

Matt excuses himself to go to the bathroom, leaving me to mingle throughout the room. When I've noticed Matt has taken longer than usual, I go off in search of him and find him sitting on the edge of our bed somberly staring down at the frame that was once in my purse. His body is slumped forward and a slight pang of fear takes over inside of me from not knowing how Matt will react to me having taken the picture.

He looks up as if he's heard me enter and quickly wipes at his eyes. My steps quicken to get to him as he stands from the bed.

"I'm sorry. My lips were dry and I thought maybe you'd have some chap stick in your purse," he says, as if he feels he needs to explain how he found the frame. My earlier fear when I walked in is now replaced with sorrow.

He cocks his head to the side as he asks, "Why was it in your purse?"

Now I'm the one trying to explain myself. "I thought it was appropriate for her to be there when you graduated. Besides the photo album I put together, this is the only other picture we have of Emily." I catch myself referring to the pictures as if they belong to both of us. The thought makes me catch my breath as Matt's eyebrows curiously lift.

"I guess that makes sense. That photo album would *not*

fit in this purse. Your bigger one, maybe, but definitely not this one," he says with an added chuckle. "Thank you for bringing it, it really means a lot to me that some part of her was there."

My earlier fear and guilt has now been replaced with joy as I let out the breath I was holding in one giant gush as I laugh at his words. "You're welcome," I reply, wrapping my arms around his neck. He pulls me up against his body and lays a kiss upon my lips.

"You make me feel like the happiest girl in the world sometimes," I tell him against his mouth.

He jerks his head back in astonishment. "Only sometimes?" he asks, looking as if I've offended him.

Playfully swatting at his chest, I say, "You know what I mean."

A faint knock at the door tells us that we're not alone, and when I turn I see David and Kelly standing at the door. "Sorry to interrupt, but Mr. Johnson wants to give a speech and asked us to come find you."

"No problem," Matt tells him. Instead of walking out as I had expected Matt to do, he looks over to the both of them, but his eyes wander down to Kelly's hand where she is currently wearing her engagement ring. "So you're finally going to make an honest man out of him?" he asks her.

Kelly bursts out a light laugh. "He's always been an honest man," she says, her eyes locked onto David's as she declares the words.

"True. Out of all of us, he was always the good boy," Matt expresses.

"I knew what I had from the beginning," David adds while smiling and lifting Kelly's hand to kiss the back of it. Kelly returns his smile.

"Yeah, well, I'm not the only one who needs to be made an

honest woman," Kelly dryly expresses out loud.

"Yeah, well, it's really up to her when. Hopefully soon," Matt replies. The words make my heart skip and I'm afraid to look at Matt for fear of his expression. I'm afraid I'd be looking at the face of a man who feels as if his heart is slowly breaking from having to wait.

"Come on," Matt instructs, wrapping his arm around my waist and looking at both Kelly and David. "If we don't get out of here, Mrs. Johnson will come looking for us."

"You do *not* want to face the wrath of that lady. I've learned my lesson after today," I voice, making everyone laugh.

"We know," David comments, leading us out of the door.

Walking past our dresser on the way out, Kelly's statement reminds me of the little box still sitting in there and the future that Matt has mentioned on several occasions. I've purposely avoided trying to answer him, but I know eventually he'll be demanding I be honest with him. Fortunately, that day isn't today as we join everyone in the living room. I may have been saved this time, but I know next time I won't easily be able to avoid the subject and it may just ruin the plans I already have.

Chapter Twenty-Seven

Abigail

I'M HOLDING MATT'S hand as the doctor delivers the news.

"Your recovery has gone well, Mr. Garcia. I've never seen a more healthy heart than yours after the trauma it was put through," the cardiologist proudly proclaims. "You're free to resume your normal activities. Including sex," he emphasizes with a twinkle of his eye.

I'm biting my lip to keep from laughing, but Matt is quick to inform him. "Oh, my heart passed the sex test a week ago," he admits without shame.

With a quirk of his brow, the doctor sarcastically replies, "Why does that not surprise me?" as he looks over in my direction.

Just as quickly, he clears his throat. "I'll fill out all your paperwork and immediately send it over to give you medical clearance. Congratulations on your contract by the way."

"Thank you," Matt gratefully replies.

Minutes later, we're exiting the room with a copy of Matt's clearance paperwork and we're both smiling from ear to ear.

"Want to go on a run before your photo shoot?" Matt's eagerly asks as we reach the car.

This afternoon, I'm shooting my first promotional shots for the running company for the Seattle Marathon. I've been looking forward to this shoot all week and it was hard to keep the excitement from my face today.

"You sure you want to run already?" I hesitantly ask, wondering if it would be a good idea to push him so soon. He notices my worry as we reach the car and before I have a chance to reach for the door handle, my body is being trapped against the car.

"I'm pretty sure my heart will do fine. You usually leave it racing faster than any run I've ever been on when I have you screaming my name." My lips grimace up to the side as I narrow my eyes at him.

"I should have held out that last week just to punish you," I playfully tease.

He's smirking as he answers near my ear, "I don't think *you* would have been able to hold out. If I recall, it was you begging towards the end." His voice drops low to purposely tantalize me.

His hands are gripping at my waist and his mouth is leaving warm kisses against my skin while I bite my lip to keep from begging him to take me right here… Right now… As he's pointed out I do so well. If it wasn't for Matt holding me tight, I would drop to the ground from my knees going weak.

"I think we should go home and do another form of cardio instead," I suggest.

"That sounds like a very good idea," he replies, slamming his lips down onto mine, kissing me until I'm whimpering from the ache traveling straight to the center between my legs. Pulling away, he leaves me practically panting from the kiss as he now adds, "You don't have to say the words for me to know you're currently begging."

I'm not going to admit he's right. I'm too stubborn to do so. But I am pushing him away so I can open the door and climb into the car so he can take me home where I know I'll have him begging soon. At least that's my plan.

I'M LOOKING AT the clock on the dashboard of my car and I grimace. I'm late... Very late, and I have Matt to blame for that. But I couldn't be happier since I'd gotten my wish and gotten Matt to beg for *me* this time.

"We're almost there, beautiful," Matt says, pulling my hand up to kiss the back of my palm. Giving him a grateful smile, I'm still disappointed in myself for being late. I'd always told myself I wouldn't revert back to my old ways, and being late was one of them. According to everyone I've spoken to who can say they've worked with me in the past, I was notorious for always making everyone wait on me.

Minutes later, we're pulling up to the park the running company had chosen and see Trey's Jeep already there, which surprises me.

"Did you know Trey was meeting us here?"

Shaking his head in response, we both climb out, already rushing to meet up with him. Trey has been surprising me more often lately. He's taken to his self-proclaimed title as if he was meant to do it from the beginning. Especially in the last few days as the media had tried reverting to their old ways when they'd discovered I'd pulled out of the fashion show.

We'd known there would be speculations as to why I'd withdrawn, but we've brushed off most of the rumors. My favorite so far was that I was pregnant and the designer had refused to allow me to walk the runway with my protruding belly. Reading the story that day reminded I needed to take another pregnancy test. But as before, it returned with a negative result. We weren't in need of restocking anytime soon thanks to Trey, who was now demanding his own company credit card for God knows why.

The unprotected sex subject got brought up again the night of the graduation, and I'd admitted that I wouldn't be upset now if I were to end up pregnant. Ironically, Matt hadn't broached the subject of our future like I had expected him to do and I was happy he hadn't done so.

Helping close the distance between us, Trey meets us half-way to the area where the production crew has set up their camera equipment for the shoot. The entire time he's been holding an excited smile on his face. Next to him is Aaron, the marketing director who is extending his hand to Matt.

Matt shakes his hand then turns to give me a skeptical look, not knowing who he is.

"Hello, there. My name is Aaron. The changing tent is over this way and I've got everything set up for the both of you," he explains, already leading us away.

Trey, who is on the other side of Matt, is being questioned why Aaron said, *the both of you.* "What did you mean by the both of us?"

"I told him how you usually run with Abigail during her training runs and I suggested he feature you too," Trey explains, shocking us both. "And, I even worked it out for you both to keep some stuff from today, along with your compensation for today's shoot." I nearly miss my step from his declaration.

"Really?"

"Yup. I'm going to make a good manager for the both of you," Trey proudly states.

"When did I say I needed a manager?" Matt asks.

"Dude, you're a fucking NFL player now. You're *going* to need a manager to get you those endorsements." Smirking, he now points in my direction. "And you, too, Abigail. I'm going to have people throwing endorsement offers at you left and right."

"Trey, I don't care about the money. You know that. I'm happy just doing what I'm doing for now." My only response is a snicker of protest. "Please, don't turn into Bill," I beg.

He looks as if he's gone pale. "I would never be like that fucker," he argues. "But don't be surprised if you get them without me having to ask. You are still Abigail Adams," he reminds me.

We've already reached the tent where Aaron is waiting with an anxious smile. "I've got several different options. My main goal for both of you is to look casual, happy, and natural during today's shoot," he explains.

"In other words, you want us to do what we regularly do while running," Matt states with a quirked eyebrow. Aaron happily claps his hands together.

"Exactly!" I chuckle at his enthusiasm.

Looking at Matt, he shrugs his shoulder and grabs my hand while he leads me under the flap of the small standing tent. Already inside are several interns, including a make-up artist standing in front of a director's chair.

"I'll start with hair and make-up since I'm a girl," I tease, stretching out the last word while taking my seat.

Matt never fails to remind me that I always take longer to get ready than he does. Oddly, he stays standing at the entrance of the tent and the intern who must be in charge of his wardrobe is staring at him, as if waiting for him to step towards her. Nodding my chin in her direction, he gets the clue and goes straight for the clothes and starts pushing hangers aside. Matt grabs a pair of shorts and a shirt and begins searching the room as if looking for something.

"Where do I change?"

"Here of course," I inform him.

"In front of all of you?" Matt asks. The intern looks perplexed from his statement.

"It's not a big deal, Matt. They're used to people changing in front of them."

"Seriously?"

"If it makes you feel any better, they'll turn around while you change," I tell him. His brow is now arched as he considers my suggestion.

"Fine."

Rolling my eyes at the childish response, I'm about to order the girls to turn, but they've already voluntarily done so after his answer. What Matt hadn't expected was for there to be a mirrored vanity across from me, which is currently giving us three a clear view of Matt's impromptu strip tease. Somehow, I feel as if I should be jealous of the intern's expressions. Their eyes are gazing into the mirror without blinking as their mouths slightly hang open. Nope, no jealousy at all anymore because I know at the end of the day Matt will be going home with me and not them. That's all that matters.

He pulls his shorts over his boxer brief clad ass and all eyes are immediately leaving the mirror to avert in different directions. The make-up artist is once more stroking her brush against my face and the other intern is fiddling through my wardrobe trying to look as if she's been doing it the entire time. He looks into the mirror, confused, as if wondering if they'd been watching the entire time. When his eyes find mine, he gives me his signature smile. I have to bite down on my lip to keep from laughing. If Matt only knew…

Another minute later, I'm now the one changing and I'm

not shy about having to do so in front of everyone like Matt was. I had to learn quickly at the beginning that changing within a minute was expected of me, and it made it easier if someone else was helping you.

With my hand laced with Matt's, we're meeting Aaron and Trey who are standing with the photographer, a pretty older looking lady who is greeting us with a radiant smile. When I fully take her in, I recognize her as the same photographer from the first shoot I did for the company. Reaching her, I'm already extending my hand out to say hello.

"It's nice to see you again," I comment, watching her eyes go wide in astonishment.

"You remember?"

Nodding my head, I say, "I had fun that day."

"Excellent, because it will pretty much go the same as last time."

If I wasn't already excited for the shoot, I'd be excited now. I don't have to pretend to be happy doing something I love do-ing. After a few quick pointers to Matt, explaining what she ex-pects from him, we're soon walking down the path of a small trail in the grassy area we're in. When we've reached the starting line marked by colored duct tape, I'm already excited for what is yet to come.

Matt faces me to say, "So we just have to act like we nor-mally do on a run?"

Giving him a nod, I say, "Yup."

"Damn, beautiful, no wonder you don't complain about these shoots."

"These are actually my favorite," I admit. He stays silent, but his acknowledging smile is all I need to know that he un-derstands. Within seconds of me admitting the words, they're shouting for us to go. I take off and Matt is soon following me.

Within a minute, we reach the photographer and I come to an abrupt stop.

"That's great," she voices, "Great. It's exactly what I'm looking for. Now let's do it again."

On the way back, Matt is slightly walking behind me and I don't have to wonder for long why when he pinches my butt, making me yelp as I jump away from him. "We're definitely keeping these," he says, explaining why he kept a distance behind me. He was staring at my ass.

"You're intolerable," I say, reaching the start marker and waiting for him to reach my side before turning and quickly jogging off.

Six outfits later, we're changing into the last outfit. With every mock run, Matt was starting to grow comfortable and before we knew it, he was posing on cue when needed at the finish marker. With amusement, I was beginning to wonder if I was going to have a little bit of competition for my future shoots.

During one of our last runs when we had playfully started to compete to see who can make it back to the finish marker first, we were both laughing and smiling as we'd done with every other one, but this time the photographer shouts, "That's perfect!" The shutter of her camera being heard as she rushes to circle around snapping pictures.

"I really love the ones of you laughing, Abigail," the photographer comments. I look over to see her looking into the tiny screen of her digital camera.

"You want to see her scream with happiness while laughing?" The photographer snaps her head up with an enthusiastic smile.

"Hell, yeah."

I'm fearfully looking at Matt knowing what he plans on doing, but his body is soon ducking low and I'm being tossed into the air and over his shoulders. As he had promised, I'm screaming and laughing at the same time while he spins us both around in circles. The world blurs around me and I keep laughing along with Matt. The faint sound of the shutter is heard in the same spot in my circle and right when I feel I'm about to throw up, Matt thankfully stops and gently slides me down his body. The remaining seconds of my laughter die down as I struggle to catch my breath.

With his laughter dying down as well, Matt says, "I told you I can get her to do it," he breathlessly answers.

"You're cruel. You know that, right?"

"But, you still love me anyway."

Shaking my head, the smile lingers on my lips. "This brochure will be the best yet," Aaron excitingly remarks, catching our attention. "I can't wait to see the final product." And neither can I since the photographer has called it a wrap.

"The promotional shoots shouldn't take that long since I got some really good ones with you and Matt sprinting, so I'm going to use those," Aaron claims. "If that's okay with you," he hesitantly adds.

"I don't mind." Aaron grows excited again before turning to rush off and speak with the photographer. Now at my side, Matt tugs me flush against his body and my arms automatically wrap around his neck.

"I think I've earned my pancakes today," he says to me.

Cocking my head, I ask, "You really want *me* cooking pancakes for you?"

"I was kind of hoping we could do that whole *thrusting while mixing* thing. You mix, I thrust," he explains, pushing his hips up against my body to emphasize how it would be done. "But it would be better if I was in you from behind."

Picturing the image in my mind, my body is already responding with desire and the cool brisk air of Portland now feels as if I'm in an Arabian desert with the heat overtaking my body. How my body never tires of responding to Matt's enticing words to get me in bed never ceases to amaze me. I just pray it will forever be this way.

Chapter Twenty-Eight

Abigail

I'M ALREADY EXITING my hotel bedroom when it occurs to me I'm forgetting something. Quickly rushing back into the room, I yell over my shoulder to Matt, "Be right back!" I rush to my suitcase and dig through it looking for the item in question. I'd made sure to keep it safely tucked at the bottom corner when I'd placed it there after arriving in Seattle.

My hand finds and wraps around it to dig it out. Originally, it had traveled with me in my purse, feeling the need to protect it at all cost during our drive up here. Tucking it now into my small tote bag provided by the race organizers used as check bags during the race, I'm now rushing back out to catch up with Matt.

"Forget something?"

"Yup, but I've got it now," I say before lightly patting the bag. He returns a genuine smile before placing a kiss on my temple.

"Let's go, speed racer," he says, reminding me of the new nickname he's recently given to me while I run.

With Julio and Trey already waiting in the hotel lobby, Matt and I are soon in the elevator heading downstairs to meet them. When the elevator doors shut, Matt gives my hand a gentle squeeze to draw my attention.

"Still nervous?" he asks. He's been repeatedly asking the same question all morning. I feel nervous and it must show, which is probably why he's still asking.

"I'm terrified," I truthfully answer this time.

He laughs at my remark, which makes me grimace. Lifting my hand up to his lips, he places a kiss on the back of my hand. "You're going to do fine. Just pretend it's any other run we're on," he says, reminding me how hard he trained with me for this race. At first, I'd insisted he not run the longer runs with me, but he explained he needed to build his endurance back up as well. Training was just around the corner and he needed to be in top shape, as he was before his injury.

I let out a snicker as the elevator dings to announce we've reached the lobby. Tucked at Matt's side, we exit and are greeted by Julio and Trey a couple of steps away, patiently waiting.

"Time to rock and roll, supermodel," Trey announces with a fist pump into the air, causing me to laugh at his eagerness of this race. Of course since he isn't running it he can look at it as no big deal.

My anxiety and nerves start to rise as we step out of the lobby and into the brisk fresh air of Seattle's early morning. When I'd arrived yesterday, Matt and I had taken a walk along the water where I'd taken my first run. With the sun setting off in the horizon and Matt holding me in his arms as we looked upon the water, I stood thinking how it was because of him it all began. Had anyone told me on that very first run that almost a year later I'd now be running marathons because I loved them, I would have thought they'd lost their mind.

Briskly walking our way to the start line, we're surrounded by a mass of runners anxiously making their way to the starting line. With Trey already knowing where I need to meet Aaron at a private VIP tent the running company had reserved, we allow him to lead the way. Within minutes we spot him and when we near, he has an excited smile on his lips.

"You ready, Abigail?" he asks, looking well rested and still excited as he rubs his palms together. I wish I could feel as excited as he feels, but my stomach is in knots.

Taking a deep breath first, I tell him, "As ready as I'm going to be."

"I can't wait to see you cross the finish line."

"You sound so sure I'm going to *cross* that line," I tell him. His smile turns into a frown. "I'm just kidding, Aaron. I'll cross that line. There's no failing for me."

"That's my girl. Determination in her blood!"

"You know, sometimes I wonder if he's been smoking the Mary Jane we used to," Matt comments into my ear only loud enough for me to hear him. I have to bite my lip to keep from laughing as I see a still excited Aaron bouncing back and forth on his heels. "I mean. Come on, no one's ever that happy all the time," Matt adds, making the laugh escape my lips.

Turning to him, I wrap myself into his body to absorb some of his body heat. We stand in each other's arms up until the last possible minute before they're announcing for the runners to make their way to the start line.

"Will you help me with my bib?" I request to Matt, knowing how much he loves the task.

"Of course. It's my favorite part about our runs."

Reaching into my bag for the bib and safety pins, my motivational item drops out of the bag. Matt reaches down to grab it and my breath catches in my throat when I see it in his hands.

His body is now hesitantly standing up before he looks back to me. Taking it from his hand, I tuck it back into my bag, my heart now racing out of control.

"Why do you have that here?" he quickly asks, looking perplexed.

Nervously swallowing, I say, "I need to re-qualify for Boston and I figured it would motivate me to the finish line before qualifying time."

With a quirk of his eyebrows, he continues to push the subject. "And you thought this would do it for you?"

Shyly, I nod my head before I drop it down to face the floor. His finger probes my chin up to look at him and I'm already preparing for him to rapidly start firing more questions at me, but he surprises me by saying, "I'll make sure I'm at the finish line with it waiting for you," he replies with a sincere smile.

Taking in the meaning behind his reply, my eyes grow glassy while still locked onto his. Another announcement booms through the speakers outside the tent and Matt is reaching for the bib in my hands and proceeding with my earlier request of helping me attach it to my shirt.

When done, he places a kiss on my lips.

"For good luck," he whispers against them.

Returning another quick kiss before I leave his arms, I realize the small bag is still wrapped around my wrist. With a chuckle, he happily accepts the sack and I'm rushing through the flaps with an event coordinator and Julio to walk me over. When I'm in the crowd of the runners who will mostly be running next to me for the next 26.2 miles, my nerves are racing faster than my out of control heartbeat. The sound of the gun shot signals the elite runners and I frightfully flinch at the sound, but my lips form into a wide smile knowing I've only got sixty seconds before it's going off once more for me. Popping my ear buds in and pushing play on the shuffle attached to my sports bar, the words of Tiësto's *All of Me* are now playing in my ears, readying me for my run. The gun goes off and I'm sprinting off to reach my future.

Matt

THE CROWD IS starting to get excited as the last couple of elite runners cross the finish line. Looking up to the timer on the finishing line, I see it's coming close to Abigail's deadline and soon she'll be running through the same line. I don't know who's more nervous. Her for needing to make her qualifying time, or me for what I plan on doing. With Trey and Aaron's help after telling them what my plan was, we'd managed to get me fairly close to the finish line so I'd be able to catch Abigail when she crosses it. My palms are sweaty, I'm a trembling wreck, and I have to take deep breaths to calm myself. I'm scared out of my mind that she'll turn me down like the first time, but I keep telling myself she wouldn't have purposely brought the box unless she intended on giving me an answer today.

I feel a strong pat on my shoulder and when I turn I'm facing Julio. He'd insisted on being at my side in case the photographers began hounding us, and the last thing he wanted was for them to get out of control from snapping a picture. At first, I'd thought he was crazy, but as I stand staring down at the still elegantly wrapped turquoise box in my hands, I've already got a small crowd of photographers surrounding me. From the murmurs I've managed to catch, they know. As requested, Aaron went up to the announcer to ask him to announce when Abigail was nearing the finish line. It was more to prepare myself than to notify the crowd. Hearing her name through the speakers lets me know she's less than a mile away, the roar of the crowd grows loud as if they're just as excited she's coming as I am.

Taking another deep breath, I say out loud, "I hope this works."

"You have nothing to worry about," Julio's thick accent tells me.

"I thought the same thing the first time," I practically snap at him due to my nerves. He simply chuckles at my tone.

"She didn't know what she could have lost the first time. I was with her the day you were shot. Nobody would beg that hard for someone to come back to life if they weren't willing to spend the rest of their life with them," he conveys.

With my lips now flat as I consider his words, I can only believe him at this point. It's the only hope I have. Looking straight ahead at the runners now nearing, I spot her. Her skinny, pale body pumps her arms and legs as fast as they can go with a radiant smile on her lips. For as long as I live, I will always look forward to seeing that smile on her face. It completely lights me up every time I see it. My heart is two times larger and pumping harder, feeling as if it may burst from my chest.

She crosses the finish line a couple of seconds later, her arms high in the air and her head thrown back in celebration as she crosses. When I glance up at the clock, I see she's made her qualifying time, with minutes to spare. The photographers have been snapping away at her since before she crossed the line, keeping her from seeing me. She brings herself to a walk immediately after crossing and I didn't realize I was still standing frozen in my spot until Julio nudges me forward.

Coming back to reality, I make my way over to her and she immediately spots me as her smile widens and she rushes over to me. Catapulting herself into my arms, I catch her, spinning her in a full circle as she giggles in my ear. The sound of the shuttering cameras surrounds us while I kiss her, keeping our lips lingering longer than usual.

Pulling my lips from hers, I'm already saying, "Congratulations, beautiful!" I have to shout over the roaring crowds still congratulating the runners entering the line as I slowly walk us over to the side so we won't be in their way.

"I did it!" she excitedly shouts back.

"Yes, you did."

I start to gently slide her down my body. When I feel her feet hit the floor, I follow them down. Looking up to her, she uses one hand to steadily hold onto my shoulder as the other goes up to her cover her mouth, tears already forming in her eyes. Unwrapping the bow myself this time, I throw it aside and open up the box, my eyes never once leaving hers. I'm trembling like crazy as I say my next words.

"Abigail Adams, will you marry me?" I hold the box up so she can see the ring for herself. In that split second, it occurs to me she's never seen it before. I'm holding my breath for what seems like an eternity, but may only be a second before she nods her head and loudly whimpers out a, "Yes."

Taking the ring out of the box and placing it on her finger, I quickly stand and she's once again throwing herself at me so I can kiss her. The roaring of the crowd booms louder and a massive amount of photographers are surrounding us while I continue feathering kisses on Abigail's lips. All of it should be a distraction, but it doesn't faze me because the only thing that matters at this very moment is the girl in my arms kissing me in return. If I had to die again today, I know I'd die a very happy man.

Chapter Twenty-Nine

Abigail

TIME HAS A way of going by faster than you want it too. It's been two months since Matt proposed at my finish line. Since that day, I've felt as if I've been floating on clouds. My original plan had been to pull the box out and ask *him* to marry me later that night, but after I'd thrown myself into his arms and he'd dropped down on his knee, I knew without a doubt I was ready to say *yes*. Deep down in my heart, I knew I was ready to spend the rest of my life with him.

Of course, the media ate it all up. We made so many front-page sports headlines it was ridiculous, but eventful at the same time. Trey had taken it upon himself to get a copy of every publication that had us on it and I was now filling another scrapbook with those to give him tomorrow night.

Nervously looking into the mirror, I can't help but smile. Tomorrow I will be Mrs. Matthew Garcia, and it will be another happy day to add to my life. One I never thought would be happening the day I first dreamt of Matt. My memories have slowly begun to fade, almost becoming non-existent now, and it was beginning to worry me.

Knowing that I'm going to worry Matt if I linger much longer, I open the door to exit the ladies room and as expected, he's standing in the hallway leaning against the wall waiting for me. His dark eyes are bearing back at me with a slight smile tugging at his lips. I will never tire of that expression. My body lights up as I take the few steps and close the distance between us, my arms automatically wrapping my body into his.

"You nervous about tomorrow?" I ask into his shoulder as he kisses below my ear.

"Nope, I can't wait." His response makes me chuckle.

"It wouldn't be any different than it is now. Only you'd be legally mine and I'd have a paper to prove I can do whatever I want to this body," he says as his hand squeezes my ass. "And you can't say anything about it."

Now I'm letting out a full-blown laugh. "You already do whatever you want with me," I proclaim after laughing.

"Very true. I'm a very lucky man," he responds, kissing his way across my chin. Lately, I have learned to take advantage of the moments alone I get with Matt.

Both our lives have been running non-stop as we prepare for our future to come. Matt had insisted we marry before his season started, pointing out that if we didn't do it soon, it may be years before we could marry. Thanks to Trey, our lives were getting busier by the day and I'd quickly come to agree with Matt. We needed to marry soon. It left me to plan a wedding with only a little bit over a month to spare.

Trey had kept his promise of getting Matt those endorsement offers and he'd somehow succeeded in getting me the dream job I'd never imagine getting.

Designing.

It started with me making suggestions in regards to some of

the clothing I'd worn for my races. Next thing I knew, I was in the design room giving them ideas and modeling the outfits in their upcoming sales brochures. The best part of the job was putting the products to the test, though. That was my favorite part.

Another bonus was they were now sponsoring me to run full-time, putting me in full training mode for the various races they sponsored. They hired a trainer and I was now training to be able to run with the elite during Boston. Running and sports modeling was now my full-time career and I couldn't be happier about the choice. All the times in the past I fought so hard to prove that my choices were what was right for me at the time, but I should have known I was just lying to myself. Now I was finally doing something for myself *and* was happy about it.

Matt holds out his hand in request. "Can I change the ringtone on your phone?" Willingly, I surrender my phone over to Matt and he goes straight to doing as he'd mentioned. Minutes later, he's handing it back to me and I'm already curious to hear what it will sing. As if reading my thoughts, he sternly orders, "No checking until I call."

"Fine," I agree before asking, "Do you want me to change yours?"

"I put the same one for myself. You'll understand when you listen to the words," he explains.

With a sigh, I lean back into his chest, already dreading leaving him for the night. Matt insisted he wanted a traditional wedding, which meant we were supposed to spend the night apart. The only non-traditional part of the wedding was forgoing the church. I'd wanted to get married near the water and Matt had willingly given in to my request since we'd already be in San Diego for training camp. We'd chosen to marry at a Catalina resort that would allow us to get married on the beach.

Tonight was going to be a very restless night for me. I can

already feel it. Even when he was in the hospital, I'd snuck into his bed to sleep at his side. My mind immediately thinks back to the nights we'd spent apart. First was when Matt went to Vegas for his bachelor party and then again for my bachelorette party, which was a trip to Cabo San Lucas with Kelly.

"I'm going to miss you," I somberly say to him.

"I'll miss you, too," he whispers back into my ear.

The clacking of heels coming towards us breaks us apart and when we both turn we see Kelly smiling back at us. "You two sure have a thing for hallways," she teases. "I hate to have to break you two apart, but they're wrapping everything up."

"What time is it?" I ask her, having no clue at all. The night has been so wonderful I lost track of time

"It's almost two A.M.," she answers.

"Whoa. I didn't know it was that late."

"Yeah, everyone else started leaving over an hour ago. It's only our little group left and I think the restaurant staff wants to go home now," she explains.

Now I feel guilty for keeping them so late. "You ready to go, chica? You've got to get your beauty sleep for tomorrow," she voices. "Well, technically today now," she adds with a light chuckle.

Deeply sighing because I know I have to leave Matt, I squeeze him a little tighter before I briefly kiss him. "I'll see you this afternoon?"

"I wouldn't miss it for the world," he expresses before kissing me on my temple.

Sadly pulling myself away from his arms, I follow Kelly down the hallway with Matt at my side. The walk back to the cabanas is made with small conversation between everyone. Trey complains about how boring Matt was for not wanting a *real* bachelor party and that they still have time to remedy that problem.

Matt had flat-out refused his offer of strippers, but for as much partying that they did in those three days, I'm surprised Trey remembers anything at all. He spent the entire trip to Vegas in a drunken stupor. You would have thought it was *his* bachelor party. Matt, on the other hand, had behaved according to Julio who was invited along. Since Julio doesn't drink, he was pretty much a full-time babysitter, but according to his daily reports Matt's eyes never once wandered and he looked like he was ready to return the moment he arrived.

With every phone call I could hear it in his voice, even if he was buzzed most of the time. I couldn't complain since it's how I spent my bachelorette party, another getaway Julio had to endure for my security.

Nearing the rooms, the lack of sleep is already starting to catch up to me. Matt walks me to our door and after Kelly lets herself in, he takes me in his arms to hold me for a moment.

"You sure you don't want to come in with me?" I plead, hoping he'll change his mind.

Matt chuckles at my request. "You know if I go in there you wouldn't be getting any sleep tonight, and the last thing I want is for you to be falling asleep on me at the alter tomorrow," he says.

"But I sleep better when I'm in your arms," I whine back.

He steps back and starts unbuttoning his shirt. "Matt, what are you doing?" I whisper, looking around to see if anyone is watching, already thinking we're going to have sex on the small porch outside. Thankfully we're alone, but it doesn't mean there aren't prying eyes.

With his shirt completely off, he hands it to me. "Here, I know it's my scent that puts you to sleep. It's why your nose is always plastered to my neck," he explains with a chuckle.

Taking the shirt from him, I bring it up to my nose, and of

course it smells exactly like Matt. My eyes are practically rolling back in my closed lids. "Thank you," I say as I open my eyes and gently kiss him on his lips in reward.

"I'll miss you tonight, beautiful," he says before kissing me one more time and walking away, leaving me to watch his half-naked body disappear into the darkness. The door opens behind me and I'm yanked back.

"Get your ass in here before you're mobbed or kidnapped," Kelly playfully snaps.

Our little villa only had one large room since it's considered the honeymoon suite, where Matt and I would be returning to tomorrow night. Julio was given a room in the bigger villa where all the guys were staying. He'd offered to sleep on the couch, but I felt bad so I turned down his offer. His only stipulation was that he'd check all the locks on the windows and doors before he fell asleep, which he was just finishing up.

"Everything is good. You sure you'll be fine?"

"We're fine. Go do your guy thing with them, and Abigail and I will do our girly thing. I'm not as big as you, but I know how to kick someone's ass if need be," Kelly reprimands, already urging him out of the door.

Julio shakes his head with a smile before saying, "See you in the morning, ladies."

"Not too early, or it will be your ass I'm kicking!" Kelly shouts after him.

The front door is soon clicking shut and I'm walking off to the bedroom to take my shoes off. "Do you mind if I take a quick bath?" I ask Kelly, earning me a wave of her hand to shoo me away.

"But don't fall asleep and drown in there because Matt will strangle me."

Giggling, I place Matt's shirt with my phone on the bedside

table and head straight into the bathroom. Allowing the tub to fill, I start disrobing and when done, I lean against the counter and stare into the mirror at my reflection. I may look like the old Abigail Adams when she's all dolled up with makeup, but it's not who I am anymore and I couldn't be happier. I'm now the Abigail Adams who is happier than I was when I'd woken up in the hospital not having one clue as to who I was. Since then, I've found myself—my *true* self—and I'm not letting her go.

With a smile on my face, I turn to get into the bathtub. For a while, I simply sit there in the warm water, allowing my thoughts to wander off to the future I'm looking forward to. When the water turns cool, I start to rinse my body and hair and I'm soon getting out. Within minutes, I'm exiting the bathroom to find the room dimly illuminated with only the side lamp from where I'd placed my items lighting the room. Kelly is already passed out, lightly snoring with her arm thrown over her eyes to ward off the light. The sight makes me giggle as I start to dress in my pajamas.

My phone starts ringing to the lyrics of, *Marry You,* and I light up inside as I imagine Matt singing the words to me. Ever since his little performance at the Brewhouse, he's taken it upon himself to sing out lyrics of the songs he's chosen as my ringtones when we're alone. The performances are hilarious, but nevertheless special and I love them. It's the reason why I let him keep changing them every so often.

Answering as the final words of the chorus begin so it doesn't go to voicemail, I whisper the lyrics into the phone, "Hey handsome, I'm going to marry you.

"You sure you want to?" he asks with a hint of humor as I climb into bed next to Kelly.

"I'm pretty sure," I quietly reply so not to wake her.

"Good, because even if you'd told me no, I'd have to go all

caveman on you and throw you over my shoulder yelling, *mine,* while thumping my chest down the aisle."

The thought makes me laugh out loud, making Kelly groan. Stifling my laughter, I reply, "You do that anyways," still giggling.

"I just wanted to call and tell you I love you before you fell asleep."

"I love you, too. I can't wait to marry you." The other end goes silent, quickly worrying me. "Matt, is something wrong?" I bravely ask.

Silence lingers for another couple of seconds. "I just wish Emily could be here," he answers, with a crackle in his words, as if he's holding back tears.

"Oh, Matt, she'll be there. I promise," I tell him.

"I'll let you go now, beautiful. I love you," he says into the phone, but the words are full of sadness and remorse.

"I love you, more," I reply right before there's dead silence, notifying me he's hung up. Sitting in bed feeling a pang of sadness, the thought of how he must feel from the loss of Emily not being present overtakes my mind. I'd known from the beginning he'd feel this way on our wedding day, which is why I took it all into consideration when planning the wedding. I just hope he loves the details as much as I do.

Plugging the phone into its charger on the nightstand, I grab for Matt's shirt, bringing it up to my nose to inhale its scent. I may not have him physically next to me tonight, but this is the next best thing. Reaching for the switch to turn out the light, my ring reflects with the gleam of the light making me bring it up so I can take a better look at it. The sight of it always brings a smile to my face. Matt was worried from the moment he'd slipped it on my finger that I wouldn't like it, insisting that I can always have it exchanged for something I'd prefer, but there was no better ring I would have chosen myself.

Turning the light off to engulf myself in darkness, I fall asleep clutching Matt's shirt tightly to my chest, my nose deeply nudged into the fabric, praying Matt will keep his promise and will be waiting for me on the beach tomorrow.

THE HAIRDRESSER TUGS at my hair, making me wince while I'm stifling another yawn.

"I'm so sorry," she apologetically lets out before placing a bobby pin into my hair. "I'm almost done," she tells me, and I simply answer with a slight nod. Julio is now standing in front of me with a huge can of sugar free Red Bull with a bendy straw already inside, and I instantly smile as I take it from him.

Swallowing the delicious sweet liquid, I look up to him to say, "Thank you."

As usual, he answers with a quick nod before walking away. Half an hour later, I'm getting my make-up done and it's off to put my dress on next. As Kelly takes the dress from where it's currently hanging on one of the doors inside of our bedroom, I fully take it in, smiling from ear to ear. I'd known from the beginning a traditional princess style dress wasn't for me. What I'd wanted was something form fitting with lace. The back was open and cut low, exposing my back where Matt would be free to roam his hand up and down, and the train was long and elegant. Putting it on, my mind keeps pleading Matt will like it just as much. Kelly brings over my veil and my eyes are already watering from the sight of it, my mind wandering back to the day I'd received it.

Matt walks into the room with a slim box in his hands, look-

ing nervous as he looks down at me. I'm sitting at our dining room table surrounded by a sea of wedding details all organized in categories where I can find them.

"What's that?" I ask Matt, watching him nervously swallow before he hands the box to me. Cautiously opening it, I find a mass of tulle neatly folded inside. Perplexed, I look back up to him for further explanation.

"This was my mother's veil from when she married my father. I remember finding it in Emily's closet a little time after my parents passed away. I would take it out and wrap myself in it every time I was really sad and missing her. On more than one occasion Emily found me asleep in it," he says with a chuckle. "When Emily got married she wore it and I swear she looked like a princess as I walked her down the aisle."

Staring down at it as Matt runs his finger across the delicate material in the box, my vision is starting to become obstructed from the tears now forming in my eyes.

"I don't know if you've already chosen a veil, but if you haven't I was hoping you wouldn't mind wearing this one on our wedding day. I know it may seem like a weird request, but somehow it feels like it's the closest thing to having my mom and Emily there," he voices just above a whisper.

I can no longer contain the tears as they fall from my eyes while I look at Matt with a smile. "Are you sure?" I doubtfully ask.

"Never mind," he says already reaching for the box, but I yank it back before he can take it.

"Matt, I'd be honored," I answer.

"Are you sure?" he asks me.

"I promise."

My thought is broken when Kelly lets out a gasp. Turning to face the mirror, I'm soon replicating the sound as a single tear cascades down my cheek from the sight now staring back at me. Taking a few moments to run my fingers against the tulle cascading around my body, it reminds me of my present to Matt. Rushing over to the bouquet of flowers that were prepared for my wedding, I grab the box I intended to be delivered to Matt along with the note I'd written days ago.

Stepping into the living room, I hand the small box over to Julio. "Can you please take this to Matt?" I kindly ask, hoping he hasn't left his room yet. Giving me his usual nod, he takes the box from my hands and is soon heading out of the door.

Kelly is walking into the room to meet me. "He's going to love it," she comments, knowing exactly what's in the box. With a tight smile on my lips, I rapidly blink away the remaining tears.

"You ready?" she asks and the question couldn't have come soon enough. I've been ready since the moment I'd answered Matt with a *yes*.

She hands me my bouquet and I double check to make sure I have everything needed to walk down the aisle. My hand reaches to touch my bracelet, which is my something old, but with a new addition of a charm from Matt, which is my something new. Just a couple of days ago he'd added a winged charm to represent my running, but I'd told him it looked more like his tattoo. Either way, it was a perfect addition to all the others he'd given me. The veil of course would represent my something borrowed, and the sparkling sapphire studded earrings Matt had given me last night during the rehearsal dinner was my something blue. Looking into the mirror one last time to fully take in my reflection, I stare back at myself with awe.

Kelly steps up behind me, her eyes glassy. "Oh, God, Abigail. You look so beautiful," she says before she starts fanning her eyes.

"Do you think Matt will think so, too?"

She lets out a laugh from my question. "Of course he will!" The photographer is snapping away at her camera as I lean in to hug Kelly, grateful she's my maid of honor today. "Come on girl, lets go get you hitched," she says into my ear, making me laugh.

"Let's go," I happily reply, eager to say *I do*.

Chapter Thirty

Matt

THE KNOCK ON the door brings my rowdy crowd to silence. Trey had just finished commenting how Abigail had me by the balls since the day I'd met her, so a legal paper wasn't going to change anything. He was right, which is the only reason why I wasn't currently regretting my decision to choose him as my best man.

David goes to open the door and I see Julio enter with a small box, handing it to me moments later. Everyone is surrounding me as I open up the small envelope to read the note inside.

I may have the honor to wear such a beautiful veil, but I thought you should also be wearing something of theirs, too. In that same box was a ribbon I'm assuming belonged to them. It was wrapped around what looked to be a bouquet. I've taken it and had it wrapped around your corsage. Place it near your heart and know they are with you on this day I plan to marry the man I first dreamt of. The man who I fell in love with on the night that changed my life.– Love, your beautiful, Abigail.

My eyes are now filled with tears as I hand the note over to Trey who is requesting to see it. Opening up the white box that is tied with a bow, inside is a single red rose elegantly wrapped with a ribbon I'm all too familiar with. It was the ribbon my mother had given Emily that she wore in her hair. Emily had wrapped it around her bouquet for her wedding day, stating it was her something old. It looks worn from age, but nevertheless stunning as it's elegantly wrapped around the rose.

"Here, let me help you with that." Trey's voice breaks me from my memory.

Sniffling through my tears I didn't realize I'd shed, I hand the corsage over to him. The shuttering of the photographer's camera overtakes the silence of the room as I force myself to blink away the tears. When done, Trey steps back to look at me and he, too, has traces of tears in his eyes.

"There, now you're ready to rock and roll," he quietly says. "Let's go claim your woman," he bellows with a fist pump in the air, making us laugh.

Looking around the room, I'm surrounded with the group of guys who have been with me through so much. I consider them more family than friends.

"Let's go," I reply, anxious to see Abigail and seconds later we're all filing out of the room.

Nearing the beach where the wedding ceremony is to be taking place, the first thing I notice is a huge sign announcing our wedding. Taking a moment to read the message, my vision is soon clouding again.

"Ramon, Irene, and Emily Garcia cordially invite you to the wedding of Matthew Garcia to Abigail Alexandria Adams."

The sight of my parents' and Emily's name leaves me breathless. I know the invitations didn't have their names on them, only Abigail's and mine, and suddenly I remember the exact moment she'd asked me for my parents' name. She was in the midst of all her planning and at the time she had simply lifted her head up, asked the question, and as soon as I'd answered she'd lowered it back down and continued her scribbling. I pushed her question aside thinking she was having a lapse in her sanity. It was during one of the many times she was on the verge of turning into a bridezilla over details of the wedding. She kept insisting that everything needed to be perfect in such a short amount of time. There were several times I had to drag her away from the piles of notebooks and samples spread across the dining room table before she went insane from stress. Because of those same papers, we've been eating out or in the living room because she didn't want anything misplaced.

"I didn't know your mom's name was Irene," David says, breaking my trance. "It's also my grandma's name," he comments. I answer him with a smile since I can't speak around the lump lodged in my throat.

The event coordinator spots me and is already urging me off into the direction of the beach. Obeying, my bare feet start walking me in the direction I need to go. Walking down the aisle, my eyes take in three empty seats at the very front on my side of guest seats; each with a single white rose sitting on them. The sign nearly had me in tears, but the sight in front of me has made them erupt from my eyes. I have to take a moment to catch my breath as I stare down at the sight.

Trey is already shoving a handkerchief at me, looking as if he needs one as well. "Here, man."

The event coordinator is once more at my side, this time patiently waiting to catch my attention. "She's coming," she says, making me turn to see Abigail off in the distance walking towards the beach.

Her words urge me to take my steps to where I'm needed

to stand and soon my eyes are finding Abigail again. When she's close enough for me to fully take her in, she literally leaves me breathless from how beautiful she looks.

It isn't long before she reaches me and I'm saying down to her, "Hey, beautiful."

Her radiant smile greets me in return. "Hey, handsome. How about we get married today?"

"I think that sounds like a great idea," I tell her, feeling like the luckiest man in the world because I'm about to marry this girl.

The preacher starts off with the usual opening, but when it nears the part where we are asked to speak our vows, I'm a nervous wreck hoping Abigail likes the words I've chose. I'd been insistent we write our own vows, but it was only because I've had them written for months. Nervously, I pull out the pieces of paper where I'd written them down the day Abigail had run her marathon. The same day she said yes. We'd returned to the hotel room and as usual after a long run, she'd fallen asleep after showering. I was so high on emotions that I couldn't sleep so I'd taken the notepad on the desk and starting writing out the words I wanted to say on this day. Taking a deep breath, I look into Abigail's eyes and start speaking.

"Today I stand before the girl who I know without a doubt was sent by an angel. You showed up at my door with a part of my soul I feared I'd lost forever. You came with part of that angel to save me from the darkness that had me trapped until you arrived. From the moment you told me why you came to me, I knew without a doubt you'd be in my life forever, because I was never letting you go. *I wasn't letting my angel go*. At first, I fought so hard to ignore my love for you, but with your own love and perseverance, you opened up my heart and showed me what true love is. I once promised I would protect you forever, and in front of our friends and family, I make that promise to you once again. Through sickness and in health, all our riches and a faithfulness to you from this day forward, I promise to never leave your side until death do us part."

When finished, I'm swallowing around the lump of tears I'm holding back. But Abigail wasn't strong enough as tears cascade down her cheeks. Finding the handkerchief I used earlier, I hand it to her. She gladly takes it from me and blows her nose into it, making me chuckle.

When done, she takes a deep breath before saying, "Wow, I don't know if I can top that," she jokes and everyone begins laughing. Her eyes lock with mine for a brief moment as she smiles, but breaks contact when she looks down into the paper in her hands.

"It all began with a dream. The same dream that lead me to my future. I knew it in my heart the moment I saw you that you'd forever be in my life. They were not my memories to claim, but every memory since then has shown me a piece of who you are and with every day that passes, you've given me memories of my own. I don't need to know my past to know that my future is with you. As much as I belong to you, you belong to me. My heart is yours, and your heart is mine. I made a promise one night, which I will forever be grateful for. With that promise, I also vow to love and cherish you for all the days of my life."

I stare down at Abigail and her eyes are full of tears. Lifting my hand, I push them away as best as I can without smearing her make-up, mouthing the words *I love you* and receiving in them return.

"The rings," the preacher orders and we're both turning to take them from their holders.

Several minutes later, the rings are on and I'm now kissing my *wife,* making sure our lips linger longer than needed as we both cherish this moment. She smiles against my lips and I can't resist doing the same. The preacher clears his throat, telling us we've taken long enough, causing us to laugh into each other's mouths.

Pulling apart, I see her eyes smiling back at me. "I love you," she says up to me and my heart feels as if it may burst from happiness. Giving her another quick kiss, I let her go so we can face the crowd. They're already cheering back at us before I lead my wife back down the aisle to begin our future.

Chapter Thirty-One

Abigail

I'M HESITANT, YET anxious to know which song Matt has chosen for our first dance. He kept reassuring me it would be one that both of us would love, but I can't help but be nervous—no matter how much I trust him.

The D.J. announces our first dance and it takes every ounce of energy to make me stand up. I'd much rather hide at this point. Grabbing my hand, Matt slowly leads us onto the dance floor, my stomach is in knots the entire time. Reaching the center of the floor, I feel like I can barely breathe.

"Nervous?" he asks with a hint of laughter in his eyes that are staring back at me. Shaking my head in response, Matt's lips go up to one side. "Liar."

I let out the breath I must have been holding. "I'm scared I'm going to make a fool out of myself," I truthfully tell him. "You do realize this is the first time we've ever danced with each other, don't you?"

Realizing the truth in my words, he nods. "Which is why is makes it even more special, beautiful. Another memory we can add to the list, and I promise many more to come."

His words are all I need to make me smile, but just as quickly the nerves return when the music starts. Matt wraps his arms around my waist, tugging me tightly against his body. Instantly, every ounce of nervousness disappears and is replaced with giddiness. My body is blissfully filled with sparks as his dark eyes gaze back at me, my body lighting up from head to toe. My mind hasn't registered the song or the words. Instead, I'm completely focused on the man currently holding my heart.

Slowly swaying us side to side, I hold onto him, allowing him to lead me. Laying my head against his shoulder, I finally relax as I try to take in the words of the song. But I don't need to focus too hard as I feel Matt place a quick kiss on my neck, his soft deep voice begins to sing the words into my ear.

Pulling my face up from his shoulder, wanting to see eyes I love so much, I see him already passionately looking down at me. His arm squeezes me tighter, his smile never leaving his lips as he continues to sing, hypnotizing me with his voice.

The song comes to an end and our bodies slowly come to a stop and I'm already saddened it's over. His lips meet mine and as I close my eyes, all my sadness is quickly pushed away.

"I love you, Matt, now and forever," I whisper against his lips.

"Now and forever, beautiful," he says back to me—a promise I know that will never be broken or forgotten

I'M NERVOUS. MY stomach is in knots and I'm willing myself to keep the pancakes Matt cooked me this morning from coming up. Sucking in another breath, I try to calm the nerves coursing

through my body. Coming to see Emily is one of our special moments and my nerves are increasing with every step I take to see her.

As we near her, I remember the first time Matt had brought me to meet her just weeks before our wedding. It was the moment I'd been waiting for since the day Matt told me my memories were Emily's. That day, I'd taken the steps up the hill with Matt holding me at his side to guide me, although my body felt as if it were being tugged to her. My desperate need to be near her had taken over and led me straight to where she lay. It was as if our bodies are two magnets fighting to be pieced together. My nerves had made my heart race faster than it ever had in my life, but when we'd reached her I felt a sense of relief. Somehow, my soul felt at peace as I looked down at her grave marker and Matt had started speaking to her.

"Emily, this is Abigail. The love of my life." His words were simple, but full of love, tugging a smile onto my lips. "I promised when I came back I'd bring her with me, and as you know, I keep my promises," he proclaimed during that first visit.

Since that day, Matt and I have made sure to visit as often as we can. On some occasions, I have even come alone. When I feel as if I need a sense of guidance, this is the first place I seek. Somehow, Emily always helps me find the answer I've been searching for.

Reaching her, Matt wraps me in his arms and we stand there in silence for the next couple of minutes. My eyes tear up as he begins to speak.

"Hey, Emily. How have you been?" I can't help but chuckle at how he begins the conversation. "I'm sorry we couldn't come sooner, but things have been a little crazy."

"But we're here now," I finish saying for him as I look into his eyes.

"Yes, we are," he whispers back to me, holding me tightly to his body.

"There's something I want to share with the both of you," I nervously say, hoping to find the courage to let it out. Matt arches his brow, waiting for me to speak.

"Matt, remember on our run the other day I felt sluggish and could barely keep up?"

"You said it was because you felt exhausted. Is this what it's about? Your running?"

"Sort of. I'm going to have to postpone some of my races next year."

He looks confused again, but just as quickly grows worried. "You're not sick are you?"

With a coy smile on my lips, I admit, "I am most of the time, but I'm pretty sure it will go away after another four and a half months. Hopefully sooner," I tell him, waiting for his reaction.

It takes him a moment to understand the meaning behind my message and his face suddenly goes pale in reaction.

"You're pregnant?" Sounding as if he's still unbelieving while asking.

Nodding my head with a smile, I confirm just above a whisper, "I'm pregnant." His eyes rapidly light up and his lips slam down onto mine. Pulling back he's asks, "Are you serious?"

My excitement has risen just as high as his as I answer, "Yes."

He reaches forward and scoops me up into the air, spinning me around in his arms. With the world swiftly whooshing by me, my earlier nausea is now returning. "Matt, please stop before I throw up," I beg, hoping I don't throw up on him.

He immediately stops, gently placing me down on the ground. His concerned eyes are looking at me. "Is this why you've been so sick lately?" Remembering the times most recently I'd been throwing up, thinking I'd had the stomach flu.

It hadn't occurred to me I may be pregnant. Matt and I have been trying for over a year now with no results and my irregular cycle was due to my intense running schedule. The doctors had explained my inability to conceive might be a side effect of taking the Depo shot. In some cases, it can take years to conceive. We'd both left the appointment disappointed, but promised we wouldn't give up, agreeing that with time it would happen.

"Yes," I answer after taking a slow breath to push the nausea aside. "I thought it was the flu at first, but after the throwing up stopped and the nausea stayed, my trainer made me go to the doctor just to make sure," I explain.

He looks excited again as he looks between Emily and me. "You're going to be an aunt, Emily!" he excitingly shouts down to her. "I'm going to be a dad!" he adds, shouting it up to the sky. I barely suppress a giggle before he's kissing me again.

"I love you," I say against his lips, feeling just as ecstatic as he does.

"You've made me the happiest man alive today, beautiful," he says, causing my heart to feel as if it may just burst from my chest from delight.

"And I'm the happiest girl alive because I have you," I tell him before looking down at Emily with tears in my eyes to silently say, "Thank you."

My heart is so full of joy as I think, if it wasn't for her, I would have never found Matt, and I would have never felt as complete as I do now.

Matt

LOOKING OVER AT Abigail, a sense of contentment takes over my body. Seeing her in our home, the home Emily once raised me in, and now the home where we're raising our own family makes me smile every day I wake up next to her in it. With each day my love for her increases as she unselfishly proves how much she loves me in return.

It was her decision to settle in our modest family home when the previous family had moved on to buy their own house. We could have easily afforded a mansion in San Diego, but she insisted on raising our daughter here. The commute on training days can be a bitch sometimes, but it's worth it when I know it's what makes her happy.

Originally, I wanted to sell the house in Portland, but she also refused to let me do that. She couldn't find it in her heart to let go of the house that held most of our beginning. She said maybe one day we could part with it, but she just wasn't ready to let it go, yet. And who was I to argue with her? It was the house where I fell in love with her. Now we use it as an alternative residence during her intense training seasons in Portland.

The little girl in my arms starts clapping with excitement when she eyes her mother walking out from the kitchen area with the cake in her hands and a radiant smile on her lips. If possible, motherhood has made Abigail even more beautiful than before. Abigail's eyes meet mine and she joyfully smiles over to me as she leads the room in the chorus of the *Happy Birthday Song.*

Looking down at my daughter as Abigail nears, Emily's eyes are wide with delight as she takes in the cake now being placed in front of her.

"Blow out the candles, boñita," I whisper down into Emily's ear as Abigail kneels down on the other side of her, pointing at the candle waiting to be blown out. Emily leans forward with her little hands as if to grab for it, earning a shouted, "No!" throughout the room. Her body trembles before she lets out a wail, making everyone sympathetically say awww. Wrapping my hand around her head to tuck it closer to my chest, my lips find her temple to kiss her while still whispering my comforting words. "Ya, ya, boñita. No llores, mi amor." Her cries quickly fade down to a whimper.

Abigail had begun speaking to Emily in Spanish while she was in her womb, and since the day she was born she has insisted we continue so she can be bilingual. Abigail's Spanish has thus improved as well. Holding out her arms, requesting I surrender Emily, I selfishly deny her request. It earns me a small snicker from Abigail before she says, "Why does it not surprise me? And you say I spoil her," she remarks. Her words making me laugh. Within seconds, I have Emily calm and smiling again, and this time Abigail and I blow out her candle together.

It's only been a year since she's been born, but with every day that goes by, I fall in love with her even more. She was our blessing in disguise the day she was born. Abigail and I had made the decision to not find out the sex of the baby, we'd wanted it to be a surprise. But the moment they told us it was a girl, Abigail had turned to face me and the first words out of her mouth were, "Our Emily," making me cry as they handed her to me first.

"Quieres una mordida, boñita?"

"Matthew Garcia, don't you *dare* smash her face into that cake?" she scolds. Her eyes are narrowed in warning. It's become her signature *you're going to pay for it later,* look. I like testing her half the time because the make-up sex is worth it.

"Let's eat some cake!" Trey shouts.

I never thought I'd see the day when Trey would have a girl wrapped around his little finger, but I was proven wrong with Emily. If it's not Abigail or I fussing over her, it's Trey or Julio. Julio is still sticking around now that we have Emily. Abigail was very adamant she wanted to raise her own children, which is why the only time we depend on a nanny is when she has to leave for her training. Even when we're on the road, Emily gets handed off to either Julio or Trey while she races if I can't be there, which is very rare since Trey is really good about handling both our schedules to coincide with each other's.

Another thing I've been amazed by is Trey and his management skills. He's taken on the role and has yet to disappoint either of us. He's still the same goofy guy as before, but thanks to a girl he's recently started seeing, he's left his player days behind. At least I hope he has.

The sound of laughter filling the room breaks my thoughts, and when I look down to Emily, she's lifting her little fisted hand full of cake up to my mouth. Happily, I lean down to take a bite, causing her to giggle. She reaches for the cake again and takes another fist full and now Abigail is leaning down for the next bite.

"Baby girl, I didn't know it was that kind of party," Trey says, reaching into the cake with his fingers to take his own sample. He lifts it to his mouth and lets out a satisfied groan.

"Trey!" shouts his *friend*, as they're still calling each other for now, but in all reality has been more like a girlfriend nowadays. "Use a plate," she scolds.

Trey ignores her and dips his fingers back into the cake before bringing it to her lips, encouraging her to take the bite. She's skeptically looking at him at first, but eventually she gives in to his request and takes his fingers into her mouth. Trey's eyes roll back and he lets out another groan. She swats him on the chest and he catches her hand, bringing it up to kiss it.

"I'll make sure to take some cake home. For later," he huskily says to her.

"And you both claim there's nothing serious going on," Abigail snickers.

Trey's girl looks as if she's now blushing and Trey's lips go into a flat smile. Emily holds her hands up to for him to pick her up and he happily gives in to her request. "Come on, baby girl. Let's go see what uncle Trey bought you."

I watch Trey and his girl take Emily out into the backyard to the small play set that Julio and Trey recently put up for her. Abigail comes over to me and I tug her to sit on my lap. My arms wrap around her waist and she leans in to kiss me.

"I love you," I tell her, and as usual she responds, "I love you, more," before kissing me again. She sighs, worrying me. "What's wrong?"

She looks out to the backyard where Trey is playfully chasing Emily around as she takes her wobbled steps, his girl in the front prepared to catch her if she stumbles forward.

"I just don't understand them sometimes," she voices her concern. Rubbing my hand up and down her back, I tell her, "It will all work out."

"I just wish they would stop denying what they both want."

The words make me laugh. "Yeah, I remember when we were both like that, and it was hell," I remind her.

She turns to face me with a smile on her face. "Who would have known I'd land the guy of my dreams?" she says with a wiggle of her brows. Tucking her hair behind her ear, I say, "Me. Which is why I refused to make you one of my friends with benefits," I tell her before bringing my lips to hers and kissing her with every ounce of happiness inside of me.

Abigail

TUCKING THE BLANKET snugly around Emily's body so she doesn't grow cold, my eyes stare down at her in awe. It's still unbelievable that Matt and I have created this little girl. Without a doubt, she is an exact replica of Matt, taking more of her features from Emily. It's what I'd wished for from the moment I discovered I was pregnant. Leaning down to give her one more kiss, my lips linger longer than usual as I inhale her sweet baby scent.

Quietly turning to leave the room, I slam into Matt's body, startling me to lose my balance. Holding his finger up to his lips in a warning to be quiet, I shake my head at him. Of course I know to keep as silent as possible. She's my daughter and throughout the past year I've come to discover how light of a sleeper she is. She startles awake at any little noise. Thankfully, Matt has been very considerate with helping me when she wakes in the middle of the night. There couldn't be a more helpful father, even if I asked for one.

Tugging me with him, we slowly start retreating from the

room. The moment I quietly close the door, I'm gently shoved against the wall and taken into Matt's arms. Instinctively, my arms wrap around his neck and I pull him to our bedroom. My feet lead us through the all too familiar steps to the bed to pull him down on top of me.

"You tired?" he whispers into my mouth.

Shaking my head, I know if I were, it wouldn't stop me.

I've been craving this all day.

Impatiently removing his clothing as quickly as I can, it isn't long before Matt and I are connected as one. Whether it's fast or slow, each time with him feels just as special; my body never tires of making love to Matt. Within minutes, my quiet whimpers are growing louder as my body rises to find its completion.

"Shhh, you're going to wake the baby."

His statement reminds me of how many times our urgent cries have awoken her. Moving my mouth to the hollow of his neck to muffle my cries isn't helping. Matt's body thrusting into mine has a way of making me moan uncontrollably.

Locking my mouth to his, Matt's plunging quickens and I'm meeting his frantic thrusts, sending my body higher until I'm reaching the all too recognizable peak of my climax. His mouth catches my screams of desire before his hands are digging into my thighs as he explodes with me. My body is still shuddering from my orgasm as he slowly brings his body to a stop. The earth shattering after effects are still traveling through my body when he rolls to my side, tucking me snuggly into his body.

He chuckles as he places a kiss against my hair. "Someone was horny," he says, sounding breathless as his chest rapidly rises and falls.

"You're the one who came looking for me."

"I was going to ask if you wanted to watch a movie with me, but I'm too tired now." His response makes me laugh, reminding me how quickly parenthood has caught up to both of us.

Soon his breathing has calmed and from how tightly he's still holding me in his arms, I know he's asleep.

"I love you," I tell him, knowing he's probably not heard me, but he doesn't need to hear my words to know how I feel. Just as exhausted and spent, my eyes start to drift close and I'm dragged into slumber.

I'm standing in a meadow surrounded by a sea of flowers, unsure of where I'm at. My confusion is replaced with fear for a few moments before I see Emily off in the distance. It's been a while since I've last seen her in my dreams, but her smile is all too familiar since it looks back at me every day.

"Hi," I shyly tell her when she's reached me.

"Thank you."

Confusion has now replaced all my earlier emotions.

"Whatever for?"

"For keeping your promise."

Remembering her request on that very first night I met her, the tears are now building up in my eyes. I had unselfishly made that promise so long ago knowing without a doubt it would be my future, regardless of what happened between Matt and me.

She steps forward and pulls me into her arms, her kindhearted spirit radiating into our embrace. Not long after, she's pulling away with tears in her eyes, making my heart ache from the sight.

"I'm going to miss all of you."

Feeling baffled as to why she'd say such a thing, I'm about to request clarification when she begins to explain.

"I couldn't let myself move on until I knew he was truly happy. It's why I sent you to him. I've known since the day I ar-

rived you were meant for each other," she says with a tear now cascading down her cheek.

"Wait, what do you mean move on?" I ask, now taking in our surroundings. "My time here was limited. I have my own love I need to be with now, but my promise to always be there for Matt is what kept me from moving on. But I know through you my promise will live on," she explains.

Understanding her words, I nod in agreement. Giving me another brief hug, she slowly turns, telling me she's preparing to leave, but I stop her.

"Wait, why have the memories stopped?" I ask, knowing how often I've been asking myself the same question.

She brings her hand up to my cheek, instantly feeling a sense of comfort traveling through my body. "My dear, Abigail. Those memories were to help you find your future. You've already done that with Matt. You don't need me to send them to you any longer."

"That's why I stopped getting them?"

"Yes."

It's the answer I've predicted for over a year now, but knowing the truth behind the confirmation still stabs at my heart. I'd grown to look forward to receiving her memories. They became a part of me the moment I'd woken in the hospital and experienced that first one. To know I was no longer going to experience them was heartbreaking, leaving me to feel as if a part of my soul was no longer going to be with me.

As if reading my thoughts, she begins to speak. "Those memories will always live on through Matt. He's just as much a part of you now as those memories once were." She takes me into her arms, and without a doubt, I know deep down in my heart her memory will never be forgotten, because I won't allow it to happen.

My eyes open and I'm gasping for air, frantically searching my surroundings.

"You alright, beautiful?" Matt's worried voice whispers to me.

Needing the comfort of his body, I roll to my side to find myself bumping into our daughter.

"Sorry, she woke up a little bit after you fell asleep and I was too tired to take her back after she fell back to sleep," he explains.

"It's okay," I whisper as my arm pulls her closer to my body. Bringing my lips down to place a kiss on her soft little head as I tell her, "I love you, Emily."

Carefully leaning over Emily, I give Matt a kiss and lean down on the bed next to them. With the moonlight glowing through the windows, I watch Matt's eyes slowly drift close right before his hand reaches over to rest on my hip. My running thoughts keep me from drifting off to sleep. Instead, I lie awake staring down at the two most important individuals in my life. I may have never found the answers to my past, but it's no longer my past I'm hoping to discover, but my future. And lying next to me are the two most important people who will help me find it.

Memories have come and gone, promises have been made and kept, but my heart knows I have finally found my unspoken ending.

You can catch a glimpse of Matt and Abigail's future in Unspoken Temptation.

Coming Spring of 2015

Unspoken Temptation

Chapter One

Trey

I WATCH ABIGAIL walk away, irritated at myself for agreeing to come to this stupid event. I only did it because Matt made me feel guilty about Abigail coming alone. Now I'm regretting letting myself be convinced, but no more. From now on, when it comes to Abigail, I will not cave. She obviously belongs to Matt, so her shit is his to deal with. Turning my head, my eyes lock onto the rigid princess they left behind.

From the moment I walked up to them, I knew she was part of this crowd. If her pinched up nose wasn't sign enough she came from money, then her designer clothes and jewelry are a dead giveaway.

"What?" she snaps out as I stare at her. Her attitude doesn't faze me. I'm used to stuck up bitches like her turning their noses up at me. This one isn't any different.

"Nothing," I clip out, trying to find the nearest exit to make my escape. When my eyes find her again, she's already turning to leave when she runs into an older gentleman. Her body bounces back and she loses her balance, causing me to catch her out of pure instinct. She lets out a giggle that is clearly a result of her drunken stupor.

"I'm sorry, sir. She clearly didn't see you there," I apologize for her, earning me a curt nod before he irritably walks off.

With my help, she steadies herself. "Thank you," she says, looking embarrassed.

"No problem," I reply, taking the empty glass in her hand and placing it on a passing waiter's tray. She's about to reach for another drink when I stop her. "I think you've had enough," I tell her.

"What, now you're my babysitter?" she asks with a scowl on her face.

"No, the last thing I want to be is your damn babysitter, but you've obviously had enough for the night," I state.

She sways in my arms and it's clear my words are true.

"How about we get you some fresh air," I suggest, already tugging her towards the nearest exit. Thankfully, it's the same one I entered when I arrived with Abigail, which tells me I can easily bail when I'm done with this chick.

"I'm fine," she states as we walk, but somehow I don't fully believe her. I stay silent as I lead her from the room.

"You have a room here?" I ask, hoping she does so I can happily dump her ass in it and leave.

I'm left disappointed when she shakes her head at me. "I have an apartment, but I can't seem to remember where it's at right now," she blurts out, tilting her head to the side as she lets out a sigh.

"How can you not remember where you live?"

"Because I just moved there. I know it's on the Upper East Side," she says.

Great. It's further proof that she's made of money.

"Look, how about I take you back to my place and let you sleep it off?" I ask her, knowing full well I'm probably out of my mind.

"Oh, I bet you use that line on all the girls."

"No, it's not the one I usually use because they're not usually sleeping," I say, unable to resist throwing it back at her.

"Look, it's obvious you're wasted and since you know Julio, he'd probably kick my ass if I left you here in your condition," I admit. "Julio is staying with us anyway. I'll take you back to our place and let him deal with you," I tell her.

She gives me a drunken nod, making her sway again. Leading her outside, I flag down a taxi. Once inside, I give him the address to Abigail's hotel.

When we arrive, I reach for my credit card to pay for the taxi, not expecting the outrageous fare. The girl reaches into her small, dangly purse and yanks out a hundred before shoving it through the plastic window.

"Keep the change," she orders.

I feel a pang of aggravation from knowing she's just paid for the taxicab without hesitating over the price. I tell myself that she's made of money and that a hundred is probably petty cash to her.

Pulling her out of the car and guiding her to the elevator, she's already clinging to my arm. In the elevator she starts to doze off against my arm, causing her to keep losing her balance. Giving up the notion that she'll actually be able to walk, I scoop her up into my arms and wait for the elevator doors to open. She wraps her arms around my neck as her face relaxes into the crook of my shoulder. Her nose nudges against my skin and I hear a contented moan. The sound alone is enough for me to get ideas in my head that don't need to be there.

Thankfully, I'm saved when I hear the familiar ping of the elevator. Briskly walking out, I rush over to our door and upon reaching it, I realize the key card is still in my pocket.

I shake the girl to get her attention, earning me a grumble. "I need you to reach into my coat and grab the key card," I tell her.

Without hesitating, she does as I request. When her hand slowly glides against my chest, I start to grow hard. How the fuck is one simple touch making me react this way? Pushing the thought aside, I start to think of ugly old ladies as she continues to search, trying to force my dick to go limp again.

Eventually, she digs the key out and swipes it. When the green light appears, she pushes the handle down and I shove the door open and enter. Kicking it shut behind us, I lead her straight to Julio's room.

On the way, she starts nuzzling her nose into my neck again, this time letting out a moan as she licks it. I nearly fucking trip on my own feet when she does it. I quicken my steps towards the bedroom and place her on the bed. I reach for her arms to unwrap them from my neck, but she tightens her grip and tries to pull me down. I have to force myself to breathe as I brace my arms on the bed to keep from collapsing on top of her.

"I don't think this is a good idea," I groan out, knowing damn well that it isn't. She ignores my words and starts kissing and sucking on my neck, still trying to pull me down on top of her. I try to gently shove her away so I can make my escape, but I lose the battle when her lips find mine.

She opens up her mouth to allow me inside, our tongues slowly glide against each other's and I can taste the alcohol she was drinking. She moans into my mouth as my tongue continues to explore hers, the breaking point of my struggle to keep away from her.

I don't know how long I hover above her as I kiss her, but when we eventually pull away, we're both breathlessly panting as I stare down at her.

"Please," she begs for God only knows what, but I know what I want.

"I'll be right back," I tell her, giving her one quick kiss on the mouth before rushing out of the room to my bag that's sitting in the living room. Scrambling through the side pockets where I put the condoms I brought, I grab the entire box, hopeful I'll put them all to use.

Entering the room again, I lock the door behind me. With the glow of the city lights entering through the windows, I take in the view in front of me. She's completely naked as she lies back on the bed. How the fuck did she manage to get her clothes off that fast? At this point, I tell myself to be grateful she's ready and willing. Within a minute, I have every piece of clothing removed from my body and I'm back on top of her, this time snuggly between her thighs.

Slamming my lips back down onto hers, I deeply kiss her, already needing to have my tongue in her mouth again. Ending the kiss, I start trailing my tongue down her body to taste the rest of her. Her skin is soft against my lips. I don't know whether to take my time and savor each inch of it or get straight to the point. Since I'm an impatient man, I choose the latter and make my way down.

When my mouth finds the heat of her, she's already wet. Lapping my tongue against her lips, the sound she delivers drives me wild. I continue tasting every inch between her thighs, her nails digging into my scalp as she tries grabbing onto my head, but unable to because of the lack of hair on my head. Instead, her hands find their way onto my shoulders and she lifts her hips to further grind against my mouth. Within minutes, she's screaming at the top of her lungs as my mouth keeps sucking at her clit. Her juices explode into my mouth and the taste of them is practically making me come as I lap up every ounce she released.

When I lift my head, she's staring down at me with a satisfied smile on her lips. Slowly, I start to kiss my way up her body and make my way back up to her.

"Do you want me to keep going?" I cautiously ask, not wanting to force her, knowing damn well she's drunk. This isn't the first time I've fucked someone while they were drunk, but somehow this time it doesn't feel right. I feel like I'd be taking advantage of her.

She answers me with a nod, and it's the only sign I need to pull away to grab a condom. She watches me as I roll it on, the entire time her eyes never leaving my dick as she hungrily stares at it. Normally, with a look like that, I'd make the girl service me back, but I can't wait to be inside her.

I grab her leg to hook it around my waist and she automatically pulls me towards her with it. Her arms move to my shoulders as her eyes lock onto mine as I gradually enter her. Inch by tantalizing inch, I push myself inside her. She's so fucking tight and the thought of her being a virgin occurs to me, but I'm proven wrong when I don't meet any resistance as I thrust the last couple of inches inside her. She does lets out a gasp when I'm all the way in to the hilt.

I stay still above her, knowing from the clutching of her eyes and the digging of her nails into my shoulders that she must be in pain. Already regretting seeing her like this, I start pulling out. When the tip of my dick is at her entrance, her other leg wraps around my waist. She lifts her hips and begins urging me forward. Giving in to her request, I thrust back into her, earning me a pleasured whimper.

At first my thrusts are slow and cautious, not wanting to hurt her any further. Her screams demand more, causing me to completely lose it. In the midst of thrusting in and out of her, Julio starts banging on the door. His angered request to open the door should be enough to make me stop, or go completely limp. The encouraging words being screamed from below me are enough to shut Julio's words out.

I know I'm going to get my ass kicked him when he finds out who I'm fucking, but at this very moment as my dick glides in and out of her tight walls, it's worth taking the beating for.

It isn't long before I feel her walls clamping down around my dick and she explodes, screaming at the top of her lungs. It's all I need to quickly follow her over the edge as I explode right after her. When I'm done, I stay hovering over her, keeping my weight on my extended arms at her side as I look down at her. She looks just as breathless as I feel as I finally collapse at her side. My heart is racing and my body is drenched in sweat as I stare up at the ceiling. She rolls over to drape her body over mine and I can't resist wrapping her closer to my body. I've never once allowed a girl to cling to me after sex. Normally, I'd be pushing her off the bed or jumping off it to get dressed. This time I do neither as I tilt my head to the side to take in the scent of her hair. She smells of something fruity and I leave my nose buried in her hair, enjoying her scent.

I start drifting off to sleep when I feel her leg rubbing back and forth over my groin. I'm about to warn her not to tease me when she climbs up to straddle my hips. She places her lips onto mine as her pussy grinds against my dick. Within second it's hard again and my last thought before I grab for another condom is: Fuck sleep. It's overrated when you have a girl as horny as the one on top of me.

Victoria

I ROLL OVER, refusing to wake just yet. Clutching the pillow, I take in its scent, realizing it's unfamiliar. My eyes snap open, alarmed by my surroundings. This is not my room. In the distance, I can hear a shower running. Panicking, I try to figure out where I'm at as my eyes search the room.

Frantically sitting up, I realize I'm naked. My heart is racing as I try to remember why I'm here. The act of sitting up makes my head hurt, as if I have hammers pounding in my head. Groaning, I'm still trying to take in my surroundings. By the looks of it, I'm in a hotel room. Closing my eyes, the last thing I remember is being at the charity event. Searching my mind, I further remember speaking to a redneck guy.

Oh, God. Did I really go home with him? Let alone have sex with him? The panic inside me is increasing with every second. Doing the only thing I can do, I climb off the bed and search for my clothes. I *have* to leave before God knows who gets out of the shower. I can't even remember his name.

Although I can't remember most of the night, now that I think about it… Just thinking about it makes my cheeks blush as I recall the things we did and the way he made me feel. Pushing the thought aside, I have to focus on getting dressed.

In record time, I'm dressed and rushing to the door, relieved to be leaving the evening behind me. Opening the door, a smile lifts my lips as I make my escape without him knowing. My face falls as I unexpectedly walk into a room full of people—recognizing two of them.

"Victoria?" I hear the familiar voice ask.

Shamefully, I hang my head as I focus on the front door, quickening my steps. My cheeks that were blushing from the thoughts of last night are now red in shame. My legs can't move fast enough as I yank open the door and pray nobody will follow me. The last thing I need is to have to explain why I woke up in a stranger's room.

Now in the hallway, I take in my surroundings. Finding the elevator, I push the button to demand its presence on my floor. Within seconds, the elevator doors open in front of me and I let out the breath I was holding since I stepped out of the room.

I watch the doors close and tell myself I should be grateful this part of my life is behind me.

Trey

AS I STEP out of the shower, I grab the towel off the rack and dry myself. Once done, I wrap it around my waist and head into the room. My need to wake Victoria with sex is overtaking me. The only reason why I'd taken a shower is because I woke up smelling of sweat and I didn't want her smelling me that way.

As I open the door to the bathroom, I find the bed empty.

"What the fuck?"

Perplexed, I search the room for any sign of her, but there isn't any besides the rumpled bed I'd awakened from. I'm pretty sure I wasn't dreaming about last night. When I woke up, she was still in bed. I know because I was staring down at her angelic face.

Turning to the door, I see it cracked. Rushing over to it, I open it to find Julio and Abigail in the living room wearing confused expressions as they look at me.

"Where is she?" I ask.

Abigail's jaw looks like it might fall off her face as it continues to hang open. Her speechless expression tells me she knows exactly who I'm talking about as she points to the door with her finger. I don't hesitate to run out the door in hopes I can still catch her.

Rushing down the hallway still in my towel, I head straight towards the elevator, but I'm too late. When I reach it, it's already closing. Pushing at the button in hopes it will re-open, I'm disappointed when it doesn't. Banging at the aluminum door staring back at me in anger, I contemplate whether or not it would be worth taking the stairs.

Laying my head against the door, I bang at it, feeling a sense of heartache and loss. I knew last night she was out of my league, but that doesn't mean I would ever forget her. No, her smile will be forever engraved in my memories.

Acknowledgements

To my husband and children. Thank you putting up with my attitude throughout this experience; every book is a journey, but I wouldn't change it for the world. You stood by me during the frustrations that came with the process of writing this book and I love you so much for never giving up on me.

To my mom, Rosa, who I love more than words can ever express. You helped me discover my passion for reading, which led to writing, and you've never let me give up. I love you dearly, Mommy.

To Matt and Abigail. It began with an idea; from there it took courage to write your story, but I never gave up on you. You never once steered me wrong. This isn't a goodbye, but an unspoken ending for now. Because of you, I am the author that I am today and you'll always live in my heart. I will love you both forever.

To Cezanne, who gave me thrust and mix, touché, and all the other brilliant lines during our blue box conversations. Yamara, who gave me DP, you know that girl was you ;). Both are my BFFs who live in a blue box and I don't know what I'd do without them. Good morning and goodnight.

To my editor and heroine, Edee Fallon. You were always a text or phone call away to convince me to not kill a certain person, but most of all, you helped pull me from my writer's block by talking me through it.

Missy Stegman and Janett Gomez, thank you for being my second pair of eyes. You ladies rock and I'm keeping you.

Chelsea Camaron, thank you for all the phones calls that dragged me out of my slump.

Renee, aka Reading Renee, thank you for answering my endless medical questions concerning how to keep someone alive.

To Becca Manuel, without your persistence to give Matt and Abigail a FaceTime conversation, it would have never occurred. That scene is dedicated to you.

To my street team, The Beautiful Girls, thank you for all your support and helping me believe this story was worth writing. To my beta group, thank you for guiding me in the right direction.

To Sarah Hansen of Okay Creations, without a doubt you've made my stories come to life with your amazing covers. You always know how to take my breath away.

To Erin McKinley Carnevale, who gave me permission to add her in these acknowledgements. Thanks for being such an awesome fan.

Last, but not least, to all the readers, and bloggers who took the time to read the Unspoken Series. Without you I wouldn't have a reason to write. Thank you from the bottom of my heart.

About the Author

Gabbie is a Southern California native, who lives with her wonderful husband, two amazing kids and a senior citizen kitty. When she's not writing you can find her reading or sneaking off for a run. Some might say it's a crazy life, but she wouldn't change anything about it.

Author links:
Author page: http://gabbiesduran.com/
Facebook: www.facebook.com/authorgabbiesduran
Twitter: @gabbiesduran
Goodreads: https://www.goodreads.com/author/show/7093957.
Gabbie_S_Duran